Praise for the Cal Clax

Matters of Doubt The first Cal Clax

"Warren Easley has created a character you can root for—a man who has experienced loss but still believes in a better future, a lawyer who vigorously pursues justice for the most vulnerable clients. *Matters of Doubt* proves that legal thrillers can indeed be thrilling."

–Alafair Burke, *New York Times* bestselling author

Dead Float The second Cal Claxton Mystery

"A fast-paced, tightly woven whodunnit that kept me guessing to the end. Easley's vivid landscapes and well-drawn characters evoke comparisons to James Lee Burke, and Cal Claxton is as determined and resourceful as Burke's Dave Robicheaux."

–Robert Dugoni, *New York Times* bestselling author.

"When someone tries to drown Cal, he uses his fishing skills to good advantage. What a showdown finish! Easley's folksy style belies an intense drama revolving around corporate greed and espionage. The second outing in this action-packed Oregon-based series succeeds in quickly bringing readers up to speed."

–*Library Journal*

Never Look Down The third Cal Claxton Mystery

"Easley exquisitely captures Portland's flavor, and his portrayal of street life is spot on. Readers of John Hart and Kate Wilhelm will delight in trying this new author."

–*Library Journal*

"The Portland cityscape is as much a character as the colorful graffiti artist and the lawyer who walks Portland's streets with his dog, Archie."

–*Ellery Queen Mystery Magazine*

Not Dead Enough The fourth Cal Claxton Mystery

"Masterfully crafted, this tale of greed, deception, and revenge has an added benefit—the stunningly beautiful descriptions of the lush landscapes of Oregon's Columbia River country. Easley's characters bring enough complex complications to keep you reading long after regular bedtime."

–Anne Hillerman, *New York Times* bestselling author

"With a very likable sleuth, Not Dead Enough is sure to appeal not only to mystery lovers, but also to those interested in Native American history, Oregon culture, and environmental issues like salmon migration. Although *NDE* is the fourth in the series, it can be read as a standalone, allowing fans of Tony Hillerman or Dana Stabenow to dive right into Cal Claxton's life."

–*Shelf Awareness*

Blood for Wine The fifth Cal Claxton Mystery.

A Nero Wolfe finalist for 2018

"If you enjoy wine and a really good mystery, Blood for Wine is a must read."

–Phil Margolin, *New York Times* bestselling author

"Warren C. Easley blends my favorite subjects—wine, food, a really cool dog, and of course a murder—into a tasty thriller set in Oregon's wine country. With more twists and turns than a rain-swept coastal road, *Blood for Wine* is the fifth in this series with a tantalizing backlist just waiting for me to get my hands on. It promises to be a mystery maven's haven."

–*Bookreporter.com*

"Senseless acts of violence that hit too close to home upend Cal's personal life—but only serve to strengthen his resolve. Oenophiles and aspiring vintners will enjoy the wine lore in this well-wrought tale of love and betrayal."

–*Publisher's Weekly*

Moving Targets The Sixth Cal Claxton Mystery

"Intelligent dialogue, evocative descriptions of the landscape, and sly pokes at the current cultural climate make this a winner."

–*Publisher's Weekly*

"Easley continues in every installment in this series to get a better handle on his characters and the vital balance between principal and supporting plots."

–Kirkus Reviews

No Way to Die The Seventh Cal Claxton Mystery

"In Easley's satisfying seventh mystery featuring genial Oregon attorney Cal Claxton [he] creates authentic characters and relationships, and his eloquent descriptions of the Oregon wilderness are sublime. This well-plotted, character-driven series just keeps getting better."

–Publisher's Weekly

No Witness The eighth Cal Claxton Mystery

Winner of the 2022 Spotted Owl Award for best mystery written by an author in the great Pacific Northwest.

"Easley should win new fans with this one."

–Publisher's Weekly

Also by Warren C. Easley:

The Cal Claxton Mysteries

Matters of Doubt

Dead Float

Never Look Down

Not Dead Enough

Blood For Wine

Moving Targets

No Way to Die

No Witness

FATAL FLAW

FATAL FLAW

A CAL CLAXTON MYSTERY

WARREN C. EASLEY

Cover and interior layout by Masha Shubin

Publisher: Lucasian Press

Paperback 979-8-218-15648-0
eBook 979-8-218-15650-3

1 3 5 7 9 10 8 6 4 2

In memory of Jay Tanzer, Stuart Burgess,
and Jerry Siebert. Friends like these
come along once in a lifetime.

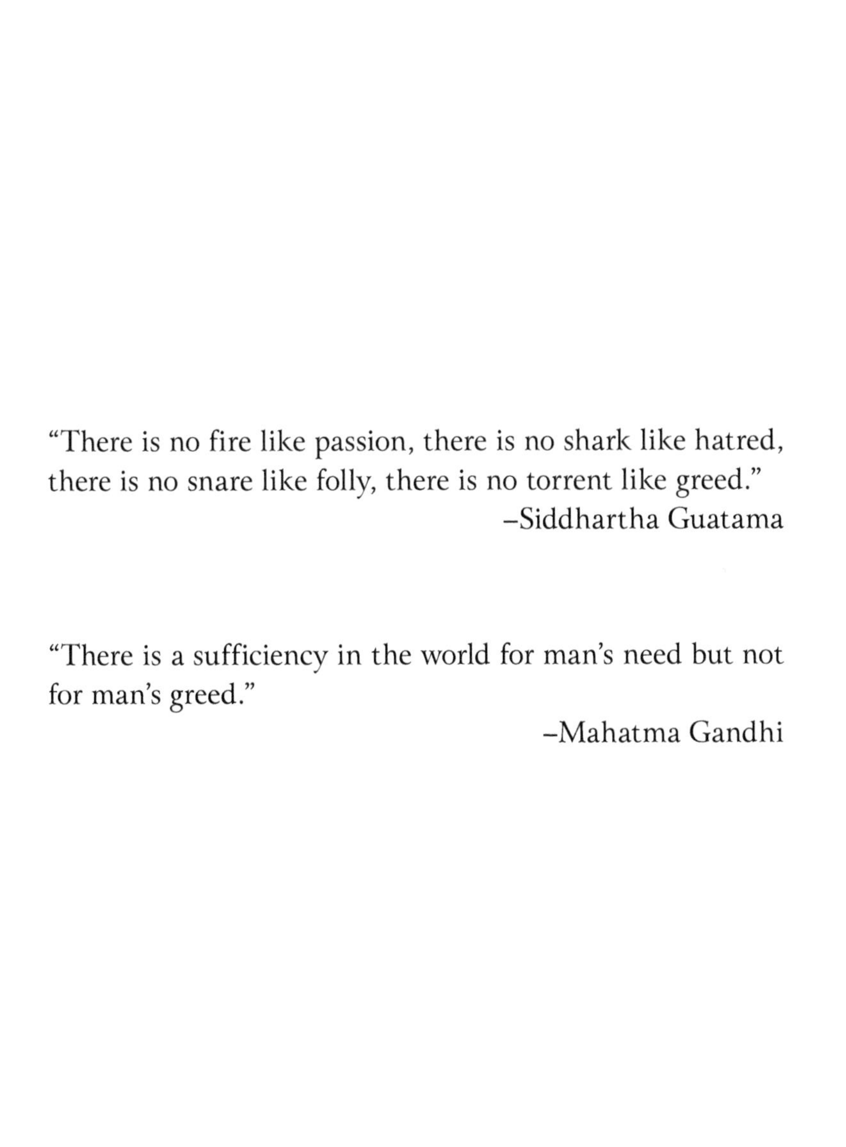

"There is no fire like passion, there is no shark like hatred, there is no snare like folly, there is no torrent like greed."

–Siddhartha Guatama

"There is a sufficiency in the world for man's need but not for man's greed."

–Mahatma Gandhi

CHAPTER ONE

THE WINTER THAT BROUGHT THE PANDEMIC BEGAN LIKE any other, at least in the wine country where I live. The fall harvest was as bountiful as it was promising, the grapes were crushed, and the magic of fermentation well underway. The rain arrived on schedule—it was Oregon, after all—and for most of us in the Northwest rain is a blessing. Not just because it makes this slice of the country the wonder that it is, but because it signals a slowing of activity and a time for reflection. And rest and reflection back then were certainly in order for me. I'd been involved in an intensive, gut-wrenching investigation of the murder of a young woman, and after the persons responsible had been brought to justice I was ready for some down time.

But you know what they say about rest for the wicked. There isn't any.

My one-man law practice is located in Dundee, a small town between the Willamette River at the northern end of the Willamette Valley. But on this particular day I was in Portland at my second office. Dubbed Caffeine Central after the coffee shop it once was, the small building was the site of my pro bono practice. Once a week I came there to offer legal representation to the homeless and other people of limited means.

Aside from washing your hands and not touching your face, there wasn't much advice out there for curbing the spread of the new virus from Wuhan, China that was being talked about in the media. However, it seemed obvious to me that holding meetings with clients in my small office was not a particularly good idea, since even a common flu bug usually kicked me like a mule.

So I posted the following sign on the front door of my Portland office that morning:

> Caffeine Central Legal Services is open, but not for in-office consultations. If you need to reach me, call 503-555-7623 and we can arrange an optimum place to meet.
>
> Cal Claxton

I just finished filing a stack of papers late that afternoon when a call came in.

"Are you Cal Claxton?" The female voice was firm.

"I am," I answered, "And you are...?"

"Willow, Willow Daniels. I know it's kind of late, but I'd like to talk to you about a legal matter. I'm out in your parking lot."

"I was just closing up. We can chat out there if that's okay with you?"

She agreed, and I grabbed a notepad in case I needed it. Archie, my Australian shepherd, got up from his mat in the corner with a stretch and was ready to go. He had enough Portland lawyering for one day and was undoubtedly longing to return to his five-acre domain in the Red Hills of Dundee.

Willow Daniels was nearly my height and fit looking in jeans and a sweatshirt with *Cartopia Rocks* across the front.

She was a redhead with a spray of freckles, a silver ring in one of her nostrils, and almond-shaped eyes whose color landed somewhere between brown and green. She stood next to a street bike with a kiddie trailer on the back. A small child, maybe a year old, was tucked inside, wearing a pink bike helmet and sleeping soundly.

When Willow saw Archie, she looked alarmed and stepped between my dog and the bike trailer. "This is my daughter, Tanya, but I call her Tater. Is your dog okay? I don't like dogs getting too close to Tater. I saw a little boy on the street get bit once."

"He's fine, loves kids, actually, but I can understand your concern." I turned to my dog and said, "Lie down, Archie, and *stay*." He gave me a look but did what I asked him. I turned back to the young woman. "How can I help you, Willow?"

"First of all, I want you to know I appreciate you taking the time. I've heard about Caffeine Central, and I respect the work you do here, Mr. Claxton. But I'm not looking for a handout. I just need a lawyer."

I nodded. "It's Cal."

"Okay, Cal. Here's the thing. My uncle died recently, and I guess I'm one of his heirs. My cousin, Donny Romano, is the only other one. He's ten years older than me. Uncle Mal never had any kids, and my mom and Donny's parents passed too early in life."

"Your uncle was unmarried?"

"He got divorced two years ago. Anyway, Donny's attorney called me the other day and said he wanted to meet about my uncle's estate." Her eyes narrowed, revealing a hint of steeliness. "I, um, I think I should probably have my own lawyer."

"I'm sorry for your loss. And yes, I think it's wise for you to have your own attorney, Willow. Your cousin's lawyer represents his interests and his only."

"Thought so. Donny and I never got along all that well." A faint, wistful smile. "I think he was jealous of my relationship with Uncle Mal."

"What's Donny do for a living?"

"He works at a gun shop on 82nd. R and J Firearms, I think it's called."

"Did your uncle leave a will?"

She shrugged. "I don't know. He hated red tape, anything having to do with business, that kind of stuff. I know he got in trouble once for not paying his taxes. So, it wouldn't surprise me if he didn't. He loaned me some money on a handshake four years ago." Her look turned resolute. "I want to make sure that gets accounted for."

I eyed her for a moment. "You want to pay back the estate?"

"Yeah, before things get divided up. I pay my debts."

"That's commendable. How much money are we talking about?"

"Fifty-five thousand dollars. It was to help me buy a food cart. I've paid back fifteen thousand so far."

"What's your uncle's name?"

"Malcolm Bainbridge. You might have heard of him. He's, um, *was* a partner in a high-tech startup here in Portland called Spectro Systems. They make spectroscopic widgets of some kind. He was kind of a technical genius."

I hadn't heard of Bainbridge or Spectro Systems, which wasn't surprising. There were a multitude of tech startups in Portland. "When did your uncle pass?"

"January fifteenth at his house in Portland near Mount

Tabor." Her face clouded over. "There's something else... Uncle Mal supposedly committed suicide—"

"Supposedly?"

"That's what they're saying, but I don't believe it."

"You don't think he took his own life?"

"He had bouts of depression now and then, so I guess it wasn't surprising to a lot of people. But, no, I don't think he killed himself."

"Accident? Murder?"

"They said he died of a gunshot wound." Her eyes flashed at me. "It was no accident, so I'm thinking that leaves one alternative."

"What makes you think it wasn't suicide?"

She watched a car cruise by on Couch Street for a few moments, then brought her gaze back to me. "First of all, I saw him two days before he died, and he wasn't depressed."

"Would you have known? People learn to disguise their disorders."

"Oh, yeah. I could always tell when he was down. It doesn't make any sense. And it isn't just me. Denise—she's a friend of mine who works at Spectro Systems—said the same thing."

"Have you considered going to the police with your concerns?"

"I did go, a week and a half ago. I talked to a young detective. He took a few notes and said he'd pass my comments along to the investigating team. An investigator called me, and I met her for an interview, but I never heard anything after that."

"Did he talk about his work much?"

"Not really." She paused for a moment. "Well, he did say he was working on something pretty important the last time I spoke to him—some kind of new virus test technology. Oh, and he mentioned he'd nixed a proposal by his partner to sell Spectro Systems. That didn't surprise me. Uncle Mal loved the company."

At that point, Tater woke up and began to fuss, which prompted Willow to produce a sippy cup from a backpack in the trailer. The child had a pair of big fawn eyes the color of cinnamon. She took the cup with two hands, but not before displaying a broad smile that revealed a couple of recently acquired teeth.

Willow turned back to me. I said, "I can understand how you feel. Losing your uncle is a terrible shock." What I didn't say was that disbelief or denial that a family member committed suicide was a very common reaction. I should know, having experienced the suicide of my wife. "I'd be happy to represent you in the estate settlement. The question of how your uncle died is a much more complex issue. I'm not sure what I could do about that. I'm a lawyer, and what you're asking for is more in the realm of a private investigator."

Her shoulders slumped. "I know. It was probably stupid of me to bring it up, but I heard you're good at solving crimes." Her eyes, shaded to green in the ambient light, locked onto mine. "Something's off about the suicide, I just know it. The police told me he was found in his photography studio." She looked incredulous. "No way he would harm himself there. He *loved* working in his studio. I was hoping you could just look at the findings, you know, talk to some people, that sort of thing. My uncle deserves it."

I stood mute for a few seconds. I didn't know Malcolm Bainbridge from Adam, and what she was asking me to do was ill-defined and open-ended, the kind of task that caused my bookkeeper to roll her eyes. But Willow Daniels had asked for my help for all the right reasons, and besides, the question of how Malcolm Bainbridge died roused my curiosity.

"Okay, Willow, tell you what. If I can get my hands on the investigation report of your uncle's suicide, I'll look it over. That's a big if, because the report is confidential unless there are public interest reasons for releasing it, which I assume isn't the case here. And even if I succeed, chances are there won't be anything I can do to help you. The investigators at the medical examiner's office are good at what they do."

The corners of her mouth, which were perpetually upturned, seemed to lift her lips in a smile. "I understand. All I'm asking is for you to take a look."

"Alright, then." I quoted her a fee based on the sliding scale I used for my Portland clients who had some ability to pay. She agreed and gave me the phone numbers for her cousin's attorney and her uncle's ex-wife. I said, "If I decide to get involved in the issue of your uncle's suicide, we'll have to talk again about expenses, okay?"

She nodded curtly, and I watched as she stowed the sippy cup in the trailer and put her own bike helmet on. Tater gave up the cup willingly and was now wide awake and focused on Archie, who studied her with equal curiosity. "Stay safe," I said as she pulled out onto Couch with her daughter in tow, a strobe light flashing on the back of the trailer to protect its precious cargo.

I looked at Archie and shrugged with a sheepish smile. "Okay, I admit it. She had me at Tater."

CHAPTER TWO

"YOU'RE *SURE* THIS IS A GOOD IDEA?" I SAID TO MY PRIVATE investigator, Hernando Mendoza. I'd slept over at Caffeine Central in the studio apartment above my office and was driving my friend to the Portland airport the next morning. "I mean, how do you know you can trust the Cuban government?"

He opened his big hands. "Can any government be trusted? They have told the world that exiles like me are now welcome to visit without prejudice. I am willing to take the chance. It has been fourteen years since I have seen my mother and sisters." He closed his eyes for a moment and smiled wistfully. "And I want to enjoy some good Cuban food."

"What about this corona virus situation? What if they start restricting travel and you get stuck in Cuba? The WHO has declared a global health emergency, you know."

He waved a hand dismissively. "Ah, I am certain there will be no problems. I am only staying for a month. What could happen in such a short period of time?"

"I hope you're right. Are you going to see Manuel?" I was referring to the friend of his whom I had heard about so many times. Manuel had helped Nando secretly gather the materials for the raft that he eventually rowed to the Florida Keys during four arduous days.

"I will, but I am not looking forward to it so much. Manuel has the Alzheimer's. My sisters have warned that he will probably not recognize me." Nando sighed. "It is very sad. I owe him much. Helping me was a great risk for him."

We arrived at the departure area, and as Nando removed his luggage from the back of my car, I said, "Have a great trip and give my love to your family."

"I will," he said, flashing his trademark brilliant smile. "And remember, Esperanza can help you with anything you may need."

He was referring to Esperanza Oliva, the manager of his PI office, the Sharp Eye Detective Agency, one of many businesses my entrepreneurial friend owned. "Of course," I said. "Fortunately, things are quiet right now." I didn't mention the fact that I needed copies of the Medical Examiner's reports on the death of Malcolm Bainbridge. This would have been a simple task for Nando, who had a female contact in the ME's office that he could count on for various favors. I would have to find another way, and if I couldn't, well…I hadn't promised Willow Daniels anything.

I intended to head home to Dundee after dropping Nando off, but on an impulse, I called Captain Harmon Scott of the Portland Police Bureau. Harmon and I had worked together over the years, forging a friendship and a deep respect for each other, although seldom seeing eye to eye. I saw him as a man longing for a past that was long gone, and he most certainly saw me as a man whose philosophy he couldn't begin to fathom.

"Cal Claxton," he said when I reached him, "let me guess—this isn't a social call. You want a favor."

"That's cold, Harmon. What are you up to today?"

"It's a Saturday, but I'm working. I was just going to grab a bite of lunch."

"Where?"

"The Virginia Café, where else?"

The VC was Harmon's go-to spot. I said, "How about that? I was just thinking of lunch. I'll meet you there in twenty minutes. I'm buying."

"I knew it," he responded. "Can't wait to hear your sad tale."

Archie, who was looking forward to getting home, gave me the stink eye when I parked in downtown Portland and cracked a couple of windows. "I won't be long, Big Boy," I promised.

Over one hundred years old, the Virginia Café was a bar and eatery with globe chandeliers, a mahogany bar and high-backed booths adorned with filigree. The place was practically deserted, and I found Harmon sitting in a booth near the back.

The gray in Harmon's thinning hair matched the color of his eyes, which regarded me through the thick lenses of frameless glasses. You wouldn't take him for a cop except for those eyes—they had that I've-seen-it-all look that every cop eventually acquires. He'd put on a little weight since I'd seen him last, and his jowls were more pronounced. We chatted for a while, mostly about what we didn't know about the potential pandemic, and it wasn't until after we'd ordered that Harmon showed the hint of a smile. "Okay, Claxton. Let's have it. What's on your mind?"

I cleared my throat. "A young woman stopped by my office yesterday, claiming a recent suicide here in Portland was actually a murder." I sketched in what Willow had told me about the Malcolm Bainbridge suicide.

"You got nothing except this young woman's emotional reaction?" he said when I finished. "Pretty thin stuff."

"That's where you come in," I countered. "I'm going with my gut, here, Harmon. She seemed credible. Does the case ring a bell?"

He furrowed his brow. "The name's vaguely familiar. We might've been peripherally involved, but nothing came of it. The ME's got the ball on suicides." He brought his eyes up to mine and waited...

"Any chance you could slip me a copy of the death report and the unredacted autopsy? I told the young woman I'd look them over, if possible. It will be for my eyes only, and I'll destroy the copies after I read them. Chances are it won't go any farther than that."

Harmon kept his eyes on me but didn't speak for the longest time. I figured a flat "no" was in the offing. He finally exhaled noisily and shook his head. "I gave up trying to understand what motivates you a long time ago. It is what it is as far as I'm concerned." He paused. "I heard about the murder of that young Latina out in the wine country. The bastards that did it got theirs, thanks to you. I'll see what I can do out of general appreciation for that piece of work." A thin smile spread across his face. "And I know you'll protect your source. He likes his job a lot."

Our food came—beer battered onion rings and a cheeseburger for Harmon and a grilled chicken sandwich with avocado and tomato for me. Our conversation drifted to more pleasant topics. Harmon surprised me when he said, "I've taken up meditation." I probably looked stunned, but he ignored my reaction. "Yeah, I get up and spend forty minutes or so before I have my coffee. It's guided, on an app my daughter suggested."

"What's it like?"

"Subtle. You kinda let your thoughts flit through your head until they play out. But you know what, it calms me down some, and I come into work a lot more focused. God knows, everyone at the Bureau could use that these days.

"That's great, Harmon. Maybe you could start leading some sessions for your fellow officers." I turned my palms up in front of me and closed my eyes. "I'm trying to picture you meditating."

He laughed. "Screw you, Claxton. You should try it."

I got the check as promised, and when Archie saw me approaching on SW 10th, he gave a high- pitched squeal of delight. We made good time to Dundee, the self-proclaimed heart of the Oregon wine country. Strung along the Pacific Highway some twenty-five miles south of Portland, the town had languished for years as not much more than a bottleneck for Portlanders hell-bent on a day at the coast. That all changed when a group of intrepid vintners decided the Red Hills was a good place to grow pinot noir grapes. It turned out they were right.

I passed my one-man law office, once the town's only barber shop, and turned off the highway and began the climb into the Red Hills. The vineyards were still battalions of brown, inanimate skeletons, and it was hard to believe that in another two months "bud break" would cover the vines in a blaze of lime green shoots, a clarion call that the sap was flowing and spring had arrived in wine country.

I let Archie out at our gate, and he rushed out into the upper field, scattering a half-dozen robins mining for worms. A hand-carved sign on a thick slab of red cedar read "Claxton's Aerie, Welcome." A gift from my daughter

Claire, it was now so weather-beaten that I made a mental note to take it down and try to restore it.

Zoe Bennett's Forester was parked up near the garage. Zoe was...well, men my age didn't use the term "girlfriend," and I'd never heard her refer to me as her boyfriend. I suppose you'd say we were in a relationship, although that sounds less than romantic. In any case, we were on a glide path to real commitment. At least, that's what I hoped.

I found her hunched over her laptop on my side porch wearing a pair of trail pants, a light fleece pullover, and low-cut boots. Her ash blond hair was pulled back and tied off, except for the strands that weren't, and her deep blue eyes looked nearly black in the waning light. Archie had followed me around the house and went straight to her. She sat up, gave him a hug, and closed her computer. "Did Nando get off okay?"

"He did. Didn't seem too worried about traveling. I gestured toward the laptop. Get any writing done?" A Ph.D. psychologist, Zoe was on a sabbatical from teaching at the University of Puget Sound and was writing a book. The book was literary fiction, not the treatise on psychology her department head was expecting. She wasn't sure how that was going to be received, but she was committed to the project, I can assure you.

She curled up one end of her mouth and shook her head. "I finished a chapter, but I'm not happy with it. Dialogue's a bitch. I can't seem to write anything that sounds authentic, like people really talk."

I paused for a moment. "You know who writes great dialogue?"

"Who?"

"Elmore Leonard."

Her head tilted back, and she arched her brows. "*Get Shorty*? That Leonard?"

"Yeah. He's written a ton of mysteries. His dialogue's always spot on, at least to my ear."

She smiled, and her eyes acquired a playful twinkle, something I loved about her. "Are you suggesting this writer of *mysteries* could help me with my *literary* masterpiece?"

"Maybe. *Crime and Punishment* is a mystery, right?"

She laughed. "Do you have any of said books?"

"Yep. There must be a half dozen in my study. Help yourself."

The twinkle persisted. "Noted. I'll take it under advisement. Meanwhile, how was your pro bono day in Portland?"

"Slow, but I did get a potential new client." I told her about my encounter with Willow and Tater Daniels.

"Interesting," she said when I finished. "Denial runs strong in the face of suicide, but you're well aware of that. This man died in his photography studio. I don't know about scientists, but artists have been known to kill themselves in their studios. Mark Rothko comes to mind. He slit his wrists and bled out in front of an unfinished painting."

I opened my hands in partial surrender. "I hear you. I know nothing about him or the case. It was his niece. She seemed credible."

Zoe rested her eyes on me. "The dust has hardly settled on the Olivia Fuentes case, and you're willing to take on another?

I sighed. "If it comes to that, yeah. I guess I am. Pretty compulsive, huh?"

She smiled, but her eyes looked worried. "That young woman must have impressed you." She sighed and took my hand in both of hers. "But I know how much that last investigation took out of you, Cal."

I dropped my eyes. "Yeah, but she could have easily let that loan from her uncle slide." I looked at Zoe and shook my head. "Integrity's a rare commodity these days."

She looked back at me without responding, but her eyes said, *Sure, but is that enough?*

CHAPTER THREE

I HAD A COURT APPEARANCE ON MONDAY AND A COUPLE of client conference calls that afternoon, so the Bainbridge issue was put on hold until I was back in my Dundee office on Tuesday. The first thing I did was pull up his obituary in *The Oregonian*, a perfunctory piece that could have been written by an AI app:

> Dr. Malcolm Edward Bainbridge
> March 20, 1953 - January 15, 2020
>
> Dr. Bainbridge passed away unexpectedly on January 15 at his home in Portland. Bainbridge was a partner at Spectro Systems, a Tigard machine and medical imaging company. He grew up in Seattle, where he obtained a Bachelor of Science degree at the University of Washington in 1973. He went on to earn a Ph.D. in chemistry from the University of California at Berkeley in 1977. Dr. Bainbridge was a brilliant scientist who authored more than thirty technical papers and was granted thirteen US patents in molecular spectroscopy and machine vision. He will be missed by his partner and coworkers for his creativity, sense of humor, and generosity.

I sat there for a moment after reading it. A man's life summarized so briefly, so dispassionately, was not a pretty sight. No mention of friends, relatives, or even his hobby, photography. One thing seemed clear—if a machine didn't write the obit then someone from Spectro Systems probably did. I Googled the company, jotted down the name of the remaining partner, and called the listed number, intending to ask for a few minutes of his time to get a sense of how he viewed Bainbridge. A recording answered and promised me a return call, which confirmed, once again, my contention that the answering machine was the worst invention of the twentieth century.

"Have you heard from Nando?" I asked Esperanza Oliva, when I called her next.

"Just a text that said he arrived in Havana safely," she answered. "How can I help you, Cal?"

I'd called Clete Bower, the attorney for Willow's cousin, and left him a message to call me back, but the number for the ex-wife was no longer in service. "I need you to find a phone number. The name's Gloria Talbot, previously Gloria Bainbridge, divorced two years ago. I think she's still in the area, but no White Pages listing. I kind of miss the old analog phone books, don't you?"

She laughed. "Yeah, I remember those innocent days when almost everyone listed their phone number, but, hey, it's job security for me."

I had just disconnected from Esperanza when my office assistant, Timoteo Fuentes, came in carrying two lidded coffees from the market across the highway. He wore a pair of sharply creased khakis, a button-down oxford shirt, and highly buffed loafers, quite a contrast to my jeans, black turtleneck, and lowcut hiking boots. He was set to start in the fall at the University of Oregon in pre-law. "So, we're going virtual, huh?" he said as he handed me a cup and sat down.

He was referring to the sign I'd posted outside that was similar to the one at Caffeine Central. I shrugged. "I figure it can't hurt until we get a clearer picture of this Covid thing. I'm no fan of viruses of any kind."

"Probably a good idea. I just read this morning that people coming back from China have to quarantine for fourteen days. *Fourteen days!* That would really suck, man." He glanced around the office. "What about you and me?"

"I guess we've already exposed each other, but we should stay separated as much as possible going forward."

"Will do," Timoteo said. "I hear there's a pretty good video conferencing site people are using called Zoom—"

"*Zoom?* Never heard of it but check it out." I smiled at my young protégé. "I like having a tech-savvy twenty-something around here. How are things at the vineyard?" Timoteo lived with his mother and father at Angel Vineyard, one of the largest in the Red Hills, where his father supervised the viticulture operation.

"Of course, this is a slow time, but, yeah, one of Popi's crew came down with a bad flu. Is it the corona virus? Who the hell knows? There's no way to get him tested." His face tightened into a look I knew all too well. "Should I worry about Popi and Mamá? They say older people might be more at risk."

"I think the risk's fairly low around here," I responded. "And in the whole country, for that matter."

"Right," Timoteo said, "we've got the best technology. I don't think we should worry too much." On that optimistic note, we set to work. Me on a brief at my desk and Timoteo on a stack of papers that needed filing.

—//—

Later that afternoon, Esperanza called back and gave me Gloria Talbot's address and cell phone number. "It wasn't that easy," she told me. "She seems to value her privacy. I also learned she works at the Wy'East Athletic Club in case you need that."

I wanted to talk to Talbot to get a sense of how she viewed Malcolm Bainbridge's suicide. She picked up after a half-dozen rings. I introduced myself and asked if she could spare some time to chat. I kept the reason vague, saying I was involved in settling Bainbridge's estate on behalf of his niece. "I don't have time to talk right now," she replied in a slightly petulant tone. "No offense, but I'm not a big fan of lawyers."

"A cross I have to bear daily," I said in a light tone that elicited a laugh. "It won't take long, I promise." She relented, suggesting we meet me at the Fresh Pot, a coffee shop on N. Mississippi Avenue in North Portland the next day at ten a.m. I agreed, which meant a trip into the city, but I figured it was worth it. Bainbridge's ex-wife might speak candidly about him.

Timoteo left early that day, but I was still hammering away on that brief when Archie finally got up, came over to me, and demanded a walk. Too proud to beg, it was his expression and the look in his big coppery eyes that made it clear. An Aussie tricolor, he was black with a white muzzle, chest blaze, and boots, and a bit of the same coppery eye color on his legs, cheeks and above his eyes. "Okay, Big Boy," I told him, "Let's get out of here."

We were across the Pacific Highway on our way to

the market when Clete Bower called back. "Mr. Claxton," he began, "thanks for getting in touch." His faux-cheerful, Chamber of Commerce tone grated on me. I stopped at a grassy strip that Archie promptly began to water. Bower went on, "We don't have a will, Mr. Claxton, but the situation looks reasonably straightforward to me. Once we get the probate judge to agree, our clients can evenly split the estate post liquidation since they're the only two living heirs."

"There's one item you should be aware of," I responded. "Ms. Bainbridge borrowed fifty-five thousand dollars from her uncle. She's paid back fifteen thousand. We'll have to account for the remaining forty in the agreement."

"That should be no problem."

"What about Bainbridge's partnership in Spectro Systems?"

"That's off the table. His share will go to the surviving partner per an agreement they entered into when the company was founded."

We talked for a while longer and agreed to meet on Friday to discuss how to proceed on the evaluations. Meanwhile, Bower offered to get us a probate petition hearing, the first step in what would undoubtedly be a lengthy process. Willow's comments about her uncle's disdain for red tape notwithstanding, I was surprised to hear that a man like him, a scientist, didn't leave a will. On the other hand, it wasn't that uncommon. Gloria Talbot wasn't the only person on the planet who didn't like dealing with lawyers.

A squall blew through that afternoon, but by the time I left the office, the skies had cleared. The gnarly grapevines on either side of Worden Hill Road glistened with a soft sheen in the late afternoon light. Once home, I changed into a pair of jogging shorts and a sweatshirt and was stretching in the driveway when Willow Daniels called.

"Hi, Cal. I don't want to bug you, but I'm just wondering how things are going." After I gave her a quick rundown, she said, "Thanks so much. Um, there's a couple of other things I didn't mention last Friday..."

"What are they?"

"I left an entire photoshoot at Uncle Mal's. He was printing the series for me. He has great equipment. I don't know if he finished or not, but I'd like to retrieve the prints along with the memory stick as soon as possible. I also left one of my best cameras with him. He wanted to play with it."

"No problem. Do you have a key by any chance?"

"Nope."

"I'll call Bower back, see if he has one."

"There's one last thing—Uncle Mal has a collection of Ansel Adams photographs. We shared a love for Adams' work. He told me once that I was to have it someday, that he knew I would appreciate it. Do you think that's possible? Maybe I could give half of what it's worth to Donny, something like that?"

"If he promised it to you, you shouldn't have to give Donny a cent. Is the collection valuable?"

"I know they're all originals. Uncle Mal's been collecting them for years, but I don't know how much they're worth. He never said, and I don't really care, to be honest."

After we disconnected, I finished stretching and began to jog. Archie trotted out ahead, yelping with delight as he led me out Eagle Nest Lane on the way to the Pioneer Cemetery at the top of the hill. The air was crisp and cool, and it felt good to run without a lot weighing on my mind.

But as the saying goes, all good things eventually come to an end.

CHAPTER FOUR

THE NEXT DAY A PRIVATE COURIER FROM PORTLAND dropped off a large envelope with my name on it and no return address. I tipped the messenger ten bucks and opened the envelope. A handwritten note clipped to a sheaf of papers read: *Here you go. Stoddard's thorough, and she determined this was a straight-up suicide. Aside from a few interviews, PPB took a pass. .Stoddard did get a request for the report from a Northwest Mutual investigator, so insurance is apparently in play. Lots of luck—Harmon.*

The package consisted of a detailed summary of the investigation carried out by medicolegal death investigator Elizabeth Stoddard, the medical examiner's complete autopsy report, and the resulting death certificate stating that Malcolm Bainbridge had died from a self-inflicted gunshot wound.

I examined Stoddard's investigative report first. Willow was right. The body was discovered the following morning in Bainbridge's photographic studio, by a cleaning lady, it turned out. There was no sign of forced entry into the house. The studio was essentially undisturbed. I studied several photographs and a sketch of the layout. Bainbridge's body was sprawled on the floor face down in a pool of blood with his right arm extended. The body was next to a workbench that held a jumble of electronic equipment—a rack of four large monitors, a couple of large printers, and other gadgets I didn't recognize.

"No darkrooms these days," I mumbled to myself.

A semi-automatic pistol lay on the tile floor a few inches from his outstretched hand. The weapon was identified as a Ruger-57 in the report, which also stated there were no bullets in the gun, and a box of shells was sitting on the workbench with one shell missing. It was concluded that Bainbridge was sitting on the stool next to the workbench when he shot himself. A check of the serial number confirmed that the pistol was purchased by Bainbridge five years earlier. The time of death, based on body temperature, rigor mortis, and lividity, was estimated at 9:30 p.m., some thirteen hours before the body was discovered.

Fingerprints on the gun matched those of the deceased. The fatal shot was administered to the right temple, and the victim was confirmed to be right-handed. Gunshot residue on the victim's hand, arm, and shirt confirmed that he had, indeed, fired the shot. However, Stoddard concluded that the size and shape of the entry wound and the surrounding stippling from the gunshot residue indicated the muzzle of the gun had not been in direct contact with the temple at the time the fatal shot was fired.

I examined the enlarged images of the wound carefully, noting the small entry point, maybe a quarter of an inch in diameter, surrounded by a tightly stippled pattern that was partly obliterated by charring from the hot gases expelled from the muzzle. I knew that with direct contact wounds the skin is torn by the gases into a markedly different star-shaped or stellate pattern. Stoddard estimated the distance at which the shot was fired to be between six and twelve inches. Her estimate seemed reasonable to me.

It was noted that a pistol vault was found open in the victim's bedroom. Also, there was no suicide note and no evidence of forced entry into the house.

I examined the autopsy report next. It consisted of an external examination and a toxicology screen only. Bainbridge's organs were not examined, but the bullet was extracted intact from his skull, allowing for a rapid and reliable ballistics match. The left side of his face was scraped due to contact with the tile floor when he fell, and a small bruise the size of a quarter observed on his left bicep was unexplained. The conclusion was that no defensive wounds or other evidence of a struggle were noted. The tox screen showed that, aside from an insignificant blood-alcohol content of .03, Bainbridge was free of drugs.

In sum, the autopsy findings were consistent with suicide as the cause and gunshot wound as the manner of death.

When I finished reading, I sat back in my chair and absently tapped my steepled fingers on my lower lip. The report was thorough, as Harmon Scott had promised, and I could understand why Elizabeth Stoddard arrived at the conclusion she did. However, the lack of a suicide note was an obvious issue, but maybe it was consistent with a man who hadn't bothered to leave a will.

A second concern was the geometry of the fatal shot. It was known in law enforcement circles that people who use a gun to kill themselves usually do it with the muzzle in direct contact with the body. With my index finger pointing at my temple, I moved my hand six or eight inches away from my head. Even at that short distance, an errant shot might wound and maim rather than kill. On the other hand, maybe Bainbridge couldn't bring himself to touch the muzzle to his temple. It was an observation only, not a swing factor.

There was apparently some life insurance involved in Bainbridge's death, and I would need to understand that better. The final thing that bothered me was more diffuse, a vague feeling that there was something about the physical scene that seemed if not off then at least bothersome. I went back and poured over the photographs again, but that didn't help.

I filed that kernel of skepticism away, knowing from experience that there could be something behind it. Or not.

The next morning at nine-fifty, I parked on Mississippi Avenue a block down from the Fresh Pot coffee shop, cracked the windows, and told Archie to chill. The place wasn't as busy as I'd anticipated. I wondered if that was in response to the virus threat, at least for those who paid attention to current events. I found Gloria Talbot in the back of the shop nursing a large coffee concoction of some kind and, after getting a double cappuccino, sat down across from her.

Wearing a scoop neck blouse that revealed a goodly amount of cleavage, she regarded me with a look of curiosity bordering on flirtation. Her wideset eyes were iceberg blue, and she had fiercely blond, stylishly tousled hair framing a handsome if not beautiful face, although the cut of her jawline lent a certain hardness to it.

"How's Willow?" she said after I thanked her for meeting with me.

"Missing her Uncle Malcolm. Did you know her well?"

"Not really, but Mal had a soft spot for her, and they both were interested in photography." A bitter smile. "With the amount of money Mal spent on equipment, he should've been famous or something. But Willow, that girl has real talent."

"Were you shocked when you heard he killed himself?"

She puffed a dismissive breath. "Not in the least. He was a nut-case depressive, and he wouldn't take any medication for it. For a scientist, Mal had a lot of blind spots when it came to objective reality."

"Did he ever talk about or threaten suicide?" She cocked her head slightly and eyed me with a questioning look. I smiled affably. "Willow mentioned that she was surprised Mr. Bainbridge killed himself. I'm just curious about your take."

She shook her head. "Mal never mentioned it, but when he was depressed, it was clear he wasn't real crazy about living."

"Did he own a gun while you were married?"

"We were broken into once, so he bought one. Never shot the damn thing...well, I guess he shot it *once*, didn't he," she added, barely concealing a smile.

"Unfortunately," I said. "As I mentioned on the phone, I'm representing Willow in the estate settlement. Willow and her cousin, Donny Romano, are the only two heirs. Does that agree with your knowledge of the family?"

"Yes. Willow was the only child of Mal's younger sister, Mimi. She divorced her husband early on and raised Willow on her own. Died of ovarian cancer, oh, maybe a decade ago. Donny's the son of Mal's older sister, Marilyn. She and her husband died in a car crash when Donny was in the service."

"That's tragic," I said, thinking of Willow raising Tater alone just like her mom. "Do you know if the estate has any large debts or if there are any other issues that might come as a surprise in the settlement?"

"Well, there's a collection of photographs in the house that Mal promised to Donny. They're by a guy named Allen Adams. Donny always loved those photographs."

I did a double take. "You mean *Ansel* Adams?"

She blinked as her head kicked back slightly. "Yeah, that's the guy."

I saw no reason to dispute her claim at that juncture. "Anything else?"

A faint smile showed itself. "An insurance policy's coming due." I raised my eyebrows. "It was negotiated as part of our divorce settlement. I'm the beneficiary."

That explains the reference to Northwest Mutual in Harmon Scott's note, I said to myself, swallowing an urge to ask what the payout was. That would've crossed a courtesy line. Instead, I said, "Mal didn't leave a will. Does that surprise you?"

"Not really. I made sure both of us had wills when we were married. He probably never bothered to write a new one after the divorce, just tore up the one we had."

"Would that kind of inattention explain why he didn't leave a suicide note?"

She curled her lip. "Oh, yeah. Just like Mal to leave a mess behind. Will the lack of a will make your job difficult?"

"We'll have to see. The cousins have already agreed to an even split."

Gloria's eyes narrowed down. "Mal loaned Willow a lot of money, you know. I doubt she's paid it back."

"Not a lot of money in the grand scheme of things," I

responded. "And she plans to pay it back to the estate prior to the distribution." I smiled. "What about your insurance payout? Knowing insurance companies, it's probably moving at glacial speed."

"*Jesus*, you said it. It's pretty simple, you know? Mal's dead. Where's my money, Northwestern?" She opened her hands and swung her eyes to me, searching for sympathy. In a quieter voice, she said, "This is my compensation for suffering through ten years with that crazy bastard." A self-satisfied smile. "The life insurance bet paid off, and I earned that money, every cent of it."

Not long after that exchange, I got up to leave. Gloria straightened in her seat in a way that stretched tight the fabric covering her breasts and rested her eyes on me a beat longer than decorum demanded. "It was nice meeting you, Cal."

Chalking the body language up to a kind of flirtation reflex, I said, "Yes, nice meeting you, too. Good luck with the insurance."

As I pulled out onto Mississippi Avenue, I turned the conversation over in my head. It was clear that Gloria considered Bainbridge's suicide probable if not inevitable, perhaps even betting on it by taking a life insurance policy as part of the divorce settlement. She also provided a possible rationale for the lack of a suicide note.

Who was right? Gloria or Willow? Truth be told, I wasn't sure at that point, but I did wonder about the size of that insurance payoff. It sounded like it could be substantial. And another issue welled up—Willow mentioned the divorce had taken place two years earlier. I knew that life insurance policies written in Oregon only covered suicide after a two-year period. How close was Bainbridge's suicide to the exclusion period? Although a suicide in close proximity didn't prove anything, the actual timing was of interest to me. I made a mental note to track down the Northwest Mutual investigator.

Finally, there was the apparent inconsistency regarding the disposition of the Ansel Adams collection. *What was up with that?*

CHAPTER FIVE

"I'M IN TOWN," I SAID TO WILLOW ON THE PHONE AS I headed back toward center city. "Can we meet somewhere? I can come to you."

"Sure. I'm prepping for lunch, but it doesn't look like we're going to get slammed today. I'm at Cartopia, a food cart pod on Hawthorne and 12th. My cart's called the Plat du Jour. Can't miss it."

"I know the pod," I said. "See you in ten."

Like mushrooms in a rain forest, food carts had sprung up in clusters dubbed "pods" all over Portland. The food was uniformly good, and they offered not only Northwest cuisine but fare from all over the world. I found a parking spot on 12th and attached Archie's leash. A large, white circus tent and a huge, elevated sign marked the pod, one of Portland's most popular. I spotted the Plat du Jour in a line of carts on the far side of the tent, all complete kitchens on wheels painted every color in the rainbow. Arch and I weaved our way through a throng of picnic tables and elevated, outdoor heaters as the aromas from the carts mixed and mingled. My stomach began to growl.

Willow was writing the menu for the day on a whiteboard in front of her cart. "Hello," she greeted us, beaming an effortless smile. Archie went up to her for some attention.

She extended a tentative hand, withdrew it after his quick sniff, and said to me, "Let me finish this, then we can talk." Unaccustomed to getting the cold shoulder, my dog sat on his haunches and cocked his head at Willow.

"Salmon steak frites and a butter lettuce salad with apples and walnuts," I said, watching her finish writing. "Sounds delicious. Kind of Northwest-French fusion, huh?"

She laughed, and it crinkled the corners of her eyes. The cold air had reddened her cheeks, the color blending with her freckles some. "Yeah, it's sort of what I'm going for. French inspired, most days, but always using local ingredients. This morning I picked up some nice chinook filets, so, yeah, steak frites sounded good." She pointed to a picnic table. "Have a seat. Tater's in the cart. I'll grab her and join you."

She reappeared with Tater from behind her red-trimmed, bright yellow cart. The little cherub wore a fleece, hooded jumpsuit with bear ears. Her big, bright eyes went straight to Archie. She stretched an arm out in his direction, pointed with a tiny index finger, and said with great conviction, "Gog."

Willow and I both laughed. She said, "That's right, Tater. He's a *dog*." She turned to me. "She knows dogs from her favorite cloth book, but the pronunciation needs some work. She's quite taken by Archie." On cue, he got up and approached the mother and child, his stump of a tail wagging slowly, his eyes locked on Tater.

"I think the feeling's mutual," I said.

Willow wrapped her arms around her daughter protectively and swiveled away from Arch slightly. I took the hint and told Arch to lie back down. Clearly, my dog was going to have to earn Willow's trust. I said, "I was able to get a copy of your uncle's autopsy and suicide investigation reports, and I've talked to Gloria Talbot. I want to go over some details, okay?"

"Of course. Boy, you work fast." Tater squirmed, and Willow produced a ring of brightly colored plastic keys, which her daughter grasped with both hands and began to chew on.

I chuckled, then took her through the physical evidence surrounding her uncle's death. "On the face of it I can see why the investigator reached a finding of suicide." Her shoulders dropped, and she winced perceptibly. "But," I said, raising a finger for emphasis, "I do have some questions. First, your uncle didn't leave a suicide note, which is odd. Gloria felt that was in keeping with his contrarian nature. How do you see it?"

Her eyes welled up, and a single tear broke loose and slid down her cheek. "Uncle Mal wouldn't leave without saying goodbye to Tater and me, without *explaining* why he had to do such a terrible thing." She wiped the tear with her fingertips and looked at me straight on, her lips compressed. "No, he would've said goodbye somehow. I'm sure of it."

"Alright. The gun that was used was a Ruger-57. It was registered to him. He bought it about five years ago. Do you know why he bought the gun?"

"Yeah, there was a burglary and Gloria had him buy it."

"It was Gloria's idea?"

"Yes. I know because he complained to me about having to buy it to placate her. I don't think he ever shot it."

"Did Gloria ever shoot the gun?"

Willow shrugged. "I don't know."

"The ME's report said he had a pistol vault. Did he use it to keep the Ruger secured?"

Another shrug. "I know who could probably answer

that question—uncle Mal's cook and housekeeper, Wanda Jenkins."

"Good," I said. "I was coming to that. I'd like to talk to her. She found his body."

Willow flinched at the reference. "No problem. I'll set it up. She helps me out at the cart sometimes and watches Tater when I'm in a pinch."

At this point, Tater chucked the keys onto the ground and pointed at Archie again with a grin that mimicked her mother's. "Gog Gog, Gog Gog."

Archie got up and whimpered this time. He wanted to approach the little creature. But I could see the uncertainty in Willow's eyes, so I told him to lie back down. "Do you know anything about a life insurance policy that named Gloria as the beneficiary?"

"No, I don't know anything about that." Her eyes—nearly green in the midday light—narrowed down some. "So is Gloria's going to come into some money now?"

"I don't know how much yet, but yes, she's the beneficiary of a policy that your uncle maintained as part of the divorce settlement."

Willow's nostrils flared. "She doesn't deserve a penny. I don't trust her, Cal. I never did."

"I'm going to try to find out the size of the payout," I responded, "and I've got a call into your cousin's attorney to get a key so we can retrieve your photos and camera at Malcolm's house."

"That's a relief."

"There's one other thing," I said. "Gloria said the Ansel Adams collection was promised to Donny. I didn't dispute it because I wanted to talk to you first."

She rolled her eyes with a disgusted look. "That's not

true. Donny wouldn't know an Ansel Adams from a comic book cover. Uncle Mal would have never done that."

"No worries," I said. "It might be just hearsay or a misunderstanding. I'll get to the bottom of it." We left it there after I answered a few questions and she had given me Wanda's contact information. I decided not to mention the details about the fatal shot to spare her the mental picture it would undoubtedly conjure up.

I was Willow's first customer for lunch that day, and when I finished eating I said, "That was delicious. I love what you did with the salmon, a little brown sugar and lemon, right?"

She laughed. "Is there any other way? This is the Northwest."

"And the fries," I went on. "Perfectly crisp. Best I've ever tasted. How do you do that?"

She showed a modest smile. "I start with the best russets I can get my hands on and slice them really thin, but the secret is I fry them twice—once to cook them through, and once right before I serve them to crisp them up."

"Belgian style."

"That's right. They one-upped the French on fries. Not many people know that. Do you cook?"

"A little. Nothing fancy." A line of customers started to form behind me. I waved goodbye to Tater, who sat in a highchair at the back of the kitchen, then paused for a moment, trying to find the right words to leave with her. I settled for, "Keep the faith, Willow. If there's something there, we'll find it."

To myself, I added, *if.*

—/ /—

Zoe Bennett lived two or three miles down the undulating slopes from me in a modest rental home on SW Red Hills Drive. Her aunt, Gertrude Johnson, who also happened to be my accountant and neighbor to the north, found the place for her. Gertie grew up in the five-acre plot above me and knew nearly everyone in the wine country. Zoe had come to the Red Hills to care for her aunt after she suffered a heart attack and had decided to stay, write her book, and perhaps start a psychology private practice rather than go back to teaching. The ranch style house had a couple of cherry trees in the front yard, mature foundation plantings—rhododendrons and the like—and a small deck out the back with a nice view of the Willamette Valley stretching to the southern horizon.

"Hey, what about me?" I said as she lavished a warm hug on my dog after letting us in. Archie and Zoe were tight, to say the least. She laughed, and after she gave me an equally warm greeting I followed her into the kitchen, where two glasses of Oregon pinot awaited us on the kitchen table. Zoe was cooking, a rare treat. Let's just say that culinary skills were not her forte, although her spaghetti from sauce in a jar wasn't that bad. I'd promised to make a salad.

"How did it go with Elena today?" I asked as I washed some fresh spinach. I knew it was her day to counsel Elena Fuentes, the mother of my assistant Timoteo. Elena was struggling with PTSD after the murder of her daughter the previous year. The counseling was informal, more like a chat between the friends they had become.

"She's doing well, getting her energy back and the ability to focus." Zoe smiled with a hint of pride. "She made you something." She extracted a swath of intricate, multicolored bead work done in a repeating geometric design from a drawer and handed it to me, smiling. "It's a bracelet in a Huichol pattern." She put it on my right wrist and fixed the clasps.

I held it up admiringly, recalling vaguely that the Huichol were an indigenous people from Mexico who perfected this art. "Very cool. You tell her I'm wearing it, that I love it."

"I will. She stopped beading maybe a decade ago, but I encouraged her to start again. I think it's helping her get her life back. She told me it will bring you good luck."

"Good to hear. I always need plenty of that. How are things at Angel Vineyard?"

She drew her eyebrows toward each other. "A worker went down with pretty serious respiratory symptoms a few days ago."

"I know. Timoteo mentioned it, said he couldn't get tested. What do you think?"

She shrugged. "I hope it's not the virus. The migrant community's pretty isolated, you know, which might make them less vulnerable.".

She went on to tell me about her day as I busied myself microwaving some bacon and slicing a couple of hardboiled eggs. I added them along with croutons to the spinach and dressed the salad with a whisked concoction of olive oil, red wine vinegar, and Dijon mustard. Our conversation didn't turn to the suicide of Malcolm Bainbridge until we'd finished eating and were out on her deck, bundled in sweaters and scarves, sipping coffee, and watching a gold-red sun die against a deep lavender sky.

"By the way," Zoe said, "what was the name of the company that Bainbridge was a partner in?"

"Spectro Systems," I answered.

"That's what I thought. Did you read *The Oregonian* business section this morning? I shook my head. "There was a big spread about Spectro Systems and a virus test they're developing. They claim to have shown they can detect the Covid-19 coronavirus in one second."

"One second?"

"That's what they're claiming. The article said they've invented a device about the size of a computer mouse that looks at saliva or blood serum using some kind of spectroscopy to determine if the virus is present. Apparently Covid-19 leaves a unique signature. It sounds pretty cool to me."

"I'll say. A test that fast could be important. Right now, most people can't even get tested, and turn-around times can be, what, a week or two?

"Some of the test kits sent out by the CDC are faulty, as well," Zoe added. "Spectro Systems is bullish on the device, that's for sure. The CEO—can't remember his name—was quoted as saying it could revolutionize epidemiology and allow viral outbreaks to be stopped in their tracks. Was this Bainbridge's work?"

"I don't know for sure, but Willow said he was a technical genius. And she said something else—that he mentioned he was working on something important the last time she saw him. Maybe this is it. How far along is the development?"

"The article mentioned a provisional patent and the start of clinical trials, so, not that far along."

I whistled. "A device like that could be worth a ton of money. The demand would be worldwide."

"No doubt." She showed a knowing smile. "I figured you'd find that interesting."

I did, indeed, and decided to put a meeting with Bainbridge's partner at Spectro Systems on the front burner. It had been my experience that money, especially a lot of it, had a way of driving behavior, usually in all the wrong directions.

CHAPTER SIX

A wreck on the notorious Terwilliger curves section of the I-5 the next morning jammed up traffic, so I didn't get to Caffeine Central until half-past nine. I'd just gotten off a call from a young, homeless woman inquiring about how to get her shoplifting record expunged when, as luck would have it, another call came in: "Mr. Claxton, this is Bradley Nielsen at Spectro Systems returning your call. I apologize for the delay. We've been busy around here."

"Not a problem," I reassured him and went on to explain why I wanted some of his time.

"I can't talk now, but I've got a window today at eleven, if you want to come to our headquarters." I told him I did, and he gave me the address. I was relieved that a busy CEO like Nielsen didn't insist on a phone conversation and even found it a little curious. Perhaps he was as interested in meeting me as I was to meet him.

Located in a business park ten miles south of downtown, the start-up company was housed in a large, non-descript, two story building with a sign in front that read:

Spectro Systems
Machine Vision Products for the Future

I was buzzed in and escorted up a flight of stairs and

down a hallway. We passed an office door with a nameplate that read *Malcolm Bainbridge, Technical Director* and stopped at another that read *Bradley Nielsen, Chief Executive Officer*. Nielsen stood from behind his desk, and after we exchanged pleasantries I said, "Before we get started, do you mind if I get your take on this new virus from China?"

He raised his eyebrows. "It appears to be highly transmissible. We're going to need to respond on a national scale to keep it in check, but we've got the strongest epidemiologic infrastructure in the world, so we'll be fine. It's the rest of the world that's at risk." A big man with a receding hairline, Nielsen wore a turtleneck, jeans, and Allbird sneakers. Four deep furrows creased his wide forehead, and the bridge of his nose seemed pinched by a set of narrow, unreadable eyes. He motioned toward a chair and sat back down. "So, how can I help you, Mr. Claxton?"

"As I mentioned on the phone, I need to understand the full extent of Malcolm Bainbridge's resources, prior to a court hearing that will divide them between my client, Willow Daniels, and her cousin, Donny Romano."

"Of course. I've already met with the other cousin's attorney, Clete..." He looked at me for help.

"Bower, Clete Bower," I said.

"Yes, Bower. Like I told him, the partner's agreement Mal and I drew up stipulated that all financial interest in the company reverts back to the other partner if one of us dies."

"That's it? No other financial entanglements, debts, leans, mortgages, something that could come back at Bainbridge's estate?"

"Well, we're carrying some debt, but that's addressed in the agreement. I can get you a copy of it for your records."

"I'd appreciate that." I paused. "Willow Daniels was shocked at her uncle's suicide. Were you?"

He gave a slight eye roll. "Nothing Mal did surprised me, and it's no secret the man had his demons."

"You mean his depression?"

"Yeah. He definitely had his bad days."

"Was he depressed in the period leading up to the suicide?"

Nielsen waved a hand dismissively. "Hell, I don't know. To tell you the truth, I don't pay much attention to people's moods. I figure it's on them to keep their heads straight."

"Were you aware that Bainbridge owned a gun?"

He paused, regarding me with more attention. "We're straying from the topic a bit, aren't we?"

I smiled with a hint of you-caught-me. "My client's having a hard time accepting that her uncle committed suicide. I'm just looking for corroboration that would help her move on. She's young, you can understand."

His brows lowered slightly, signaling that he didn't really understand. "Yeah, I knew about the gun. Mal bitched and moaned that Gloria, his ex, made him buy it." He laughed. "He hated guns and the NRA with a passion."

"Given his demons, did you ever worry he might use it on himself?" I asked, but I knew the answer by that time.

"I never thought of it that way. I mean, it's his damn gun. What he does with it is none of my business." Nielsen picked up a pen and tapped it on his desk a couple of times, a not-so-subtle signal our chat was nearing an end.

I said, "Congratulations on the virus detection device. These must be exciting times for your company. Looks like good timing given this Covid virus threat."

He dropped the pen and seemed to puff up before my eyes. "Yeah, we got lucky. We were developing the technology for other applications, but the device has great potential for detecting Covid 19. We just came up with the name InstaVision20 today. What do you think of it?" I smiled approval and he went on, "Investors want in on this. My phone's ringing off the hook."

"I'm curious. How does it work?"

He broke a broad smile. "Basically, on one side of the device we have a light source, and on the other a hyperspectral camera that can rapidly record the different transmitted wavelengths," Nielsen said, spreading his hands and launching into full sales mode. "The sample vial goes in the middle. If the virus is present, it absorbs certain wavelengths that the camera captures, a unique signature, if you will. And it all happens in a second or two."

"Impressive."

"There's more," Nielsen said, beaming. "The algorithm we've developed is enhanced by artificial intelligence. This allows us to differentiate between the various coronaviruses, which aren't identical siblings, but close to it."

"Is InstaVision20 costly?"

His narrow eyes widened. "Hyperspectral cameras are exceedingly expensive, but we've innovated a low-cost version that employs a single, cost-effective silicon chip. Our device can be used in hospitals, at remote sites, even at home."

"Was this Bainbridge's work? His niece said he was working on something important shortly before his death."

"Mal had his hand in everything technical at Spectro Systems. I'm not sure his name's going on this particular patent, but he was as pleased as I was about the preliminary test results."

"Yet he shot himself?"

Nielsen opened his hands. "It was Mal. What can I tell you?"

"What are the next steps?"

"We're gathering enough test data to go for an FDA emergency use authorization. Our goal is to have our system ready for the pandemic we think might"—At that point Nielsen's phone rang. He answered, then cupped his hand around the speaker and looked at me. "I've got to take this. Can you find your way out?"

When I got to the car, I let Archie out for a stretch, and we headed back into Portland. I didn't hear anything from Nielsen that tipped the scales one way or the other relative to the suicide. However, I did learn that the important work Bainbridge told Willow he was engaged in was almost certainly InstaVision20. Willow's question was a good one—why would her uncle kill himself in the face of what was apparently a breakthrough? And, of course, Bradley Nielsen was now in a position to reap *all* the rewards that might result from the new technology.

Hmm.

—/ /—

It was a good day for connections, because as I turned onto the Naito Parkway I got a call from a woman named Kiara Jones, the Northwest Mutual insurance investigator. I'd left her a voicemail the day before. She agreed to a rendezvous, and on a whim I said, "Have you had lunch? I know a great little food cart at Cartopia on Hawthorne. I'm buying." She laughed and said she'd meet me there in twenty minutes.

After we exchanged greetings under the Cartopia tent,

Jones stayed back with Archie while I waited in line to order our lunches at the Plat du Jour—a cup of French onion soup and a *croque madame*—a grilled sandwich with Black Forest ham and Gruyere cheese. "Nice crowd," I said to Willow when my turn came.

A smile lit her face. "Oh, hi Cal. Yes, this sandwich is a favorite." She looked past me. "Who's your friend?"

"The insurance investigator who's vetting Gloria's policy. She finally called back." Willow raised her eyebrows while making my change. I waved to Tater who sat in her highchair at the back of the cart.

Her eyes got big, and she pointed at me. "Gog Gog."

We both laughed. Willow said, "Don't get your feelings hurt. She likes you, too." She glanced at my wrist. "Is that a Huichol bracelet? I love it."

"My law clerk's mother made it for me. It's supposed to bring me good luck."

When our food came up, I carried it back to Kiara. She had a quick smile and casual manner but projected an unmistakable air of professionalism. I liked her immediately. We ate, both of us marveling at the food, and after some get-acquainted talk, she said, "So your client doesn't think Malcolm Bainbridge killed himself."

"That's right. Willow was very close to her uncle, and I'm just doing some fact-gathering to make her feel a little more comfortable with the reality. It's a hard thing to accept."

She looked at me for a couple of beats, then smiled. "I Googled you, Cal. You've been known to do more than just gather facts."

I smiled back. "Okay, I'm looking around, but I haven't committed to anything yet. Where are you coming out, Kiara?"

"My job is to determine if there's any reason Northwest Mutual shouldn't make good on the policy benefit. The hard evidence points in one direction—suicide." She paused and studied me for a moment. "And the beneficiary has a rock-solid alibi for the night of Bainbridge's death, in case you're wondering. I'm about ready to close out the investigation."

"The lack of a suicide note and the position of the gun when the fatal shot was fired doesn't bother you?"

"Not everybody leaves a note or has the courage to press a gun barrel against their head. The medical examiner called it suicide. In the absence of any other evidence, I don't have any other option but to sign off." A wry smile. "Not sure how my boss is going to react."

"Your boss is less sanguine?"

She laughed. "Always, and he makes the final call."

"Can you tell me how long the policy has been in force?"

"Twenty-six months."

"Two months past the minimum, I said. "I assume it's for a substantial amount."

"I don't investigate small payoffs," she answered with a hint of pride in her expression.

"Over a half-million?" I asked. She nodded. "Over a million?" Another nod. "Over two million?" She looked back at me without responding.

My eyebrows raised involuntarily. "Okay. Thanks for that, Kiara."

She smiled with a hint of slyness. "For what? I didn't give you anything. But if you feel indebted, I'm sure you'll let me know if you come across something material to my investigation." She looked at her watch and stood up. "I've got to run, Tell your client the lunch was delicious. She knows what she's doing."

Willow was busy, but when I waved goodbye she managed to call out, "Tater wants to see Archie. Can you bring him around to the back of the cart?"

I did, and when Tater saw Gog Gog her eyes became enormous. Willow took Tater out of the high chair and put her on her feet. I took the hint and let the pressure off Arch's leash. My dog inched forward, and Tater smiled ear to ear. She reached out, then pulled her hand back and laughed with the pure delight of a one-year-old. Mom picked her back up and said, "Okay, that's enough Gog Gog for today."

I laughed. "I think this is the beginning of a beautiful friendship."

—/ /—

On the way back to Caffeine Central, I thought about the two meetings I just had. The truth was Malcolm Bainbridge was worth an awful lot of money dead. For Bradley Nielsen, Bainbridge's death would double his take on InstaVision20, and for Gloria Talbot it meant somewhere in the neighborhood of two million in cold cash. And the timing in both cases couldn't have been much better.

Potential motives, big fat ones, raised their ugly heads, and questions, serious ones, began swirling around in my brain like a bunch of angry wasps. At the same time, my rational side reminded me there was no hard evidence to suggest murder rather than suicide. The lack of a suicide note? Explainable. The lack of contact between the gun and Bainbridge's temple? Bothersome, at best. Bainbridge's mental state at the time of his death? An open question.

The death scene photographs came back to me—Bainbridge stretched out in front of that high stool, the gun just out of his reach. What was it about that scene that bothered me? I still couldn't put my finger on it.

I shrugged and kept driving. *Give it some time,* I told myself. *Whatever's bothering you will bubble up.*

CHAPTER SEVEN

"SORRY I'M A LITTLE LATE," CLETE BOWER SAID WHEN I met him at the door to my office at Caffeine Central later that day. Well short of my height, he was heavyset with squinty eyes and a wide nose that veered to the left a few degrees, making me wonder if he'd ever boxed. As he drew near, I was greeted with an odor of stale cigars. "I've taken the liberty of collecting some information on Bainbridge's assets for us to look over," he added, holding up a legal-size envelope, "and I've drawn up a draft settlement agreement."

"Good," I said a bit hesitantly, "I appreciate that." I was peeved that he'd ignored the sign out front about calling first but stepped back to let him in. The virus was still more theoretical than reality at that point in time. "Come in, but let's keep our distance, okay?"

"Sure, whatever." He took a seat and looked around, ignoring Archie, who lay in the corner sizing up our visitor. "So this is your pro bono gig, huh?"

"Essentially, although I use a sliding scale in some situations."

He lowered his bristly brows. "Law school cost me a bundle. No offense, but I figure if they can't pay me, fuck 'em." I didn't react, so he opened the envelope and removed some papers. "I've ordered an appraisal of Bainbridge's house in Mt Tabor. I looked at some comparables to get a ballpark. The place is worth a mil and a half, easy, which means around a million one after the mortgage is paid off. We can split the cost of the appraisal."

I shook my head. "We'll get our own appraisal. The probate judge will make us do that, anyway. Must be quite a place."

He showed a toothy, tobacco-stained grin. "Suit yourself on the appraisal. Yeah, the place is fucking awesome. Set back on a big lot on Belmont. Columns, balconies, the whole nine yards. We won't have any trouble unloading it. There's some pictures hanging on the walls that are worth a bundle, too."

"The Ansel Adams collection?"

He showed momentary surprise that I knew about the photographs but chose to let it slide. "Right. All black and white photos. I had a curator at the Portland Art Museum take a look." A sly grin. "Told him the heirs were thinking about donating the pictures. He got real cooperative, said we were looking at three, maybe three fifty."

"Thousand?"

"Yep. Of course, they're spoken for. Bainbridge promised them to my client."

I paused for a moment and looked him straight in the eye. "Does Donny Romano have that in writing?"

"No, but my client told me Gloria Talbot can back up his claim."

I held a neutral expression. "I see." I would fight that battle down the road.

Bower got up and slid two stapled stacks of papers across my desk. "The top one's the draft agreement. You can look that over at your leisure and get back to me. I figured we might as well get the ball rolling."

I picked it up and scanned the first page, noting a misspelled word and the misuse of an apostrophe, the latter being one of my particular pet peeves. I put the draft aside without comment.

Bower pointed at the second stack. "That's a copy of Bainbridge's most recent statement from a Fidelity mutual fund he owned. It's taken a hit with this virus talk, but the balance is still around seventy-five thou, all conservative investments managed by a broker here in Portland. I told him to carry on until we're ready to divide it up."

"That's fine with me."

"There's also a checking account with about fifteen thousand cash in it. We can use an estate sale firm to sell the furnishings and other items in the house, and that plus getting Blue Book on a couple of motorcycles and a beat-up Land Rover pretty much does it."

"I'm surprised," I admitted. "I had no idea the estate was that valuable. Do you have a date for the probate petition hearing yet?"

"Nah, the clerk hasn't gotten back to me. I'll let you know when I hear. We need to run an ad in *The Oregonian*, too. Let the public know Bainbridge croaked in case there's some heir in the woodwork we don't know about."

"I'll handle that," I volunteered. "If memory serves, we can't liquidate anything until four months after the ad runs."

"That's right, he said, then paused for a moment, his squinty eyes becoming slits. "Of course, we'll have to account for the loan your client owes the estate. How much did you say that was?"

"Fifty-five thousand, but Ms. Daniels has paid fifteen thousand back."

"We'll need a copy of the promissory note and any other records pertaining to the loan."

"There are none. The deal was done with a handshake."

"I see." Bower's lips sagged at the corners. "This, ah, could be a bit of a problem. My client, Donny Romano, recalls his uncle telling him the loan was for one hundred and fifty thousand dollars, not fifty-five."

I was taken aback, but I didn't show it. "I have no reason to doubt my client's word. Does Mr. Romano have proof of this amount?"

"Well, I think that was what Gloria Talbot understood, as well, but I'll talk to him." Another toothy grin. "I'm sure we can work something out. There's plenty of money in the estate, after all."

A small red flower of anger bloomed in my chest. I locked onto his squinty eyes. "My client is crystal clear on the amount we're talking about, just so you know."

"Well, let me talk to Donny. Maybe I got the numbers wrong."

"Yeah, that must be it," I said, knowing full well that wasn't the case. Bower stood to leave. I added, "Did you bring the key to the house?"

"Oh, that. I almost forgot. Donny has the key, and he would prefer to be there when Ms. Daniels visits, you know, in case there are any questions." Bower drew near, and I got another whiff of stale tobacco as he handed me the card. "His cell number's on the back. You can call him to arrange it."

After Bower left, I turned to Archie, who stood up, stretched languorously, and cocked his head. "I'm with you, Big Boy," I said. "Let's go home. I feel like I need a shower."

—/ /—

I poached some rockfish in white wine that night and served it with saffron rice and grilled asparagus spears. While we ate, Zoe talked about her book, mentioning she was halfway through one of the Elmore Leonard's books I'd loaned her. "You're right," she said, "Leonard has a gift for dialogue." She made a face. "If I can get past his violence, I just might learn something." She laughed. "Turns out people hardly ever speak in complete sentences, but you have to have an ear for it. Not sure I do."

We ate, sipped some local pinot gris, and I listened as she talked about her work, marveling at her passion and insight. At one point, I said, "Can I be a first reader?"

She looked at me, horrified. "Oh, God, no. They say *never* share your work with your, ah, significant other. That's a recipe for disaster."

I smiled. "So, I'm your significant other?"

She smiled back over the rim of her wine glass. "Yeah, I guess you are."

After dinner, we sat out on my side porch, huddled around a fire pit fueled with propane. A waxing moon shimmered through the Douglas firs lining the east side of my property, and a pack of coyotes yipped in the abandoned quarry below us. Lying next to Zoe's feet, Archie's only response to his canine cousins was to raise his head off his paws and give a single, halfhearted 'ruff.'

The conversation had turned to what I'd learned about the scientist Malcolm Bainbridge. After I poured us each a little more Rémy Martin to fight the cold, Zoe took a sip and said, "Bainbridge turns up with a bullet in his head.

The medical examiner calls it a suicide, and you can't find much in the death report to criticize, except there's something about the scene that looked staged to you, but you don't know what it is."

I couldn't help a sheepish smile. "That's right. And there's Willow Daniels's disbelief it was suicide. That started the whole thing."

Zoe rolled her eyes. "Her strong relationship with her uncle is what makes it so hard for her to accept what he did. It's the ultimate rejection for the young woman, amplified by the loss of her own mother."

I felt a twinge of annoyance. I understood the denial argument. I started to comment but thought better of it.

Zoe went on, "Turns out Bainbridge's ex-wife is the beneficiary of a sizeable life insurance policy, and his business partner will accrue all the benefits of his virus test invention. And today you learn that Bainbridge's only two heirs will split a bundle once his assets are liquidated."

Her mouth curved into an ironic smile. "*Cui bono?*"

"Yes. Who benefits? Four people by my count."

"Why aren't the police interested in this?"

I shrugged. "Good question. The ME called it a suicide, and I don't think Portland police bothered to put the whole picture together. There's an insurance investigator looking at the ex-wife, but I don't think that's going anywhere, either."

"What's your take on your list of potential suspects?"

I had to laugh. "Gloria Talbot has a raging sense of entitlement. She can't wait to get her hands on the insurance money, fair compensation for living with Bainbridge, she told me."

"Entitlement in the extreme is narcissism, which can lead to nasty behavior," Zoe offered.

"Noted. She's got an alibi, according to the insurance investigator. Also, I think she's lying about the Ansel Adams Collection being promised to Donny. And judging from my first brush with the nephew's attorney, I'd say Donny Romano is a liar as well."

Zoe smirked. "Sounds like Bonnie and Clyde to me."

"Yep, there could definitely be some collusion. Finally, Bradley Nielsen is utterly compassionless and literally drooling over the financial potential of InstaVision20. I got the impression he thinks the Covid-19 thing's going to escalate across the globe. Bainbridge's death doubled Nielsen's potential take. And the timing of the death couldn't have been better for Nielsen."

Zoe tilted her head and raised an eyebrow. "What about the young mother? She stands to gain, as well."

"Willow came to me, remember?"

"You really think she didn't know how much the Adams collection was worth?"

"Yes, I do. The value surprised me, and her story makes sense. She and her uncle shared a passion for photography." I tapped my heart with a folded fist and smiled. "And besides, some things you just know."

Zoe smiled and shook her head. "It's a real rogue's gallery. She looked at me over the flickering flames. "Are you going to take your findings to your detective friend, then?"

I returned her gaze. It wasn't the encouragement I hoped for. "Not at this point. I don't have enough to stir any interest. My staying involved will burn time and resources I don't really have, but I feel I owe it to Willow. I admire her and, damn it, the truth matters."

She smiled knowingly. "Figured this is where you'd come out. It's a noble challenge, the kind you can't resist." She sighed and got up, looking at her Fitbit. "I've got a big day tomorrow at the vineyard. I'm going to slip on home." She gave me a short peck that passed for a kiss.

"Yeah, uh, sure. Me, too," I responded. "A big day tomorrow."

After she left, I turned to Archie and said, "Significant other. Really?" Then I went upstairs and took the shower I'd promised myself. It was a cold one.

CHAPTER EIGHT

SPRING WAS A MONTH AWAY, AND WINTER SHOWED NO signs of loosening its grip. I stood at my kitchen sink the next morning sipping a cappuccino and gazing out at the vineyards that fell away in orderly, if cadaverous, rows below my property. The sky over the valley was a gray boil of swirling clouds and there was, of course, no sign yet of bud break—that point in time when the vineyards awaken and push out the first green of the new growth cycle. Theories and rumors about the Covid-19 virus seemed to be growing as fast as the infection rate in Hubei province in China. But our sitting President promised the scourge wouldn't threaten our shores, especially with the coming warmth of spring.

After breakfast I called Willow and told her I wanted to talk. "Fine," she said, "Saturday's a big day, so can you come to my food cart? I can squeeze in some time with you, and Wanda has agreed to help me out today, so you can talk to her, too."

Two hours later Archie and I crossed under Cartopia's big tent and waved to Willow, who was busy at the Plat du Jour. She pointed in the direction of 12th Street. "Wanda's taking Tater for a walk in the stroller. I told her you wanted to talk to her."

"Gog Gog," Tater cried out when Arch and I caught up with her and Wanda. Archie sidled up next to the stroller and Tater reached out, touched his fur, and giggled with pure joy. It felt good to hear it. I introduced myself.

Wanda was past middle age with hair gone gray and a face that worry had left its mark on. As we walked and chatted, she said with a twinge of a southern accent, "I'm real sorry about Mr. Bainbridge." Her face clouded over, and she shook her head. "He was, ah, different than most but always kind. After Hank—he was my husband—passed, I thought I was gonna lose the house until he gave me the housekeeping job. Easiest man in the world to cook for."

"How long did you work for him?"

She stopped and cocked her head. "It would've been three years next month."

"Oh, so you overlapped with his ex-wife, Gloria, for a year or so?"

She expelled a breath. "I did. That woman...well, I'm not gonna gossip."

"Did she and Malcolm argue a lot?"

"Oh, Lordy, there was no pleasing her. Mr. Bainbridge tried. That's why he hired me. She got tired of doing the cooking." At that point, Tater reached out and grasped one of Archie's ears. Wanda gasped. "Tater, let go of—"

"It's okay," I said. "He won't react." My dog let her tug on his ear, and when she let go he nuzzled her hand to show there were no hard feelings. Tater giggled, pointed at her new friend, and they repeated the process. We watched as the two got better acquainted, but I finally broke the mood, saying, "Do you have any recollection of Mr. Bainbridge's mental state around the time of his death?"

Her face tightened and lost some color. "I was out with

a cold most of the week before, so I can't say for sure. When I came back, he seemed more or less normal, I guess."

"More or less?"

She managed a smile. "That man was always changing, you know? Unpredictable. But he seemed okay last time I saw him."

"What time did you leave that last evening?"

"Fixed him some fish and chips and left around seven."

"Did anything unusual happen while you were there? Any visitors?"

"No."

"When you discovered the body the next morning, did you notice anything odd or out of place in the photography studio, something you might have thought of since talking to the police?

She grimaced. "No, nothing comes to mind. It's all a blur to me."

"You must have seen the gun on the floor. Had you seen it before? Do you know where Malcolm kept it?"

Her face grew tighter, and she lost a little more color. "No, I know nothing about the gun. I don't even remember seeing it that morning."

"You never saw it while you were cleaning either that day or earlier?"

"I know nothing about the gun," she repeated in a firm tone. Too firm.

At that point, we turned around and headed back toward Cartopia. The line in front of the Plat du Jour had dwindled to nothing, so Willow joined me under the tent while Wanda tended to Tater. As she sat down, I said, "I've got big news on your uncle's estate." I went on to explain what the assets she and her cousin were about to inherit would be worth.

The news literally rocked her back, and as her mouth fell open, she reached up and absently touched her bottom lip. "That much? I had no idea. I guess I never really thought about selling Uncle Mal's house." She scrunched her brow and frowned. "That seems obscene. And *stocks?* I'm going to make money from corporate America? Oh, shit."

I chuckled. "It'll be your money. You can be as socially responsible with it as you want."

I took her through the probate process next and answered a slew of questions before I moved to my second topic. "I'm still undecided about the question of your uncle's death, but I've uncovered some significant issues." I outlined where the investigation stood before adding, "If we go forward, I'll fold the charges into the estate work."

Her eyes, shading to green again, lit up and she flashed a broad smile. "Let's keep going. I'll have the money to pay you now."

"Okay, and remember, Willow, my investigation is confidential. The cover story is the work I'm doing to settle your uncle's estate. Got that?"

"Got it."

"Since your food cart is closed on Sundays, would it be a good day to retrieve your pictures and camera at the Mt. Tabor house?" She said it was. "Okay, then I'll call your cousin and try to arrange something for, say, the early afternoon. He insists on being there, by the way."

She ran a hand through her russet hair, and her smile took a sarcastic turn. "Why am I not surprised? I might sneak off with the family silver, right?"

"Two other issues have popped up," I went on. "First,

Donny's lawyer informed me that he's claiming your loan was actually for one-hundred and fifty thousand, not fifty-five."

Her eyes flashed, and her face tightened with anger. "That's vintage Donny. He's never had much of a relationship with the truth." Her look turned anxious, and she wrung her hands. "Will the probate judge believe him?"

"This is an attempted shakedown. He doesn't want it to get to the judge. He's hoping he can get you to agree with something lower that will still pad his take. He's also claiming Gloria Talbot will back his story. I haven't talked to her about it."

She rolled her eyes. "That's not surprising. She and Donny, well, Gloria treated him like he was her little puppy dog, and he was only too happy to play along."

"There's more," I said. "It turns out the Ansel Adams collection's quite valuable. According to Donny's attorney, it appraised at about three-hundred and fifty thousand dollars."

Her jaw dropped again, and her eyes got enormous. "You're kidding. I knew some of the photos were rare, but I had *no idea.*" She eyed me cautiously, as if she knew another shoe was about to fall.

"They're pressing their claim that your uncle promised the collection to Donny."

She paused, her eyes narrowed down, and I saw a toughness I always sensed was there. "Of course they are."

I leaned in. "Look, Willow, the burden of proof's on them. We're going to continue to ask for your half minus what you legitimately owe. And we're going to ask for *all* of the Ansel Adams collection. We may not prevail, but that'll be our opening position. Okay?"

Her face lit up. "*Really?*" But it clouded over just as quickly. "It's their word against mine, two against one."

"Let me worry about that."

Tater began to cry, and Willow stood up and forced a smile. "I gotta get back."

"One last thing," I said. "About your uncle's gun—would Wanda know anything about it?"

Willow's brow furrowed for a moment. "As a matter of fact, there was an incident. She was straightening up in Uncle Mal's bedroom closet and she knocked his gun on the floor. It really freaked her out, you know. I think she screamed and Gloria rushed in." Willow paused and studied me for a moment. "Did you ask her about that?"

"No," I lied, not wanting her to bring the question up with Wanda. As Archie and I walked back to the car, I turned over the exchange with Wanda in my mind, feeling slightly unsettled. The shock of finding a bloody corpse can addle anyone's mind, but still... Wanda's apparent amnesia seemed odd to me, It was a loose end that needed further scrutiny.

CHAPTER NINE

THE MT. TABOR NEIGHBORHOOD WAS CLUSTERED around a massive city park, a gentle rise in southeast Portland that was an active volcano vent 300,000 years ago. There's still a chunk of exposed cinder cone at the top of the park to prove it. Malcolm Bainbridge's house sat on the north side of the park on a large, heavily wooded lot laid out over a hundred years ago. I arrived first and parked in front of a set of marble steps bordered by low stone walls that marched at least two hundred feet up to the mansion, which sported a portico and second-floor balcony fit for Scarlet O'Hara. I'd offered to pick up Willow, but since no rain was forecast, she insisted on biking from her place in the Hawthorne district, and our arrivals coincided perfectly. She'd left Tater with Wanda.

After Willow locked her bike, we climbed the marble steps and waited on the porch for Donny Romano to show up. With a bit of mischief in my eye, I said, "Were you given the name Willow, or did you grow into it?"

She laughed. "I was born twenty-three inches long. The story is that when the nurse brought me out to show my dad, he said, 'Oh my, she's as slender as a willow.' And the name stuck."

"Well, it's a beautiful name," I said, and then shifted

my gaze toward the bike. "Is that your sole means of transportation?"

"If it's pouring rain I resort to my car, a twelve-year-old Prius with a hundred and fifty-thousand miles on it."

"Do you feel safe on the road with your bike?" I asked the same mother who worried about her daughter touching my dog.

She gave me a sober look. "There are places I won't bike to, but Portland's pretty bike friendly. You have to know the territory."

"That must be him," I said as a man began trekking up the steps. We stood and watched as Donny Romano approached. I said under my breath, "Let me broach the subject of the loan and the photos, okay?" I saw her nod out of the corner of my eye.

Donny was well built with glossy black hair, close-set eyes, and a carefully manicured three-day stubble beard. He stopped at the porch steps, looked up at us, and laughed. "Damn nice place, huh? It's gonna be a shame to sell it."

"We missed you at the funeral," Willow replied, refusing to take the bait.

"Yeah, sorry about that. Something came up."

"I'm sure it did."

He climbed the steps to our level. After Willow introduced me, Donny glanced at her, then back at me and scowled. "Maybe I should have brought Clete Bower along."

"No need," I said. "I just wanted to see the place and give Willow a hand if she needs it."

Donny smirked, but instead of a smart remark he produced a key and let us into a spacious foyer and switched on the lights. The house was tomb-silent, the air cold and musty smelling. A staircase swept an elegant curve up to the second floor, but we followed Donny down a central hall to the back of the house, passing formal living and dining areas and a couple of closed doors. Willow pointed to the framed photographs on either side of us and said under her breath. "These are the Ansel Adams."

There must have been at least twenty of them, all dramatic black and white landscapes. I caught a glimpse of desert expanses, dramatic mountain vistas, swirling storm clouds, and one large print I'd actually seen before—Half Dome in Yosemite. I'd heard of Adams, of course, but seeing the large photos, even in the weak hall light, was impressive. "These are spectacular," I said, half to myself.

As we entered what was obviously Malcolm's photo studio, Donny turned to me. "Can you believe it? Only one person lived in this joint." His eyes lit with a kind of manic glee. "Can't wait to sell the dump." He turned to Willow, glancing at his wristwatch. "Get your snapshots, kiddo. I don't have all day."

Willow glared back at him as she removed her backpack. "News flash, Donny. You don't own this place. In fact, you owe me a key."

He crossed his arms and remained silent.

The workshop was as I remembered it from the photos in the death report: a large workbench on the right held all Bainbridge's photo equipment, and shelves and open cabinets on the left wall were crammed with all manner of supplies. Photographs—some framed, others not—covered the right wall. One door on the back wall led to a bathroom, and another door led outside.

Willow went straight to the workbench and picked up a camera with a large telephoto lens attached. She looked at me. "This is the camera I loaned Uncle Mal. The one I told you about."

Donny placed his hands on his hips as his eyes narrowed down. "Yeah, right. Prove it."

Willow unzipped a pocket on her backpack, produced a sales receipt, and handed it to her cousin.

"Are you kidding me?" he said, looking up from the receipt. "You paid over three thousand bucks for that thing?"

She rolled her eyes. "It's not a *thing*. It's a Canon R5, one of the best cameras on the market." She pointed at the barrel of the attached lens. "And this is a Tamron 200 telephoto lens."

Donny tossed the receipt onto the workbench. "Whatever."

I had to work to suppress a chuckle. Donny was clearly no match for his nimble younger cousin.

He pulled up a high stool and sat down while Willow began gathering up her photographs, some of which were on top of the workbench and others in a large, sliding drawer underneath. I caught a glimpse of one large print and said, "My favorite Portland bridge—the Saint Johns."

She smiled with modesty. "Yeah, this is part of a bridge series I've been working on for a long time." She held up the print, which captured one of the bridge's iconic gothic suspension towers in silhouette before an explosive, golden red sunrise.

"How'd you get that unusual perspective?"

"I was on the other side of Route 30 on the Ridge Trail hanging from a tree limb." She laughed. "Fell climbing down and sprained the heck out of my ankle."

"Well, it's a stunning piece."

"Thanks." She laughed. "Of course, every photographer

in Portland does the bridges, but I took that as a challenge—how do it without being derivative."

Donny shifted impatiently on the stool.

I said, "I'd say you succeeded."

While Willow worked and Donny stewed, I reimagined the last moments of Malcolm Bainbridge's life. I saw him perched on one of the stools to the left of the workbench. His right arm came up, and he fired the gun at his right temple. He pitched forward, scraping his face on the tile floor, his right arm outstretched, the gun just beyond his reach. The small bruise on his left bicep remained unexplained.

I looked at the stool again. It was high, and the fall a long way down. That's when I realized what had bothered me about the scene. Why was the gun so near his hand? Why hadn't it skidded across the tile floor on impact? It wasn't hard to picture someone placing the gun there after the fact to tidy things up.

But that was no breakthrough. While the minute detail raised the specter of a staged scene, I realized it would be impossible to predict the final resting place of the gun.

A seed of doubt was planted, but the matter would need more thought.

I was yanked from my reverie when Donny hopped off his stool and said, "For Christ's sake, Willow, how long's this going to take?"

Willow looked up from a stack of photographs, her eyes flashing daggers at him. "Some of these are mine, some are Uncle Mal's. I'm trying to sort them out. You can leave, you know."

He got back on the stool with a sour expression.

Willow held up another photo and said to me, "This is my favorite of this series."

The photo caught the majestic, semicircular arch of the Freemont bridge bathed in the soft, dusky rose light of a sunset. It was shot from the surface of the Willamette River. "Magnificent," I said. "How did you shoot this one?"

"From a kayak. I got lucky and caught the sunset just right."

A few minutes later, she was packed up. She looked at Donny. "There are several pieces of equipment here that I'd like to buy before we settle up. You okay with that?"

Donny hopped off the stool again. "Sure, as long as the price is right, and it comes off your share. Be my guest."

She looked at me. "Will that be a problem?"

"No," I said. "We have to sell all this gear in any case." I turned to Donny and fixed my eyes on him. "That reminds me, are you still claiming that Malcolm told you he loaned Willow one hundred and fifty thousand dollars?"

He swallowed and broke eye contact. "That's what the old fart told me. One hundred and fifty big ones."

"Liar," Willow shot back. "Prove it."

He smiled defiantly. "Why don't we just split the difference, Cuz? It's my word and Gloria's against yours. Whataya say?"

Willow faced him and placed her hands on her hips as color pooled in her cheeks. "Fuck you, Donny. You're lying about that and about the photographs." She laughed. It was laced with contempt. "What a joke. You don't know Ansel Adams from Pablo Picasso. Uncle Mal would've *never* given you those photographs."

The two cousins stood glowering at each other. Returning my gaze to Donny, I said, "This won't get settled here, but the burden of proof rests with you. Make no mistake about that."

"We'll see," he said with a bitter smile as he spun

around and walked out. We followed, and when we exited the house, Donny locked the front door, put the key in his pocket, and started down the stairs.

Willow called after him. "I need a key, too."

Without turning around, he raised his hand and displayed his middle finger.

Willow shot me a do-something look. "Don't worry about it," I said. "I'll demand a key from Bower."

She smiled sheepishly as she grappled with the large cardboard folder she'd put her photographs in. "Do you think you could drop this by my place? I should've realized it would be hard to carry all this on my bike." I told her sure, and she reached into the folder and pulled out a clasp envelope. It was unmarked. "Oh, I almost forgot. This was on the bottom of the drawer. I tossed it in, probably some of Uncle Mal's stuff. It should probably be put back in the studio."

"Depends what it is. Take a look."

She opened the clasp and removed a stack of eight and half by eleven photographs. Her eyes got huge. "Oh, God, no!" she cried out. She turned her head and thrust the photos in my direction with her eyes closed. "I think I'm going to be sick."

I took the photos. They were copies of Gloria Talbot and Donny Romano, buck naked in a bed *in flagrante delicto.*

I slid the photos back in the envelope. "Well, well," I said, "this is interesting."

CHAPTER TEN

WE SAT ON WILLOW'S FRONT PORCH AFTER OUR VISIT TO Bainbridge's mansion. It had begun spitting rain but wasn't too cool to be outside. Tater sat upright next to Archie, who lay like a big Sphinx next to her. She'd already learned not to pull his ears. Instead, she stroked the black fur on his broad back, retrieved her hand, and repeated the process. With each stroke Archie closed his eyes in utter contentment. Their friendship was sealed, and I knew Archie saw Tater as family, precious family.

"Uncle Mal must've set up a spy cam in their bedroom," Willow was saying. The bike ride had allowed her time to gather her wits after the shock of the photographs. "It would've been a trivial task for him." She cocked her head at me. "What do you think this means?"

"He obviously suspected something, and my guess is he used those photographs to precipitate the divorce." I paused for a moment. "Do you think your uncle left that envelope in the drawer for you to find?"

She shook her head. "Nah, I don't think so. I think he stuck it in there and forgot about it. The time stamps on the photos were three years old. He would have just told me outright, but I guess he thought better of it." She drew a breath in, then released it. "Did Gloria and Donny kill Uncle Mal? I wouldn't put it past either one of them."

I shrugged. "They were lovers, and they both stand to gain from your uncle's death, but if they killed him, I don't know how they did it." I didn't mention my questioning of the gun placement on the floor. It was too flimsy an idea. "The insurance investigator told me Gloria had an alibi. Now I'm interested in what Donny was up to that night."

Willow leaned in, her eyes blazing. "Can you find out?"

I shook my head. "It won't be easy. He doesn't have to tell me anything. But we're in negotiations with him, so some opportunities might present themselves." I met her eyes. "Trust the process, Willow. If we get anywhere at all, it won't happen overnight."

She forced a smile. "I understand."

"In the meantime, let me keep the photos, and, of course, you can't breathe a word of this to anyone, okay?"

"Sure. What are you going to do with the photos?"

"I'm not sure yet. The photos, per se, aren't that valuable, and there are ethical rules about their disclosure that I'm bound by. It's what they *suggest* about Donny and Gloria that could be important."

Our conversation eventually turned to Willow's photography. "You have a real gift," I told her. "Did your uncle do all your printing?"

Her look turned wistful. "Most of it. Sometimes he was too busy. I do limited-edition prints, usually forty per image, signed and dated, and I'm a stickler for quality. If I get Uncle Mal's equipment, I can do my own printing. It's something I've always dreamed about, but coming into the equipment this way doesn't feel right, you know?"

"I can understand how you feel, but I think your uncle

would have wanted you to have it, Willow, just like the Ansel Adams photos. Do you show your work anywhere?"

"Yes, at the Alberta Street Gallery. I'll be hanging the bridges there next month, and I'm working on another series I hope to include." I raised an eyebrow and she explained. "There's a number of abandoned boats on the Columbia, even some old naval vessels. They're totally cool. I've been shooting them, too, but only when the light's right." The modest smile again. "Anyway, I'll have an entire wall at Alberta. You can see my work on willowpics.com, too."

"Can I afford a copy of your Freemont Bridge photo? It would look great in my Portland office."

She laughed, and I saw where her daughter got her joyfulness. "I haven't priced the series yet, but I'll give you the bro rate."

—//—

I was heading back to Dundee when a call came in. "Calvin, how are things in Oregon?" Nando Mendoza's voice came through as though he were sitting in the seat next to me.

"No complaints. How's Cuba?"

"It is good to be home." He went on to describe his visit in rhapsodic terms, saying at one point, "I am afraid my mother and sisters are spoiling me. I don't think they want me to leave."

"Speaking of leaving," I said, "I read the virus has reached Cuba. Have you thought about leaving earlier?"

He laughed dismissively. "Yes, a few cases have been documented, but there should be no problem. Cuba has a good healthcare system. Are you still looking into the suicide that might not be?"

"I am," and after a brief description of the case, I summed it up, saying, "I'm still not convinced Bainbridge was murdered, but there's a lot of money involved, and I've got more than enough suspects who stand to benefit from his death."

The car filled with his basso profundo laugh. "Indeed. Money draws trouble like nectar draws bees, but not so innocent, yes? If this man was, in fact, murdered, you are dealing with someone very clever. Be careful, my friend."

"You, too, Nando."

—/ /—

It pelted rain that evening. I grilled a pork loin and served it with stir-fried spinach, sauteed red potatoes, and a five-year-old pinot noir. Zoe and I kept the banter light while we ate, a rule we tried to stick to. I did stray into some shop talk when I related the discrepancy between Wanda Jenkins' claim that she knew nothing about Bainbridge's gun and what Willow told me. "What's your take on the psychology of that?"

She paused for a moment and sipped some pinot. "Memory's often a casualty of severe trauma. From what Willow told you, the episode of finding the gun in the closet was pretty jarring for this woman. Then she finds the body with a gun lying next to it. The *same* gun. Yeah, it's possible she blanked on the thing completely."

"That makes sense," I said to close the topic. But I still harbored some doubt. Chalk it up to my suspicious nature.

After dinner, we sat in front of the fireplace. We were

quiet for a while, probably because we both knew a serious discussion was in the offing. The fire crackled as Zoe leaned her head against my shoulder and sighed. "I'm sorry about the other night, Cal."

"Don't apologize," I said. "I understand. You didn't sign up for a relationship with Don Quixote."

She chuckled. "It's me. I'm too sensitive. The past is hard to get over, you know?"

"Tell me about it. I know you've got your reasons, but you've never said much about what you've been through." I laughed. "Most of what I know comes from your Aunt Gertie."

She smiled and shook her head. "Well, I knew she'd talk, knowing my aunt, and I figured that was probably enough said." She sat up and turned to me. "Anyway, it's not that big a deal. My first husband brought his work home with him one night. It was one of his graduate students. I walked in on them."

"Ouch. That must have hurt."

"It did." She smiled with a trace of bitterness. "He wanted me to brush it off, but I couldn't. The trust was gone, shot to hell."

"I get that."

"My second husband was passionate about mountain climbing. He'd done practically every tough ascent in the Northern Cascades, and he kept looking for the next challenge, always more difficult, of course." She looked at me, her eyes pleading. "I didn't want him to stop climbing, but I could see where it was headed. It just seemed so inexorable, and it made me wonder where I was in that equation." She sighed. "He finally fell up on Mt. Rainier—Liberty Ridge." She looked away, but not before I saw her eyes brighten with a film of tears. "It was a closed-casket funeral."

I pulled her close and hugged her. "I'm sorry, Zoe" was all I could say. I knew that cutting sense of loss all too well.

She dabbed her eyes with a folded index finger. "It sounds trite, even selfish, but I don't want to be anybody's second fiddle ever again."

I started to respond but thought better of it.

She went on, "It's just, I, ah, I think I need some more time. I know you're going to be who you are, Cal, and I respect you for that. And God knows I don't want you to change anything on my account."

I felt my heart sink a little. Respect wasn't exactly the word I was looking for. "Hey, we're in no rush here," I said. "This is just a bump in the road. Take the time you need." I smiled and met her eyes. "For what it's worth, I'm clear as a bell about how I feel about you. I want this relationship to work."

That night after Zoe left, I sat on my bed with a book, but I found myself reading the same sentence over and over again. My body was tired, but my head buzzed like a hive of summer bees. Archie sensed my restlessness and had plopped down next to the bed instead of on his matt in the corner. Every so often he would sit up and place his head on the bed and wait until I absently scratched it.

I finally tossed the book aside. "She's right," I said out loud. "I'm not going to change. But I don't want to lose her either." Archie looked up at me. "Is there any way to square this circle, Big Boy?"

He wagged his stump of a tail. I took it as a yes.

CHAPTER ELEVEN

THE FRONT CLEARED OFF OVERNIGHT, ALLOWING ARCHIE and me to get a jog in before heading down the hill to my Dundee office. Timoteo was already there when we arrived. "You've got a municipal court appearance in Portland this morning," he said after greeting us. "The Hallinan case." He held up a file folder.

I feigned a forehead slap. "Right. Thanks. It's just a preliminary. I'm good to go. How are things at the vineyard?"

"Another worker is sick. He's just staying home. No tests, of course. It's worrisome."

"How's your mother?"

His face brightened. "She's doing so much better. Zoe's a miracle worker. She's got Mamá talking, cooking, even doing some bead work, something she used to love to do. She's starting to act more like her old self."

My heart swelled a little. "Yeah, Zoe's good at what she does." I pulled my right sleeve up and displayed my beaded bracelet. "Your mom gave me this. It's exquisite."

A gleam of pride showed in Timoteo's eyes. "She doesn't give her work to just anybody, you know." I smiled, and he pointed at two bottles sitting on my desk. "Those are bottles of hand sanitizer I picked up. One's for the office and the other's for your car. Oh," he added, "I got us a

Zoom account, too. I can check you out on it when you have time."

I smiled to myself. I could count my good business decisions on one hand with fingers left over, but hiring this young man was a master stroke.

On the way into Portland that morning, I mulled over what to do with the fact that Donny and Gloria—who both stood to gain handsomely from Malcolm Bainbridge's death—had and could still be having an affair. I considered alerting both insurance investigator Kiara Jones and Harmon Scott but thought better of it. No, I decided, best to let it ride until I got a better handle on the situation. My default position, to be sure.

With Timoteo holding down the fort in Dundee, I decided to stay in Portland after the court appearance. It was mid-afternoon when I answered a call on the office phone. "Mr. Claxton? My name's Stuart Burgess," a youngish male voice said. "I'm a tech assistant at Spectro Systems. I'm wondering if you have some time to talk."

"Of course, Stuart. What's on your mind?"

"Is what I say protected by confidentiality?"

"Yes, if that's what you want."

"Okay. I, ah, I heard you visited my company, that you were hired by Dr. Bainbridge's niece to investigate his death."

I snapped to attention. "That's not completely accurate. I'm representing Ms. Daniels, but only in the settlement of her uncle's estate. Where did you hear I was investigating Bainbridge's death?"

"The rumor mill at work. See, some of us think his death was kind of weird, you know?"

"Wait a minute. Back up. Rumor mill? Tell me more about that."

"I think it started with Denise Howard. She's a secretary at Spectro and a friend of Dr. Bainbridge's niece. Anyway, the rumor spread like crazy."

Oh, shit. "I see. Why do you say the death was weird?"

"Dr. Bainbridge's nickname at Spectro was Albert—you know, for Einstein. We all called him that behind his back, but it was in fun and out of respect. He could be weird sometimes, you know, depressed and easily frustrated, but he was brilliant, and everybody loved him." Stuart paused for a moment. "Well, not everybody. That's why I called."

The back of my neck started to tingle a little. "Go ahead."

"See, one of our senior scientists at the lab and Dr. Bainbridge were in a battle royal. Eric Trenton's his name. He's aggressive, ambitious, wants his name on the InstaVision20 patent. Dr. Bainbridge said no. He said Trenton's only contribution was to run the experiments and tests he was directed to run. Trenton now claims the whole concept was his idea and that he did all the work to prove it out."

"What's having his name on the patent worth to Trenton?"

"Mega bucks. Spectro Systems has an incentive plan that says, basically, an inventor gets twenty percent of any profits earned by the invention. With InstaVision, the sky may be the limit." He laughed. "We call InstaVision the golden goose around here."

"What about records?" I asked. "You need documented proof of who did what to secure a patent."

"I'm not in that loop. I'm sure Bradley Nielsen's looking at that question. Anyway, I thought it was important for you to know about Eric Trenton. Nobody at my level trusts him."

"You think he killed Bainbridge?" I tried not to sound incredulous.

He sighed deeply. "I'm not accusing him or anything like that, but the idea that Dr. Bainbridge killed himself just doesn't compute, Mr. Claxton."

"Did anyone at Spectro Systems mention this to the police?"

He laughed. "Quickest way to lose your job. Nielsen runs a tight ship, doesn't want any dirty laundry aired in public. I figured if I came to you, I could stay anonymous."

I thanked him and before I let him go said, "Look, Stuart, this is important information. I'd like to share it with my client, Willow Daniels, but no one else. Is that okay with you?"

He paused for a moment. "As long as she doesn't reveal I'm the source."

"I won't even use your name."

"Okay, then go ahead."

Since I was on a roll, I decided to ask one more favor. "I'm also wondering if, going forward, you'd be willing to be my eyes and ears inside Spectro Systems. Not to do anything unethical or illegal, mind you, but just to keep me apprised of what you're hearing from the rumor mill about the patent and anything else you pick up."

"Cool. I can do that."

After we disconnected, I turned to Archie. "Whataya know, Big Boy, another suspect joins the rogue's gallery." I laughed out loud. "What we have here is an embarrassment of suspects but no proof of a murder."

—/ /—

Willow called just as I was pulling onto Couch Street after locking up Caffeine Central for the day. Her voice had a nervous edge to it. "Hi Cal. Are you in Portland?" I told her I was, and she went on, "I'm hesitant to ask, but I need a favor."

"Sure. What's up?"

"I'm over at my exercise class and Wanda's got Tater at her place. She was supposed to swing by here and pick me up, but she's over thirty minutes late. And she's not answering her phone, which isn't like her. Could you possibly go to Wanda's house? I'll stay here in case she shows up." I told Willow I would, and she gave me the address. "Oh, and Cal, if she's not home, she might be taking Tater for a walk on 103rd. It leads into Kelly Butte Park."

I was in front of Wanda Jenkins's house on SE Clinton in fourteen minutes. While Archie waited in the car, I rang the bell and when no one answered tried the front door. It was locked, but the back door wasn't. I opened it, called out, and after no response went inside and looked around. A couple of lights were on, and nothing was disturbed.

I leashed up Archie, backtracked on Clinton, and took a left on SE 103rd at a full jog with my dog leading the way. Wooded and sloping away on either side, the road leading into the park traced a gradual ascent for maybe a quarter of a mile before veering into a hairpin turn to the left. A pathway on the right accommodated bike and foot traffic. I saw nothing along the straightaway, but when I rounded the turn, I saw what looked like a clump of discarded clothing in the pathway on the right, or at least that's what my subconscious mind wanted it to be. When I got closer, I realized what it was, and my heart began to beat violently against my ribcage.

I skidded to a stop next to Wanda Jenkins and went down on one knee. Her head was turned to one side. An unblinking, unseeing eye stared out across the road and blood from her nose pooled in the dirt. She was utterly still with her arms splayed in front of her and one leg tucked beneath the other at an angle that made me wince. I checked for a pulse to confirm she was dead, then jumped to my feet, looked around, and unleashed Archie. "Where's Tater, Big Boy? Find her!"

He took about ten steps forward, then dove into the underbrush and vanished down the slope. He barked once, a single, sharp chord. I crashed through the brush right behind him. Halfway down the slope, Tater Daniels sat facing downhill in her stroller, which was wedged beneath the arching fronds of a huge sword fern. Her head was turned toward Archie who stood next to her. She was pointing at him. "Gog Gog, Gog Gog."

I pulled her out of her stroller and hugged her to my chest like she was my own child. She stiffened but didn't cry. It was me who did the crying.

Arch led the way back up the embankment, and once we reached the street I made sure to shield her from the sight of Wanda's body. While holding her, I reached for the cell phone in my jeans pocket, called 911, then Willow. "Tater's with Archie and me," I said when she answered, "but Wanda's had an accident." At the same time, I heard the distant wail of a siren.

"*What?* What happened?" she gasped.

"I don't have time to explain right now. Your daughter's fine. Not a scratch on her."

"I'm coming. Where are you?"

"On the road into Kelly Butte Park, 103rd."

I stood there holding Tater as the sound of a second emergency vehicle chimed in. A vivid image of the stroller wedged beneath that big sword fern kept coming back to me. It was as if the fern had tucked Tater beneath its fronds to protect her. And the jogging stroller—my God, it's three wheels and wide berth kept it from tipping over on its way down the embankment.

I shook my head and exhaled a breath of gratitude.

Tater was still tense with a wary look in her eyes, but she was holding back tears. "She's tough like her momma," I said to Archie. He whimpered softly and brushed my leg, so I knelt down and let Tater pat his back. She did it again and smiled. My dog knew instinctively how to comfort her.

I felt horrible about Wanda Jenkins, whose body lay unattended in the road. But by the time a police cruiser pulled up, I'd figured out what must have happened. Wanda Jenkins was a hero. No question about it.

CHAPTER TWELVE

"YEAH, I'M PARKED DOWN ON CLINTON," I TOLD A UNIformed police officer, who had arrived on the scene with her partner. "I came down here looking for them, because the child's mother told me they often walk into the park. Wanda was late dropping the child off, and the mother was worried." I pointed past Wanda's covered body to where Tater went down the embankment in her stroller. I shook my head. "I think Wanda heard the car bearing down on them and gave the stroller a shove in a last ditch attempt to save the child."

The cop looked at Tater, clasped in my arms, then back at me. "I think you're right." Her eyes grew hard, and she let a non-professional comment slip. "Some idiot fiddling with his cellphone, most likely. No skid marks. The driver just swerved off the road, hit the woman, and kept going. She did a courageous thing getting the little girl out of the way." The cop shook her head. "A miracle."

—/—

When Willow arrived, she rushed to take Tater from my arms. She closed her eyes as she embraced her child but shed no tears. Her stoicism didn't surprise me. The investigative team and the paramedics paused for several moments out of respect and a recognition of just how close this had come to being an unthinkable double tragedy.

We both gave statements, which included Willow informing the investigators that Wanda had a brother named Benny Boykin, who lived somewhere in Portland. We left the scene and walked slowly back to Wanda's house with Archie leading the way. After retrieving Tater's car seat from Wanda's unlocked car, we set off for Willow's place. Still seemingly stunned by the knowledge that Wanda had made a split-second decision that saved her daughter, Willow was quiet while Tater clucked and laughed about riding in a car with Gog Gog.

"Please come in," Willow said after we pulled up in front of an old Craftsman with tapered porch columns. "I can make us some coffee after I put Tater down."

"Do you own this house?" I asked as she poured me a cup. Tater had been fed and was safe in her crib, fast asleep. The house had handsome Doug fir flooring and built-in dining room cabinets with cut glass doors. It needed a ton of work, but its bones appeared sound.

"Oh, don't I wish! I just rent the place. It strains my budget, but I love old houses." She allowed a smile that rippled the freckles on her cheeks "I've probably photographed half the old houses in Portland, the ones with character, at least." But the smile quickly faded, her face grew tight, and she locked onto my eyes. "Wanda's accident...it isn't connected to Uncle Mal's death, is it?"

I held her gaze. "I honestly don't know. I mean the visibility in the park was fine. The first cop on the scene said it was probably someone distracted by a cell phone." I paused for a moment to choose my next words with care. I didn't want to alarm her. "There's one thing—remember when I asked you if Wanda knew anything about your uncle's gun, like where he kept it?"

"Yes."

"Well, she told me in no uncertain terms that she knew nothing about a gun."

Willow's eyes widened. "That's weird. That's not what she told *me*."

"I know. It seemed a little strange to me, too. She seemed too emphatic. But after talking to a psychologist friend of mine, I chalked it up to the shock of her finding your uncle's body. She said she didn't even notice the gun that morning. Memory, it turns out, can be unreliable in the face of a traumatic shock."

Willow looked somewhat relieved, but I still wasn't there.

"How well did you know Wanda?"

"Good enough to trust her with Tater, but the truth is I didn't know her all that well. Uncle Mal thought the world of her, and that was good enough for me. I know she doted on her younger brother. Uncle Mal didn't like him because he was always hitting her up for money."

"Benny Boykin?"

"Yeah." She closed her eyes and began softly crying. We sat for several moments in silence. Finally, I said, "The police will be all over this. A car involved in a hit and run's not easy to conceal. Maybe they'll make a quick arrest."

She sniffed and wiped her eyes. "I hope so."

She filled my coffee cup back up, and I continued, "There's one more thing, Willow. Apparently, you're not the only one who doesn't believe your uncle killed himself." I went on to tell her about my conversation with the Spectro System lab technician, Stuart Burgess, without using his name.

When I finished, she said, "But how did this guy know to come to—" She stopped in mid-sentence, looked at me, and blushed enough that her freckles nearly vanished. "*Denise*. Oh, shit, I'm so sorry. I thought I could trust her."

"Apparently not. The whole company's buzzing with rumors about my investigation." Willow looked horrified, but I had to smile. "I hope you learned a lesson, but if you hadn't said anything, I don't think I would have heard about the feud between your uncle and Eric Trenton. Did he ever mention Trenton?"

She shook her head. "No. I don't think so. But I can tell you this—if Trenton deserved to have his name on that patent, Uncle Mal wouldn't have stood in the way. He wasn't that kind of person."

As I was leaving, I commented on a series of photographs of the Oregon coast that lined her dining room walls. One caught my attention. I pointed and said, "I know that spot. Yachats, right?" Her photo caught one of several blow holes on the coast at full height, the fine spray set ablaze by a setting sun. It looked like an erupting volcano with the thrashing Pacific as a backdrop.

"Yes, that's Yachats, the blowhole behind the Fireside Motel." She laughed, that delightful sound. "That shot nearly cost me a camera. I got in too close and a sneaker wave nearly took me out."

I walked up to the photo for a closer look. "It was worth it, I think."

On the front porch, Willow actually hugged Arch, then looked up at me, her face ringing with resolve. "I won't slip again, Cal. You can trust me." I nodded, knowing I could. "And I'm going to use my Prius until this thing gets cleared up."

"That would be a wise precaution," I answered, relieved I didn't have to bring up the question of being cautious.

Once Arch and I were on the road, a scene of what could have happened out on that park road played across my mind like an obscene video. I felt equal parts revulsion and anger. I thought about what Willow said. I wasn't quite sure if this investigation was a *thing* yet, but if it was, I knew I was in all the way. I thought of Zoe next. It was clear this news would not make things any easier between us. But if we had a future, I knew it wouldn't come from my holding things back.

I called her and described what happened.

"Oh, God," she said when I finished, "whoever did this must be a monster, Cal."

"We don't know if this is related to Bainbridge," I said. "It could be a simple hit-and-run. Portland has lots of those."

She laughed, a single, sarcastic note. "What do they say about coincidences?" I didn't respond, and she went on, "Do you have enough now to interest the police?"

I pushed down a twinge of annoyance at her pressure disguised as a question. "Not quite. It'll take more to get them to reopen a settled suicide case. That's what I'm focused on."

"Well, Willow's lucky to have you on her side." It was said as a compliment, but did I hear a hint of resignation in her voice? The conversation drifted off from there, and when we disconnected, I was left with that hollow feeling again. This wasn't the first time my work and personal life had collided, and the results were never pretty. Was my focus on this case an exercise in avoiding commitment?

No, I told myself. Maybe I'd gone down that rabbit hole a time or two, but not this time.

CHAPTER THIRTEEN

THE NEXT DAY IN DUNDEE PASSED WITHOUT INCIDENT until a call came in from Esperanza Oliva late in the afternoon. I'd called her first thing to see if she could find an address for Wanda Jenkin's brother. "I found your Benny," she said when I picked up. "His name's Benjamin Boykin, younger brother of Wanda Boykin Jenkins. He's moved around a lot. The last address I have is on SE 84th." She read off the house number. "Been there fourteen years. Before that the Florida panhandle, Panama City. He's got a rap sheet, too, B and E, a couple of marijuana busts, nothing major. You want that, too?"

"Sure. Send it on. Heard from your boss?"

"Yes. He is having a grand time." She sighed into the phone. "I'm a little worried he'll get stuck in Cuba, or worse, he'll get sick. I'd offer to move up his return flight, but I doubt he'd listen to me. Maybe you could talk to him, suggest that?"

"I have. But I'll try again." I was touched by Esperanza's concern as a shadow of worry for my friend crossed my heart. There was something ominous about this outbreak, like the whole world was slipping into uncharted territory, or at least territory that hadn't been trod for a hundred years. *But we're the most technically advanced country in the world*, I reminded myself. *We can handle this.*

—/—

I was in no mood to sit on a potential lead, so I locked up my office, loaded Arch into the car, and headed back to Portland. It was nearly dark by the time I pulled up in front of Benny Boykin's house, a one story bungalow with uncut grass, untrimmed shrubs, and faded paint. The lights on the porch and in the front half of the house were off. I tried the doorbell, heard it buzz, but got no response. I knocked on the front door. Nothing. I stood still and listened. Did I hear a noise from the back of the house? I wasn't sure, but I hadn't driven all the way to Portland to miss this guy.

I followed the driveway around the house and unlatched a gate in a rickety privacy fence. A back porchlight shone dimly. I stepped into the backyard, and just as I sensed movement to my left, a dwarf star exploded behind my eyes and shards of light ricocheted around in my brain. I staggered and put a hand up, fearing another blow was on the way.

"Who the fuck are you?" a voice said. I tried to focus, but all I saw through a thick fog was an extended arm attached to a hand holding a very large gun. It was pointed at my head.

I stepped back and felt a wet, growing welt above my left ear. Unless my assailant had a steel hand, he'd struck me with the butt of his gun. "Name's Claxton, Cal Claxton. I'm a lawyer looking for Benjamin Boykin. Why the hell did you hit me?" I blinked a couple of times and was able to focus a little better. I pointed at the gun. "And could you point that damn thing somewhere else? I'm unarmed and you're making me nervous."

"That's the idea. You're tresspassin'."

"If you're Benny Boykin, I've come to talk to you about your sister, Wanda."

"Too late. She's dead."

"I know. I found her body."

He lowered the gun slowly. "What the fuck, man? Wanda's gone. Ain't nothin' can be done about that now." The porch light reflected off his eyes. He'd teared up.

"Can we go inside and talk?"

"Why?"

"Because I don't think it was an accident, that's why. Your sister was babysitting my client's little girl when she was killed. I know you're grieving, but I'd like to ask you some questions. Please."

He stood there and looked at me for the longest time, his right arm dangling at his side with the gun pointed at the dirt. He raised his arm and wagged the gun in the direction of the back door. "You go ahead a me." I passed through a screened-in porch into a small, dingy kitchen. A big orange cat lounging on the counter between the stove and a stack of dirty dishes watched me with obvious curiosity. "Have a seat."

Benny Boykin was tall and thin with a long, equine face, straggly goatee, and careworn eyes that reminded me of his sister's. His hands were huge, his fingers long and spidery. He stripped off a paper towel and handed it to me. "Here. You're bleedin' on my floor."

I dabbed at the welt and winced. "I'm so sorry for your loss. I—"

"Cops said she saved that little girl she was watchin'. Pushed her outta the way. Is that true?"

"Yes, it's true. Your sister acted heroically as far as I'm concerned. The mother of the little girl feels the same way."

His eyes got shiny again and his face registered pain. "That would be Wanda. Never had no stingy bones in her body." His eyes narrowed to slits. "You don't think it was no accident? That's not what the cops tol' me."

I leaned in, pressing the paper towel against my head to staunch the bleeding. "She cooked and cleaned for a man named Malcolm Bainbridge. He died of a gunshot wound last month. It was ruled a suicide. Did she say anything about that to you?"

His face stiffened slightly, and he licked his lips, avoiding my gaze. "Yeah, she was upset. She was fond of the old man, thought he was some kinda genius or somethin'. And she needed the job."

I decided to ask the next question even though Benny had placed the pistol on the table in front of him. Although he'd smacked me with it, my gut said he wasn't a killer, that the chances were low he'd shoot me. "Did Wanda ever mention the gun that Bainbridge kept in his closet, the one he was shot with?"

His face tightened again, and he swallowed, his Adam's apple bobbing in his slender neck. "I don't know nothin' about no gun." The tone of the denial matched that of his sister's. "I think you oughtta go now. I'm havin' guests for dinner."

"Of course." I got up and tossed a business card on the table. The cat got up, too, stretched, and hopped off the counter. When I got to the kitchen door I turned and said, "You know what I think, Benny?"

"No, what do you think?"

"I think you know more than you're telling me. And I think you're afraid of something. That's why you're carrying a gun and why you hit me out there. You're afraid of someone. Who is it?"

"Shee-it, you don't know what you're talking about. I got nothin' to say and nothin' to hide. And if you go siccin' the cops on me you'll be damn sorry."

"I'm not going to the cops, but if you're in danger you should talk to me. Maybe I can help." I pointed toward the card on the table. "My number's on the card. Think about it, Benny. Your sister deserves justice."

I turned my back on him and walked out. I was still pretty sure he wasn't going to shoot me, but that didn't keep rivulets of sweat from snaking down either side of my rib-cage. When I got in the car, I dabbed at the knot on my head, which had grown to the size of a walnut. Archie sniffed at it and licked me on the ear in sympathy. I said, "It was well worth it, Big Boy. This case is definitely a *thing*, and the key appears to be that Ruger that killed Malcolm Bainbridge."

—/—

I scrambled some eggs that night and sprinkled in some scallions and smoked salmon to make it interesting. After dinner, I heard a familiar tap on the kitchen door leading out to the side porch. When Zoe entered the kitchen, she looked at me, horrified. "What happened?" By that time my head had stopped bleeding, but the welt was more the size of a golf ball than a walnut.

"I'm fine. Just bumped my head in the garage."

She eyed me skeptically. "Are you concussed?"

I shook my head. "I'm okay. Look, Zoe, I'm glad you came, I—"

She extended her arm and placed an index finger against my lips. "Shhh." She took my hand and led me upstairs to my bedroom and slowly undressed me. When she was through, I undressed her. When we finished making love, I dropped into sleep out of sheer exhaustion. When I awoke later that night she was gone.

CHAPTER FOURTEEN

"HOW'S THE MEDITATION GOING?" I SAID AFTER CAPTAIN Harmon Scott answered his cell phone at nine the next morning.

"It helps me cope with people who call me and just start talking." He waited, and when I suppressed a chuckle, he said "How's that suicide you're looking at?"

"More interesting by the day."

He moaned. "Uh-oh, don't give me anything else to do, Claxton. I've got two detectives out sick and a caseload that's already ridiculous."

"I was just wondering—do you know anything about that hit and run up at Kelly Butte Park?

"The one where the little girl in the stroller survived?" he asked, caution creeping into his voice.

"That's the one." The line went quiet. I said, "Come on, Harmon. I wouldn't ask unless it was important."

"Important how?"

"The victim was Malcolm Bainbridge's housekeeper."

The line went quiet again. "Oh. The case didn't land on my desk, but I skimmed the preliminary report. The vehicle was found—a truck, actually. A Dodge Ram 2500. Hardly a mark on it. Those Rams are built like brick shit-houses. It was stolen, which suggests joyriding. The truck was left in the parking lot at the top of the butte. The perp probably took one of the hiking trails down the other side."

"Anyone in the park see anything?"

"No, no witnesses, and the truck was wiped clean inside. No prints, probably no DNA as well." He paused. "What else have you got on the Bainbridge suicide?"

"Not much except for a list of people who stand to gain handsomely as a result of Bainbridge's passing. Something your detectives glossed over."

"It was ruled a suicide, open and shut," Scott said. "No reason for us to take a deep dive. The man's estate's going to get divvied up, of course. That can look like motive, I suppose."

"Look, Harmon, I'm not casting any aspersions, and I'm just nibbling around on the edges of this thing right now. If I find anything solid, I'd be glad to make you the hero. My client just wants the truth about her uncle. And if someone killed him, she wants justice."

"Well, you do owe me," he said, and I pictured his sardonic smile, "but I won't hold my breath."

—/—

Timoteo arrived shortly after the call, carrying two coffees. He stopped dead when he saw me, and the coffees would have sloshed without the lids. "What happened to your head?"

I waved a dismissive hand. "It's a long story. I'll get to it in a minute. But first, how are things at the vineyard?" I asked, because I'd just read that the governor formed a Coronavirus Response Team in preparation for potential outbreaks in Oregon.

He handed me a coffee and took a chair well away from my desk. "No new cases," he began, biting his lower lip, "but the person who got sick last week had to be taken to the clinic." He was referring to a health facility in McMinnville for laborers and their families who lacked health insurance. It was named after his late sister, Olivia Fuentes, who had worked at the clinic before her untimely death. "They have a couple of beds there, but that's it."

"Still no testing?"

He sipped some coffee and eyed me with his luminous brown eyes. "Not yet. The clinic's working on it. They're low on masks and gloves, too. Everything's in short supply, it seems. You think it could be Covid-19?"

"Could be, but it's hard to imagine how a vineyard worker could've contracted the disease." I couldn't help thinking about Zoe at that point. Was she being careful when interacting with Elena Fuentes and others at the vineyard? Probably not. What about my contact with Timoteo and his contact with me? Were we all potential threats to one another? There were no clear answers and few guidelines, so I pushed down the troubling thoughts.

Things still needed to get done.

While Timoteo brought my billable hours up to date, I sketched in the latest on the Bainbridge investigation. After we kicked it around for a while, I said, "I need you to follow someone. You up for that?" He'd done some surveillance work for me, and I had a lot of confidence in his ability to stay safe and go unnoticed.

He flashed a brilliant smile. "I mean, working here's great, but surveilling someone is a hell of a lot more fun. No offense."

I laughed. "None taken."

"You want me to follow that sleaze-bag nephew, right?"

"Exactly. I want to know where he goes and who he makes contact with. I have a home address and his work address, a gun shop on 82nd called R and J Firearms. He doesn't look like the stay-at-home type, so I think your best bet is to catch him when he leaves work."

Timoteo showed a sly smile. "You got any other photos besides the ones of him naked in bed?"

I laughed again. "I don't. Try to pull some headshots off Facebook or something. Otherwise, I'll see what Esperanza can come up with."

"No problem." He paused and leveled his gaze at me. "What about the asshole who pistol whipped you? I can alternate nights if you want. Find out what both of them are up to."

I paused for a few moments. "Benny Boykin's a much higher risk. He's already looking over his shoulder. Besides, what about your studies?"

"I can handle Benny, and there's no problem with school. I'm only taking two classes and they're a snap."

"Okay, we'll try it for a week. Give Benny plenty of space and stay in your car."

His eyes lit up. "Roger that. I'm on it."

Although I had nothing but the vaguest outlines of this case, there seemed to be a quickening pace and a growing momentum about it, as if it were taking on a life of its own. I could feel the shift in my bones. It came as no surprise, then, when Bradley Nielsen, CEO of Spectro Systems, called later that morning.

After an overly cordial greeting, he said, "Mr. Claxton, I'm wondering if you could spare me some time today? I've got a media engagement this afternoon, but I should be free any time after, say, three p.m."

I told Nielsen I'd see him at three and then asked Timoteo to hold down the fort in Dundee. "It looks like a slow rest of the week," I said. "I'll stay in Portland till the weekend." He glanced at my calendar to check for himself. My assistant ran my office better than I did.

—/ /—

At two fifty-five that afternoon, I parked near the Spectro Systems headquarters and cracked the windows for Archie. He gave me an anxious look and whimpered a couple of times. I told him he couldn't come along, that I'd be back soon, and left feeling the usual pang of guilt. A creature of infinite energy and curiosity, he detested waiting in the car.

I arrived at the front of the building just as one man carrying a shoulder-mount camera exited, followed by two others, one with a clipboard, and finally, a tall, stately woman with long blond hair. She smiled at me, and I realized I'd seen her on one of the local TV channels. The networks, it seemed, had an endless supply of tall, stately blondes.

I announced myself and was escorted directly to Bradley Nielsen's office. He sat behind his desk looking very much the CEO in a conservative, dark blue suit, white button-down shirt, and red tie.

"I saw channel eight coming out," I said as I was shown in. "How did the interview go?"

His eyes strayed to the knot on my head, but my question brought a smile. "It's just some local coverage, but the timing's perfect. We've got interest expressed by Italy,

Spain, and the UK. We might need to produce a half-billion test kits, so we've got venture capitalists to woo and deals to cut."

"Are the feds interested?"

"They're waiting for our test data. But if we contain the outbreak here there won't be much of a domestic market."

"Are you still bullish on our ability to contain the virus here in the US?"

"If we nip it in the bud, we should be okay."

"How would these tests be deployed?"

"Good question. We're thinking drive-through test stations initially. All people will have to do is drive up and spit in a vial. No swab stuck up your nose. A second or two later they'll have a diagnosis. Down the road, maybe a test kit in every home." He broke into a self-satisfied smile. "Who knows?"

"How's the approval process going?"

His smile vanished. "Slower than I'd like, but we're getting there. FDA approval's key no matter where we deploy. Those bastards make you jump through too many goddamn hoops. It's a wonder anything ever gets approved." He motioned for me to sit, and when I did he came around and sat on the edge of his desk, eyeing me with sudden, unblinking intensity.

"We're a small company, Mr. Claxton, and rumors travel fast." He paused, but I didn't respond. "Rumor has it you're not just representing Malcolm's niece in the estate settlement like you said. The word is you're looking into his suicide, questioning it. Is that true?"

"Would that be a problem?"

His face stiffened. "A problem? Are you kidding me? I just told you I'm in the middle of sensitive negotiations. The last thing I need is you picking at that scab. Even the hint of a scandal will scare investors away. Mal killed himself. That's bad enough. Leave it at that."

I shifted in my chair and looked at him straight on. "I'm representing Willow Daniels in the settlement of Bainbridge's estate, like I told you. If in the course of that work I come across evidence suggesting it wasn't a suicide I'm certainly not going to suppress it."

He leaned in. "Come on, it was ruled a suicide by the medical examiner. Have you found any evidence that would dispute that?"

I kept my demeanor neutral. "Nothing I'm willing to disclose."

He leaned back and opened his hands. "Look, I'm sure you can understand my concern here, Cal," he said in a softer tone. "Maybe you could keep me in the loop. I mean, I need to stay out ahead of any surprises. You think you could do that? I could pay you for your time, of course. I'll make it worth your while."

I paused for a moment to give the impression I was thinking his offer over. "I'll see what I can do," I said. Of course, there was no way I would share anything sensitive, nor would it be ethical for me to represent both Willow and him. But he didn't need to know that. And, who knows? A communications link with Bradley Nielsen could come in handy down the road.

He smiled with a hint of smugness. "Well, then we have an understanding. Keep me informed and keep track of your billable hours."

"Always." I paused for a moment. "Since you brought it up, what can you tell me about the feud between Bainbridge and one of your scientists, Eric Trenton?"

His eyes lost their friendliness. "Oh, *that*. It's no big

deal. Two headstrong scientists squabbling over a patent. Happens all the time in this business."

"How's it going to turn out?"

He shrugged. "Our patent lawyers are still looking at it. It's critical in patent work to get inventorship right."

"Could be a big payday for Trenton, right?"

He eyed me cautiously. "What are you suggesting?"

I made a dismissive gesture. "Not a thing. Just an observation." After a pause in the conversation, I thanked him for his time and got up to leave. At the door, I turned back to him, and in my best Columbo-like manner said, "Oh, one other thing. Where were you the night Bainbridge died?"

His head rocked back as if my words had physical force, and his neck took on some color. "You've got a lot of nerve, Claxton," he said, apparently done with the first-name familiarity. "That's an insulting question." But he caught himself. "If you must know, I was home with my wife the entire night." His tone rang with righteous indignation.

"Thanks. I'll be in touch," I said and stepped into the hall. I also wondered where he was last Tuesday afternoon when Wanda was killed, but that would have to wait.

CHAPTER FIFTEEN

"HEY," ZOE SAID BRIGHTLY OVER THE PHONE, "HOW'S your head?"

"It looks worse than it feels. What's up?"

"I stopped by your office, and Timoteo said you were in Portland. Turns out I'm coming in to meet with my department head. He's got an alumni gig—you know, academia is like politics. Fundraising comes first. He wants to touch base with me, to use his term."

"Are you going to tell him you're not writing the book he expects?"

A long pause. "I think not. I guess I'm not quite ready to pull the plug." She sighed. "I'll have to bullshit my way through our meeting. It won't be hard. He's not a good listener." She paused again. "Does that make me a bad person?"

"No, you earned your sabbatical. Besides, in your novel your protagonist's character arc involves healing from grief and loss. That's psychology, right?"

She laughed. It was a good sound. "Yeah. I guess all fiction is about psychology when you boil it down. Why the hell do people do what they do? That's the question. But what I'm writing is a long way from a text on clinical psychology."

"Take more time, then. You don't have to tell him tonight that you're not coming back."

"I know. Anyway, you want to meet for dinner? I'm thinking seafood at Jake's. The place has high ceilings, plenty of ventilation, so we won't get the plague."

We agreed on an early dinner, before her appointment with her boss. After we disconnected, I sat back and thought about the exchange. I was relieved Zoe wasn't placing the communication burden entirely on me. That was a good sign, wasn't it? And I believed her when she said she just needed some time, and I was willing to give it to her. But I couldn't help feeling a little deflated. Her plan was to quit teaching, write her book, and hang a shingle out for private practice in the wine country. But she just admitted she wasn't ready to "pull the plug" on her job at Puget Sound. Was her hesitation because of me?

I wasn't sure.

—/ /—

Jake's was moderately busy that evening—unusual for one of the most popular restaurants in Portland. Zoe and I shared a bottle of Domaine Serene sauvignon blanc and feasted on horseradish-crusted steelhead and Dungeness crab cakes. The mood was light, like old times. When Zoe hurried off to meet her boss, I headed back to Caffeine Central. The parking area was dark, but when I got out of the car and walked toward the building, a motion-sensing light illuminated part of the lot. I saw a figure move on the periphery of the lighted area. I stopped dead.

"Evenin', Mr. Claxton," Benny Boykin said as he stepped out of the shadows. His arms hung at his sides.

I didn't see a gun, and his demeanor didn't telegraph a threat. "I was hopin' you'd show up here tonight."

"Hello, Benny. What's on your mind?"

"It's BB. Everyone calls me BB. I want to talk. You're a lawyer, says on the card you gave me." He started to step toward me.

I raised a hand. "Let's keep some space between us, okay? You know, the virus thing."

He stopped and hesitated before speaking, as if searching for the next words. "I think I could use a smart lawyer. Are you a smart lawyer, Mr. Claxton?"

I had to smile. "It's Cal. Everybody calls me Cal. Yeah, I'm a smart lawyer. How can I help you, BB?"

His eyes gleamed in the overhead light, and a tear started down his cheek. He quickly swiped it with the back of his hand. "I might know somethin' about my sister's death. I need to get it off my chest, but I don't want no trouble with the Portland Police."

"What do you know, BB? Is this about Malcolm Bainbridge's gun? Your sister didn't want to talk to me about that."

He eyed me with suspicion. "I ain't talkin' to nobody till I got a deal of some kind." He coughed a couple of times. I moved back several steps. "How would that work?" he said.

"The first step would be to get you a lawyer. I know a—"

"What about you? I read you don't charge all that much sometimes."

"I'm flattered, but I can't represent you. I found your sister's body. A lawyer can't participate in a case he's also a witness in. It's a potential conflict of interest."

He blinked a couple of times. "Makes no sense to me. You know a good lawyer who ain't too expensive?"

"Sure. I can put you in touch with one. Give me your

cell number." I handed him a business card and a pen, and he scrawled a number on it with his left hand. I paused and met his eyes. "I want to catch the person who killed your sister. Is there *anything* you can tell me right now that might help, BB? I'll keep it to myself."

He looked away, and a long silence ensued. "It wasn't no accident. And it was my fault it happened. Thank the Lord that little girl's okay." That said, he turned and walked away.

I watched him disappear into the shadows. Despite the lump on my head, I was moved by the man and the guilt he carried for his sister's death. I knew a lawyer who might be interested in taking on his case. I would call him first thing in the morning. I was frustrated, too, that BB hadn't told me more, but I was getting a clearer sense of what might have gone down.

Be thankful for small favors, I told myself.

I contacted Ned Gillian, a highly successful lawyer out of McMinnville, first thing the next morning. He'd taken on a pro bono case at my urging a while back. To his surprise, but not mine, pro bono work gave him a sense of satisfaction that was wholly missing in his regular practice. We were now good friends. After I explained the situation, he laughed. "What are you getting me into now, Cal?"

"All he wants is indemnity in exchange for what he knows. I'm convinced he holds the key to this case, and his information might bring the police back in, which is what should happen. They've washed their hands of it."

"What, you don't want to crack the case all by your lonesome?"

"Not if I can help it. Zoe's calling me Don Quixote these days."

He laughed again. "She's got a point, you know. How much danger is BB in? I mean, you think his sister was murdered?"

"He said as much, and yeah, I think he's scared shitless of someone. But he's pretty wily, too."

A long silence. "Okay, give me his contact information. I'll call him and see what I can do."

—/—

After disconnecting from a prospective client later that day, my phone rang again. "Mr. Claxton? This is Stuart Burgess, the TA from Spectro Systems. Remember me?"

"Of course, Stuart. What can I do for you?"

"I have some information that might interest you."

I heard street noises in the background and on a hunch asked, "Are you outside?" He said he was, and I invited him into my office. I would risk virus exposure if it meant I could observe him more closely this time.

Stuart had a strong jaw, intelligent eyes, and bushy eyebrows that matched the shade of his blond hair. I watched with interest how he and my dog interacted. He got high marks for not only acknowledging Archie's presence but offering a hand to be sniffed. Archie responded with an enthusiastic butt wag, another plus for my visitor. My dog was an excellent judge of character.

He took a seat well away from my desk and held up

what looked like a surgical mask. "I saw your sign out there. Want me to wear this? It's an N-95 surgical mask."

"Sure. Where can I get some of those?"

Stuart shook his head. "We're rationing ours at work right now. They're in short supply across the country, even in some hospitals and nursing homes." He put the mask on and continued, "Most of the US personal protective equipment's made in China, and the supply chain's getting hammered by Covid."

"Don't we have a strategic stockpile of this stuff?" I said with an incredulous look.

"In theory, yes, but somebody dropped the ball."

I shook my head. "What's on your mind, Stuart?"

He ran his fingers through his hair and squared his shoulders. "I've been talking to Marsha Coates. She was Dr. Bainbridge's TA. She told me something weird is going on with the laboratory notebooks at Spectro Systems."

"Notebooks? Like for recording scientific data?"

"Yes. Our scientists keep detailed records of their work in notebooks, for patent purposes. You can't get a patent unless you can show the date the idea was conceived and what experiments were performed to prove the concept. And all notebook entries have to be dated and witnessed."

"I see. What did Marsha say?"

"She told me the notebook Dr. Bainbridge was using during the InstaVision work is missing, or at least she can't locate it." He opened his hands, and I sensed a sheepish smile beneath the mask. "Okay, that's not too unusual. Dr. Bainbridge was forgetful. Sometimes he took his notebook home and left it there. She'd have to remind him to bring it in. He'd forget. That kind of thing."

"We could look for it at his house," I offered.

"That's already been done. Marsha told the patent attorneys about this, and Nielsen got someone to let them into the Mt. Tabor house—Dr. Bainbridge's nephew, I think."

"Donny Romano?"

"Yeah, that's the guy. Anyway, they didn't find it. I heard Nielsen had a screaming fit, blaming Dr. Bainbridge for being careless." Stuart's brow furrowed. "Can you believe that? I mean, the man just died."

"Is Marsha sure he took the notebook home?"

"No, I don't think so."

"But she's positive it existed, right?"

"Oh, yeah. And this one couldn't have been more crucial. Notebooks are where an invention starts." Stuart came forward in his chair. "Meanwhile, Eric Trenton has made *his* notebook available to the attorneys. I heard it's got entries that explain how to recognize that the hypercamera is showing you spectra from Covid-19 and not one of the other human coronaviruses—you know, the ones that give rise to the common cold. There are four of them."

"Sounds like a tough job, picking one out of five."

Stuart nodded emphatically. "Right. The molecular structures of the spike proteins are almost identical on all the coronas, so they yield very similar spectra. Is it a cold or is it Covid-19? Telling the difference is at the heart of the invention behind InstaVision. Trenton's saying *he* figured it out, not Dr. Bainbridge."

"Who witnessed his entries in the notebook?"

Stuart laughed. "Good question. His TA, Anthony Grimes. The guy's a complete kiss-ass climber. He'd do anything to get ahead, and Trenton gives him his performance reviews and raises."

"So, without Bainbridge's notebook, Trenton could get full credit for the patent. Is that what you're saying?"

"Exactly." Stuart's eyes grew hard. "It seems awfully convenient that the key notebook suddenly goes missing right around the time Dr. Bainbridge dies. And a lot of us at Spectro doubt Trenton's clever enough to have come up with the breakthrough on his own."

He paused, and I sat there as the message sank in. The young technical assistant was sitting on the edge of his seat. "Was there anything else you wanted to tell me, Stuart?"

He absently adjusted the mask, then shook his head. "No, that's all I got right now. What do you think, Mr. Claxton?"

"I think you did the right thing, telling me about this. It's important information, and I'll hold it in the strictest confidence." I locked onto his eyes. "You need to do the same, Stuart. Not a word to anyone that you've told me this. Agreed?" He nodded with an earnest look, and I added, "And keep your ear to the ground at work."

After Stuart left, I leaned back in my chair, laced my fingers behind my head, and studied the dimpled moonscape of my ceiling for a while. The suspicious death of Malcolm Bainbridge and the missing laboratory notebook appeared to be synchronous. That elevated Eric Trenton in the rogue's gallery pecking order.

Would someone kill to claim the inventorship of the golden goose? I asked myself. *Someone driven by greed and ambition? Most assuredly,* I answered.

CHAPTER SIXTEEN

A LIGHT RAIN BEGAN FALLING ABOUT THE TIME I LOCKED up Caffeine Central that afternoon. Arch followed me up the interior staircase to my studio apartment and stood by anxiously as I donned running attire. If looks could hurry a person, I'd have been dressed in an eye blink. Before exiting the back of the building, I put on a raincoat and ballcap, and as I leashed up Archie, he let out a couple of high-pitched yelps that set my ears ringing. I locked up, replaced the key in the chink in the bricks, and headed east on Couch.

At 1st Street we crossed over to Burnside and took the stairs at the bridge down through Ankeny Plaza and out to the river. The rain had eased off, and the gathering sunset lit the sky in pale lavender and orange. Archie was out ahead of me, prancing like a proud pony.

The Willamette River was broad, smooth, and silent, and when I spotted a single kayaker, I thought of Willow's moxie in getting that spectacular shot of the Freemont bridge at sunset. We passed under the Morrison and Hawthorne Bridges, both of which doubled as shelter for homeless people. I was unsettled by how much the camps had grown since the last time I jogged the river.

Homelessness was bad enough. Adding a contagious virus to the mix was unthinkable.

We reached the Marquam Bridge and were turning around when my cell went off. I fished it from my raincoat, hoping it was Zoe. It wasn't. My phone didn't recognize the caller, but I answered anyway.

"Clete Bower here, Claxton. You sound out of breath. Are you okay?"

"I'm out jogging," I explained. "What's on your—"

"In the city? Is that safe? Where are you?"

"Under the Marquam Bridge at the moment. What can I do for you, Bower?"

"That far? I'm impressed. Are you heading back, or are you a marathon man?"

"Get to the point, Bower," I said with mounting irritation. "I'm cooling off here."

"We've finally got a hearing date. March twenty-fifth. We need to talk, see if we can work through the minor issues we've got."

"They're not minor, they're bullshit, and you know it. But if you want to meet, that's fine. I'll be at my Portland office tomorrow, and my morning should be free."

"Fine. I'll drop by."

"Call first. And bring a key to the Bainbridge house. Your client apparently has the only one."

It was nearly dark when we got back to Caffeine Central. I was sure I'd left the light on above the rear entry, but it was off now. I activated the flashlight in my phone and illuminated the fixture. The bulb was broken. I shone the light on the door. It was ajar.

I stepped back as a chill snaked its way down my back. I pushed the door open, stood still, and listened. Not a sound. And Archie was nonchalant, which led me to believe the prowler was long gone. I called the police and was informed a unit wouldn't arrive for at least an hour. Muttering to myself, I went to my car, extracted the tire iron from the trunk, and with Archie at my side, went through the building to make sure no one was inside.

Both my office and the upstairs apartment had been rifled. File and desk drawers were open with the contents scattered on the floor. A mess, to be sure, but I was thankful there wasn't any major damage. All the cash—fifty or sixty bucks—had been stripped from my wallet upstairs, along with my credit cards. Aside from the pain of having to cancel the cards and get new ones, it appeared the biggest loss was my laptop.

I looked at Archie. "When's the last time I backed up my hard drive?" I groaned pathetically. "Like *never.*" He looked back at me without much sympathy. Clearly, he was more interested in getting fed.

I went back outside and looked around for the key on the off chance the prowler dropped it, but there was no trace of it. I berated myself for being so cavalier about the hiding place, which I'd used for years. Then again, that chink in the bricks was well to the right of the entry and behind a scruffy potted lemon cypress. Somebody must have seen me put the key away, I decided.

The parking lot was deserted when we left for the river, I recalled. I looked across the lot to a gap between the backs of two buildings, the most likely observation spot. A possible explanation was that someone seeking to score drug money had seen me stash the key from there. But two other possibilities sprang to mind. First, I thought of the visit from BB the night before. He'd been standing in the shadows over by the gap in the buildings. Had he come back and broken in? I couldn't rule it out, but it didn't seem likely.

Second, I thought of Clete Bower, who seemed awfully interested in where I was this evening. And I'd been very obliging, telling him I was a good thirty-five or forty minutes away under the Marquam Bridge. I walked over to the gap, turned my cell flashlight on, and looked around. Nothing caught my eye except for a few fresh scuff marks in the soft mud that I took for footprints. I didn't see any cigar butts, but I liked Bower for this a lot more than BB or some meth head.

I went back inside to wait for the police, feeling a strong sense of déjà vu. Caffeine Central had been broken into a decade earlier. The backdoor lock had been smashed in, and Nando came to help me resecure it. He brought me a gun for protection, too. I smiled at the memory and realized how much I missed my friend. And it wasn't just his companionship that I missed. I had a sense I was going to need his help before this case was over, something I realized I'd taken for granted over the years.

No worries, I told myself. He'll be back soon.

The police finally showed up and were gone in forty minutes. I got the look and the lecture for leaving a key in an outside hiding place. I deserved it. "No, we're not going to dust for latent prints," a young, uniformed officer explained before leaving. "We just don't have the manpower to do forensics on property crimes." I said I understood. They did find some muddy footprints I'd missed on the staircase. Alas, like the ones outside, they were not clear enough to be of any use.

I'd just finished lining up a twenty-four-hour locksmith

when Timoteo called. "Hey, boss," he began, "I've got good news and bad news."

"Give me the bad news first."

"Donny Romano went out tonight, but I lost him on the I-5. I got behind an eighteen-wheeler and didn't realize he'd turned off on the 405. He drives like a wild man."

"Are you sure he didn't spot you?"

"Positive. It was a fluke. I'm sorry."

"No problem. There'll be other chances. What's the good news?"

"Since I lost Bainbridge, I decided to see what BB was up to. I parked a half block down and across the street from his place. Wasn't there more than ten minutes when out he comes wearing a backpack and carrying a suitcase. I figured he was making a run for it, but it turned out he drove to a motel over on SE 91st. The Stasson, a real fleabag. He parked in the back, away from the lighted area, and checked in. He's on the second floor, room twenty-eight, facing the street."

"That *is* good news. If you hadn't gone to his place, we wouldn't know where he's hiding out. Nice work."

"You think that's it—he's gone into hiding?"

"Yeah. He's worried about getting killed like his sister."

"Wow, can't blame him. What's the next step?"

I told Timoteo about my conversation with my lawyer friend, Ned Gillian. "So, even if Gillian helps him out," I summed up, "I want to keep an eye on BB, see if he makes contact with anyone. I think he's feeling a lot of guilt about his sister's death, but I still don't trust him."

"Sure. I can do that. There's a spot across the street where I can easily watch his room. Want me to start tomorrow?"

I paused for a moment. "No. Let Gillian contact him

first. Try tailing Donny again." Changing the subject, I added, "There's been an incident here at Caffeine Central." I went on to tell him about the break-in.

"You think it's related to the case?" he said when I finished, his voice tinged with a kind of gee-whiz excitement.

"Maybe. Then again, it had all the earmarks of a typical burglary for drug money." I didn't mention my suspicion of BB or Clete Bower. That was pure speculation. "If it was related, they didn't come away with anything. I haven't put word one about the case on my laptop."

"That's good," Timoteo responded. "And don't worry about your hard drive. I backed it up on the cloud just last week. You couldn't have lost much."

"That's the best news I've heard all day. Thanks for the foresight." To myself I asked, how did I ever get along without this kid?

—//—

"Hey, what're you up to?" Zoe asked later that evening.

I was busy in the galley kitchen of the studio apartment, holding my phone to my ear. I'd cleaned up most of the mess, and a locksmith had already come and gone, installing a new dead bolt. "I'm sautéing some Kalamata olives and anchovies for puttanesca and missing you." I regretted saying the last phrase the moment it left my mouth. It wasn't wise to admit how I felt at this point. It might be construed as not giving Zoe the space she needed. *Shit, shit, shit.*

"Oh, that sounds delicious." I just had the last of some

lamb stew Aunt Gertie gave me—a care package. She's the only person I know who can outcook you. How does she do it?"

I laughed. "That's a question I've been asking for the last decade. How did the discussion with your department head go?"

She huffed a breath in frustration. "You don't get a Ph.D. in psychology without learning how to sling some bullshit." I laughed again, and she added, "I told him I was still working on a first draft. I just didn't tell him *which* first draft, and he didn't press me." She sighed. "And now I feel shitty about it. Lying by omission is lying. No way around it."

"If he had pressed you, would you have told him the truth?"

She paused for a moment. "Yeah, I would have, no question. He was more interested in telling me how much money he raised than the book I was working on. The guy's low on intellectual curiosity."

"Then don't worry about it."

"How's the investigation going?" she asked with the clear intent of changing the subject.

I told her about BB's visit and what Stuart Burgess had said about Eric Trenton and the scientific notebook. But when I came to the break-in, I hesitated. A lie by omission would've served me well here, because I knew the burglary would upset Zoe. But I thought better of it. "There's one more thing," I added, then went on to describe what happened.

She sighed when I finished. "First the hit-and-run, now this. I'm getting worried about you, Cal."

"Hey, I've got this."

A long pause ensued. "That's what my second husband said."

I had no comeback for that.

CHAPTER SEVENTEEN

"LOOK, CAL, YOU REALLY OUGHT TO CONSIDER CUTTING a deal here," Clete Bower said. It was the next day in my office. Bower wore a tweed blazer with leather elbow patches and rumpled slacks that looked like they'd never known a hot iron. He smelled of cigars again, although not quite as strongly, owing to the fact it was only mid-morning. "I mean, it's your client's word against mine, but I've got a witness who'll back up my client." He gave me a look of faux bewilderment and shook his head with his palms upturned. "Who do you think the judge's going to believe?"

I swallowed a contemptuous laugh. "What do you have in mind?"

He opened a battered briefcase, extracted a single sheet of paper, and cleared his throat. He squinted at the paper and looked up at me. "It's straight forward. We liquidate everything in the estate except the Ansel Adams photos. Your client gets her share minus seventy-five thousand, which is half the amount she owed her uncle." He raised his chin and managed a self-righteous look. "And the photo collection goes to my client to satisfy his uncle's wishes."

I had an urge to throw Bower out by the scruff of his neck, but I kept my cool. "I agree we should liquidate everything except the photo collection. As for payment to your client, Ms.

Daniels will pay him half of what she owes the estate, which is twenty thousand dollars. The Ansel Adams collection goes to *her*, per her uncle's request. That's our position."

Bower's eyes widened in disbelief. "That's it? You're gonna take *that* to the judge?" He opened his hands again. "Look, even though we've got a witness and you don't, we're willing to cut down what Ms. Daniels owes from seventy-five to, say, fifty thousand. We keep the pictures, of course."

I looked him straight in the eyes. "No deal. As for your witness, Gloria Talbot, we have reason to believe she's not credible. There are rumors that she and your client were lovers while she was married to Malcolm Bainbridge, that the affair broke up the marriage."

"Rumors?" He laughed. "That's not gonna fly and you know it."

I gave him a look that said I had more but decided this was not the time to reveal the photos Willow had found. "Regarding the Ansel Adams collection, we can establish that my client and Malcolm Bainbridge had a close bond owing to their mutual interest in photography. It follows that he would have wanted her to have the photo collection." I chuckled for effect. "And I doubt he'd have wanted the collection to go to the person who broke up his marriage." I stood up. "I think we're done here. We'll see you at the probate petition hearing."

Clete Bower was shaking his head as I showed him out. I glanced down at his shoes. There were slight traces of mud on the edges. I said, "Hope you didn't get that mud on your shoes from my parking lot. It's a mess out there sometimes."

His face froze for an instant. *A tell?* I wasn't sure. "It's winter in Oregon, lots of mud everywhere. Looks like I'm about due for a shoeshine."

I stood in the doorway after he hurried off, mulling over the exchange. Had Bower broken in and taken my computer to gain advantage in our negotiation or to learn where my investigation stood? His reaction made me a little suspicious. On the other hand, he was right. Oregon's a muddy place in winter.

Back at my desk, I realized Bower had failed to give me a key to the Bainbridge house, an annoying little ploy to suggest dominance in the negotiations. I bristled at that and the two-bit shake down attempt. I wondered what else that kind of greed could give rise to.

—/ /—

By the time the lunch hour rolled around, I had doled out pro bono legal advice on two lengthy calls. After a walk, I loaded Archie into the car and took the Hawthorne Bridge across the river, scoring a parking spot a block from Cartopia. It had sputtered rain most of the morning, but the sodden clouds had moved north, and a decent lunch crowd had gathered under the big tent. Willow's menu that day featured "Chicken Kebabs Française"—skewered chunks of marinated chicken, fennel, and black olives—served with wild rice. It was so good, I shamelessly got back in line for a second plate.

The rush subsided, and Willow and Tater joined us under the tent. She stood her daughter next to Archie and placed Tater's hands on his back for balance. I moved down the bench and gently motioned to Arch. We both watched with delight as he slowly came toward me, and Tater moved with him, taking cautious steps with a huge grin. This went on until Tater finally took a couple of steps on her own, her very first.

"Oh, my God, did you see that?" Willow said, her eyes sparkling with pride. "I caught the whole thing on my cell phone." She swept Tater up in her arms, hugged her, and—after handing her off to me—knelt and hugged Archie.

Chalk up another convert to my dog's fan club.

As for me, well, the experience opened the floodgates on memories of my own daughter I hadn't dwelt on in a very long time. They were bittersweet, and I kept them to myself.

When Tater finally went down for a well-earned nap, Willow rejoined me, and I began updating her on the case. She was wide-eyed and furious after I described Clete Bower's visit and the "deal" he offered.

"Don't worry," I said. "I doubt Bower will have the nerve to raise this in front of a judge. He was trying to shake us down *before* the hearing. Since there's no will, my guess is the judge will simply rule to divide everything equally."

She smirked. "If I hadn't offered to pay my debt, I doubt this would have ever occurred to Donny."

"No good deed goes unpunished, you know. Given the actions of your cousin and his lawyer, you could consider not paying Donny the twenty thousand. I doubt the judge will care one way or the other."

Her jaw flexed, and she drew her lips into a straight line. "I think of it as owing the money to Uncle Mal's estate, *not* Donny."

"Of course," I said.

"What about the Ansel Adams collection?" she asked. "I'm still willing to buy Donny's half if it comes to that. I'll have enough money, right?"

"You will, but I told Bower we're going for the entire

collection." Her face brightened and then I moved on to the visit from Stuart Burgess. "Did your uncle ever mention a scientist at Spectro Vision named Eric Trenton?"

Her brow furrowed and she shook her head. "Not that I recall. As I mentioned, he didn't talk much shop with me, but he did complain now and then about the work environment at Spectro."

"What did he say?"

She cocked her head for a moment. "Oh, that it was too cutthroat, that sort of thing. He felt science should always be collaborative. I think he chafed at working at a for-profit organization, even though he was a partner. He saw science more as a gift than a money-making operation." She paused before adding, "I wonder how hard they looked for that notebook at Uncle Mal's house?"

"You think they could have missed it?"

"It's a big house, and he was notorious for putting things in unusual places." She laughed. He once put some fresh fish in the pantry instead of the fridge. It took him three days to find it." She eyed me for a moment. "We could take a look, you know. I want him to have his name on that patent if he deserves it."

Another visit to the house was in order, we decided.

I mentioned the break-in at Caffeine Central the night before but downplayed it so as not to alarm her. I did extract a promise that she would check the locks on all her first-floor windows and make sure she kept the doors deadbolted. She shot me an impish grin. "And I promise I won't hide a spare key in a flowerpot."

As the conversation on the case wound down, I said, "Do you mind if I ask if Tater's father is in the picture? Just curious."

"No. Not at all." She smiled softly. In the winter light,

her short, choppy hair looked almost burgundy-colored, and her freckles were reduced to a subtle patina. "Tater's father's out of the picture. I was in love, he wasn't. And he has zero interest in his progeny. He's made that clear."

"Is he paying child support?" I asked, although I was pretty sure I knew the answer.

"No. I don't want *anything* from him," she answered, the words barely escaping a clenched jaw.

"Is he in Portland?"

"No. He's teaching English in Japan." She looked away with a hint of wistfulness. "Maybe he'll grow up someday." She brought her eyes back to mine. They were more brown than green in the low light. "What about you? You have a family besides Archie?"

I went on to explain that I was a widower with a grown daughter, who had just started working as an environmental scientist for the state of California. We swapped stories about raising daughters for a while, and then she eyed me again with another impish grin. "What about now? Is there a significant other?"

I smiled. "Yeah, there is. Her name's Zoe. She's a prof at the University of Puget Sound, psychology. She's on sabbatical, living up in the wine country near where I live."

I must have telegraphed something in my demeanor, because Willow held my gaze and said, "Are things good between you two?"

"Yeah, we're fine," I said, trying perhaps too hard to sound more upbeat than I felt.

I hoped she wouldn't press me, and she chose not to, although I was sure she picked up on my unintentional ambiguity. Instead, she looked past me and sighed. "Well, as far as I'm concerned, being in a relationship is overrated. Tater and I are doing just fine on our own."

I didn't buy it, but I extended her the same courtesy, figuring that if I asked her to elaborate, she would, in turn, ask the same of me. And that was not a conversation I was ready to have with this precocious young woman.

As Arch and I headed back to our car that afternoon, I realized something that should have been obvious from the outset—Willow Daniels reminded me an awful lot of my daughter, Claire. No wonder I was willing to go out on a limb for her.

CHAPTER EIGHTEEN

IT WAS A SLOW FRIDAY AFTERNOON AT CAFFEINE CENtral until my cell phone buzzed. "Cal Claxton?" a somewhat familiar female voice asked. When I answered yes, she continued, "What did you tell that goddamn Northwest Mutual investigator, Tiara Jones?"

"Nice to hear from you, Gloria," I answered.

"Well, she's back asking a lot more questions and delaying the whole damn process. This is ridiculous."

I figured Gloria was fishing, since I doubted agent Kiara Jones would've used my name. But I sensed an opportunity. "Look, I was just doing my job. Tell you what, why don't you let me buy you a drink and explain. Maybe I can help." Surprisingly, she accepted and agreed to meet me at the Haymaker on Killingsworth in an hour.

A popular watering hole in North Portland, the Haymaker had a handsome L-shaped bar, a beamed ceiling, and a friendly vibe, although it wasn't all that crowded for a Friday. I got there first, took a table along the wall, and ordered a Mirror Pond pale ale. I waved when Gloria entered and stood as she approached my table. Wearing yoga pants and a tight-fitting tank top beneath a windbreaker, she turned the heads of more than one male patron. She was curvaceous and moved with the elan some athletes exhibit, with more than a pinch of flirtatiousness thrown in.

She eased into her seat, made a face, and said, "So, explain."

I smiled affably. "Order a drink first." The waiter appeared a moment later and Gloria asked for a whiskey sour. "Thanks for meeting with me," I said, in full nice-guy mode.

She waved a dismissive hand. "Yeah, I was able to get away. Things are slowing down at work. The virus, I guess." A bitter smile. "I had to go back to work after the divorce."

"What do you do?"

"I manage the office at an exercise club, The Wy'East. That's where I met Mal." She shook her head. "He wasn't that committed to getting in shape and dropped his membership after a month."

"But a romance was kindled?".

A grudging smile. "Yeah, somehow I found his dislike of physical activity endearing. Go figure."

I sipped some beer. "I'm sorry your insurance payout is still hung up. I did speak briefly to agent Jones. To be honest, I was interested in her take on the suicide."

She flashed her eyes at me. *"Why?* Mal shot himself. End of story."

I sighed. "Well, you know, my client's having trouble accepting that. I thought getting agent Jone's perspective might help me convince her." It was a bullshit answer, but I figured it would suffice.

Her glacial blue eyes narrowed down. "If that's all you did, then why did Jones come back with more questions and more attitude?" Her drink arrived, she took a healthy swallow, and returned her gaze to me, accompanied by a thin smile. "You're not as innocent as you say you are. You're stirring up doubt about what happened, aren't you?"

I smiled with feigned sheepishness. "Well, I did ask some questions, but I can assure you Jones vouched for you. She said you had an alibi for the night Malcolm died."

She lowered her slanted brows, and her face tightened. "I was with someone the entire night. I'm sure the insurance investigator checked that out. I gave her the person's name." Her delivery sounded like something she read off a teleprompter.

"Care to share a name?" I ventured.

"That's none of your business."

I opened my hands and smiled reassuringly. "See? There you go. You have no problem." I paused for a moment and fixed her wintry eyes. "While we're on the subject, you don't happen to know what Malcolm's nephew was doing that night, do you? I've heard you're very fond of him."

She summoned an indignant look. "He was at a Blazers game, but what are you suggesting?"

I broadened my smile and raised my hands this time. "Nothing. Nothing at all. Was he alone?"

Her face went from tight to granite hard, and her voice dropped an octave when she answered. "He was with his lawyer, a guy named Bower."

I didn't let up. "Are you still insisting that Malcolm promised the Ansel Adams collection to Donny and not Willow?"

She pushed her shoulders back and thrust her chin out. "That's what Mal told me. Donny was his favorite."

I smiled at that. "Well, be advised that you'll be under oath at the probate hearing. Perjury's a serious crime, Gloria."

She leaned forward to speak, her chin trembling slightly. "I should have known that little bitch Willow would try to fuck things up. Mal's dead. I want my insurance money, goddamn it. And Donny wants the pictures and the money Willow owes the estate." She glowered at me. "Back off if you know what's good for you."

"Is that a threat?"

She curled her lip contemptuously. "It's advice you should take." She stood abruptly and sashayed out of the bar.

I finished my beer, and when I returned to the car Archie licked my right ear in an enthusiastic greeting. I said, "Just received my first threat of the week, Big Boy." Always a good listener, he waited for me to continue. "Bradley Nielsen was home with his wife the night Bainbridge died, Gloria was with an unnamed person, and Donny was at a Blazer game with his lawyer. How utterly convenient. And Gloria Talbot has a flinty edge to her, too."

—/—

After a quick galley-kitchen meal that evening, I packed up in preparation for the trip back to Dundee. I said a couple of choice words when I picked up my empty computer case and remembered that I no longer owned a laptop. I would consult with Timoteo in the morning on what to buy as a replacement.

We were heading to my car in the Caffeine Central parking lot when Archie began to growl, a low, menacing sound. I stopped dead as the hair on the back of my neck began to tingle. Benny Boykin appeared like a specter out of the shadows. "Hello, Cal, it's me, BB."

I greeted him, and as he moved farther into the light I added, "Are you okay? You don't look so good." His face was flushed, and his creased forehead gleamed with a sheen of sweat.

He forced a grin. "Thought you'd be goin' out tonight. I got a cell phone, but I don't use it much. The gov'ment can track you when you use 'em." He cocked his head. "How's your head? Sorry I hit you."

I raised a hand to what was left of the welt above my ear. "It's better. What's on your mind, BB?"

He stepped forward, closing the distance between us. I matched his steps in retreat until he stopped. "I ain't got the virus," he said, forcing another grin. "Just a touch of fever's all. You know a lawyer name of Gillian, Ned Gillian? He tol' me you sent him."

"Yeah, I did send him. Ned's a good man and he'll make sure you get that deal with the police."

"Okay, I was just makin' sure about it, that's all. I ain't got much trust left." He studied the ground for a few moments. "Gonna bury my sister tomorrow. You believe in redemption?" he asked, raising his eyes back to mine.

"Yes, I do, BB. In my experience, it doesn't come easy. You have to work for it."

He shook his head slowly. "Never shoulda happened, never shoulda done what I did. Maybe I can make it right, somehow."

"What did you do, BB?" I asked in a soft voice, hiding the urgency I felt.

He wiped some sweat from his brow and raised his hand. "I wanna deal first, you know that. I'm gonna go ahead and meet with your buddy Gillian on Sunday to talk about it." With that, he turned and melted back into the shadows.

On my way to Dundee, I called Nate Gillian, described my encounter with BB, and after I finished, added, "When you meet with him Sunday, I'd keep my distance. He looked like he was coming down with something."

"Like that Covid virus?"

"Probably not, but I'd keep my distance."

"Thanks for the tip."

After we disconnected, I felt a surge of frustration. Sure, BB might reveal what really happened to Malcolm Bainbridge, but Gillian would be bound by lawyer-client confidentiality, which meant he couldn't talk to me about it. On the bright side, if BB knows what happened, Gillian could initiate an early resolution of the case through police involvement. That would give Willow the satisfaction she was seeking and relieve the pressure between Zoe and me, wouldn't it?

The answer was yes, of course, but the *real* question was—why didn't I feel better about it? Was Zoe right about my doggedness? Did my ego demand that I solve the case on my own? Sure, it was natural I wanted to follow through on an investigation I'd sunk time and emotion into. But where was the end point?

CHAPTER NINETEEN

IT WAS COLD AND CLEAR WHEN I GOT OUT TO OPEN THE gate at the Aerie, and a gibbous moon hovered like a lop-sided silver coin behind the Doug firs. Archie popped out of the car and dashed across the upper field in a burst of pent-up Aussie energy. All I could see were his white boots galloping along like a strange, four-legged apparition. He began to bark, and then two deer appeared out of the shadows. I laughed. It was a game they played—Archie, obeying a genetic impulse, would herd them to the fence line, and the deer, moving with unconcerned nonchalance, would escape over the fence at the last moment.

I was fumbling for my house key when my cell phone went off. "Cal, it's Timoteo. Just checking in."

"Where are you?"

"I'm staked out across from the Stasson Motel. I saw BB enter his room about twenty minutes ago, so if he comes back out, I've got him covered. I think he was drunk or something. He was staggering."

"*Staggering?* Are you sure?"

"Oh, yeah. He barely made it up the stairs."

I described my encounter with him earlier that evening. "He's definitely up to his neck in the Bainbridge death, and he doesn't like cell phones. If he's working with somebody, he might lead you to them. Good luck and stay safe."

"Will do."

I'd just hung my coat up in the hall when my phone sounded again. I hoped it was Zoe, but it was her aunt Gertie, my next door neighbor. "Have you eaten dinner?" she asked, and when I told her I had, she said, "Well, come over for a drink then. I haven't seen you in a while."

I put my coat back on and trekked across the acreage separating my place from hers. Archie followed, and when she let me in the backdoor, he lay down dutifully on the back porch. A Dutch oven sat on the stove, and I smelled the remnants of something tasty. Notes of garlic and thyme suggested a hearty stew, and I found myself wishing I hadn't eaten.

Gertie's pewter-colored hair was pulled back and tied off, accentuating the nests of fine lines bracketing her mouth and her robin's egg blue eyes. Her demeanor, as always, was no nonsense, as she handed me a generous glass of Macallan single malt Scotch, neat. "So," she began after we clinked glasses and sipped the peaty liquor, "I gather this new investigation you've launched is gaining momentum."

"It looks that way. Didn't mean to leave you out of the loop, but things have moved fast. I assume you've spoken to Zoe." She nodded, and I went on to sketch out where the case stood while we sipped our Scotches. As expected, I got the lecture about how these forays don't pay the bills and how I shouldn't neglect my clients who pay at the full rate. This was Gertie, after all—my business conscience.

As that exchange wound down, she got around to the topic I sensed was front and center in her mind. "What's going on between you and Zoe?" she asked after topping up my Scotch. "I'm concerned about you two."

I turned my palms up. "It's nothing serious, you know. We're taking it slow."

Her look told me she didn't buy it. "Then why is she all pouty and more emotional than I've ever seen her since she moved here? Are you having problems?"

I sighed and rubbed the back of my neck absently. "I don't know. It's mainly my fault. She, uh, she's concerned I'm just jumping back in after the Fuentes case, that I'm some kind of adrenaline junky."

Gertie rolled her eyes. "Well, yeah, you are, Cal. You and I both know that. And you haven't even recovered financially from the Fuentes case."

I raised my hands in mock surrender. "I know, I know, and she worries about my safety and how she ranks in my priorities."

"Well, you're as stubborn as a bulldog once you latch onto something. I don't blame her for worrying." She paused for a moment and eyed me carefully. "How *does* she rank in your priorities?"

"At the top. I care for her, Gertie," I said without hesitation. "But I have to be honest about who I am and what I value."

"Of course you do. Look, she's as stubborn as you are, Cal, but I know for a fact that she cares for you, too." Gerties eyes got a little shiny, the closest thing I'd ever seen to her tearing up. "I hope you two don't blow it. That would be a damn shame." She forced a smile. "And that's all I'm going to say on the subject."

We finished our Scotches, and Arch and I were halfway across the field connecting our properties when Timoteo called. "Something's up, Cal!" he began. "An ambulance just showed up in the motel parking lot, and two paramedics rushed up to the room BB's staying in."

"You're sure it was his room?"

"Positive. They're in there now. The door's shut, so I can't see anything. I'll call you back when they come out." Ten minutes later: "Here they come. I've got my night-vision binocs on them. Oh, shit! BB's on a stretcher. He's got a mask on, too. Looks like they're giving him oxygen or something."

"Follow the ambulance," I said. "Find out where they take him. You didn't see anyone go in or out before they arrived, right?"

"No one. And I had eyes on the room the whole time. I'll call you back."

Twenty minutes later, Timoteo informed me BB had been taken to Adventist Hospital on SE Market. "I parked and watched them unload him," he explained. "He was definitely on oxygen. I followed the stretcher into the ER, and one of the attending nurses asked if I was a friend of BBs. I said I was, thinking they might tell me what was going on. Instead, she asked if I'd had close contact with him. I told her no and asked why. 'Just procedure,' she told me, but I think they were worried about Covid-19 exposure."

"I was afraid of that."

CHAPTER TWENTY

"ANY LUCK?" I SAID TO ESPERANZA FIRST THING THE next morning.

"Well," she said, "I had to make four phone calls, but I got some information. Boykin has a severe respiratory illness. They're running tests. He's diabetic, which puts him at greater risk, I was told."

"Does he have the Covid virus?"

"My source didn't say, but I don't think his prognosis is very good, Cal."

My heart sank. My key witness was out of circulation just when I needed him, and he might die on me, too. "Thanks, Esperanza. I'm not going to ask about how you got around the HIPAA rules."

She laughed. "Don't. It wasn't easy. I don't feel bad about it, though. Like you suggested, no names were used, just the time of his arrival at Adventist and the fact that he was being administered oxygen when he was admitted."

"Have you heard from Nando?"

"Yes, just yesterday."

"Is he worried he'll get stuck there or quarantined because of the virus? I understand Europe's restricting travel now."

An exasperated sigh. "Does Nando worry about anything?"

I laughed. "Yeah, that was a dumb question. Keep me posted. And thanks again, Esperanza."

Afterwards, my gut turned sour. I was concerned about Nando staying safe in Cuba and, closer to home, what his absence meant for me. It was like being on a high wire without a net. I missed my wingman.

I called Ned Gillian next and gave him the bad news. "This damn virus is worrisome," he commented. "I read there's been quite an outbreak at a nursing home in Washington. How do you know BB didn't expose you?"

"He looked a little feverish, so I gave him a wide berth, and we were outside."

"That was wise, my friend."

Archie and I left for Willow's place in Southeast Portland next. We were on our way to Malcolm Bainbridge's house to search for his laboratory notebook. I'd warned her about my exposure to BB, and we decided that as a precaution she would ride in the backseat with Tater and Archie, and despite the early morning chill we would put the windows halfway down. After she nestled a sleeping Tater into her car seat, Willow looked at me and shook her head in disgust. "Donny wouldn't give me the key, of course. He insisted on meeting us there."

I'd warned her that might happen. "They're playing keep away with the key so they can keep an eye on us," I explained. "I've written Bower a letter with a copy to the probate judge demanding a key. This won't happen again."

Wearing a heavy Carhartt jacket and a flat-billed ball cap with 'Zero Fucks Given' emblazoned on it, Donny Romano was slouched on the front porch steps when we arrived. He stood, smiled without warmth and looked at

Tater, who was still snoozing in her mom's front pack. "Jesus, Willow, you ever hear of *babysitters?*"

"You can open up and leave the key, Donny," she answered, her voice level but her face rigid with defiance. "No need to waste your valuable time here."

"That's okay. I think I'll stay around." Another arctic smile. "We can catch up, Cuz." He opened the front door, slipped the key into his jacket pocket, and hung the jacket on a corner coat rack.

We were halfway down the front hallway when Willow, who was leading the way, stopped abruptly and gasped. "The Ansel Adams photographs. Where are they?" The hallway walls were bare, where more than twenty large prints had been the last time I was in the house. She spun around and glared at Donny, her eyes burning with anger. "What did you do?"

He stepped back and opened his hands. "Whatdaya mean? I didn't do anything. What the fuck did *you* do?"

Willow looked at me, tears brimming in her eyes. "What happened to them?"

"Let's check the house for signs of a break-in," I said. When we got to the studio, Willow gasped again. A side window was wide open, and the back door was ajar. After checking the rest of the house to make sure the photographs were indeed gone, I called 911 and reported the theft.

The animosity between the cousins was palpable, and I was relieved when Donny chose to isolate himself in the living room with his cell phone while Willow was distracted by the act of feeding and changing her daughter. Archie and I waited on the front porch. It took twenty minutes for a patrol car and two officers to arrive.

The lead officer's eyebrows rose in surprise when

he was told how much the photographs were worth. He immediately called in to request a full investigative team. Meanwhile, he questioned us, saying at one point, "Do you have any idea who could have done this?"

I shook my head and Donny shrugged, but Willow narrowed down her eyes and pointed directly at her cousin. "He did it. I know it."

Donny's face contorted with rage. "You lie, you little bitch!" He took a threatening step toward Willow and Tater, and I instinctively moved between them. He shoved me hard, and in the exchange his nose somehow found my elbow. Imagine that. He cried out and dropped to one knee, catching a few drops of blood in his palm. He looked up at me, then the officer, his expression dripping with self-pity. "He assaulted me. Arrest him."

The officer rolled his eyes and after examining Donny's nose said, "You all need to calm down. I'm not arresting anybody at the moment, but don't tempt me again." He separated us, and by the time he and his partner finished their preliminary questioning, a forensic team arrived along with a detective from the robbery division.

The detective cut us loose a half hour later, but not before requesting that we stop by the police bureau building the next morning to leave our fingerprints. Donny scurried out to his car and took off with squealing rubber. That was the moment Willow reached into her coat pocket, withdrew her hand, and held up a key. "Well, at least we can get in the house now," she said with a triumphant look. "I lifted it from Donny's jacket. He was so anxious to get out of here he didn't think of locking the door. Now we can look for that notebook without him being around."

We locked up, got in the car, and rushed to Cartopia to

give Willow enough time to prepare for the Saturday lunch traffic. Trying to contain a smile, I said, "You sure didn't hold anything back in there."

I caught her concerned look in the rearview mirror. "Did I go too far by accusing Donny?"

I had to laugh. "Not in the least. The cops needed to hear that. You project a kind of righteous indignation that's very persuasive."

"Well, there's no doubt in my mind. Donny took them." She paused for a moment. "But I doubt he acted alone. Initiative's not his strong suit." She frowned. "I'll bet Gloria planned this and used her puppy dog to do the dirty work."

"Could be," I said, "and my guess is Bower's involved as well."

"Will we ever get the pictures back?"

"Hard to say, but they're hot, so it'll be hard for whoever it is to unload them for a while. That works in our favor."

She sobbed, a single gasp. I glanced in the mirror again. Tears were streaming down her face. "Those photographs were the only thing in that house I cared about." She sniffed. "I learned so much from them—composition, lighting, perspective. Uncle Mal and I used to pour over them, sometimes for hours. I can't believe they're gone."

"Well, between what I told the detective and what you said, I'm sure they're going to look hard at Donny."

"I hope so," she said. "Maybe they'll recover them before he does something unthinkable, like destroy them if he can't sell them. They're evidence, after all."

"I doubt that will happen," I reassured her. The real danger, I said to myself, is that they'll wind up on the walls of some billionaire collector with no scruples. "Let's look for that laboratory notebook first thing tomorrow." She agreed.

I had a quick lunch at Cartopia and then headed back across the Hawthorne Bridge. Willow said she was closing Plat du Jour early to attend Wanda Jenkins's funeral, a funeral Wanda's brother would not be able to attend. Before I left, I reiterated the need for her to be cautious, although I didn't go so far as to name what had become obvious—if BB was right about his sister's death not being an accident, then we were dealing with two brutal murders, not one.

An unsettling thought.

CHAPTER TWENTY-ONE

AS I CROSSED THE WILLAMETTE LATER THAT AFTERnoon, I called Spectro System CEO Bradley Nielsen, hoping to catch him in the office. He picked up, and I said in a bright, cheery voice, "Working on a weekend, I see, Bradley. This is Cal Claxton."

"It's all-hands-on-deck around here," he replied, his tone all business. He went on to say he was glad I called, that he'd been wondering how my investigation was going. It was just the response I was hoping for, and I said I'd drop by to update him in within the hour.

The parking lot adjacent to the Spectro Vision building was filled, and I had to park out on the street. I announced myself and waited at the reception desk until an escort showed up, a harried-looking young man wearing a stained lab coat and high-top North Face hiking boots. Nielsen was on the phone but waved me in anyway. I took a seat just as he thanked the caller and hung up.

"That was a contact in the New York State Department of Health I was talking to," he said, referring to the phone conversation. "They're starting to see some Covid-19 cases, but the test kits sent out by the CDC fail half the time."

The comment—which seemed like something inappropriate to share with me—caught me off guard. "That sounds bad," I said.

"Bad for New York but good for us. If Covid-19 takes off in this country, we could be a major player. Put a test kit in every home." He smiled, relishing the thought. "We weren't even counting on the domestic market…and now this."

Rooting for the virus seemed obscene, but I swallowed a sarcastic comment. "I thought you said we'd have no trouble containing the virus."

"We can if we get on top of it, but I'm beginning to wonder. I think the man in the White House is more worried about the economy. The Chinese are shutting their cities down, and Italy is heading in that direction."

"How are the InstaVision tests going?"

"The key tests are underway. Meanwhile, more of our internal results are in from Trenton's tests. They look tremendous." He paused. "We could own this market. Malcolm's gone, but we haven't missed a beat."

"Has the issue of inventorship between Malcolm and Eric Trenton been sorted out?" I asked.

He swung his eyes to mine. "That's company confidential."

"Trenton's got a credibility problem, you know."

He kept his eyes fixed on me. "What do you mean by that?"

"A lot of his co-workers don't believe he invented InstaVision. They're saying Malcolm Bainbridge deserves the credit, that he was the brains behind the breakthrough. What's your view?"

His neck bloomed reddish, and his jawline flexed like he was biting down on something hard and flat. "Who's saying that?"

I smiled to provoke him even further. "I can't reveal my sources, or they'll dry up. You wanted me to keep you apprised, right? Well, this is what I'm hearing."

He waved a dismissive hand. "Actually, I don't give a shit. I own the patent in either case. And Trenton's got notebook entries that back up his claims. But if this palace intrigue shit gets out, it could be very damaging." He paused and cocked his head. "What else have you heard?"

"Some of your employees aren't buying the suicide, despite the medical examiner's findings. I'm also hearing that the animosity between Bainbridge and Trenton was intense. Is this true?"

Nielsen came forward in his chair. "Meaning?"

"It's just a question."

He sighed and shook his head. "We're about ready to close a major deal. Like I told you last time, just the appearance of a scandal could blow it. Who the hell's spreading these conspiracy theories? I need to know."

I looked at him straight on. "What you need to know is the *truth*. I'm no patent attorney, but I know that misidentification of inventorship can invalidate a patent." I waited for that to sink in. "I need to talk to Eric Trenton. It would help if you could set something up." It was a blatant bluff I wasn't sure Nielsen would buy, but it was worth a try. "Tell him you've asked me to identify who's spreading rumors or something along those lines."

Nielsen leaned back in his chair and massaged his temples with his brow scrunched up and his eyes closed. "I'll think about it."

With that, he called someone to escort me out. I stopped in the entryway at a photo display of company executives. Malcolm Bainbridge was in a prominent spot, and next to him was a smiling Eric Trenton. Now at least I knew what Trenton looked like.

As I walked back to my car, I wondered about the

relationship between Trenton and Bradley Nielsen. Bainbridge's death, after all, benefitted them both in a timely, substantial way. Was Nielsen too cavalier about the patent issue? Wouldn't he be concerned that Bainbridge's notebook could turn up and complicate the process? Maybe he knew for certain it wouldn't.

My persons of interest list, I realized, was divided into three distinct populations, each potentially driven by different motives. The Gloria, Donny, Bower cohort benefitted from the value of Bainbridge's estate, and Nielsen and Trenton gained from having Bainbridge out of the picture at Spectra Vision. I wasn't sure what Benny Boykin could've gained—probably cold, hard cash—but I suspected he'd done some, if not all, of the dirty work and because of the death of his sister, he was now ready to spill his guts.

Get well, soon, BB, I said to myself.

CHAPTER TWENTY-TWO

WHEN ARCH AND I ARRIVED AT THE AERIE THAT EVENING, Zoe's Prius was parked in the driveway, a sight that did my heart good. I found her on the side porch, sitting next to my blazing propane fire pit wearing a ski jacket and a knit cap. A bottle of wine sat next to her along with two wide-bowled glasses, the kind you drink a big red from. After greeting Archie, she stood, and I wrapped my arms around her and hugged her hard, breathing in a scent of lavender. Stay cool, I told myself. Keep your emotions in check.

"I missed you, too," she said as we uncoiled. She motioned toward the wine. "I brought a *Le Petit Truc* pinot. Gertie gave it to me. She said you'd appreciate it."

I studied the bottle for a moment. "Wow, a 2012. Probably Jim Kavanaugh's best vintage ever." I laughed but didn't say what I thought—that Gertie was playing Cupid. "I suppose this means I'm cooking tonight."

She smiled the smile that came so easily, that bloomed on her face like a flower. Her blond hair, aged to a pleasing ash color, brushed her shoulders, and her big, expressive eyes shone slate blue in the fading light. "Would you?"

"I'll see what I can come up with," I said, "but you're the sous chef." I uncorked the wine, poured us each a glass, and after savoring the deep, fragrant bouquet we clinked glasses and sipped while catching each other up.

"I finished three chapters this week," Zoe began. She talked with animation about her book, lifting her chin to say, "Even wrote some pretty decent dialogue, I think." She paused for a moment, her eyes brightening with what she was about to say. "Something pretty crazy happened, too. I planned to bring my protagonist's daughter in for one chapter—you know, a cameo—then send her on her way, but guess what?"

I smiled at her enthusiasm. "What?"

"She refused to go! She's demanding a bigger part in the book. And it seems so easy to write her that I think I'll do it." Zoe laughed and shook her head. "I sure didn't see that coming."

I joined her laughter. "That's a daughter for you."

We'd finished a first glass of wine by the time we got around to my news. I poured us another—it was Saturday night, after all—and hit the high points, the biggest being the hospitalization of BB and the theft of the Ansel Adams photographs. When I finished, she said, "That's rotten luck about BB. Any way to get your lawyer friend into the hospital to talk to him?"

"Maybe, but I think it's touchy because of the virus."

"Oh, right, there's that. Seems like—"

My phone interrupted us. I glanced at the screen. "It's Timoteo. I should take this. Hold that thought."

"Hey," he said, "just checking in. I followed Donny from the gun shop to his apartment. An hour later, he led me straight to...wait for it—Gloria Talbot's address. I got some photos of him going in, just to document the visit.

Five minutes later, another dude arrives and goes in. Got shots of him, too, and I'll send them to you now."

"Excellent work, Timoteo. I'll take a look as soon as I have a chance. Stay on your toes."

Zoe and I went into the kitchen and began preparing dinner. I popped some potatoes in the oven, then took out a couple of filets that an appreciative client had given me from one of his grass-fed cows. I was pounding some peppercorns when my phone pinged. Timoteo's telephoto lens caught a couple of clear images of Donny on a well-lit front porch with Gloria standing at her open front door. No surprise there, but it was good to have hard evidence of their collaboration. The next arrival was also no surprise—Gloria's attorney, Clete Bower.

I called Timoteo back to tell him I got the pictures. "What should I do when the party breaks up?" he asked.

It was a good question. I paused for a moment. "Don't bother following Donny or Bower," I answered, and then added, "Watch Gloria's house for an hour or so, see if anything else happens. If not, call it quits."

"Roger that."

"Looks like Bonny and Clyde and their lawyer are having a pow wow," Zoe quipped after I punched off.

"Yeah. My guess is they're discussing what happened today at the Bainbridge house."

"Do you think all three of them are in on the heist?"

"Hard to say, but this certainly suggests that. Willow swears Donny couldn't pull something like this off solo. Planning and organizing are apparently not his forte. I don't think he counted on Willow being so direct with the cops about his possible involvement. That robbery detective got the message loud and clear."

Zoe smiled with an almost gleeful look. "Will the cops swoop down on him, search his place?"

I shook my head. "They have no probable cause to request a search warrant, but that could change if they uncover something in their forensic work, a fingerprint on the window frame or in the hall where the pictures had hung, for example"

Zoe, who was washing some fresh asparagus spears, eyed me. "You look disappointed. Is this theft kind of a distraction?"

I paused to think for a moment. "Not really. I don't think those pictures were stolen by some covetous Ansel Adams fan. It was an act of greed. Malcolm Bainbridge was probably murdered out of greed, so maybe it fits a pattern. And all three of them—Donny, Gloria, and Bower—would benefit from a staged theft and, of course, from the murder." I took a breath and let it out. "And the other thing is the theft pisses me off. Willow loves those photos with a passion. I hope they turn up undamaged."

Zoe eyed me again. "Do you really think she didn't know how valuable the collection is? I mean she's a professional photographer."

I pushed down a twinge of annoyance. It was a fair question. I smiled and met her eyes. "I do. I think the question of value simply never occurred to her. What's the opposite of greed? That's Willow Daniels."

I cut the shop talk after we sat down to feast on *steak au poivre*, grilled asparagus, and baked Yukon Gold potatoes. The *Le Petit Truc* pinot provided a perfect pairing. It was a sparkling clear night with a nearly full moon, so we went back out and huddled around the fire pit after dinner. We were deep into a discussion of Zoe's book when my cell sounded again.

"Hey, something's up here, Cal," Timoteo began. "Both of Gloria's visitors left, and I was getting ready to take off when another dude arrived on foot. I saw him go by and park a block down from her place. I don't think he wanted his car to be seen near her place. Anyway, I got a couple of shots of him entering." He chuckled. "She was really glad to see him. You'll see what I mean from the images I just sent you."

"I'll be damned," I said as I clicked on the two photographs and enlarged them. The first was a clear shot of a man stepping onto the porch. The second shot showed the man embracing and kissing Gloria Talbot at her open front door.

"Who is that guy?" Zoe asked.

I immediately thought of the photo display at Spectro Systems. "That's Eric Trenton, the scientist who claims he invented InstaVision."

"Whoa," Zoe said, "that's interesting. Gloria takes another young lover, and he's the scientific rival of your victim." She leaned in for a better look at the photo and giggled. "Excuse me for being sexist, but he doesn't look like much of a catch."

"Neither was Donny."

She looked at me, her eyes wide with curiosity. "What do you make of this?"

"It's another connection, a totally unexpected one." I leaned back in my chair, ran a hand through my hair, and sighed. "This case is like a Rubik's Cube. I have, what, six solid suspects? Any one of them could have done it, or they could be teamed up in almost any combination, or, hell, they could all be in it together for all I know."

"Shades of *The Orient Express*, huh?" Zoe quipped.

I laughed. "I can't rule that out. And to top it off, I have a few hunches but no good theory of *how* the Bainbridge suicide was staged." I looked at Zoe and shook my head with disgust. "This case is kicking my ass."

To my relief and her credit, Zoe commiserated without a hint of judgment. After we sifted back through what I knew for a while, she yawned, stretched, and stood up. "I think we—"

I stood and put my index finger against her lips. "Shh." I took her hand and let her up the stairs. This time we reversed the undressing sequence, and once again, when I awoke later that night, she was gone. I was wide awake, so I switched on the lamp to read for a while. Archie awoke and came over from his corner and lay his muzzle on the mattress. I scratched him behind the ears.

"What if I lose Zoe and screw this case up, too?" I asked him. He looked back at me, but his big, coppery eyes held no answer.

CHAPTER TWENTY-THREE

AT SUNRISE THE NEXT MORNING, THE EASTERN HORIZON was a strip of polished gold, and above it the night sky was surrendering to a swirl of purple fading to lavender. I'd given up on sleeping any longer, so I stumbled down the back staircase with Archie leading the way and busied myself with the tasks of feeding him and making my usual cappuccino. Archie cleaned his plate and went down the hall to the front door and looked back at me longingly. He wanted a run.

"Okay, Big Boy," I said, "but let me finish my coffee first."

Archie and I jogged up to the Pioneer Cemetery and back, and after a hot shower, a big breakfast, and a leisurely read through the digital Sunday *New York Times*, I called the lead detective on the Ansel Adams theft to make sure they'd finished working the scene and that it was okay for us to reenter the Bainbridge house. He said it was.

I called Willow next and told her I'd pick her up in forty-five minutes. "We can swing by the Police Bureau first to get fingerprinted and then go back to your uncle's house," I told her.

Despite it being a Sunday, I next called the insurance investigator, Tiara Jones. I figured she'd forgive the intrusion. After we exchanged greetings, I said, "I need a favor,

Tiara. You mentioned that Gloria's alibi checked out. I know she was with someone that night. I, uh, I'm wondering if you could tell who that was?"

The line went quiet...

Finally, I said, "Okay, I get it. It's confidential. How about this—I think I know who she was with. If I'm right, could you confirm it by staying silent?"

She sighed. "Jesus, Claxton, you've got a lot of nerve, but okay, take your shot."

"She told you she was with a man named Eric Trenton, who works for Spectro Systems, the company your client co-owned."

The line went quiet again.

"Thanks, Tiara. I owe you another one."

—/—

Riding in the back seat of my car with Archie had to be one of Tater Daniel's favorite things. Bundled up in a knit cap with a big pink tassel and a polka dot snowsuit, she chattered like a magpie and stroked Archie's fur. For his part, my dog nuzzled her and gave loving glances. It was a mutual admiration society.

The Police Bureau was quiet, and we cleared it in record time. When we pulled up in front of Bainbridge's house, the place looked smaller and less imposing than the last time I visited. Familiarity probably explained the impression, but it seemed the house had shrunk by virtue of standing vacant, and I felt a surprising twinge of sadness.

We let ourselves in with the key Willow had pilfered from Donny and decided to search Malcolm's photo studio first. Willow plopped Tater down in the center of the floor, and I produced a tennis ball I'd taken from the trunk of the car. "Watch this," I said, and in no time, I had Tater rolling the ball onto the floor and Archie retrieving it for her. Each retrieval was followed by a scream of pure delight, and the activity kept them both busy.

"What's a laboratory notebook look like?" Willow asked, looking around the studio.

I'd done a little homework with Stuart Burgess. I spread my hands. "They're large with a textured black cover, a maroon spine, and "Property of Spectro Vision" printed on the front. We set to work, going through every drawer, cabinet, and shelf without finding the lab book or anything else of interest. We moved to Malcolm's study next and searched his desk, a stuffed-full filing cabinet, an entire wall of books, and even looked under the cushions of his leather couch. Nothing.

We went upstairs to check another likely place, Malcolm's bedroom. Willow gasped and pointed at a framed picture, one of several sitting on the dresser. "That's Uncle Mal and me at Crown Point in the Gorge." The photo caught her and her uncle standing together with the Columbia River curling behind them in the distance. She smiled wistfully. "That was such a fun photo shoot."

I pointed to another, smaller, framed photo. "Isn't that Bradley Nielsen with your uncle?" They were standing next to each other dressed in white martial arts workout suits. "Looks like happier times."

Willow looked at the photo. "Yeah, Bradley talked him into taking a mixed martial arts class. Uncle Mal didn't take to it, but that's where he met Gloria. She was working at the gym where the classes were held."

"Yeah, Gloria mentioned that when I talked to her."

After coming up empty in the bedroom and adjoining bath, we moved to a large, walk-in closet. We found nothing of interest until we came to a grey metal box resting on an upper shelf. It had an inset door equipped with a large digital keypad. "This must be the pistol vault where Malcolm kept the Ruger. The vault was heavy but portable. I pulled it forward on the shelf and attempted to open it.

"It's locked," I said. "One of the investigators must have shut it, because the ME's report said it was open when they found it." I swung my gaze to her. "You wouldn't happen to know the combination, would you?"

Willow scrunched her brows, then her face brightened, and she snapped her fingers. "It's his birthday unless he changed it. I remember him making jokes about it, you know, kind of pooh-poohing the whole gun thing. Try 5-18-66."

As Willow looked on, I punched in the numbers and the vault opened with a satisfying click.

It was empty.

"Aw, crap," Willow said, "I was hoping we'd find the notebook in there. Wouldn't that have been cool?"

I laughed. "Who else knew the combination besides you and your uncle?"

She cocked her head at a slight angle. "Gloria for sure." She smirked. "Donny, I guess. Gloria could have told him."

"What about Wanda? You told me about her knocking the gun off the shelf when she was cleaning one day. What happened after that?"

"That's when Uncle Mal got the pistol vault."

"Would he have shared the combination with Wanda?"

Willow opened her hands and shrugged. "Maybe.

Wanda knew *everything*. And, like I said, Uncle Mal made a big joke out of the combination being his birthday. She might've overheard that." Willow raised her eyebrows. "What are you thinking?"

As I stood gazing at the vault, something crystalized in my mind. "It was BB. He either had his sister swipe the gun or he took it himself using the combination she gave him."

Willow shook her head vehemently. "No way Wanda took the gun. She was scared to death of the thing."

"Then she arranged a time for BB to go in and get it, a time when the coast was clear."

Willow's eyes narrowed down, and her face turned to stone. "You think he killed Uncle Mal with it?"

I hesitated for a few moments. "I don't think so. BB wants to trade what he knows for immunity. I doubt he would've come forward if he was the shooter. Too risky."

Willow's face crumbled. "*Wanda?* You think *Wanda* gave him the combination? She wouldn't..."

"That's the best fit. I think the gun was taken in advance of the murder, and the vault was closed so your uncle wouldn't notice the gun was missing."

"That's why Wanda was killed? She knew too much?"

"She was probably seen as a weak link who might talk after I started poking around." The possibility, until that moment unspoken, shot a twinge of guilt through me.

Willow put her hands on her hips and scowled, reminding me of my daughter, Claire. "If Wanda was involved, she was either forced or tricked into it somehow. She would have *never* knowingly betrayed Uncle Mal."

Willow's defense of Wanda was admirable, but I kept a neutral expression and didn't respond. My experience in criminal law told me that acts of betrayal were not all that uncommon.

She eyed me carefully but didn't challenge my lack of support. "What about Gloria and Donny?"

"Good point," I said. "But if Wanda was murdered, it was for a reason, and her brother knows what the reason is."

"Why haven't they killed BB?"

"Since Wanda's death, he's been watching his back like a hawk. He even moved into a motel to hide out."

She rolled her eyes. "But now he may have the virus."

"Let's hope not."

—/ /—

An hour and a half later we finished searching the house, including a semi-finished attic filled with boxes of books and papers and a basement with an amazingly well-equipped workshop. Malcolm Bainbridge's laboratory notebook was not to be found. However, our spirits were high. As we headed back to Willow's place, she said, "We didn't find what we were looking for, but it feels like we—I should say, *you*—made a breakthrough."

"Yeah, it does. This gives me the first inkling of how this thing could have gone down."

She leaned forward in her seat. "Explain it to me."

"Okay. Someone wanted your uncle dead. They knew that his housekeeper had a sketchy brother. Somehow, they induced BB—probably with money—to break into your uncle's house and steal the gun. Wanda probably aided this—either wittingly or not—by giving him the combination to the vault, and perhaps a key to the place to make it easy to get in when Malcolm was away."

"When did BB take the gun?"

"Unknown, but certainly prior to the night of the murder. From what you've said about your uncle, he was unlikely to miss the weapon with the empty safe locked."

"So, this person gets the gun from BB and just comes into Uncle Mal's house and shoots him?"

"There's a good chance your uncle knew his assailant, because there were no signs of forced entry or a physical struggle. But *how* the murder was actually carried out is another unknown." I had some thoughts about that, but nothing I was willing to share at that juncture.

Willow leaned back in her seat and exhaled. "My God, I can't believe this. So cruel and premeditated. And Wanda, look what they did to her. And Tater—they almost killed my baby." She looked at me, her expression an equal measure of fear and anger. "I mean, why would someone do this?"

"Greed, Willow, unfettered greed."

We drove in silence for a while. Willow leaned forward again and squeezed my shoulder. "Coming to you for help was the smartest thing I ever did, Cal. Thank you for taking the case."

I cringed inwardly. "What I outlined is all speculation, Willow, nothing more than a working hypothesis. I've yet to find any hard evidence."

CHAPTER TWENTY-FOUR

"MALCOLM BAINBRIDGE DIDN'T COMMIT SUICIDE. HE was murdered," I said to Captain Harmon Scott the next day at lunch. I'd talked him into joining me at Cartopia, where we could eat outside in a well-ventilated, albeit chilly, space.

"Oh, shit," he said as he lowered his baguette before taking a bite. "I was afraid of that. You got something solid, do you?"

I shook my head. "Nothing I can hang my hat on yet, but there's no doubt in my mind." I went on to brief him on what I knew and some of what I suspected.

He looked relieved when I finished. "Interesting, but you're right. You don't have squat I could use to reopen the investigation. Do you think this guy Boykin needs protection?"

I waved a dismissive hand. "I don't think so. I don't think anyone knows he's at Adventist, because the ambulance picked him up at the motel where he was hiding out. And besides, the hospital's scrutinizing everyone who comes in due to the virus, so I think he's safe."

"That's good," he said. "I doubt I could make a case for assigning someone to watch him." He shook his head. "And it'd be tough to find a patrolman who wouldn't bitch about doing it these days. People are starting to take this

Covid-19 threat a little more seriously. He glanced around the sparsely populated picnic tables under the tent. "This pod's one of the most popular in Portland and look, half the tables are empty."

"Yeah. It feels a little like the slow build of a tsunami." But, reluctant to get off on a virus tangent, I brought him back to what was on my mind. "Anything new on the Wanda Jenkins hit and run?"

He'd taken a bite of his sandwich, and before he could answer my question said with his mouth full, "This sandwich's great. You weren't kidding. Your client's a damn good cook." He chewed and swallowed the bite. "We may have caught a break. Our best forensic tech was off skiing at Mt. Bachelor when the truck that killed Jenkins was processed. We had him take another shot at it when he got back, and, whataya know, he found two human hairs that don't appear to belong to the owner. One has root material attached, so maybe we'll get a DNA profile. It's a long shot, but who the hell knows?"

"Good," I said. "Are you still calling it an accidental hit and run?"

"Officially, yeah, but the investigating team is beginning to think otherwise. They just can't prove it."

"How's that?"

I caught him with another mouthful. He put a finger up while he chewed and then swallowed. "They think the truck was too squeaky clean. Somebody's out for a joy ride and they hit someone, they don't have the foresight to wipe every surface down, inside and out. They're in shock. They just park the truck and run like hell." He cocked his head slightly and raised an eyebrow. "What about you? You got anything new on this?"

"No, but I think Wanda Jenkins was killed to keep her

quiet about Bainbridge's murder. If I get something, you'll be the first to know."

He leaned back and leveled his watery gray cop eyes at me. His jowls had a day's growth, and his complexion was borderline sallow. "You know, Cal, you're the only civilian I'd ever do this dance with. The moment you get something solid, you call me in, okay? And no cowboy shit."

I smiled. "Got it. No cowboy shit. How's the meditation going?"

He returned the smile. "I'm a new man, can't you tell?"

I gave him a skeptical look. "You look a little tired to me, Harmon."

"Comes with the territory. I'll rest when I'm dead."

I'd heard it before. It was vintage Harmon Scott.

—/—

When I left the food cart pod, the first thing I did was call an old friend, Semyon Lebedev, who had some familiarity with the car theft business in Portland. We'd had a violent confrontation a decade earlier but had since grown to hold the highest respect for each other. He was the floor manager—meaning he supervised the bouncers—at a strip club in southeast Portland. I called because I was having a hard time imagining any of my suspects—with the possible exception of BB—actually hot-wiring a truck. It was a loose end that bothered me.

"It has been a while," Semyon said after we exchanged greetings. "What is on your mind?"

I explained the situation. "I'm wondering if this could have been a contract job, somebody wanting a sturdy truck stolen and delivered. Of course, the thief would've known nothing about the intended use." I left out the fact that the thief might have left DNA behind. That information was given to me in confidence.

He chuckled. "I see. With you, Calvin, it's always about my past in the automobile appropriation business. You know I no longer work in that area."

"I know, Semyon. It's a lot to ask. I only want to know if it happened this way. I have no interest in knowing who the thief was, and I'm sure the thief doesn't know the name of his client."

A lengthy pause ensued before Semyon answered. "People need stolen trucks for parts now and then, but it is an unusual request. I will make some inquiries. Because of the death of the woman, I doubt my contacts are going to be very forthcoming, but I will try, Calvin."

I thanked him, and after disconnecting I checked in with Timoteo, who was tending my office in Dundee. "Anything up?"

"One caller this morning looking for a divorce lawyer. She's computer savvy, so I sent her a link for a Zoom meeting for tomorrow. I—"

"You'll be there, right?" I said, feeling slightly intimidated. "I don't know a Zoom from a broom."

He laughed. "Sure. It's no big deal, trust me." He paused for a moment. "Any more thoughts on the affair I stumbled onto last night?"

"Well, Eric Trenton and Gloria Talbot make an unexpected pair, that's for sure. With Bainbridge's death, of course, Gloria gets two million in insurance and Trenton lines up for a big payoff for inventing InstaVision."

Timoteo whistled softly. "Wow, that's a humongous

payday. If Trenton did it, he probably didn't want the notebook to surface, the one that's gone missing, right?"

"It's plausible. And Trenton has more than a financial motive—he gets the ego gratification and the professional recognition of being named the inventor of a breakthrough technology. The recognition could be worth a lot more down the line."

"What about the earlier meeting between Gloria, Donny, and that lawyer, Bower?"

"Suspicious as hell. My gut says it was about the theft of the Ansel Adams collection. Could be a separate issue. Maybe they tried to make a fast buck and needed to get their stories straight."

"Gloria's playing both sides?"

"Maybe."

Timoteo whistled again. "What people will do for money."

"How are things at the vineyard?" I asked, changing the subject.

"Tense. The wife of one of the workers who went down is sick now. Still, no one's been tested, but the symptoms point to Covid-19. It seems to be spreading."

"Is your mother being careful?"

"More or less. I've talked to her, but, jeez, she's just coming out of her funk and now she's supposed to socially distance or whatever they're calling it? That's *not* her. It really sucks, Cal."

"I know, but stay after her and your dad, too. The threat's real, Timoteo." What I didn't say was how worried I was about Zoe, who was being exposed every time she interacted with Elena. Timoteo was right. The situation did suck.

CHAPTER TWENTY-FIVE

WHEN ARCHIE AND I GOT BACK TO CAFFEINE CENTRAL that afternoon, I was relieved to see that no one was queued up in front of the building. If that held, it meant I would have some time to check my email, in case some of my paying clients were trying to reach me. I went up to the apartment first and made a double cappuccino to fortify me for the afternoon, and two hours of undisturbed bliss later I'd responded to a half dozen messages and made several phone calls.

I looked over at Arch, pumped a fist, and said, "I'm caught up. Let's go for a run."

My dog sprang to his feet, but, alas, my cell phone buzzed at that moment. It was Eric Trenton. The seed I planted with Bradley Nielsen had apparently germinated. He introduced himself and said with obvious antipathy, "Nielsen told me to call you. He said you're chasing down rumors in the company, that you wanted to talk to me." Trenton wanted to make it a phone conversation, but I persuaded him to meet me in person.

When I disconnected, I looked at Arch, who was standing in front of me. "Sorry, Big Boy. I'll make it up to you." His ears dropped and his big, coppery eyes registered unmistakable disappointment. Do dogs feel emotions? You bet they do.

—/ /—

"I did my undergraduate work at Stanford and got my Ph.D. in virology at Princeton," Trenton was telling me in response to my asking about his background. A ring on his right hand with a cardinal red stone—gaudy by my standards—attested to his Stanford days. We were seated in a small bakery and coffee shop near the Spectro Vision headquarters at five that afternoon.

"You must have gotten a ton of job offers," I said.

"Yes, I did, but I wanted to go with a high-tech startup with potential."

"Risky," I said.

"That's where the really big money is," he countered with a look that said, 'Is there any other reason to take a job?'

"Looks like you chose right," I said, adding a measure of envy to my voice. "How long have you been with Spectro Vision?"

"I just had my five-year anniversary." Narrow through the shoulders with long arms and slim hips, I put him at around thirty-five. He had short sandy hair, a wispy blond mustache, and brown eyes that looked almost owl-like behind thick-lensed, circular wire rims. He took a sip of water from a stainless-steel bottle he carried with him and leveled his gaze at me. It was surprisingly confident. "So, what's this all about?"

"Bradley is worried about rumors that are going around Spectro Systems. As I'm sure you know, he's in some delicate negotiations to secure the kind of financing needed to scale up InstaVision. If rumors get into the media, well..."

A knowing smile creased his lips. "What? Are you

talking about Bainbridge's supposed missing notebook? I've been all through this with Bradley and our patent attorneys. I know nothing about the damn thing, if it ever existed. Malcolm was very cavalier about documenting his work."

"What about your TA, Anthony Grimes? Did he ever see the notebook or have any idea what could have happened to it?"

Trenton rolled his eyes in frustration. "Anthony knows as much as I do. Nothing."

"Did you collaborate with Bainbridge during the development of InstaVision?"

"Of course I did. And I ran some of the experiments he requested." Trenton elevated his chin. "But I did my own work, too, and that's how I came up with the breakthrough. It's all laid out in *my* notebook. It's all there."

"Yet there's talk among your coworkers that it was Malcolm Bainbridge who invented InstaVision. How do you explain that?"

He curled a lip in disdain. "What can I say? Everybody loved the guy. He did some great work at Spectro Vision, but he'd lost a step. I beat him to the punch this time. I'm sorry he's dead, but *I* deserve the credit for InstaVision, not him." He gave me the confident look again.

Instead of reacting I cleared my throat. "There's another issue I'd like your perspective on. A lot of Bainbridge's coworkers find it, uh, hard to believe that he took his own life. What's your opinion? I'm just curious. You were a close associate of his."

Trenton held my gaze, but his face grew tight. "You mean, was it an accident or was he murdered?" He laughed, a short bark. "That's what you're really after, right? I've heard about you, Claxton."

I held a neutral expression and didn't respond.

He finally gestured dismissively. "That's ridiculous on its face. It was investigated, right? The man had a history of depression. Look at the statistics for people who suffer from that disorder. A lot of them choose suicide as a way out."

"Good point," I said, keeping my eyes on him. "Then I'm wasting my time asking where you were the night of January fifteenth, the night Bainbridge died?"

A vein appeared in his neck and began to pulse, and his eyes bulged perceptibly. "Who do you think you are, a cop or something? You can't ask that question."

I smiled and kept my eyes locked on his. "I just did, Eric. Where were you?"

He stood up and grabbed his water bottle. "We're done here," he said and stomped off.

I leaned back in my chair and watched through the front window of the shop. He crossed the street and got into his Lexus, an expensive car but a bit of a staid choice for a person his age.

I ordered another cappuccino and sat sipping it, deep in thought. Not one of my better interviews, I admitted. Trenton was tough to read and unwilling to state if he had an alibi for the night Bainbridge died. Was that just righteous indignation or did he have something to hide? Hard to say, but one thing was apparent—he may have been physically unimpressive, but his ambition and desire to enrich himself shown through like a bright light.

CHAPTER TWENTY-SIX

"HAVE THE GRAPEVINES TURNED YET?" NANDO SAID IN his baritone voice. He'd called from Cuba the next morning just as Archie and I arrived at my Dundee office.

I laughed. "Bud break's still three or four weeks out. Why do you ask? Are you missing Oregon?"

"I am a creature of the tropics, you know. The rain. It lasts so long in Oregon. But I admit that I have great fondness for your neighborhood in springtime."

"You're not thinking of staying in Cuba, are you?" I asked, half in jest but only half.

"They say you can't go back to your home, right? I have businesses to run and payrolls to meet in Portland. Besides, I am only welcome in Cuba as a visitor."

"What's the latest on the Covid-19 situation there?"

"Ah—it is not so bad. I am being cautious, and I'm heading back in three weeks."

"Three weeks is a long time, Nando. Have you thought of returning sooner?"

"I am having too much fun, my friend," he said, then changing the subject, added, "I am curious about your new investigation. Esperanza tells me you are making progress."

"She's being generous." I said and began bringing him up to date.

"A Rubik's Cube is a good—how do you say it—metaphor?" Nando remarked after we'd thrashed out the case with its myriad suspects and combinations of suspects. "The first murder was one of stealth and cunning," he went on. "But if you are right that the hit-and-run was no accident, that the driver was willing to accept a child as collateral damage, then you are dealing with a person or persons who will stop at absolutely nothing." He sighed into the phone. "I regret that I am not there to assist you. Be careful, my friend."

Timoteo arrived shortly after the call, bearing cups of coffee. "Your Zoom call's at 9:30, he reminded me. At that time, with my assistant at my elbow, I tapped the link he'd established and opened the meeting. "Your client's already in the waiting room," he observed, pointing at the screen. "Invite her in." I clicked on the tab, and a middle-aged woman appeared on my screen like magic. I started to introduce myself and immediately noticed a puzzled look on her face and turned to Timoteo, who was off-camera.

He laughed. "Unmute yourself, Cal! She can't hear a word you're saying."

After that shaky start, the call went well and when we signed off, I'd acquired my first Zoom client, a harbinger of things to come. Unexpectedly, the call left me with a vague feeling that I had inadvertently seen something of interest, although I didn't know what or why. It wasn't the image of my new client per se, but something *behind* her. I closed my eyes and tried to picture the background—a well-stocked bookcase, some wall space with hung art, a floor lamp—but I couldn't put my finger on what it was that caught my attention.

Timoteo left for his afternoon classes around noon, and I was having a quick sandwich at my desk when a call came in. "Mr. Claxton, this is Detective Kohler, lead on the Ansel Adams theft case. I have some additional questions for you."

"Of course, Detective. How's the investigation going?" I said, hoping he might open up to me.

"It's early days. We're, ah, looking hard at the nephew, Donny Romano. He was unable to verify his location on the night we think the burglary took—"

"You know when it happened?" I interrupted, surprised.

"We think we do, yes. A neighbor with insomnia saw a van parked at the back of the Bainbridge property on Yamhill Court at around three a.m. on the 28th. She didn't observe any activity, but it's unlikely a van would park in that neighborhood for any other reason. Also, we found indications of recent foot traffic from the back door to the street. It would have taken several trips to get all the photos loaded."

"Usable footprints?"

"One clear one. A size ten Nike cross trainer. About the size shoe Romano wears."

Amazed he'd shared this much, I said, "So, how can I help you, Detective?"

"We'd like to talk to the people Romano associates with." He paused for a moment. "Captain Scott suggested you might be able to give me some names."

Oh, I said to myself, Harmon Scott's behind this. This is quid pro quo.

"You should talk to Gloria Talbot," I said, and sketched in what I knew of her background, including the fact that she and Donny had been lovers and were collaborating to shake down my client over the estate and the stolen photo collection. "In addition, you should talk to an attorney in Vancouver named Clete Bower. I believe he's in on the attempted scam." I gave him their contact information. "Give them my love," I said, which drew a chuckle from the detective.

After Kohler thanked me and ended the call, I thought about Harmon Scott's sly gesture. It was a sign he was starting to believe me, and as a smart cop he knew that an information exchange between Kohler and me could prove to be critical for both the theft and the murder. It was also clear, although left unspoken, that Kohler and I would continue to trade information.

I looked over at Archie, who was watching me from the corner with his chin resting on his big paws. "How about that, Big Boy?" I said, "We've got another ally in the Portland Police Bureau."

That afternoon I wrote a summary memo of my Zoom conference call with my new client and got caught up on my billable hours, the latter chore having been made simpler and more accurate by a spreadsheet Timoteo had created. Late that afternoon, I called Esperanza Oliva. We talked about Nando for a while and the fact that we were both concerned about his blithe attitude concerning the virus. "But there is nothing to be done except to worry," was the way she summarized it.

"Any word on Benny Boykin's condition?" I asked.

"Yes, I meant to call you but got tied up. I have a contact

at Adventist. He is a cousin, or he wouldn't do this. He told me Boykin has been put in the ICU and placed on a ventilator. It's called being intubated."

"And it's not good," I added. "I read the other day that intubation is an act of desperation in severe respiratory cases."

"Sorry, Cal. I wish I had better news."

He may be intubated, but he's not dead, I told myself after I thanked her and ended the call. *Thoughts and prayers, BB.*

—/—

I stopped by Zoe's place on my way home that evening. "Hey," I said when she answered the door, "I've got some nice rockfish I could thaw if you're interested in joining me for dinner."

She stood with the front door only half open. "God, I must look horrible. I—"

"You look fine to me, you always do. What's the matter?"

She closed her eyes for a couple of moments, then opened them. "I don't feel very well, that's all. Maybe you should keep your distance."

I felt my stomach drop. "What are your symptoms?"

She stroked her throat absently. "Throat's a little tender. Some achiness."

"Temperature?"

"A hundred point one."

"Okay," I said. Probably just a flu. It's the season, you know. You need to get in bed right now. I'll go to my place and make you some soup."

She managed a faint smile, but her eyes registered concern. "Thanks."

Back at my place, I fed Archie and then whipped up some soup from leftover chicken, broth, noodles, and vegetables. Bland but nutritious. Hey, I told myself while I was busy cooking, even if it's Covid, she's younger and in better shape than me. She'll beat it.

I wanted to believe that with every fiber in my being.

I put the soup in a quart thermos bottle I used for fishing trips and took it back to her. She was asleep but awoke at the sound of me bringing the soup to her on a tray. She sat up with some difficulty and when I placed the tray on her lap waved an arm at me. "Thanks, but don't linger, please."

I stepped back after placing her phone and a thermometer on the nightstand. "I'll call in a couple of hours to see how you're doing. Okay?"

She nodded. "Don't touch your face until you wash your hands thoroughly." Another faint smile. "That's what Dr. Fauci's saying."

"Who's he?"

"An infectious disease expert, the best we've got in this country."

"Got it." However, halfway back to the kitchen, I caught myself rubbing my tired eyes. *Shit.*

When I called later that evening, Zoe's temperature had gone up another degree. I told her I was coming over to check on her and clear her dinner tray, but she talked me out of it. "I'll be okay," she told me. "I'll call you in the morning."

I spent a fitful night, awake a good deal of the time, and

when I did sleep, I dreamt I was moving through a kind of dystopian landscape with a stark sense of foreboding.

"This can't be happening," I kept saying in my dream. But no one was listening.

CHAPTER TWENTY-SEVEN

ZOE WAS NO BETTER THE NEXT MORNING, WHICH ONLY ratcheted up my concern. I went over to her place and made a poached egg on dry toast and a pot of Earl Grey tea and brought it in to her. She looked flushed and complained of achiness. Her temperature was a hundred point two, but her breathing was okay. "Looks like a garden variety flu," I offered, trying to put a positive spin on it.

"Yeah," she said with a weak smile. "Never thought I'd be hoping I had the flu." She went on to insist I go about my business, adding, "I'll manage lunch, and don't tell Aunt Gertie I'm sick. She'll insist on coming over, and I don't want to expose her."

I told her I'd check in on her that evening and left feeling only slightly less anxious.

I had no meetings booked that day so I decided to head into Portland, figuring I would stop by the gun shop where Donny Romano worked and see if he would talk to me. Stuart Burgess, my mole at Spectro Systems, called on my way into the city. He said he had an errand to run in town and could drop by at lunch. I suggested we meet at

Cartopia and he agreed. "I've got some new information," he promised.

I was unexpectedly busy at Caffeine Central that morning and didn't get around to calling Zoe until I left to meet Stuart Burgess. "I'm no worse, she told me. "Slept all morning."

I took that as a positive sign. "I'll fix you something nutritious tonight," I said. "I'll be back early." We left it at that.

The food pod was moderately busy. Willow was featuring a crowd favorite—French onion soup and *Croque Madame*—and the line at the Plat du Jour was putting the other carts to shame. Stuart arrived shortly after Archie and me, and we queued up after I told my dog to stay at our table. When it was our turn to order, I introduced Stuart to Willow.

"We met at a Spectro Systems picnic once," he said to her as a broad smile spread across his face.

"We did?" she said, and then looked embarrassed at having not remembered him.

Food in hand, we took our seats under the warmth of a raised heater. Like Harmon Scott, Stuart was an immediate convert to the Plat de Jour. He slurped some soup and held up his sandwich after a big bite. "This is outstanding. These pods are a treasure, I mean they add so much to the Portland vibe."

I nodded in agreement. "Judging from the lines, Willow's got quite a following. It's all French today, but she blends French and Northwest cuisines in some creative ways."

We talked Portland food for a while. "I was a chem major but when I got out of college, I wanted to be a chef," he said at one point. "But I couldn't earn enough as an apprentice to make my student loan payments, so I took the Spectro Systems job. The pay and benefits are great."

"Do you see yourself there long term?" I asked out of curiosity.

"He shook his head emphatically. "No way. You need a Ph.D. to go anywhere in this field, and I'm done with school, man."

When we finally got around to the business at hand, he said, "Rumor has it that a mega-deal is going down at Spectro any time now. Either heavy investors are coming in to bankroll the InstaVision scaleup or the company's being sold outright. Nobody seems to know which it is."

"I'm curious about something," I said. "Has the death of Malcolm Bainbridge hurt these negotiations, whatever they are? After all, you're a high-tech company, and he was a partner and your top scientist."

"It could have been devastating, but that's where Eric Trenton comes in. We have a staff of good scientists, but he's being positioned as our top gun now."

"And the missing notebook's key to that?"

"Right. If Trenton's the inventor of InstaVision, not Bainbridge, then Bainbridge's death is not such a big deal, and the company is worth a whole hell of a lot more. That brings me to my second piece of news—Trenton is to be named the inventor and is being promoted to Principal Scientist."

"Looks like the search for the notebook has ended," I said.

"Yes, and get this—Nielsen fired Marsha Coates, Bainbridge's technical assistant, yesterday."

I lowered my soup spoon and leaned in. "The one claiming the notebook exists?"

"Right. I heard she threatened to get a lawyer but then settled for a big severance deal and signed a non-disclosure agreement. All of us TAs are up in arms. Marsha was loved by everyone. Clearly, Nielsen doesn't want her spoiling his coronation of Trenton."

"Is that the view of the TAs now, that Nielsen and Trenton could be colluding in some way?"

Stuart swallowed a bite before speaking. "There seem to be two points of view. One is that when Dr. Bainbridge died, Nielsen panicked because Spectro Systems was on the cusp of something huge—InstaVision—and Bainbridge was the brains behind it."

"And somebody was waiting in the wings to buy the company or invest heavily in the new technology?" I asked.

"Right. So Nielsen disappears Bainbridge's notebook and starts to position Trenton as the inventor to reassure the big money."

"A reaction to the ill-timed suicide?"

"Exactly. The other point of view is much darker—it wasn't a suicide. Bainbridge was murdered by either Nielsen or Trenton or both of them." He rested his eyes on me. "What about you, Cal? Where are you coming out on this?"

I was spared the decision of what to hold back, because I didn't have much to tell him. But I felt I owed him something. "I've got some theories, and I've identified some people of interest, including Nielsen and Trenton. But that's about it."

His eyes widened. "You have evidence it wasn't a suicide?"

I held his gaze and didn't respond.

He finally smiled. "Okay, I get it. You can't share anything right now. I'm cool with that."

Before he left, Stuart went over to Willow's cart and spoke to her. He came back bearing the broad smile again. "I told her the Plat du Jour was now my favorite food cart."

He hesitated for a moment before adding, "She's, um, really something, too."

I smiled. "She is that."

—//—

I handled a couple more calls for legal advice that afternoon and then around three I loaded Arch in the car and took the Ross Island Bridge across the river and headed east on Powell Boulevard. R and J Firearms was located on 82nd, just south of the Powell intersection. The shop was housed in a one-story building with a large, vertical sign on the roof that pulsed "Guns" in red neon. I parked a half block down, cracked the windows for my dog, and walked into the store.

I spotted Donny Romano before he saw me. His three-day stubble was neatly trimmed, and he wore a ballcap that had *2A 1791* stitched on the front. It took me a moment to realize the caption was a shout-out to the Second Amendment. He was waiting on a customer at the counter. I browsed around until he was free and then approached him. It was time to rattle his cage.

"Hello, Donny. How's business?"

A flicker of surprise in his eyes instantly dissolved into wariness. "What do *you* want?"

"A word when you have time. Detective Kohler came calling. Your name came up. I thought we ought to have a chat."

He crossed his arms and smirked. It was unconvincing. "Why should I talk to you?"

I looked around the store. "You're not busy. Take a

break and I'll tell you." I paused. It was like waiting for a trout to bite after casting a fly.

He held my gaze but lost the smirk. I could almost hear the gears turning in his head. He said, finally, "I get off in twenty-five minutes. There's a bar across the street, a block north. I'll meet you there."

Roscoe's Place was dimly lit and sparsely populated. I took a table in the back and ordered the usual—a Mirror Pond Pale Ale. Donny showed up thirty minutes later and ordered a draft beer with a whiskey chaser.

"So, what's this all about?" he said, drumming his fingers on the table. His face was tight, his eyes narrowed down. "I already talked to the cops. You were there."

I gave him a knowing smile. "I'm wondering, Donny. Maybe you thought you were just sort of stealing from yourself when you took those pictures. I can see how you might think that. But your uncle's estate hasn't cleared probate, so they were *not* yours. And now you're looking at a felony charge." I wasn't positive about the law in this situation, but he didn't need to know that.

He set his beer down and leaned back like I'd slapped him. "I didn't take those damn pictures."

"This is the twenty-first century, Donny. You think you could haul all those frames out the back door of your uncle's place without leaving some physical evidence behind, something that traces back to you?"

He popped the shot in one gulp. "Bullshit. I didn't take the fucking pictures."

I glanced up at the ceiling for effect. "Did they talk you into it? I mean, it was practically your house. 'Go ahead, take them, make it look like a burglary. We can unload them and split the profit.' Is that what they told you?"

"They? Who's they?"

"Come on, Donny. Gloria Talbot and Clete Bower, that's who. Their first scam was aimed at convincing a probate judge the collection was promised to you. But when I told them I knew you'd broken up your uncle's marriage, they knew that wouldn't work. I—"

"That's a lie," he said, snarling like a wounded animal. He pointed a finger at me. "And leave Gloria out of this."

I rolled my eyes. "So they talked you into the fake burglary. Is that how it went down? How much of the take are they asking for? *You* took all the risk."

"I don't have to listen to this bullshit," he said and sprang to his feet to leave. But I saw pain in his eyes, and I actually felt a pang of guilt, like I'd crushed this man's world by revealing an ugly truth.

He took a step, and I fired my last shot. "What else have they talked you into, Donny? They're using you. I can help you if you let me."

"Fuck off," he said without looking back.

I definitely got to him, I told myself as I sat nursing my beer and musing over the brief encounter. I had to chuckle. Donny left in a huff just like Eric Trenton had, although Donny seemed more hurt than angry. And the look in his eyes when he said, 'Leave Gloria out of this' told me he still had feelings for her, strong feelings. And I was sure he'd taken the Ansel Adams photos. He was Gloria's and Bower's useful idiot.

Was he in deeper? Could he possibly be involved in the murder of his uncle?

CHAPTER TWENTY-EIGHT

"THE SILENCE IS YOUR ANSWER," SEMYON LEBEDEV explained. He'd called while I was heading back to Dundee that afternoon. "None of my contacts would tell me anything about a contract theft of a pickup truck. Not a yes, not a no, not a maybe. *Nothing.* That's a sure sign there was *something.* The powers that be obviously put a clamp on things.

"Why would they do that?"

"Perhaps they know the stolen truck was used for a homicide. They have a business to run. A crime like that is bad publicity. The next thing you know the police decide on a crackdown, form a car-theft task force or something. The bosses do not want this."

"Okay. You didn't expose yourself, did you?"

"No. I trust my sources."

"Thanks, Semyon. I owe you for this."

"Always a pleasure, Calvin."

—/—

By the time I got to Zoe's place a brisk wind was blowing in off the valley, and the sun was down except for a blood red streak silhouetting the Coast Range. She was asleep, so

I quietly rummaged around in the kitchen for something to fix her for dinner. To say the cupboard was bare would've been an overstatement. I did manage to find a can of vegetable soup and a box of stone-ground wheat crackers. I fixed a tray for her and when I brought it in to her bedroom, she was awake with a thermometer in her mouth. Her color was off, and her cheeks looked a little sunken. But it was Zoe. She always looked good to me.

She removed the thermometer and squinted at it. "Christ, it was down earlier this afternoon, but it's a hundred and one now." She looked at me. The alarm in her eyes blew a cold wind across my heart. "Thanks, Cal. Just set the tray down and get out of here. I'm radioactive." She grimaced as she sat up. "I don't think I can eat anything."

"Try," I said, backing away. "How does your chest feel?"

She put a hand on her breasts and took a deep breath. "Okay, I guess. I just ache all over and pay a price every time I swallow."

"How's Elena?" I asked, thinking of what Timoteo had told me.

"Okay, as far as I know."

"I'm going to the Aerie now to get Archie and me something to eat. I'll come back later to check on you." She smiled a thanks.

After dinner my dog and I went out on my side porch, and I lit the fire pit. It had cleared off and the lights in the valley had a nice twinkle to them. I sipped a snifter of Rémy Martin and listened to the distant call of a great horned owl that nested in one of my Douglas firs. The four-note call squeezed at my heart, because Zoe and I jokingly referred to it as 'our song.' I tried to think about the Bainbridge case, but thoughts of Zoe blotted everything out. *No chest pain,* I told myself. *That's a good sign. She's strong. She'll beat this.* This became my mantra.

—/ /—

"Your timing's impeccable," I said to Timoteo the next morning. "I'm having a coffee jones."

"What else is new?" he said as he handed me a twelve-ounce, double cappuccino and backed off. We were trying our best to stay separated.

We went on to discuss the situation at the vineyard, and when I asked about his mother, he said, "She's fine, but another field hand came down with respiratory symptoms, and some of the other vineyards are seeing the same thing."

"Still no testing?" I asked.

"Not that anyone in the migrant community can access, but I guess that's the case for just about everyone." When I told him about Zoe, he studied me for a moment before responding. "I thought you looked worried. It's probably just the flu, Cal."

I managed a smile and a nod, and not wishing to dwell on the subject, began describing my confrontation with Donny Romano and my hunch he was being played by Gloria and Bower. By the time I finished, his grin was broad, and there was a sparkle of excitement in his eyes. "That was a gutsy move, confronting him like that. You want me to research whether, as an heir to the property, he can still be charged with theft?"

"Hold that thought for now. Just the threat of it's probably enough. All three of them are going to get a visit from the detective working the Ansel Adams case. That's going to stir things up even more."

Timoteo's grin got broader. "What do you think Donny might do?"

"If we're lucky, he'll panic and come to me for help or cooperate with the police. Who knows? Maybe we'll get the pictures back."

Timoteo laughed. "You tossed a grenade right in the middle of them." I could see the gleam in his eye. My assistant loved the chase as much as I did. *What have I done?* I asked myself half in jest.

I told him about my visit with Stuart Burgess next, describing how both Bradley Nielsen and Eric Trenton could be working together to delegitimize Bainbridge's technical contribution for mutual gain. He scratched his head and scrunched his brows down. "Interesting, but I keep coming back to Gloria. Trenton's another young lover she can manipulate."

"A black widow, huh?

"Yeah, maybe she got Trenton to kill Bainbridge, not Donny." He paused for a moment and scrunched his brows down again. "Whoever it was, how do you think they went about making it look like a suicide?"

I just shook my head.

—/—

Early that afternoon, I had a follow-up call with my new Zoom client. Her name was Phoebe Tyson, and she was very rich and very angry with her soon to be ex-husband. In Oregon, divorce is 'no fault,' meaning a divorce can be obtained by either party simply if that party has had enough of the marriage. In this case, Phoebe had definitely had enough, and I had to suffer through a litany of her spouse's transgressions, even though I'd heard them all the last time we talked.

At the end of the call, after she'd calmed down and I'd taken her through the next steps, I said, "There's an interesting piece of art hanging on the wall behind you, Phoebe, the one showing two men in hand-to-hand combat. Can you tell me what it is? I'm just curious."

She looked behind her, then back at the camera. "Oh, the bas relief? It's an artifact from the Khmer empire that I picked up in Cambodia years ago. I collect bas reliefs." She smiled a little self-consciously. "I suppose it looks a bit violent. It depicts some kind of chokehold used in Khmer martial arts, I think. I just like the fluid grace of the two fighters. Do you want a closer look?"

I said I did, and she picked up her laptop and held it next to the ancient artifact. The intricate lines and raised surfaces of the jade carving shone with a soft patina. It was worn smooth in some areas, but the images were clearly discernable. One fighter was behind the other with his arm clamped around his opponent's neck, his legs spread, his back bowed. The choker's eyes were wide open, his look triumphant. The victim clutched the attacker's arm with his hands, but his head was thrust forward, his mouth downturned and eyes closed.

"Game over," Timoteo said softly from behind me.

I praised the artistic merit of the bas relief and thanked Phoebe before clicking off. I turned to Timoteo. "Know anything about chokeholds used in martial arts?"

"Not much except that you can knock someone out that

way." He smiled as the light bulb went on. "I see where you're going with this."

"Out for how long?" I asked.

"Wait a second," he said as he pulled his cell phone from his pocket. A few clicks later he had an answer. "The hold we saw in the bas relief is called a blood choke, because it compresses the carotid artery without compressing the airway. Looks like the period of unconsciousness is roughly proportional to the time the choke is held." He read some more and looked up. "There's a big difference between chokes of the carotid artery and chokes of the windpipe, which are called air chokes. They suffocate and take a long time to knock someone out. Blood chokes shut off blood to the brain and work quickly."

"How quickly?"

"A twenty or thirty-second choke can put someone under for about the same amount of time." He read more and looked up again. "Looks like the blood choke is used a lot in martial arts these days. Cops use it, too, but some jurisdictions have banned it. There's all kinds of YouTube videos on it."

We watched a couple of videos together. Afterwards I shook my head. "I saw that bas relief the first time I talked to Phoebe, but I couldn't quite put my finger on why it caught my attention. I don't know much about martial arts, but I knew there was a hold that put people under."

Timoteo laughed. "Apparently you knew just enough to trigger your subconscious."

I snapped my fingers. "Let's try something. Grab that step ladder in the bathroom."

When Timoteo returned with the small ladder, I said, "It's about the height of the stool Malcolm Bainbridge was sitting on when he was murdered." I motioned for Timoteo to sit on the ladder. "Okay, I come up behind you like this and..." I placed my right arm around his neck and gripped my left elbow in the manner I'd learned from the videos. "Once I've secured you, I lock down and constrict your carotid artery, and while you flail and squirm I hold the pressure. The blood stops flowing to your brain, and you black out in ten seconds or so. I hold it for another ten seconds...Go limp now," I requested.

He slumped on the ladder, and I released my right arm and grasped his left bicep with my left hand to keep him from toppling over. "Now, I pull out Bainbridge's Ruger"—I simulated this by withdrawing my cell phone from my right front pocket—"and place it in his right hand and...*shit*," I said as my phone hit the floor with a clatter.

After retrieving my phone, which was still operable, I said, "That's the tricky part of the operation. I only have twenty to thirty seconds before Bainbridge regains consciousness. Can the killer manage to place the gun in Bainbridge's hand or at least near his hand and then pull the trigger in that short a time? There has to be gunshot residue on Bainbridge's right hand for it to appear like a suicide."

"Let's try it again," Timoteo said. "I'll count out the seconds."

"Go limp," I said, after placing him in another simulated chokehold.

Timoteo slumped forward and began counting as I steadied him with my left hand. "Mississippi one, Mississippi two, Mississippi three..."

I pulled my phone out again and after some fumbling managed to grasp his right hand with mine and pull it next to his temple. "Bang," I said as Timoteo reached a count of Mississippi sixteen.

I stepped back and Timoteo sat up, his eyes wide with excitement, "I think it's doable."

"I agree, and it explains two things that were bugging me. First, the barrel of the Ruger wasn't flush against Bainbridge's temple in the murder. It would have been a lot harder for me to do that in the simulation. Your head was practically between your knees. I think the killer settled for proximity to save time. Second, the autopsy showed that Bainbridge had a bruise on his left arm that was unaccounted for. I think it was caused by the killer's left hand as he grasped his unconscious victim."

Timoteo rubbed his left bicep and grinned. "Roger, that. You've got a hell of a grip, Cal." He moved his hand to his neck. "And if you do the chokehold correctly, you don't bruise my neck, which would have been a dead giveaway."

"Right. It's apparently easy to pinch off the carotid without doing any collateral damage. Now," I went on, "after the fatal shot's fired, the killer lets go of Bainbridge, who falls forward, scraping his left cheek on the tile floor. Then he may have rearranged the body, particularly the right arm, which he probably stretched out to make it appear authentic—"

"And he puts the Ruger on the floor just beyond Bainbridge's hand," Timoteo interjected.

"Yes, and that explains the third thing that bothered me, the one that caused me to question the scene in the first place—why was the gun so close to Bainbridge's hand? That position was possible, but it just didn't seem probable."

We both sat down, and the room fell silent for a few moments. Timoteo said, "So the killer pays a visit to

Bainbridge with this whole scenario planned out ahead of time. Is that what you think?"

"It looks that way. It was someone Bainbridge knew, so getting behind him wouldn't have been a problem."

"What about the gun?"

"The killer had already obtained it from BB Boykin and had it on him, well concealed, of course."

We fell silent again. Finally Timoteo said, "So, it all rides on a well-executed stranglehold that leaves no trace on Bainbridge's neck and provides just enough time to put a bullet in his head with his own hand."

"Right. And guess who's no stranger to the art of mixed martial arts?" I went on to tell him about the picture of Bainbridge and Bradley Nielsen in their workout suits I'd seen in Bainbridge's bedroom.

"Holy shit," Timoteo responded, "You think the CEO could have done this?"

"Maybe. But Gloria Talbot works at the Wy East, so she's no stranger to the martial arts either. And besides, a blood chokehold isn't that hard to learn. You saw all those videos on YouTube showing exactly what to do."

Timoteo swallowed and shook his head. "It's hard to picture someone being this calculating and cold-blooded, you know? I can't imagine it."

I felt a twinge of sadness as another chunk of my young assistant's innocence was swept away. *At least the murder's hard for him to imagine,* I consoled myself.

It was easy for me to imagine, too easy.

CHAPTER TWENTY-NINE

TIMOTEO HAD GONE FOR THE AFTERNOON, AND ARCH and I were getting ready to leave when the front door of my office swung open, and Clete Bower appeared. Wearing a once-white shirt, faded chinos, and trademark tweed blazer, he tossed a cigar butt onto the sidewalk before entering.

"Afternoon, Cal. I was in the area and thought I'd stop by," he said. "The probate hearing's coming up at the end of the month and things have, well, taken a turn, haven't they?" He launched a counterfeit smile and set his scuffed briefcase on the floor next to him. "We should review the bidding."

I stood from behind my desk and pointed at a chair a good six feet from me. Archie watched from his corner without moving. He remembered people who paid him no mind and returned the favor with canine indifference.

"What did you have in mind?"

He clicked open his briefcase and removed a couple of sheets of paper. "Of course, we liquidate the assets like we discussed and split everything down the middle. I've talked to my client again about the loan indebtedness. He wants to get this over with and move on, so he's still willing to take fifty thousand and let the matter drop." As he said that, he looked up from the papers to gauge my reaction.

"*Still willing?* Our position hasn't—"

He put a hand up. "Wait, I'm not finished. Hear me out. My client doesn't want there to be any hard feelings between him and his cousin, so he's still willing to take fifty thousand instead of the seventy-five he's owed, *and* when the Adams photographs are recovered, he'll accept half their value instead of the entire amount as his uncle promised him, and your client can have them." He held the papers up. "This is an addendum covering our new offer."

I sat back and studied him for a moment. He was on the edge of his chair with his neck bowed and his squinty eyes boring holes in me. "I'll run this by Willow," I said, trying to keep my temper in check. "But I can tell you right now she won't take it. She owes Donny for half the balance on the loan—twenty thousand—and that's what she intends to pay him. Not a nickel more or a nickel less. As for the stolen photographs, she'll maintain her assertion that they were promised to her, if they're ever recovered, which is doubtful." We locked eyes, and I added, "I hope Donny hasn't done something foolish here."

His face stiffened, but his look fell well short of righteous indignation. "What are you implying?"

"Come on, Clete, cut the bullshit. Looks to me like Donny saw an opportunity he couldn't resist. Trouble is, the theft of the pictures could easily splash on you. Why not intercede now, tell him to claim it was all just a big misunderstanding, that he thought he owned the pictures? It might just work with the Portland police."

His eyes became slits. "It's one thing for your little Miss Innocent client to accuse Donny, but I'm betting you set that dickhead detective on me and Gloria. He's treating us like we're fucking suspects. And your meddling has slowed the insurance settlement, too."

I opened up my hands. "Hey, Detective Kohler is just doing his job. First degree, aggravated theft's a felony, after all." Bower sneered back at me, and I decided to turn the screw. "How was the Blazer game?"

He gave me a blank look.

"You know, the one you and Donny attended the night Bainbridge died. Gloria mentioned it. Did they win that night?"

His jaw flexed, and his nostrils flared. "Who the fuck do you think you are?" He pointed a nicotine-stained finger at me. "You better watch your step, Claxton."

"Funny, that's what Gloria told me." I stood up and sensing the tension so did Archie. "I don't respond well to threats, Bower," I said. "Get the hell out of my office."

A look of surprise rippled across his face but was gone in an instant. He'd underestimated me. "Don't get your knickers in a bunch," he said as he got up, smiling like a viper. "Try the offer on your client. Maybe she's got more sense than you do," he added over his shoulder as he turned to leave.

I stood there for a while, letting the anger drain out of me. Finally, I looked over at Archie, who was eyeing me with an anxious look. "Another day, another threat. But thanks for the backup, Big Boy. Is it just silly me, or is everyone in this case touchy about their alibis?"

—/ /—

I locked up forty-five minutes later, and as Arch and I were walking across the small lot behind my office, an early model CRV pulled up, and Stuart Burgess got out with a carton the size of a shoebox. "Hi, Mr. Claxton. Glad I caught you." He held the carton up. "Brought you some N-95 masks."

"You're kidding. I thought they were in short supply."

"We just got a shipment in. I figured these would have been used by Dr. Bainbridge and his TA, so no harm done to Spectro Vision. Use them when you're in any kind of congregant setting. They'll stop any virus particle floating around. And wash your hands a lot. Viruses can live for a long time on surfaces."

I took the box and thanked him, adding, "You drove all the way over here to give me these?"

He ran the fingers of one hand through his thick blond hair and smiled with a hint of sheepishness. "I wanted you to have these, and I, uh, thought you could share them with Willow. Maybe she could wear one when her cart gets busy, you know, to cut down her exposure. Who knows who's just flown in from Wuhan, right?"

"That's a great idea, Stuart."

He held the smile. "Yeah, well, I was also wondering if it would be okay if I contacted her." He paused before adding hastily, "For social reasons only. I wouldn't discuss any of the stuff I've shared with you."

"Fine with me, and you're right. It wouldn't be a good idea to discuss the goings on at Spectro Vision." I paused for a moment and opened the carton. "Looks like, what, a dozen masks in here?" I looked up at him. "Why don't *you* give her half of these and kill two birds with one stone?"

He flashed a broad smile. "Yeah, I could do that. Save you a trip. I'll pop by the Plat du Jour tomorrow, first thing." He furrowed his brow before adding, "Uh, she won't be put off, will she? I mean, nobody in Portland's wearing masks."

I laughed. "Nah, she's a bright young woman and a caring mother. She'll get it."

When Stuart left, I had to smile. It was nearly spring, after all, and the sap was beginning to rise.

—/—

"Honest, Cal, I don't think I can eat tonight," Zoe told me when I called about bringing her dinner. Her voice sounded alarmingly weak.

"How about a second helping of chicken soup. I have some in my fridge." She reluctantly agreed, and after I fed my dog I drove down the hill to her place.

"Where'd you get the mask?" Zoe said when I brought in a tray with the soup, a couple of crackers, and a cup of Earl Grey.

"From the young man at Spectro Vision I've been working with," I said, setting the tray down on her lap. "It's an N-95. It's supposed to stop virus particles."

"Good," she said. "You don't want this nasty stuff, whatever it is." She sighed and looked up at me. With the exception of her flushed cheeks, she was pale and wan, and her eyes lacked their usual luster. She forced a smile. "Now, mask or no mask, get the hell out of here."

I took a couple of steps back. "I'll hang around, see how the soup goes down. We can take your temperature after you eat."

I checked on her twenty minutes later. She was curled up next to the tray sound asleep. The soup looked untouched. *Sleep's good,* I told myself. *That's what her body needs right now.* I laid my hand on her forehead. It was as hot as a stove top. Anxiety began to tighten my chest like a coiling snake. I wanted to take her temperature but couldn't bring myself to wake her, so I retreated to the kitchen, warmed up the soup, and slurped it down. I then logged on to her laptop to distract myself. Always at home in Zoe's house, Archie lay snoozing at my side.

The Oregonian reported that Oregon officials had identified four new cases of Covid-19, three of them in southern Oregon. All three cases were said to be travel-related, not examples of what the article termed 'community spread,' a condition necessary for the virus to gain a foothold. The fourth case was in Portland and was still under investigation. That brought the total confirmed cases to seven, the article noted. *That total includes Benjamin Boykin*, I said to myself. *Just my luck*. On the other hand, seven cases out of a population of more than four million didn't seem that threatening. The tightness in my chest eased somewhat.

I turned to the business section, and the headline of the lead article jumped out at me:

Sale of Medical Imaging Startup Imminent

> –March 5
> Endeavor Investments, a venture capital firm located in Seattle, announced its intention today to buy medical imaging company Spectro Vision, headquartered in Tigard. Although the price was undisclosed, sources say the opening bid was more than $450M. Spectro Vision's CEO Bradley Nielsen confirmed the negotiations, saying, "We think this is the right move for the company.
>
> Endeavor's financial strength will ensure that the innovative research and development work at Spectro

> Vision continues and provides for a rapid scaleup of our new coro- navirus detection device, InstaVision 20. This technology pro- mises to revolutionize the field of virology detection at a time when the world faces a new and formidable virus threat, Covid-19."
>
> In subsequent remarks, Principal Scientist Dr. Eric Trenton said the InstaVision device "is about the size of a computer mouse and can identify and classify evidence of a virus in the body in about one second, using a sample of fluid—blood serum or saliva—inserted into a disposable test curvette."

The article went on to say that, although Nielsen would be stepping down as CEO after the transition, the company would remain in Tigard. Endeavor's CEO was gushing with praise for Nielsen's leadership and the technical expertise of the company, as embodied in Principal Scientist Eric Trenton. "We think SpectroVision has an exceptionally bright future," he was quoted as saying.

I whistled softly and shook my head. Four hundred and fifty million was a staggering amount. And with Malcolm Bainbridge no longer in the picture, it was all going in Bradley Nielsen's pocket. That amount dwarfed the two million coming to Gloria Talbot or the amount Donny Romano would inherit, or the sum Eric Trenton could realize for the InstaVision patent. From that perspective, Nielsen should move to the top of my suspect list. But I knew it wasn't always that simple, that the reason for killing someone rests solely in the heart of the murderer. People are killed for their sneakers, after all, or for the keys to their Mercedes, and for far, far less.

I told myself to follow Frank Zappa's advice: "A mind is like a parachute. It doesn't work if it is not open."

CHAPTER THIRTY

I AWOKE AT 1:55 A.M., SLOUCHED AWKWARDLY ON ZOE'S couch. I sat up and massaged my neck. Archie stirred at my feet and went back to sleep. I put on my mask and tiptoed into her bedroom. She was still asleep, but her breathing was labored and uneven. I placed my hand on her forehead. It was alarmingly hot. She awoke and looked up at me through eyes that were barely open and forced a smile with bluish lips.

"How do you feel?"

Her chin trembled. "Scared." She sucked a partial breath. "It's in my chest, Cal. It's hard to breathe." She closed her eyes and grimaced. "And every cell in my body aches."

My heart felt like it'd been stabbed with an icicle. I took her temperature. It was 102.2. "Okay," I said. "I think we need to go to the ER right now. I'll get your robe." She didn't resist, which wasn't like her. She was that sick.

Eighteen minutes later, I pulled into the ER entrance at the Providence Medical Center in Newberg, put her in a wheelchair, and endured the agonizing admissions process involving insurance cards and twenty questions. When Zoe was finally admitted, she turned to me and our eyes met. "I love you," I said softly.

"I love you, too," she responded.

It was the first time either of us had exchanged those words. As she disappeared behind a set of double doors, my chest constricted. I felt a sense of panic and helplessness. Would she make it out of there?

Before I left, I gave a sample for a Covid-19 test, the result of a swab of my nasal passage that felt like it scraped my brain. "We'll call you with results for both you and Ms. Bennett as soon as we can," the nurse informed me. "We're just now setting up our protocol, which includes not allowing any visitors. If Zoe tests positive, you'll need to come back for a second test even if your test today is negative. There's an incubation period. Meanwhile, avoid close contact with others as much as possible."

The advice seemed prudent if decidedly unnerving.

Arch and I got back to the Aerie around four in the morning, and we both managed to sleep until six. I got up feeling like I had a lead anvil on my shoulders, not from lack of sleep but because of my concern for Zoe. Much to Archie's delight, I put on my sweats and jogging shoes anyway, and he led me out into the new day for our usual jog. It was the last thing I wanted to do, but I wasn't about to shrink into some shell of worry and self-pity. I'd had too many sips out of that cup.

I felt like I was wearing cinder blocks instead of lightweight Asics, but by the time we headed up the hill toward the Pioneer Cemetery, I found my stride. I felt a pang of guilt as I inhaled a lungful of air, something Zoe couldn't manage now. At the same time, breathing deeply felt good, like giving the virus the finger. Of course, the jury was out on both of us, but the knot in the pit of my stomach was for Zoe alone. Somehow, I knew in my bones she had contracted the virus.

She's strong, I repeated to the rhythm of my strides. *She's going to beat it.*

⊣/⊢

It was Friday, my pro bono day. Before I left for Portland, I made two calls, the first to the hospital, which informed me Zoe was in "serious condition," whatever the hell that meant. I called Gertie next. She was shocked and a little hurt at being left out of the loop, but I explained it was only her niece trying not to worry her. "I have a good friend who's a nurse at Providence," she told me. "I'll make sure she keeps us updated. And I'll try to contact Zoe's parents. They're in Europe. Some kind of expensive river cruise. Always travelling, those two."

⊣/⊢

With the exception of two brief calls, my morning at Caffeine Central was uneventful, proceeding at glacial, mind-numbing speed. At noon, I called the hospital again—no change in Zoe's condition, I was told—then called over to Market Cocina and ordered a couple of fish tacos, picked them up, and ate them at my desk. I wore my N-95 in the market and got some weird looks for my trouble. I closed up at 3:30 and headed over to Cartopia to meet with Willow.

I'd called earlier to arrange a chat after she'd wrapped up her day.

When Arch and I arrived, Willow was sitting out in front of the Plat du Jour with Tater on her lap. She wore jeans, a hoodie, and a Blazer ball cap that left a fringe of her auburn hair showing. Tater had on a powder blue jumpsuit, and without a hat I could see a hint of red in her hair as well.

Tater pointed at Archie and began to laugh and chant "Gog Gog, Gog Gog." Archie went directly to her, and Willow placed her daughter down next to him. I told Archie to stay while Tater used him for balance.

"She's quite the walker now," Willow said while gazing with pride at her daughter. "She can walk to you, if you ask her."

I'd chosen a seat well away from them in the nearly empty, well-ventilated space. "We need to keep plenty of distance between us," I said. I went on to explain the situation with Zoe.

"Oh, no," Willow said, drawing a hand to her face. "You really think it's Covid-19?"

"I hope not. Some flus can be virulent, too. We'll know in a couple of days, both of us."

She studied me for a moment, her face filled with compassion. "I can understand how worried you must be, Cal. I'm sorry."

A surge of emotion caught me off guard. My eyes burned, holding back tears. "Yeah, I, uh, I'm pretty worried." I forced a smile. "Did you wear your N-95 today?"

"I did. Got some funny looks, but I don't care."

"Good. It was nice of Stuart Burgess to think of you."

A flush crept across her freckled cheeks. Another smile, more contained. "It was. I was surprised, you know? I didn't even remember meeting him at that picnic."

I laughed, "He remembered you." She shot me an annoyed look, so I changed directions again, broaching the subject I'd come to ask her about. "Did you hear that Spectro Systems is being bought?"

"Really? For how much?"

"Something north of four hundred and fifty million, according to *The Oregonian*."

Her mouth dropped open. "Oh, my God! *That* much?"

"A venture capital firm up in Seattle's buying it. My guess is they figure the virus detection device your uncle came up with is going to make them a fortune." I paused, eyeing her more carefully. "Didn't you mention once that your uncle stopped an effort to sell the company, or something along those lines?"

"Yeah, I did. Uncle Mal said he nixed some deal Nielsen was cooking up." She shook her head. "Spectro Systems was Uncle Mal's baby. No way he'd agree to sell or to dilute his share of the company, no matter how good the deal was."

"Could this have been the deal? A sale of that magnitude must have been in the works for a while."

Tater had plopped down next to Archie and was beginning to fuss. Willow hoisted her daughter back on her lap before answering. "I don't know. He mentioned turning down some kind of proposal maybe four or five months ago. That's when he told me he'd never ever dilute his ownership or sell." She turned to me and cocked her head. "Pretty sweet outcome for Nielsen, huh?"

"It is. Did your uncle and Nielsen clash over this?"

"If they did, he didn't tell me about it."

"I'm curious, what's your personal opinion of Nielsen?"

She drew in a breath and let it out. "Well, most of my opinions come from what Uncle Mal has told me. They didn't get along, and, frankly, my uncle didn't trust him very much." She wrinkled her nose and hesitated...

"And...?" I coaxed.

"Personally, I think he's a creep. I don't like the way he looks at me, if you know what I mean. Women know that look."

"I see," I said, feeling a twinge of revulsion. I went on to describe the Khmer bas relief incident and how Timoteo and I re-enacted a possible version of the shooting.

When I finished, Willow's hand came to her mouth again. "Nielsen knows all the martial arts moves, Cal. Oh, my God, it was him, wasn't it?"

I shrugged. "He told me he was home with his wife the night your uncle died."

Willow smirked. "Oh, so Darlene's his alibi? What a joke. She's half his age and totally into being a kept woman. She'll be a good girl and say and do what she's told."

"I see," I said and moved on to another subject. "Gloria met your uncle at—"

Willow's eyes widened and she cut in. "The Wy East Club. She was a martial arts *instructor* there back in the day." Her face darkened as the revelation sunk in. "God, I'm sounding so judgmental here, but you know how I feel about Gloria, especially when money's involved."

"Could she have overpowered your uncle with a choke-hold?"

She answered without hesitating. "In a heartbeat. She's strong, and she stays in shape. Would she shoot him with his own gun?" Willow looked at me, horror stricken. "How could *anyone* do something like that?"

Willow reminded me of my daughter once again. Claire had bombarded me over the years with similar questions, the kind a father wants to answer to reassure his child that civilization isn't just a thin veneer, that all's well with the world.

But my only response was to shake my head. Some questions have no answers.

CHAPTER THIRTY-ONE

Three Days Later

"YOU TESTED NEGATIVE, MR. CLAXTON, BUT MS. BENNETT has Covid-19. I'm sorry." The call came from Gertie's friend at Providence just as I was putting on my Asics for a morning jog. I'd been running each morning, figuring that as long as I could go four and a half miles, I sure as hell didn't have the virus.

"I see," I said as I felt my whole body tense up. "How is she this morning?"

"Oh, she's quite sick. She's receiving oxygen now to boost her blood oxygen level. The prognosis is uncertain. There's a lot we don't know about this virus and how to treat it."

"Any way I can see her?" I blurted out without thinking.

"I'm afraid not. No visitors are allowed, and besides, she's in our isolation ward."

After we disconnected, I sat motionless on the front porch bench. I can't say I was surprised, but the news still rocked me to the core. I shook my head thinking about the turn of events. I knew I cared for Zoe, but it took this situation to make me realize just how deeply my feelings went. Was it the same for her, or was her declaration of love more the result of our emotional parting at the hospital? I hoped it was the former and not the latter.

Archie, who sat erect on the porch watching me, began to whimper softly, a gentle reminder that we had a run to complete. It seemed he knew how much the exercise would help relieve the stress I felt. After I did some stretching in the driveway, we headed out. The air was crisp and cool, and owing to a mass of gray clouds out over the valley I could smell the faint scent of rain. Would we make it back before the front reached us? I wasn't sure, but, hey, it's Oregon. Who cares?

Running against the traffic, we rounded a broad curve on Worden Hill Road and saw a slate blue Grand Cherokee with an imposing set of grill guards facing us on the soft shoulder maybe seventy-five yards ahead. Odd to be pulled over there, I thought.

The Jeep started up and pulled onto the road. Nothing unusual about that except that it seemed timed with Arch and I coming into view. Archie was out ahead of me and instinctively moved off the pavement and onto the shoulder about the same time I did. The shoulder was narrow, bounded on one side by the road and the other by a sizeable drainage ditch. The distance between us closed, slowly at first and then faster as the Jeep accelerated. The windshield was heavily tinted. The Jeep accelerated again and was just about on us when it swung into our direct path.

"Look out, Archie!" I screamed. He ripped the leash from my hand and leaped to the right. I had no choice but to go left and into the ditch. The jeep zoomed between us, missing us both by inches. Like most drainage ditches in the Red Hills, it was home to some particularly hearty blackberry bushes, and I managed to land with a crunch directly on one that stretched maybe ten feet in either direction. I cried out as pain exploded on my left side from my ankle to my ear.

I came to rest and lay there, stunned and motionless, as the sound of the Jeep receded into the distance. Would it come back? It didn't sound like it, but I couldn't be sure. "Archie," I called out next, my heart in my throat, "Archie, come here, boy."

Time stood still until he appeared at the edge of the ditch. Unscathed, he whimpered softly with an anxious expression on his face, then paced back and forth in frustration, looking for a way to help me. I breathed a sigh of relief. "Stay there, Big Boy," I told him in a firm voice. He whimpered some more and then sat on his haunches, looking down at me.

As the threat of the Jeep returning loomed over me, I took a couple of deep breaths to calm myself and took stock of the situation. I was suspended on a bed of mature vines. They were thick and springy and bristling with needle-like thorns. Each time I moved I was greeted with a fresh set of jabs that could pass for killer bee stings. My left ankle and leg were afforded some protection by my shoe and sweatpants. My left arm, however, was wedged under me and felt like a pin cushion. The left side of my face took a direct hit, but my eyes were spared. I was thankful for that.

I looked up at Archie. "How do those yogis and mystics do it?" I asked as I grimaced with the act of gingerly retrieving my cell phone from the right pocket of my sweats. After muttering a string of expletives directed at the pain, I called 911. "No, I don't need an ambulance," I said after telling the operator what happened and describing the Jeep that nearly killed me and my dog. "I'm okay, but this was an attempted homicide. Please send someone fast, since the Jeep might come back. It's slate blue and has a big, black tubular grill guard. You can't miss it, and it can't be far away."

I called Timoteo next and explained my situation, adding, "Wear boots and leather gloves and bring a pair of loppers with you. You're going to have to cut me out of here." He said he was on his way.

I waited in agony, the mere act of breathing generating new killer bee stings. I heard a sound in the distance—an oncoming car. Was it the Jeep? I tensed up and wished I could command Archie to get out of harm's way. But I knew he wouldn't budge with me stuck in the ditch.

The car passed by, and I let out a breath.

Angel Vineyard, where Timoteo lived, was only a short distance away, and the next car I heard carried Timoteo along with his father, Carlos. They each had loppers, and in no time at all I was cut free, hoisted out of the ditch, and sitting on the back of Carlos' truck while he attended to my injuries, using a first-aid kit he had the presence of mind to bring. Aside from a tear in my left earlobe, which bled freely, and a sizeable gash on my left arm, my wounds, although plentiful and painful, were superficial.

I worried about exposing my two rescuers to the virus, but what was to be done? At least I tested negative, I told myself, and we're outside.

A Newberg-Dundee Police patrol car arrived just as Carlos finished his doctoring. After I described what happened, one of the officers said, "So at the last moment the Jeep veered off the road and came directly at you?"

"Yeah," I said. "My dog went one way, and I went the other, and the Jeep just missed both of us."

"Must have been close."

"Inches." I glanced down at Archie, who lay off to the side watching the proceedings. "I still don't know how he escaped, but I do know this was an attempt to kill me."

"Okay, let's deal with that in a minute. Notice anything else about the Jeep besides the color and grill guard—bumper stickers, dents?" the officer asked.

"No, but I'm betting it's stolen. It's probably on the side of the road between here and the Pacific Highway by now."

My wounds stung, and the adrenaline rush I'd experienced had slid into bone-weary exhaustion. But just as we were leaving, another police car—an unmarked cruiser—arrived bearing Detective Darcy Tate. Darcy and I had some history—I'd handled her divorce and subsequent to that, we'd collaborated on a brutal murder case, the one that set Zoe to wondering whether I was, at the core, an adrenaline addict.

"We found the Jeep," she said after we exchanged greetings. "Parked on Knudsen Lane," she told me. "Stolen last week up in Beaverton. We're processing it now. Any idea who would want to kill you?"

I went on to sketch the circumstances surrounding the Wanda Jenkins hit and run. "This was the exact same MO," I concluded. "I don't know who's behind it yet, but the two incidents are related. I'm sure of it. A confidential source told me a Russian car theft ring might be involved."

"Duly noted," she said with a raised eyebrow. "You figure someone was watching you, knew your morning running routine?"

"I guess, but I sure as hell didn't notice anything suspicious the last few days."

"Of course, it's well known you're a morning jogger."

I looked at her with my eyebrows raised.

"That profile of you in the *NewsRegister* after the Fuentes case. It starts out mentioning you and Archie run up by the Pioneer Cemetery nearly every day. Google your name, and it probably comes right up."

I smirked. "Whatever happened to privacy?"

"The digital age happened," she answered and then went on. "There're no houses on Knudsen Lane, but we're checking Crabtree Park and Knudsen Vineyard on the off-chance someone noticed something."

"Good," I said. "The truck that killed Wanda Jenkins was wiped clean, but one of Portland's techs found a couple of hairs in the cab that weren't the owner's. They're trying to get a DNA profile, but I haven't heard anything on that. You should ask for the same tech to have a look at the Jeep. He's their best." I gave her Harmon Scott's contact information. "Tell Harmon I sent you."

"He's my next call," Darcy said after thanking me. "Looks like the perp's weapon of choice's a five-thousand-pound chunk of steel going fifty miles an hour. Charming." After taking me back through my account of the near miss and asking several more questions, she said, "Anything else you want me to know?"

I shook my head. "No, not at the moment." Of course, I had several suspects in mind, but without a scintilla of evidence pointing to any of them it wasn't worth Darcy's time.

She chuckled. "Okay, but Jesus, Cal, you're a glutton for punishment. This looks just as hairy as the Fuentes case."

I raised my right hand—the one that wasn't dotted with thorn pricks—in defense. "I backed into this, Darcy, believe me."

Another chuckle. "Come on, Cal, you don't back into anything."

She had a point.

CHAPTER THIRTY-TWO

TIMOTEO AND HIS FATHER FINALLY DROPPED ARCHIE and me at the Aerie. I told Timoteo to open up the office down in Dundee, that I would follow after cleaning myself up. The first thing I did after giving Archie a snack was call the Newberg hospital. There was no change in Zoe's condition. After I disconnected, I felt a sharp pang of frustration. I yearned to go to the hospital, to see her, to reassure her somehow, but the damn virus stood in my way.

I spoke to Willow Daniels next. "I don't want to upset you," I began. "I'm okay, but there's been an attempt on my life."

"Oh, no!" she gasped. "Is this related to your investigation?"

"I think we can assume that," I responded and proceeded to describe what happened.

When I finished, the line went quiet until she said, "This is my fault. I got you into—"

"Hey," I said, "I made the decision to investigate your uncle's death, and I don't make a habit of looking back. But I am concerned about your safety."

"You think we're in danger?"

The thought of anything happening to Willow or Tater sent a cold chill down my back. "I think the focus is on me. I've been turning over a lot of rocks, and whoever's behind this probably thinks I know more than I actually do. But you should stay vigilant like we discussed. Keep your doors and windows locked, use your car even if it's a short trip, and stay alert to your surroundings."

"Don't worry. I will."

Upstairs, I stripped down and stepped into a steaming shower, holding my bandaged left arm out of the stream. The warm water first burned then soothed the welts that had formed over the thorn pricks on my leg. I bent my head forward and let the stream gently buffet the back of my neck. "Ahhhh."

I stepped out of the shower and swiped the mirror with a fist. My left cheek was adorned with swollen puncture marks, like a terrain of tiny volcanos. I removed the bandage on my left earlobe and shook my head. It resembled a piercing gone bad. My mustache needed trimming, I noted, and my salt and pepper hair seemed to have gotten a lot saltier. After donning a turtleneck and a pair of loose-fitting sweats—I would be seeing no clients that day—I looked over at Archie, who was dozing in the corner. Unbidden, the attack flashed back like a video—the Jeep's windshield a darkened cyclopic eye, the massive grill guard a malevolent grin. And as it bore down on us, the high-pitched whine of the engine. A shiver rattled through me, and then a fist of anger hit me hard and left me stunned. Trying to take me out was bad enough. Trying to kill my dog? That was a declaration of war.

I went downstairs and had just made a cappuccino when my cell went off. "Greetings, Calvin," the deep, cheery voice of Nando Mendoza rang in my ear. "How is your morning going?"

I had to laugh. "Funny you should ask." I told him what just happened.

"This attempt comes as no surprise," he said when I

finished. "These people you are involved with are playing with hardballs." I went on to update the status of my investigation. "You have made great progress," he noted. "A theory for the murder and a couple of suspects with knowledge of how to choke someone without leaving a bruise is a good start. What about the murdered housekeeper's brother? The man you think stole the murder weapon for the killer?"

I sighed. "Still in the ICU with a tube stuck down his throat. Esperanza's keeping me updated on his status."

"I see. This is unfortunate." He paused, and I could picture his forehead furrowing as he grappled with the implications of what I'd laid out. "There are many parts that move here, Calvin. Perhaps you should find a weak link and focus there. Someone else must know something. Maybe the cousin or the other, younger scientist?"

I went back over what I knew about Donny Romano and Eric Trenton, and after we exhausted possible new approaches I said, "Still coming back at the end of the month? I could sure use some help around here."

Nando paused before answering. "That was the reason for my call today. My return is becoming somewhat complicated. More cases of Covid-19 have been confirmed on the island. My return flight connects through Mexico, and I am told by reliable sources that these flights may be delayed or cancelled with little advance warning. It is worrisome, Calvin."

"Indeed," I said. A dark shadow descended on me as I broke the news about Zoe.

"Oh," he said. "It saddens me to hear this. I will keep her in my thoughts. I am very fond of Zoe."

"Me, too."

We ended the call on that note. I looked down at my

cell phone in disgust. My screen protector was smeared with blood from my ear. "Shit," was all I could say to that. And "shit" that my wingman might get stuck in Cuba. And "shit" that the damn virus might take the woman I love.

—/—

Esperanza returned an earlier call of mine shortly after lunch. She'd been in touch with Nando, of course, and spent the morning looking at alternative return flights from Cuba without any luck. There was no change in BB's condition over the weekend," she told me. "He's fighting for his life, Cal." I wasn't up to telling her about Zoe, so I let it ride.

After we disconnected, I gingerly stretched out on the leather couch in my study and instantly fell asleep. When my phone sounded, I jerked upright and put the phone to my good ear. "Claxton?" the voice of Donny Romano began. "I got some things on my mind. You said you could help me."

Despite the stinging, my head cleared instantly. "Yeah, Donny, I can. Go ahead."

"Any way you could meet me at that bar on 82nd?"

I told him I'd be there in an hour.

Roscoe's Place was even dimmer than I remembered and looked empty except for an older couple at the bar who were in a heated discussion with the bartender. But as my eyes adjusted I saw Donny slouched at a table in the back. I was carrying my N-95 mask but opted against wearing it. This was definitely not a congregant setting, and I could sit well away from him. Besides, this conversation could be important, and I didn't want any distractions.

"What the hell happened to you?" he asked as I sat down.

"Took a spill jogging this morning. How's the gun business?"

"Booming," he said, allowing a faint smile. "Guns and toilet paper, man. Every American needs 'em." His stubble beard was more beard than stubble and his close-set eyes had a kind of feral quality I hadn't noticed before. A half-full beer mug and two empty shot glasses sat in front of him.

The bartender looked over at me. "Mirror Pond," I called out. Donny raised the mug and one of the shot glasses. "So," I began, locking onto his eyes, "what's on your mind?"

He swallowed and licked his lips. "That asshole detective believes what Willow told him. Thinks I took the pictures. He's brought me in for questioning twice now. And I think they've got a tail on me."

"What did you tell him?"

"That I didn't have anything to do with the heist. That's it. Bower told me I didn't have to tell them anything else."

"No," I said, "you don't, but it's not quite that simple, Donny. When you refuse to talk it makes you look guilty as hell."

He averted his eyes. "I'm not saying I do, but suppose I did know something about this, ah, situation. Suppose I wanted to get it straightened out. What should I do?"

"Just so we're clear, Donny, I'm not your lawyer so I can't advise you." I paused while the bartender set our drinks down on the table. "But if you were my client, I would have you go immediately to Detective Kohler and tell him exactly what happened and where the pictures are. If others are involved, I would counsel you to ask Kohler for immunity in return for your cooperation."

He poured the shot into the beer and downed half of the mixture in a couple of long pulls. He started to speak when an incoming text pinged on his phone. He read it and said "fuck you" under his breath before turning back to me with a defiant look. "Seems like a guy in this situation would have a right to protect his uncle's valuable pictures."

"Protect them from whom?"

He brought his eyes up to mine and tried to look indignant. "From Willow, man. She's the one saying I don't have a right to them. God knows what she'd do to deprive me of what Uncle Mal promised."

"Oh, so you stole the pictures to protect them. *Really?*" I laughed out loud. "That line of bullshit would get you laughed out of any court in Oregon, Donny."

He broke eye contact. "Yeah, well, I'm just spitballing, here. Not admitting to shit."

"Of course," I said. "But the longer you dither, the harder it's going to be on you. And don't think for a moment that Gloria and Bower won't leave you holding the bag. Better to get this off your chest."

Except for a tightening of his jaw, he didn't react. He drained his beer mug, got up, and popped a couple of breath mints in his mouth. "Gotta go arm the citizenry."

After he left, I immediately called Detective Kohler and described my conversation with Donny. "He's wavering now," I told him, "looking for a way out. If you come down hard on him, I think he'll crack."

"That would be nice," Kohler said, "because I still don't have enough to even get a search warrant. I'll haul him back in, and me and my partner will try a little good-cop, bad-cop."

I spoke to Timoteo next. "Yeah, I'm free tonight," he replied to my question about the possibility of him following Donny. "I can tail him. Is he at the gun shop?"

"Yes. If you leave now, you can probably catch him. Be

careful. He thinks the Portland cops are following him, so he'll be on guard. He's wound pretty tight, and I'm betting he'll make a move of some kind tonight."

"I got something else," Timoteo said. "I went over to Knudsen Lane, where the Jeep was found, just to look around. A couple of guys were up on the hill working in the vineyard, so I talked to them. They said a cop who spoke Spanish came earlier, but they didn't cooperate, acted like they didn't see anything—"

"But they did?" I said expectantly.

"Right. They opened up to me when I told them who my father was. They saw the Jeep get dropped off, Cal."

"Go on," I said, my pulse quickening.

"The Jeep arrived first and parked on the side of the road just after sunrise. A couple of trees obscured part of the view, so they didn't get a very good look, but they agreed it was a Jeep. The driver stayed inside. Right after that, a car pulls up, two doors, red. No idea what make or model. The guy in the Jeep hops out and gets in the red car and they drive off."

"That was the delivery of the stolen Jeep alright," I said.

"Anyway, the workers go up to the barn for some tools, and when they return the Jeep's gone and another car's parked there, dark blue or black, four door. The two I talked to again weren't sure of the make or model, but a third guy was with them this time. I have his name and I'll track him down. Maybe he's semi-car-literate."

"Excellent. What time was this?"

"Around six thirty." He sighed again. "As shitty luck would have it, they took a breakfast break, and when they returned to the vineyard the Jeep was back, and the other car was gone. The timing fits perfectly."

"It was another contract theft, like with Wanda Jenkins," I said. "The stolen Jeep was dropped off at Knudsen Lane as part of the deal. And now we know the killer drives a dark-colored sedan. Every detail counts in this business, Timoteo. Nice work."

"Thanks."

I told Timoteo to contact Detective Tate and brief her on this information before we disconnected, and then I called Stuart Burgess. After we exchanged greetings, I said, "Do you happen to know what kind of car Nielsen drives?"

"An Audi A-8."

"What color is it?"

"Black. Why?"

"Just curious."

I called Semyon Lebedev next and left a message when he didn't pick up. I was giving Archie a bio break out in Roscoe's parking lot when a BMW three series that had seen some miles skidded to stop in the gravel between us and our car. Clete Bower got out. I noted it was another dark colored sedan, navy blue in this case.

"What the fuck, Claxton," he said as he approached. "You've been talking to my client, haven't you?"

I gave him a blank look.

Bower came on fast and Archie stepped between us and faced him in a crouch. He looked at my dog, stopped, then eyed me, noticing my damaged face for the first time.

"You should have seen the other guy," I said.

Ignoring the quip, he said, "I called the gun shop and they told me Donny took a break to meet someone here. I figured it might be you. I texted him, but the little fucker ignored me. Where is he?"

"Beats me. It was a chance encounter at my favorite watering hole. We just shot the breeze."

His neck flushed red like the last time I angered him. "This is unethical. I could have your ass disbarred for a stunt like this."

I threw my head back and laughed. "You're the one who should worry about disbarment."

His eyes narrowed down. "Come again?"

I met his squinty glare. "It's probably not too late to get off the hook for the Ansel Adams photos, Bower. That wasn't one of your better cons. But, you know, if they suddenly reappeared, there probably wouldn't be many questions asked. You know what they say—no harm, no foul."

He bunched his brows unconvincingly. "I don't know what the fuck you're talking about." I huffed another laugh, and his hand came up with a stubby finger pointing at me like a pistol barrel. "You're out of line here."

Archie caught the threat in his voice, and I saw his hackles rise out of the corner of my eye. "You're between me and my car," I said, keeping my voice even. "Step aside. You're pissing off my dog. And that's never a good idea."

Bower held his ground for a few moments before moving a couple of grudging steps. I caught the now familiar scent of stale tobacco as I walked past him. "This isn't over, Claxton," he said in a low voice.

I turned back and smiled cheerily. "Well, we finally agree on something."

CHAPTER THIRTY-THREE

"WHERE ARE YOU?" GERTIE ASKED WHEN I ANSWERED MY cell phone.

"Heading home from Portland. Why? What's up?"

"Can you meet me at the Newberg Medical Center?"

My heart froze. "What is it? What's wrong?"

"It's okay. My nurse friend Julia just called. They're moving Zoe from the isolation ward to the PCU in—"

"PCU? What the hell is that?"

"It's a progressive care unit, not the ICU. They're better equipped to treat her there. It's precautionary, Cal. We can see her during the transfer."

"They'll let us do that?"

"Only from outside the building. They'll bring her down a corridor that's adjacent to an outside garden area. Julia will be with Zoe and will make sure she knows we're outside looking in. It's worth it, a show of support..."

"Meet you in the Med Center parking lot," I said without hesitation.

"The garden area is on the east side," Gertie said ten minutes later as Archie and I followed her around the medical building on a flagstone path. "There's a set of glass double doors there." We located the doors, which provided access to a small rose garden with a couple of cement benches, a bubbling fountain, and a canister for cigarette butts. She looked at her watch. "They should come by here in five minutes or so." As we stood peering into the narrow hallway, Gertie took my hand and squeezed it, something she'd never done before.

While we waited, Gertie came back to my ravaged face, which I'd explained away when we met. She gave me an appraising look. "Okay, you're way too coordinated to fall while jogging. What the hell really happened?"

I heaved a sigh and told her the truth. When I finished, she said, "Good God, you've got a target on your back *again?*"

"I wasn't looking for trouble, believe me."

She rolled her eyes. "When's Nando getting back from Cuba?"

"End of the month, provided Covid-19 doesn't interfere."

"Well, keep your head down until then. You need backup."

"I'll try, but—"

"I see a gurney," Gertie cut in. We both fell silent, and I turned slightly, hoping Zoe would see mostly the undamaged side of my face.

A jumble of corrugated tubing, wires, digital screens, and swaying IV drips, the gurney was surrounded by four attendants dressed in blue scrubs and wearing masks. An oxygen mask covered most of the patient's face, but the ash blond hair was instantly recognizable. My heart swelled in my chest. One of the attendants—whom I assumed was Julia—put a hand up and the gurney stopped. She gently raised Zoe's head and turned it toward us. Zoe's and my eyes found each other. More was said in that moment than in all our previous conversations put together.

Gertie said with exaggerated expression, "We love you, Zoe," and I blew her a kiss before putting both my hands over my heart. Archie whimpered softly and wagged his butt, a clear indication he recognized Zoe.

Zoe managed a thumbs-up before Julia lowered her head back on the pillow. She was gone a moment later.

I'm not sure how long Gertie and I stood there before she said, "Well, that felt like a kick in the head, but seeing her recognize us was worth it. Thanks for coming, Cal."

"You're right. It was worth it," I responded reflexively. "Thanks for including me, Gertie." *And it was, indeed, worth it,* I said to myself. That look Zoe and I shared, that brief encounter, answered a nagging question. For the first time I felt her feelings about me might run as deeply as mine about her. At the same time, I knew that image of her strapped in a gurney ladened with medical devices would haunt me. Was all that technology enough to save her from the virus?

—/ /—

Gertie offered to fix us dinner, but I begged off. I really didn't want any company and didn't have much of an appetite in any case. Although it was nearly dark when we got back to the Aerie, Archie and I managed a good fifteen minutes of slobber ball, a game in which I chucked a tennis ball as far as I could and he raced after it, often catching it on the bounce with more grace and elan than a major league center fielder. It was a joy for him and good therapy for me.

After feeding him and downing a quick scramble of eggs with some smoked salmon tossed in, I poured myself three fingers of Remy and went into the study. With Diana Krall's *Wallflower* on the sound system, I began reading *The Oregonian*. The news concerning the virus wasn't encouraging. The Oregon Legislature approved five million in emergency funding for Covid-19 response, and although no new cases were identified that day, fifty-two people still awaited testing. Down in California, a cruise ship was held at sea after twenty-one passengers tested positive. And in Washington DC, the CDC stated that two of the three factors—illness resulting in death and person-to-person spread—had been met for a pandemic. Frightening.

The words began to swim on the screen, and my eyelids were turning to lead when Timoteo called. "I started following Donny when he left work," he began. "He went home, and two hours later he drove over to Gloria's, parked in the shadows on a side street, and is still in his car. I figure he's watching her place. He chuckled. "I'm watching him, and he's watching her. You want me to hang in?"

"Yeah. Give it some time. See what happens. By the way, what's Donny driving?"

Timoteo caught my drift immediately. "A silver Ford F-150. That tends to clear him for the attack on you and Archie."

"It would seem so."

When Timoteo called back, the *Wallflower* playlist must have cycled through a couple of times as I dozed with my chin slumped on my chest. "Hey, something's up. Trenton, the young scientist came calling, I think. I wasn't sure it was him from my distance, but I recognized his Lexus. He went in and came out an hour and ten minutes later. Must have been a quickie."

I waited for Timoteo to continue, my head clearing rapidly.

"So when Trenton leaves, Donny gets out of his car, slams the door, and stomps over to Gloria's place, a jealous lover if there ever was one. He pounds on the door. She finally opens it. Words are exchanged there on the porch, then she lets him in."

"Catch any of what was said?"

"Nah, I was too far away. I figured letting him in wasn't such a good idea on her part. The dude looked pissed, even from a distance. Anyway, the porch light goes off, and he slinks out of there twenty minutes later. He stays in the shadows all the way to his car and takes off like a bat out of hell."

"Uh-oh," I said. "That doesn't sound good."

"Yeah, it looked like he was running from something. You want me to check on her? She doesn't know me. I could make some excu—"

"No. I want you to leave right now. I'll take it from here." Although Timoteo was a DACA recipient, he was still undocumented, and brushes with the law were best avoided no matter what the circumstances.

After we disconnected, I called Gloria's cell phone, and when she didn't answer I became even more concerned. After all, I'd been trying to provoke Donny. Had his violent temper gotten the better of him? I couldn't chance it, so I left Archie snoozing in the study and reluctantly headed back into Portland, arriving in front of her place in Multnomah Village thirty-five minutes later. The porch light was still off, and I found the door slightly ajar, as if Donny had left in a hurry. I knocked softly first, then louder. Nothing.

I eased the door open and called out. "Gloria? It's Cal Claxton." Nothing. I repeated the call, and that's when I heard a low moan. I found her in a back bedroom sitting on the edge of a bed holding a towel to her face. Her thin negligee was ripped in the front and dappled with blood. She looked up at me and placed a hand on her chest to obscure her half-revealed breasts.

"What are you doing here?" she said, lowering the towel. Her left eye was nearly swollen shut, and she had an abrasion on her right cheek and a swollen, bloody lower lip.

"Are you okay?" I asked, ignoring her question.

"Do I look okay?" she snapped back, glaring at me.

"I'm calling an ambulance."

"No. I don't need any help."

"Who did this to you, Gloria?"

She lowered her eyes and didn't answer as blood dripped slowly into the towel.

"Was it Donny?"

Her eyes came back up, the surprise they registered answering my question. "Why do you say that?"

I closed the distance between us. "Just a guess. I know you were lovers once, that it broke up your marriage to Malcolm. And I've seen his temper firsthand."

"Well, it's none of your business," she answered in a weary voice. "And for the second time, what the hell are you doing here?"

"I happened to be in the neighborhood and had a couple of things to run by you, but I won't bother you with—"

"Like what?" she said, fixing me with the gaze of her good eye.

I paused for a moment, not expecting her to call my bluff. *What the hell,* I decided, *push her some more, see where it goes.* "Look, Gloria, we both know Donny stole the Ansel Adams photographs. I don't know if you're in on the theft or not, but I'm here to tell you that it's not too late to get out from under. If the photographs suddenly reappeared at Malcolm's house, I don't think the cops would—"

"How many times do I have to tell you? I don't know anything about those stupid photographs." Strong words but she'd broken eye contact. "What else is on your mind?"

I paused again. Despite her injuries, she seemed forthcoming. "I understand you used to be a mixed martial arts instructor," I began. "In the past, say, six months or so, have you taught anyone how to execute a blood chokehold?

Her brow furrowed in what looked like genuine perplexity. "No. What the hell kind of question is that?"

"Just curious. What about Bradley Nielsen? Does he know the move?"

"Of course," she snapped. "I taught him years ago. He's a good martial artist."

"What about Donny?"

She rolled her good eye. "Yeah, we used to spar around some. He's better than Nielsen. So what?"

"He got the better of you, tonight, huh?"

She glared at me again. "Size matters, even in MMA."

"How about Eric Trenton? Ever 'spar around' with him?"

Her mouth dropped open, then her good eye blazed at me. "You bastard. Have you been spying on me?"

"It's no secret, Gloria," I lied. "The rumors are all over Spectro Vision. I guess Trenton's been doing a little bragging." I stopped there, hoping she'd buy it.

She forced her swollen lip into a bitter smile. "Men. You can never trust 'em." Then, seeming to notice my face for the first time, she abruptly changed the subject. "Looks like I'm not the only one who got beat up today. What happened to you?"

The question caught me off guard, stirring the latent rage I felt about the attack on Archie and me. "Someone tried to run my dog and me over this morning. I wound up in a ditch lined with blackberries." My face grew hot. "Do you know anything about that, Gloria?"

She winced at my words, and I thought I saw a flicker of fear in her eyes, but if I did it was fleeting. "No, of course not."

A couple more drops of blood from her lip found the towel. "Let me drive you to the ER," I said. "Your eye should be looked at, and that lip probably needs a stitch or two."

"No, just leave." She exhaled a deep, weary sigh. "Maybe I deserved this."

I cringed at her words. "Don't let Donny get away with this, Gloria. Don't make excuses for him."

Her face hardened. "I said leave, get the hell out of my house."

I let myself out, noting that the car parked in her garage was a fire-engine red Miata convertible. By the time I reached my car I was practically shaking with anger. I still harbored suspicions about how deeply involved Gloria was in the murders, but she seemed trapped somehow, maybe even fearful, and I felt, if not sorry for her, a sense of pity for the emptiness I sensed in her life.

But I felt certain she was lying about the photographs. She was in on the deal, which is why she was letting Donny off the hook. Sure, she seemed unruffled by the chokehold questions, but why wouldn't she be? She had to know by now that I did my homework, that lying would have been obvious. And I reminded myself that behind it all for Gloria was the insurance money. She coveted the big payoff above all else, and that kind of greed was always dangerous.

Still, that flicker of fear I thought I saw in her eyes stuck with me. *What or who was she afraid of?*

CHAPTER THIRTY-FOUR

SLEEP THAT NIGHT WAS WHAT I GUESSED DEATH MIGHT be, a descent into a black, featureless void with the suspension of all consciousness and sense of time. But as morning light gradually filled the bedroom, I clawed my way back, and when Archie licked the wound on my ear, I became fully awake. I got dressed, and after feeding Archie and letting him out the kitchen door, I ground some dark roast coffee beans and brewed a cappuccino. The birds were all over the feeders in the backyard—finches on the Niger seed and nuthatches, chickadees, and sparrows on the sunflower seeds. Behind them on the south fence line, a thick hedge of forsythia had exploded in brilliant yellow, always the first thing, aside from the crocuses, to bloom at the Aerie.

My face stung a little, and my ear had bled on my pillow the night before, but as I sipped my coffee and watched the intricate dance of the birds at the feeders, I felt, if not at peace, at least a sense of hope. There was, after all, beauty and maybe even some order in the universe.

But was there any mercy? *That* was an open question.

The first thing I did that morning was contact the hospital to inquire about Zoe. She remained in serious condition. Phoebe Tyson, my divorce-obsessed client, called next, and after we played twenty questions and guess-what-he-did-next, I was able to convince her we were on schedule to sever her marital knot as quickly as the law would allow.

Harmon Scott called midmorning. "Heard from Detective Tate from Newberg-Dundee," he began. "She told me you had a close call."

"You could say that."

"How are you feeling?"

"Sore and pissed off. The same person who ran down Wanda Jenkins took a shot at me and my dog. I'm sure of it."

"Jesus Christ, Cal. Why?"

"Someone thinks I know too much—which I don't—but the fundamental driver is probably garden-variety greed. Turns out the death of Malcolm Bainbridge is making several people rich to varying degrees." I went on to list the growing number of suspects and my theory of how Bainbridge's suicide was faked, including the role I suspected Benny Boykin played in providing the gun.

"Some kind of chokehold, huh?" Scott said when I finished. "Sounds kind of out there to me, and the problem is you still don't have any physical evidence to back it up."

"I've got the bruise found on Bainbridge's left bicep," I offered up, "and the gap between the gun and his head, and the fact that the gun was so near his hand."

"Come on, that's not enough. I'll need a crowbar to open this case back up, and you know it. But tell you what, if Boykin survives the virus and you can get him to talk, then I might be able to do something."

"I hear you," I said. He was right and I knew it.

"Meanwhile," Scott went on, "I'm going to put the team working on the Jenkins hit-and-run in close touch with Detective Tate. I agree there could be a connection."

"Yep," I said, "and if you and Tate crack those, you'll have Bainbridge's killer, too, or at least who's behind it all."

"We'll see, won't we?" Scott said.

"You sound mellower," I said in a half-tease before we disconnected. "The meditation must be working."

"Shit. I just heard I have a new nickname around here—the Zen Master. If I hear any of my detectives call me that, I'll bust them down to patrolman."

I had to laugh. "But you'll do it with newly acquired sensitivity, right?"

—/ /—

On Thursday of that week, I was informed that my second Covid test was negative. I admit it was a relief to know that every throat tickle, sneeze, or momentary bit of congestion didn't foretell a trip to the ICU. Zoe's condition remained unchanged, as well. Was she holding her own, or was this a plateau before a precipitous decline? I didn't know, and Gertie's friend wouldn't speculate beyond saying her blood oxygen level hadn't gotten any lower.

"No news is good news," was as far as she would go.

A subsequent chat with Semyon Lebedev brought more good news—he'd located a source, a former girlfriend, who confirmed that a Grand Cherokee with a grill guard was delivered to Dundee on the indicated time and date of the attempt on my life.

"Is there any way to find out who let the contract?" I knew the answer, but I asked the question anyway.

A soft chuckle. "I was lucky to get this, but she still has

feelings for me. It cost me a bottle of Black Opium perfume, by the way."

"How much was that?"

"One hundred and forty."

"I think her feelings were for the perfume, Semyon. I'll send you a check."

"You're a cruel man, Calvin, but thank you."

After we disconnected, I crumpled up a piece of paper and took a shot at the wastebasket. It fell short, an apt metaphor. Archie eyed the crumpled ball but didn't bother to get up. The information confirmed my suspicion that the Jeep was supplied by another contract theft, but without a name or description, there wasn't much to go on. "Hey," I said to ease the sting, "Every scrap of information helps."

—//—

Later that morning, Archie's low, irritated bark announced the arrival of a visitor. It was Clete Bower, and as he was letting himself in the front door I sprang up and said, "I was just going to take my dog for a walk. Join me and we can talk outside." I really didn't want to swap air with him and have the lingering smell of cigars in my office the rest of the morning. He shot me an irritated look but backed out of the doorway.

It was another perfect morning, the sky cloudless, the air cool and crisp. "We can get a coffee across the street," I said, nodding in the direction of the Red Hills Market. Bower shrugged indifference but followed me across the Pacific Highway and up 7th Street to the market. I got a double cap, Bower got a black coffee, and Archie scored a chew treat courtesy of the barista, a big fan of his.

We found an outside table and sat down facing each other. Wraparound sunglasses shielded Bower's eyes, and his thinning, slicked back hair glistened in the morning light. A red tie decorated with a couple of coffee stains lay like a tongue against his white shirt. "What have you done with my client?" he asked.

"Which one?"

"Donny, Donny Romano. He's not returning my texts. He hasn't been at his place, and he hasn't shown up for work."

There was no reason to hold back. "You know he attacked your other client, right?"

"Gloria?" he answered, trying to look surprised.

"Come on, Bower, every time we meet you have another line of bullshit. I'm sure Gloria told you what he did to her the other night."

"So, you've been talking to Gloria?" he said, conceding my point by omission. "What is it about my clients that you find so fascinating?"

"How is she? She refused to let me call an ambulance."

He frowned in frustration. "This is about Donny, damn it. Him and his truck are gone. Has he been in contact with you? I'm worried about him."

"No. I haven't heard from him since our chat at Roscoe's. Maybe he's hiding out, afraid that Gloria's going to have him arrested for beating the shit out of her?"

"No," Bower answered, shaking his head, "that's not going to happen."

"Why is that?" I pressed. "Have you seen her face? Why wouldn't you be counseling her to have him arrested?"

His expression became pained as he squirmed in his

chair. "It's complicated. They have some history, you know, and Gloria feels, well, a bit maternalistic toward him."

I managed to suppress a laugh.

Bower frowned and opened his hands. "What did I do to deserve these clients? I mean, I'm just trying to make a living here. There's never a dull moment with these two."

I shrugged indifference. "Comes with the territory, I guess. Look, if I hear from Donny, I'll let you know" I said, although I had no intention of doing so. I paused as a question occurred to me. "You mentioned his truck's gone. Does he have a second car?"

"Yeah, a Camry, I think. He had it before he bought the truck."

"What color is it?"

"I don't know. I just heard him mention it once. Why the hell do you ask?"

"Just in case I see it around," I said, hoping the answer would suffice. "Meanwhile, I wish you luck sorting out the legal dilemma of what to do when one of your clients assaults another. You sure as hell can't represent them both."

"Yeah, well, it's not assault unless charges get filed." With that, Clete Bower downed his coffee and left.

Why hadn't Bower simply called or texted me to inquire about Donny's whereabouts, I wondered? Did he think I was harboring Donny for some reason? Confronting me in person would allow him to better read me, right? Suppose Donny *was* missing. Would Bower really be 'worried about him,' or did he want to find him for other, more selfish reasons, like preventing him from fessing up about the photo heist? I suspected the latter.

And what about Bower's reluctance to involve the police in Gloria's assault? No surprise that he and Gloria were in sync on that issue. An incarcerated Donny would be even more likely to reveal the Ansel Adams con. Much better to forgive and forget.

Finally, there was Donny's second car. I looked over at Archie. "Let me guess—his Camry's going to turn out to be a dark color. That would put him in the running along with Bradley Nielsen, Eric Trenton, and Clete Bower for the person who forced me into the ditch. Archie looked up at me and I shook my head. "Too many suspects and not enough time, Big Boy."

—/—

Later that afternoon, I caught a glimpse of a car turning into the small parking lot behind my Dundee office. I opened the back door just as Willow Daniels got out of her weather-beaten Prius. Her smile froze when she glimpsed the side of my face. "*Jeez*, does that hurt as bad as it looks?"

I shook my head. "Nah, it's just a damn annoyance."

The smile returned as the breeze riffled her russet hair, her eyes green in the afternoon light. "I hope you're not busy. I should've called."

"Not a problem. What brings you to the wine country?"

"The light's so perfect today, I just had to get out of Portland. I've always wanted to do some shooting out here in the vineyards. Thought I'd scout around a little, maybe take some shots. I guess I'm a bit early for when the vines begin leafing out, but it's still gorgeous."

I smiled. "It's called bud break around here, and it'll happen in another three or four weeks." By this time, Archie had greeted Willow and was standing next to the rear door of her Prius with his butt in full wag. I gave an eye nod in his direction. "He wants to say hi to Tater."

"And she to him," Willow said as she extracted her daughter from the back seat and stood her next to Arch. Chattering away about Gog Gog, Tater reached her arms as far around Archie neck as they would go and gave him a hug as Willow and I stood by, smiling broadly.

Willow looked at me, and her face grew serious. "How's Zoe?"

"No change overnight. No news is good news, I'm told. I got my second Covid test result this morning. I don't have the virus."

"That's a relief," Willow said and then turned back to her car. "I brought you a present." She opened the trunk, lifted out a thin rectangular package wrapped in brown paper and handed it to me. "This is in appreciation for all you've done for us."

I started to deny having done anything but thought better of it. "You didn't have to do that, Willow, but thanks." I removed the paper to discover a signed and framed copy of Willow's photograph of the Freemont Bridge bathed in a Portland sunset, the one I'd admired so much. I looked at her in amazement. "My favorite of your bridge series. I've got the spot for it all picked out. I'm honored to have a copy."

She smiled with genuine modesty. "You got the first one. The whole series goes up next month at the Alberta Street Gallery." She chewed her lower lip for a moment. "I hope Portlanders will be interested in seeing yet another collection of bridge photos."

"Don't worry," I said. "You've captured them in ways that are going to amaze people."

While Archie and Tater paraded around the parking

lot, I gave Willow some tips on where to go in the Red Hills to find interesting vistas and overlooks. Willow took notes on her phone, and when we finished, I killed the mood by bringing up my encounter with Gloria. "That's sickening, and I'm not surprised," she said when I finished. "Donny's mean streak runs deep."

"Clete Bower told me Donny hasn't been home for a couple of days. Do you have any idea where he could've gone if he wanted to, you know, lay low for a while?"

She cocked her head slightly and squinted in a gesture that reminded me of my daughter. "Not really. Who cares where he's gone?"

"I think he's running scared, that he's ready to give the pictures back if he can cut a deal with the police. Bower would like to disabuse him of that idea, and I'd like another crack at him, too."

"Oh," she said, looking a bit chastised. "Let me do some digging. He has a couple of friends who might know something. I'll get back to you."

"Good. I understand Donny owns two cars—a metallic silver Ford F-150 and a Toyota Camry. Do you know what color the Camry is?"

She closed her eyes for a moment as if visualizing the car. "Dark gray or black, I think."

Of course, I said to myself before changing the subject. "Have you seen Stuart again?"

"Yeah. He dropped by the other day for lunch and gave me a few more masks."

"He's an awfully nice guy, thoughtful."

She flicked me a look that held a gentle warning—Willow Daniels didn't need any help in conducting her love life, thank you very much.

When she and Tater left to scout the Red Hills for photo opportunities, Archie and I went back into my office. I plopped down in the seat behind my desk and shook my head. Sure, I said to myself, I might save the photographs for Willow, but that's not why she hired me. What's the connection between the stolen photographs and the deaths of Malcom Bainbridge, Wanda Jenkins, and the attempt on my life?

Those were questions for which I still had no answers.

CHAPTER THIRTY-FIVE

THERE'S A SPOT ON THE I-5 A FEW MILES SOUTH OF DOWN-town Portland that affords a clear view of Mt. Hood to the east. On that Friday morning the mountain gleamed bright white against a cobalt blue sky, a hulking, snowclad behemoth that looked much closer than the seventy miles that lay between it and the city. Despite its status as an active volcano, the sight of the mountain was always a pleasant surprise and on this particular day oddly reassuring. It looked solid and unmovable, unlike my life, caught up in a swirl of events I seemed to have little control over. I inhaled a lungful of fresh air and vowed to make the day count.

Traffic in town was light that morning, which I assumed was due to the virus that hung over Portland like a darkening cloud. At nine sharp, I checked in with the hospital to learn that Zoe's condition was unchanged. Her breathing was still assisted with oxygen, but she still hadn't been intubated, thank God.

I intended to talk to Eric Trenton but decided to leave that until the afternoon. I planned to warn him about the threat Donny Romano might pose—in case Gloria hadn't bothered—and use that as an excuse to question him again. While I was at it, I would also check in with Stuart Burgess to get the latest from the Spectro Systems' rumor mill.

Meanwhile, business that morning was as quiet as the traffic, and by the time Archie needed a walk and I needed a coffee, I'd fielded only three calls. We had just exited the back door of Caffeine Central when Stuart Burgess pulled into the small adjacent parking lot. "I'm picking up some supplies over in the Pearl and thought I'd drop by," he said, breaking into his signature smile.

"You read my mind," I said. "I was going to call you for an update."

Stuart knelt to greet Archie, who'd approached him whining softly with affection. "The biggest thing right now," he said, "is that our new owners—well, I guess I should say future owners, since the deal doesn't close for another month—want to expand the spectroscopic test technology beyond just Covid-19 testing. They want to create a platform that's something like a home pregnancy test, a test you can buy at the drugstore. Do I have a common cold or a more serious virus? What kind of virus? With this technology you can get an answer instantaneously and skip the trip to the doctor."

"Impressive," I said. "How's the testing coming?"

"No news on that front, but a lot's riding on it."

"Is there any doubt about the outcome?"

"Not according to Eric Trenton. And the timing on all this couldn't be better. Somebody in finance leaked that the company is heavily leveraged. If the sale doesn't come through, we could go belly up."

"That wasn't in the press release," I said. "What else is going on?"

Stuart shook his head and smiled with something close to bitterness. "Trenton's let his new status go to his head. He's dictating changes in research programs, shifting budgets, and reassigning personnel without consulting with anyone. For some reason he seems almost desperate. All the group managers are up in arms. That's not the way Dr. Bainbridge ran the research side of the house. Spectro Systems has always had a collaborative atmosphere. Trenton doesn't get it."

"Desperate? Desperate about what?"

Stuart shrugged. "My best guess is he's worried about the accuracy of InstaVision. The test is sensitive enough to tell one Covid virus from another, but with what accuracy? False negatives could be a deal breaker."

"What's Nielsen have to say about that?"

Stuart made a dismissive gesture. "He's a numbers guy. Doesn't know squat about biotechnology or managing for innovation. And he thinks Trenton walks on water."

"Bainbridge's notebook is still missing, I take it."

"Oh, yeah." Stuart pushed a thick shock of hair off his forehead and eyed me with curiosity. "What do you make of that?"

I decided it was worth the risk of being candid. "If it didn't turn up at work then he must have taken it home. And now it's gone."

"Someone might've killed Dr. Bainbridge for his *notebook?*" Stuart's eyes grew huge. "Someone like Trenton?"

"I haven't ruled that out. I'm being open with you, Stuart. This is just one piece of a very complex puzzle. Keep it to yourself."

He held my gaze. "Of course."

"Willow told me she appreciated the N-95 masks," I said. "She says she's been wearing them at her food cart."

"That's good," he said. "The outbreak's going to get worse before it gets better." He shook his head in frustration.

"She seemed to appreciate the masks, but she won't give me the time of day."

I smiled with sympathy. "I'm the last one to be giving advice on relationships, but I will say less may be more with Willow." I looked at him. "She's fiercely independent and focused on her business and her daughter."

"And her photography," he added. His shoulders slumped. "What should I do then?"

I scratched the back of my head. "Don't push it. Drop by for lunch, check on her mask supply, that sort of thing. Let her know about your interest in food, too. That's something you two share."

His face brightened. "I'm thinking of buying some of her photographs, too."

"Maybe too obvious? Less is more, Stuart."

He grinned with a sheepish look. "Yeah, okay. You're right. That's a dumb idea."

—/—

Around lunch time a front blew in and began pelting the city with rain that thrummed on the roof and ricocheted off Couch Street like gunfire. My stomach was rumbling, and since I hadn't gone shopping, the larder up in the apartment was essentially bare. I put on a hooded raincoat and after telling Archie to stay put made a dash down Couch to Angelina's for takeout. I was halfway through my falafel wrap and Greek salad when Detective Kohler called.

"Mr. Claxton," he began, "I stopped by to see you but saw your sign about using the phone instead. This social distancing thing makes police work a lot harder, but it's probably a good idea, given the way the virus seems to be spreading."

My stomach tightened at the mention of the virus. "I appreciate the call, Detective. It's a small office, you know. Not much ventilation. What can I do for you?"

"Donny Romano. We've tried to pick him up like you suggested, but we can't find him. Any idea where he might've gone?"

I laughed. "You're not the only one looking for him." I went on to describe what he'd most certainly done to Gloria Talbot and my most recent conversation with Clete Bower.

"Donny sounds like a real, all-around dirtbag," Kohler said when I finished. "But Talbot and Bower have to play nice with him, because they put him up to the photo heist?"

"That's my take on it. That much money just gathering dust on a wall was too much temptation."

Kohler smiled. "Sounds about right. In any case, I finally got all the missing photographs entered into the National Stolen Art File. Fencing them is going to be even tougher now and sure as hell no job for amateurs."

"What about FBI involvement?" I said, knowing their help wasn't always welcome by local jurisdictions. "They have dedicated resources for art theft, right?"

"Yep, it's called the Art Crime Team. I'm getting pressure from the Chief to contact them, but I'm pushing back. I think it's a bit premature. I heard you were a prosecutor down in LA, so you know the drill with the FBI—we'll do all the leg work, and they'll steal the glory."

I laughed at that. "Maybe we can beat them to the punch."

"My thought exactly."

—//—

After I finished my lunch, I called Spectro Systems and asked for Eric Trenton. "Why should I talk to you again?" he shot back after I identified myself.

"Because one of Gloria Talbot's ex-lovers is probably looking for you, Eric. He doesn't like it that you're screwing around with her, and he's a jealous, violent man."

"How did you—"

"That's not the critical issue here," I cut in, "and my sources are none of your business."

"Is that what happened to her?" he asked, his tone a mixture of fear and anger. "Did this guy do that to her? She told me she fell in the shower."

"That was his doing, and he's probably saving his best for you."

"What's his name?"

When I didn't answer, he finally said, "Okay, I'll meet you at the same coffee shop at three thirty."

After we disconnected, I sat there feeling a little guilty, like I might've just bashed the young man's illusions. Was Eric Trenton an innocent, love-struck bystander, a boy toy for Gloria Talbot? It was easy to cast him in that role. On the other hand, he certainly had the brains and physical strength to have pulled off the choke, and he certainly could have driven the truck that killed Wanda Jenkins, not to mention the Jeep that nearly took Arch and me out.

CHAPTER THIRTY-SIX

JUST AS I LEFT TO MEET ERIC TRENTON, A GAP IN THE latest front provided a welcome sun break. The city looked like it had been power washed, and as I made my way down the Naito Parkway, sunlight glittered on the river like freshly minted coins. It was Friday, so the traffic heading south on I-5 was already jammed with commuters, intent on getting an early start on the weekend, to say nothing of the trucks that clogged the center lane as they jockeyed to pass one another.

Eric Trenton was already sitting at one of three wrought iron tables in front of the bakery when Archie and I arrived. I cracked the car windows and left a disappointed dog in the car. Trenton sat up straight in his chair as he tracked my approach, his stainless-steel water bottle at his elbow to insure adequate hydration. I imagined him sitting in the front row of a Princeton lecture hall with the same eager beaver posture and the water bottle sitting there like a pacifier stand-in.

A young waitress appeared just as I sat down. She took our orders—a coffee and blueberry scone for me and a lemon tea for Trenton. He wore chinos, a tailored Oxford shirt, and a tasteful, black and gold paisley tie. His glasses were new—rectangular with tortoiseshell rims—which did wonders for his owlish appearance. All in all, a considerable upgrade from the last time we met. He was Spectro System's new Principal Scientist, after all.

Skipping the small talk, he said, "So who's this guy who's supposed to be after me?" His look was dismissive, his tone skeptical. "I talked to Gloria. She says you're full of shit, Claxton. She fell in the shower."

I laughed at that, knowing full well he didn't believe her. I could see the worry in his magnified eyes and the tenseness along his jawline. "His name's Donny Romano. He's Malcolm Bainbridge's nephew. His affair with Gloria broke up their marriage." Eric's dismissive façade crumbled. "He beat her up and left her bloodied because of you. This is the woman he idolizes. Imagine what he'd do to you, her current lover."

"*That* guy? Mal's nephew?" he said, dropping all pretense.

I smiled. "You've had the pleasure, I see. Yeah, that guy. He's evading the police right now, but you need to watch your back. No telling when or where he'll resurface."

"Why is Gloria protecting him?"

I paused, thinking this guy's either clean or one hell of an actor. "Look, Eric, you're swimming with sharks," I said and went on to give him my take on the Ansel Adams photo theft. "Do you know anything about that?" I asked when I finished.

Eric's eyes enlarged as he started to speak, but that's when our order arrived. After the waitress left, he sipped his tea and looked up at me, his face a shade paler. "I, uh, I don't know anything about the theft. And it sounds like you don't have any real proof."

"Oh, come on, Eric. You mean there was no pillow talk

between you and Gloria about the valuable photos that were stolen out of Bainbridge's home?"

He swallowed and raised his chin slightly. "If there's something going on, Gloria isn't part of it. She wouldn't get involved in something like that."

I lowered my brows in a skeptical look.

"Okay, she might've corroborated Donny's story that he was promised the pictures, but how do you know that's not true? I mean Bainbridge was an erratic guy."

I leaned forward. "Are you suggesting Donny might've taken the photos?"

He swallowed again and avoided my gaze. "I didn't say that."

I leaned back and studied him. "What are you hiding, Eric?" When he didn't answer, I decided to up the ante, pointing to the left side of my face as anger boiled up inside me. "See this? Somebody tried to run me and my dog down, the same person who ran down the housekeeper, the same person who murdered Malcolm Bainbridge. If you know something about this, you'd better start talking. You could be in as much danger as I am."

I didn't think his eyes could get any larger behind his thick lenses, but they did. He paused and looked past me as if turning something over, something weighty. "This is crazy," he said finally. "I don't know anything. You sound paranoid to me."

I kept my eyes on him. "I don't believe you. Look, I can understand you don't want to talk to an attorney like me. That makes perfect sense. Maybe you'd be more comfortable talking to the Portland police?" When he didn't object, I fished my wallet out, extracted a business card, and after looking up a number on my phone, wrote it on the back of the card.

"This is Captain Harmon Scott's personal number. He's a good man. You can talk to him in confidence. Tell him you got the number from me." I extended my arm, offering the card to him. "There are sharks in the water, Eric."

"I don't know anything," he repeated. I kept my arm extended. He looked down at the card for a few moments while I held my breath, and then he took it. He stood abruptly, grabbed his water bottle, and left without saying another word.

I finished my coffee, paid the bill, and left the scone, which must have been at least three days old. When I got to the privacy of my car, I called Harmon. "This guy knows something about Bainbridge's murder, Harmon," I said after explaining what had just gone down. "He's conflicted about something but wants to talk...just not to me."

"He'd better give me something good," Harmon said. "Otherwise, you're on my permanent shit list for giving out my personal cell phone number."

"I know, I know. I'm sorry about that. I wanted to give him a sense that his call would be safe, you know. And I wanted to make sure he'd get through to you. This is big, Harmon, I can feel it in my bones."

"Yeah, well, my number better not show up on some social media platform."

"That's not likely," was all I could counter with. Harmon had a point. I'd crossed a line in my zeal. It wasn't the first time, and it probably wouldn't be the last.

CHAPTER THIRTY-SEVEN

HEADING BACK TOWARDS THE I-5, I COULD SEE THE southbound traffic had gone from bad to worse. Since Zoe was in the hospital, I had no burning desire to return to Dundee, so I took the north on-ramp and drove back to Caffeine Central. Archie and I could run the river and spend a solitary evening in the apartment, which would give me a badly needed chance to unwind.

But as I was changing into my running gear Willow called and announced excitedly, "I just got off the phone with an old friend of Donny's. Turns out he hates Donny's guts now, but they were tight a few years back. He told me Donny had access to a cabin near St. Helens. The cabin belongs to some distant cousin on his mother's side. Donny isn't supposed to have a key, but he does. What a shocker."

I waited for her to continue.

"Anyway, they used to take girls there on the weekends to party. The guy didn't have an address, but he told me how to find the place. He said if Donny needed to disappear, that's where he'd go."

"Excellent work, Willow. Can you text me the directions?"

"I want to come," she said emphatically. "This might be where he stashed the Ansel Adams photographs. You can follow me and Tater. I'll meet you at Caffeine Central in fifteen minutes, okay?"

There didn't seem to be any point in arguing, but I did extract a promise that she would stay clear once she showed me the cabin.

—//—

Named for its view of the volcano that famously blew its top in the eighties, the small town of St. Helens lay thirty miles from Portland on a leg of the Columbia River that juts north before heading west to the Pacific. We took Route 30—the Columbia River Highway—and headed north before turning off at Fox Creek Road, a few miles past town. I followed Willow on the narrow road that swept a broad curve before paralleling the river. After a couple of miles, she pulled over at a driveway marked by a mailbox listing at twenty degrees. Rutted and unpaved, the drive traced a long, lazy bend before bisecting a row of poplars that served to block the view of what lay on the other side.

"This is it," she said when I approached her car. "The cabin's back there somewhere, right on the river."

"Okay. I'm going to walk in and check it out."

"I'm not afraid of him," she said.

"I know, but you agreed to wait here with Tater, right?"

She nodded with a sour look. "This is where he stashed the pictures. I just know it."

I started down the driveway, wishing my Glock 17 was tucked in my waistband instead of sitting in my closet at the Aerie. The damn gun never seemed to be around when I needed it. Once I cleared the poplars, the cabin came into view, a single-story structure with a pitched roof, a railed-in porch running its width, and a carport sans automobile. The cabin needed paint, and its roof was more moss than shingles. Behind the cabin, gold-tinged light reflected off the Columbia, and across the water a flat-topped Mt. Saint Helens dominated the horizon forty miles to the northeast.

No one answered when I rapped on the door, and what little I could see through curtains and shades suggested no one had been there recently. A path behind the house led down to a dock with an attached boathouse. I scrubbed enough grime off the window in the boathouse door to see it contained an aluminum fishing boat equipped with an outboard motor, a couple of gas cans, some foul weather gear, and nothing much else.

A toolshed on the west edge of the property caught my eye. The door was padlocked, and the lock—a brass Master Lock with a four-digit combination—looked brand new. And when I circled back around the house, I noticed what looked like reasonably fresh tire marks in a low, soddened spot in the driveway.

"We can go back to St. Helens and buy a bolt cutter," Willow said after I described what I'd found. Her eyes were big, her jaw set in defiant determination.

I had to laugh. "No, that would literally be breaking and entering, and we're not going to do that. I'm as interested as you are, Willow, but we don't know who put that lock there or why. I'll call Detective Kohler right now. Maybe he can get a judge to sign a search warrant." I didn't think he'd prevail, but I kept my doubts to myself.

Kohler was interested, of course, but non-committal on the chances of getting the warrant. When I clicked off, Willow gave me a look. "That didn't sound encouraging.

What if Donny comes back and cleans out the shed while we're sitting around debating this?"

"That's a risk," I admitted, "but Donny doesn't know that we know, so if the pictures are here, he won't move them until he has a buyer. That could take a long time. There's a good chance the cops will pick him up, too, and now Kohler's got something solid to question him about."

"Okay," she said, "but it's frustrating to think those photos are sitting in some dirty shed out here in the middle of nowhere. What if the roof leaks?"

"The roof looked fine to me. Remember, Donny has a vested interest in protecting the pictures."

"Yeah, that's true, I guess." She focused on something in the distance behind me and sighed. "I sorta get Donny taking the pictures. I mean, it's about me as much as it is about the money, you know, his jealousy and all. The pictures were such a bond between Uncle Mal and me. But I can't get my head around him being a suspect in the murder." Her eyes brightened with a film of tears. "Now, seeing this and hearing about what he did to Gloria, it makes me wonder. Do you think he could have done it? Do you think he could have killed his own uncle and all the rest of it?"

"Most murders are committed by relatives or close friends of the victim. Donny has a strong motive, he learned some MMA moves from Gloria, and his alibi is a Blazer's game that he may or may not have attended. So, yeah, he's still a suspect in my book." I met her eyes. "The question is, does he have the smarts to have pulled off a nearly perfect murder?"

Willow held my gaze. "Maybe he's smarter than we think?"

"Point taken."

CHAPTER THIRTY-EIGHT

"MS. BENNETT'S STILL HOLDING HER OWN, MR. CLAXTON," Gertie's hospital contact told me the next morning. "Be thankful for that. This virus wants to attack the air sacs in the lungs. As the body fights it, the lungs can become highly inflamed and less able to swap carbon dioxide for oxygen. That's when the trouble starts."

My chest tightened as she said this. "How are her lungs?"

"She has pneumonia, but she only needs oxygen intermittently. That's a good thing. She's strong and was obviously never a smoker. She's also the most popular patient in the PCU," she added, her voice softening. "All the nurses just love her."

"No surprise there," I managed to say as a golf ball-sized lump formed in my throat.

After disconnecting, I looked over at Archie, whose coppery eyes were ablaze with expectation. It was Saturday, and Saturday always meant a long run.

"I hear you," I told him. "But I've got to make a call first."

Esperanza Oliva answered on the first ring. "Hello Cal," she said. "I had you on my list of people to contact today."

"Sounds like you're working on a Saturday. You're supposed to be playing while the cat's away."

She laughed. "It's just the opposite, one thing after

another, and you know how careless Nando is with keeping his phone charged. Half the time, I can't reach him."

"When's he coming home?"

"Oh, don't get me started. His original return flight was cancelled without any explanation. I'm trying to rebook him now. The virus has disrupted everything, and the airlines and the Cuban government don't seem to be talking to each other. It's utter chaos over there."

"He's being careful about the virus, right?"

"I hope so, but when have you known Nando to be careful?"

"Good point. Tell him to remember he's not superman. Tell him I said that." She laughed again, and I asked, "Any word on Benny Boykin's condition?"

"Yes, I spoke to my cousin yesterday. Basically, no change—he's still being ventilated, and the prognosis remains poor. They're doing everything they can to save him."

I felt a pang of sadness, followed by a sharp stab of disappointment. "I don't suppose there's any way I could talk to—"

"Not a chance, Cal. I already asked that."

"I hear you."

After a brisk run up to the Marquam Bridge and back, I was down in the office checking my email and getting the latest Covid 19 updates from the *The Oregonian* and *The New York Times*. Despite having my "Closed" sign out, someone wrapped at the Couch Street door. It was my accountant, Gertrude Johnson.

"You weren't at the Aerie this morning, so I figured you must be here," she said when I opened the door.

I invited her in, and after she sat down, I said, "You're on your monthly trip to buy books, right?" Gertie was a voracious reader and strong supporter of one of Portland's iconic businesses, Powell's Books, just a few blocks away.

"I like the free parking," she quipped with a smile. But the smile quickly faded, and she sighed deeply. "Zoe's no better, Cal. I know, the news could be a helluva lot worse, but damn, I was hoping she'd be out of the hospital by now."

"Me, too."

She swiped a tear and eyed me. "I saw the way you two looked at each other when she went by on that gurney," Gertie said. "At least there's that, that you two knuckleheads have finally figured out how much you mean to each other."

I hope it's not too late, I said to myself. To Gertie, "Yeah, I think we finally crossed the Rubicon, at least I did." She smiled at that, and I asked, "Are her parents coming to Portland?"

Gertie puffed out a breath in disgust. "They're stuck in Budapest on a river boat that's had an outbreak. Quarantined. The Europeans aren't screwing around with Covid. Zoe's their only child. They're frantic. I have to talk them off the ledge every day."

I thought of Nielsen's warning about the looming pandemic but didn't say anything. My friend didn't need anything else to worry about. Instead, I opened my desk and withdrew one of the N-95 masks Stuart Burgess had given me. "Here, wear this when you're at Powell's today. It's a high-quality mask."

She waved a dismissive hand. "Oh, I don't—"

"Dammit Gertie, listen to me. You're recovering from a heart attack, which puts you at risk if you contract the virus. I just read about that this morning. Wear the mask or don't go shopping. *Please*."

We went another couple of rounds until she finally

promised to wear the N-95. My dear friend was as stubborn as I was, but once I extracted a promise, I knew she'd keep it.

—/ /—

Around mid-day I got restless, so I loaded Arch in the car and headed to Spectro Systems to see if Bradley Nielsen was in his office on a Saturday. At least one thing had distilled from my morning run—I had more questions for the CEO of Spectro Systems. I didn't call ahead, gambling again that I'd catch him unscripted. His black Audi was in the parking lot, and the main entrance to the building was open. Before I could ask the receptionist to see him, he came through the massive double doors leading into the interior of the building.

"Hello, Bradley," I said. "I just popped in to see if we could chat for a few minutes. I've got some new information to share with you."

He stopped and regarded me for a moment. Then he surprised me. "I'm stepping out for a quick bite. I suppose we could talk then. I was going to go to the little bakery down the street, unless you know a better spot."

I thought of the inedible blueberry scone from my meeting with Eric Trenton. "If you like Northwest cuisine with a French accent, I know a great little food cart. And we can eat outside under a tent."

With a flourish he said, "Lead the way."

—/ /—

"It's all French today," Willow said when I asked about the cassoulet she was offering for lunch. "Made it last night—white beans, pork shoulder, and duck leg confit. Hearty French peasant food." She was wearing an N-95 mask, but her eyes told me she was smiling. She nodded slightly toward the customers behind me, who were more or less observing a socially distanced six-foot separation, some masked, most not. "Lunching with Bradley Nielsen, I see," she said in a conspiratorial voice, her eyes now curious.

"Working lunch."

"Where's Archie?"

"Snoozing in the car."

"Where's Tater?"

"Snoozing in the back."

It had begun to drizzle, but the area under the Cartopia tent was warm and dry. Nielsen and I took our seats in an isolated corner. He looked around at the sparsely populated space. "I've heard this pod's exceptional. Looks like Covid's taking a toll."

"It is. This is the smallest lunch crowd I've seen here."

He took a bite of his cassoulet and leaned back in his chair. "Goddamn, this is *delicious*. Mal's niece can cook as good as she looks." He shot me a lascivious look. "What a sweet little thing, huh?"

Thing? I let the inappropriate comment slide. "I'm curious about your take on the virus."

He frowned, deepening the furrows in his broad forehead. "I just spoke to a contact at the CDC yesterday. He says the WHO is about to declare a pandemic. That's a big deal. It means we have a runaway global problem."

"But good for business?"

"Yeah, Endeavor's going to clean up, but I'm glad to be out from under."

And glad to be richer than Midas, I thought but didn't say. "I'm curious, what's your take on the situation here in the US?"

His demeanor turned grim, which didn't take much effort. "We're not likely to respond aggressively enough because of the upcoming election. It could get ugly."

Surprised, I said, "Last time we spoke you were bullish on our ability to contain the virus."

"We have the technical knowhow and resources, but we may lack the political will to do what's necessary. The virus spreads person to person, so the remedy has to involve shutting things down, and our President, well, let's just say he's in denial at the moment."

"I see," I said, but not wishing to go off on a tangent I changed the subject. "I read that you're going to stay on as CEO through the transition, so I thought you'd still be interested in what's coursing through the Spectro Systems rumor mill these days."

A thin smile. "So, the meter's still running?" When I started to respond, he waved me off. "I appreciate it, and I'll cover your time. I want to leave everything in good shape for the new owners." He held the smile, but his narrow eyes were focused on me like a couple of distrustful lasers.

"Eric Trenton has your group managers stirred up," I began. "The complaint is he isn't ready for the top job, that his promotion was premature."

Nielsen waved a dismissive hand. "Eric's the best man for the job. What you're hearing is professional jealousy."

"I hear he's being dictatorial about program direction and resource allocation. He seems desperate to shore up the accuracy of InstaVision20, that false negatives may be an issue."

"Nonsense. I've discussed this with Eric, and I've seen his data. We're in good shape. The world is salivating for a test like this."

"That's reassuring," I said. "The firing of Malcolm's TA, Marsha Coates, has also caused quite a stir. I—"

"She wasn't fired. She left cordially with a settlement."

"And a non-disclosure agreement," I added.

He made another dismissive gesture. "NDAs are standard practice in business. Talk to my lawyers about it."

"So, the missing notebook remains a mystery."

Nielsen rolled his eyes. "We're talking about Mal's notebook. Who knows what he did with the damn thing. He couldn't keep track of his own car keys, for Christ's sake. What else you got?"

"I heard that without the sale your company might go bankrupt. Is that true?"

He paused, a bite of cassoulet midway to his mouth, as his neck flushed red. "That's company confidential." He struggled to regain his composure before adding, "It's a moot point, anyway. We close in a month, and all our bills get paid."

"What if the tests fail? What does that do to the deal?"

He slammed a fist on the table and glared back at me. "That's *not* going to happen. We disclosed all our experimental and clinical data to Endeavor. They liked what they saw and snapped us up before one of their competitors could. It's their risk now."

I put my hands up in mock surrender and smiled. "Don't shoot the messenger. I'm just telling you what's out there." His glare softened and I went on, trying to sound more conciliatory. "Well, you have to feel thankful that you have someone like Eric Trenton to turn to after the loss of your partner. You must have a close working relationship with him."

"I have all the confidence in the world in Eric."

At that point I was tempted to ask him if he knew his golden boy was sleeping with his partner's ex-wife, just to observe his reaction, but I demurred. If Nielsen was the killer, that might put a target on Gloria's back. And, of course, I didn't mention that Eric Trenton had taken Harmon Scott's personal cell phone number from me, although again I would have been interested in Nielsen's reaction to that little tidbit.

Instead, while we finished up our cassoulets and baguettes, I let Nielsen set the direction of the conversation and wound up hearing a little more than I wanted to about his plans for the future, which included buying an island off the coast of Belize and dredging out a harbor suitable for accommodating a one-hundred and fifty-foot yacht.

I wanted to ask him how much is enough, but I knew better than to waste my breath.

As we were leaving, he turned to me with the lascivious grin again and winked. "Just between you and me, does working with Willow come with benefits?"

His words brushed me back like a gust of bad breath. Anger roiled up inside me. "*What?* Is this your version of locker room talk or something?" I squared my shoulders and glared at him, my face hot as a griddle. "You're completely out of bounds here. If you ever suggest something like that to me again, I'll break your jaw. Am I clear?"

He smirked, but I saw a trace of surprise in his eyes, like he actually thought the remark might elicit something other than anger from me. In any case, he turned and walked away without saying another word.

I watched him leave as the heat in my face began to cool. Bradley Nielsen's clearly an asshole, I concluded. The question is, was he a murderer?

CHAPTER THIRTY-NINE

BACK AT THE AERIE THAT AFTERNOON, I GOT A CALL from Detective Kohler telling me he struck out on getting a search warrant for the shed on the Columbia River. "But I'm working with the St. Helens police chief to get a surveillance camera set up on an adjacent property," he went on. "A friend of his owns it. Best I can do."

I told him that was a brilliant idea and found myself wondering why I hadn't thought of it.

The sky above the Red Hills was clear, but a gray, smoke-like veil hanging below a mass of clouds out over the Coast Range told me it was raining there. It was Oregon, after all, and rain in spring was never that far away.

I was on the side porch sipping a *Cara Bella* pinot and grilling a salmon steak while jasmine rice simmered and fresh broccoli steamed on the stove. A good meal generally boosted my spirits, but my effort backfired this time. Grilling on the porch reminded me of one of the first times I'd cooked for Zoe. I smiled at the memory of her almost childlike enthusiasm for the food I prepared, then grew emotional thinking of her in the hospital struggling to breathe.

With my appetite thoroughly blunted, I was easing the salmon off the grill when my cell phone rattled on the table behind me. "Cal? It's Harmon here. What are you up to?"

"Grilling some salmon and planning to get drunk. Why?"

"There's been a murder, the guy you gave my cell phone number to—"

"Eric Trenton?"

"One and the same. Look, this isn't by the book, but any way you could come over here? You know stuff I don't about this case. I'd like you to take a look, tell me what you think. You might see something we'd miss."

"Yeah, I can do that. Where are you?" He gave me Eric Trenton's home address.

I drained my wine, fed Archie, and stashed the whole damn meal in the fridge. Archie lobbied to go with me as I put on my jacket, but I left him behind with a nice bone and strict orders to guard the castle.

—/ /—

Trenton lived just off Vermont Street in Southwest Portland. I got there in twenty-five minutes. Two cruisers with flashing lights, an ME van, and two unmarked cars were parked in front of the house, a modest, two-story bungalow set back on a well-landscaped lot. I was met at the door by Sonny Harper, a veteran detective I'd seen around but didn't know well. When I gave him my name, he handed me a pair of Tyvek booties and nitrile gloves to wear. "Scott's down the hall on the left," he said. Harper's tone and the look in his eyes told me he didn't approve of my presence at their crime scene.

Scott and a woman in a white medical smock were standing in what must have been Trenton's study, judging from the bookshelves, rolltop desk, and black leather couch. I assumed the woman was the assistant medical examiner who'd caught the call. A couple of crime-scene techs were on opposite sides of the room dusting for prints. They were all at least six feet apart, a sign of the times.

Eric Trenton's body lay behind Scott and the assistant ME. He was flat on his back, arms splayed on either side, his glasses in a broken heap next to his head. His face was purplish, and his eyes were open and bulging as they stared at the ceiling. I sucked a quick breath, and my gut twisted in a knot at the sight. On the drive there, I'd gone back and forth with myself about whether I'd done enough to warn Trenton about Donny Romano.

This is not your fault, I told myself again.

Scott turned to me. "Thanks for coming, Cal. I'm short-handed right now, so I'm taking this case." After introducing me to the assistant ME, he went on, "Based on his temperature and some slight lividity, we're estimating time of death at around two-thirty this afternoon. The doc here thinks he was choked to death."

"That's right," she said. "Looks like his trachea was crushed, and he died from asphyxiation. We'll confirm that in the autopsy. I think he was attacked from the rear. Frontal strangulation normally leaves bruises on the back of the neck from the perpetrator's fingers."

My spine tingled a little. "If the attack was from behind using a forearm, it's called an air choke in mixed martial arts. The attacker positions a forearm against the trachea to cut off the air supply to the lungs. Takes a couple of minutes to kill somebody that way." I looked at Scott. "Like I told you, Harmon, I believe Bainbridge was also choked from the rear prior to being shot. In his case, the forearm was positioned on the *side* of his neck where the carotid artery is." I pointed to where mine was located. "A blood choke, and it rendered him unconscious long enough for the killer to stage his suicide."

Scott pushed his lower lip out and nodded. "Interesting possibility."

I chaffed at his lack of enthusiasm, but let it go for the moment and glanced around the room. The books on the shelves were in disarray, drawers of the desk pulled open and papers strewn on the floor.

"Anything appear missing?"

Scott shook the question off. "Nothing obvious. And he has a hundred and sixty dollars in his wallet, a stack of credit cards, and an expensive watch."

"Forced entry?"

"Nope," Scott answered. "Looks like the perp was someone known or someone who presented no threat."

"Mind if I have a quick look around?" I asked. "I won't disturb anything."

"Of course," Scott said, "that's what you're here for. I'll be around when you're ready to talk." He shot me a knowing smile. "You know something already, don't you?"

I didn't react to the comment, but thought, *damn you, Harmon, you read me like a book.* I went quickly through the rest of the downstairs rooms. The only thing of interest I noted was that the back door was unlocked, and the unfenced backyard was connected to the next street over through a vacant lot. The killer could have easily slipped in the back way unnoticed.

The first thing I saw upstairs was that a ladder providing access to an attic space had been pulled down and left in place. I climbed into a semi-finished room Trenton obviously used for storage. Books—most of them texts from his college days—along with personal correspondence and a series of old tax returns had been taken out of labeled boxes and scattered about. I sifted through the mess without seeing anything of interest.

The upstairs bedrooms appeared undisturbed except for the master, where, again, the books in a large bookcase had been rifled through in a seemingly haphazard manner, leaving some upright and others lying flat. A nightstand drawer lay upended on the floor. I skimmed the papers and looked through the books without finding anything. A teapot resting on the nightstand, together with a chipped mug and a Phillip K. Dick novel with a bookmark at the halfway point, conjured up Trenton's ghost, which passed across my heart like a dark shadow.

Confronting the finality of death was always unsettling.

When I came back downstairs, Scott was out on the front porch talking to a burly man sporting tats on both forearms and a thick ponytail trailing out of his Sea Hawks ball cap. I drew within earshot. "So yeah," the man was saying, "it was around two, two-fifteen when I noticed the F-150, because it drove by twice while I was out trimming my front hedge." He pointed down the street. "Turned left at the corner on the second pass."

"Did you get a look at the driver?" Scott asked.

"Nope. Windows were tinted."

"What color was the truck?" I chimed in.

The man looked at me, then back at Scott. "Silver."

Scott thanked him, gave him a card, and instructed him to call if he thought of anything else. Then he turned to me. "Okay, whataya got?"

I raised a hand to slow him down. "First, tell me how you found the body."

"Trenton called this morning, said he wanted to talk to me, but wouldn't name the subject. I told him fine, and we set a time for three-thirty this afternoon. When he didn't show and didn't answer his phone, I sent a patrol car over to check on him, you know, figuring he got cold feet or something. His front door was locked but the back door ajar, so the officers entered and found him."

"I'm pretty sure I know who did this." I went on to tell Scott about Donny Romano, his relationship to the case, and the fact that he'd beaten up Gloria Talbot in a jealous rage over her affair with Trenton. "And he drives a metallic silver Ford F-150," I added.

Scott's poker face didn't change, but his gray cop-eyes were almost smiling. "I need to talk to this young man."

"According to his lawyer, he's in the wind," I said and described what Clete Bower had told me. "He's been missing for a couple of days now. The truck, too."

"We'll see about that," Scott said and immediately called his office and ordered a BOLO alert for Donny. "You can chase down the license number of the F-150," he barked. "Get a picture of him, too, and add it to the notice. I want this guy in custody for questioning ASAP. He must be somewhere in the Northwest. Find the son of a bitch."

At this point, Trenton's covered body passed by us on a gurney and was loaded into the van. Scott turned his attention back to me, with a pen and notebook in his hand. "Give whatever contact information you have for the attorney, Bower, and this *femme fatale*, Gloria whatever her last name is. I'm going to talk to them next." He jotted down the information, returned his ballpoint to his shirt pocket, and cocked his head slightly. "You think this crime's related to the Bainbridge suicide, huh?"

"Looks that way to me. Both attacks came from behind and both have distinctive martial arts signatures. Similar MOs and similar means. What are the chances it's coincidence?"

A thin smile creased Scott's lips. "Now you're going to tell me Donny Romano knows some MMA moves, right?"

"Gloria Talbot told me he's a damn good martial artist."

Scott scratched at his cheek. "Been my experience that people who kill out of jealousy do it frontally, you know, so they can look their victim in the eye, make sure the message is sent. This doesn't fit that. What about the other suspects for your theory of how Bainbridge died?"

"You raise a good point. Turns out Gloria Talbot was an MMA instructor, and Bradley Nielsen was a star student of hers, but neither of them has a motive to kill Trenton, at least that I know of. And neither drives a silver pickup."

"Noted. I'll add this guy Nielsen to my short list for immediate questioning. One other question—any idea what the perp was looking for?"

I thought of Bainbridge's missing notebook, but that was so speculative I just shook my head. He thanked me and we went our separate ways.

—/—

The shock of seeing Eric Trenton's lifeless body stayed with me on the drive back to the Aerie. I'd met with him just the day before, a young scientist with his whole life in front of him. Now he was gone, and with him all he could have contributed to this world. I might have questioned some of his motives, but it seemed a terrible loss.

I brought my thoughts back to the crime. I liked Donny for the Trenton murder, because I knew his temper and had seen what he'd done to Gloria. No way Trenton would have let Donny in his house, so Donny must've surprised him. Would that explain why he used an air choke from the rear instead of a frontal attack, and did it suggest that Donny might indeed be smarter than I thought?

Maybe, but it's not smart to drive by your victim's house a couple of times prior to killing him, if it was, in fact, him that the neighbor saw. And finally, how did I know Donny was working alone? I didn't, of course, and that got me thinking about the possibilities...

Once again, I had more questions than answers. On the bright side, Archie was glad to see me when I got back to the Aerie that night, and I didn't have to prepare dinner, only warm it back up.

CHAPTER FORTY

WILLOW CALLED EARLY THE NEXT MORNING. "SORRY I didn't get back to you last night," she began. "I had a bad day, so I turned off my phone and crashed early. What's up?"

I told her about the murder of Eric Trenton and the fact that Donny was a person of extreme interest to the Portland Police. She heaved a sigh and said more to herself than me, "Jesus, Donny, what's wrong with you?"

"I know, it's a lot to process," I offered. "Rest assured the police are focused on finding him, but you need to be extra cautious right now, okay?"

She sighed and said, "Of course" in a firm voice.

"I've got some questions for you. Would you mind if I dropped by your place or the pod?"

"I'm shut down for a couple of days. My food delivery didn't arrive this morning. Some kind of glitch in the supply chain. My supplier didn't explain, but I think it's a Covid-19 thing. Anyway, the light's really nice today, and I still have a couple of places in the Red Hills to shoot. I could stop by your place if that works?"

I told her it would, adding, "I'll leave the gate open for you."

Before we disconnected, she said, "How's Zoe?" I could hear the trepidation in her voice.

"I checked this morning. She's still on oxygen, a mask

not a ventilator, and she's still in the progressive care unit, *not* the ICU." I let a breath out.

"I've been thinking about her," Willow said, her voice thick with emotion.

"Thanks," I said, deeply touched by her reaction. Willow had never met Zoe, but I knew her words were heartfelt.

—/ /—

Later that morning I was working with murderous intent in my herb garden. Archie was lying off to one side, watching with keen interest. A big, ravenous gopher had moved in overnight to feast on the tender roots of a lemon thyme plant, a discerning gourmand, apparently. I was arming a trap to place in the gopher's tunnel when my damn cell phone went off. I gingerly released the spring on the trap and wiped my dirty hands on my jeans before retrieving the phone from my shirt pocket.

"Cal? This is Bradley, Bradley Nielsen. Got a minute?" I answered in the affirmative, and he sighed heavily. "I got some devastating news last night." He described Eric Trenton's murder and his interview with Harmon Scott. I knew Scott wouldn't have mentioned my role in his investigation, so I had no choice but to feign surprise and shock at the news. "Apparently, Mal's nephew has gone missing," he continued, "but the police have a full court press on to find him. God, I can't imagine that kid doing something so brutal."

"Did you ever meet Donny Romano?" I asked, keeping my tone in the innocent question range.

He hesitated. "Oh, I suppose I did at some social

gathering or other, but to tell the truth, I don't remember him. I assume you've run into him as part of the estate settlement. What's your impression?"

"He's a hothead with a violent temper. Sounds like the police are looking for the right guy."

"Tell me," Nielsen said, "do you know what his connection was to Eric and why he would be motivated to do such a thing? Scott wouldn't tell me shit. In fact, he treated me like I was a suspect or something."

I still saw no reason to connect the dots for him. "That's what cops do in a murder investigation. Don't take it personally," I said, hoping he wouldn't notice I hadn't answered his question.

"Something else came up, too," he continued, his voice developing an edge. "Scott mentioned that Eric had an appointment with him yesterday afternoon to, ah, discuss something important. He asked if I knew anything about that, you know, what was on Eric's mind. Of course, I have no idea what that could have been." He paused. "Would you happen to know anything about that? You've got your ear to the ground at my company, after all."

"No clue," I said. "Trenton's death won't impact the sale of the company, will it? I mean, he was your new Principal Scientist."

"That deal is set," he replied, and I could almost see him salivating over his private island and deep-water yacht port.

"I gather you're confident Trenton had all the skids greased for the InstaVision tests?" I asked next.

"Very confident. We're expecting the first tranche of data in two weeks. Our new owners are going to be delighted."

"When do you close?"

"Three and a half weeks."

After we disconnected, I troweled out the gopher tunnel a bit more, re-armed the trap, and slid it into place, all the while thinking about the call. No question Nielsen was fishing for information, although in all honesty, I couldn't blame him. He was still CEO of Spectro Systems, after all. He would want to know why his Principal Scientist had made an appointment to talk to a Portland Police captain and then got himself murdered.

Still, he asked a lot of questions and sounded anxious for the answers. Too anxious?

But what really caught my attention was Nielsen's seemingly utter lack of emotion about the death of his young protégé. Like some men, was he incapable of expressing what he felt, or did he simply feel nothing? My money was on the latter, and the thought was chilling.

—/ /—

Archie announced Willow's arrival later that afternoon with a single bark. When she got out of her Prius, and it was clear her daughter wasn't with her, Archie stopped wiggling his butt and whimpered a couple of times. After greeting her at a distance, I said, "Where's Tater?"

"She's with a trusted friend." I must have looked surprised because she smiled reassuringly. "Don't worry, she's safe. Molly's practically a recluse, works from home on her computer and orders her food delivered. She knows what happened to Wanda and offered to give me a day off from mothering. I needed it."

I looked down at my dog, then back at her with a mock frown. "Archie and I are crushed."

Wearing hiking attire and a ballcap with *Nevertheless She Persisted* stitched on it, she extracted a backpack from her car. "This is a beautiful place. Mind if I bring my photo gear? Looks like you might have some nice views to the south."

I told her sure, and as she followed me around to the east side of the house I said, "We can sit out here and talk. I'll light the fire pit to keep the chill off."

"Oh, my God, what a stunning view!" she exclaimed. "The vineyards are so, so *orderly*, and there's the Coast Range and the Cascades. Oh, and the valley looks like a quilt my grandmother had on her bed."

"Yep," I said smiling at her enthusiasm. "We look straight down the Willamette Valley, and the view's constantly changing."

"When's bud break?" She smiled. "See, I know the jargon now."

I glanced out at the vista, the grapevines arrayed like teeth in a hairbrush, but still the color of sodden wood. "A few more weeks."

She set her backpack down and extracted a camera and a hefty telephoto lens. After snapping on the lens she began shooting from every possible angle on the porch. When she finished, she aimed her camera at Archie and me. "Smile," she teased. "These are for your Christmas cards this year."

She put her gear away and sat down next to the fire pit, a serious look on her face. "Full disclosure. I drove out to St. Helens this morning to check on the Ansel Adams photographs."

I snapped to attention. "And…?"

"The lock's still there."

"Good. Did you disturb anything?"

"No. I just looked around. I had to know they were still

there." She paused for a moment and shot me a mischievous look that again reminded me of my daughter Claire. "You know, with a duplicate lock and a bolt cutter we could—"

"No, we're not doing that," I said and went on to tell her about the video surveillance arranged by Detective Kohler. "I'll give him a heads up that you've made a cameo appearance."

She smoothed the strands of hair below her cap dramatically. "Gee, if I'd known, I would've done my hair and worn my dress sneakers."

I laughed at that and then changed the subject. "There's a loose end I've been wondering about—did Donny and Bradley Nielsen ever meet or have any sort of relationship that you know of?"

Willow cocked her head and scrunched up her eyebrows. "They were probably at some company events together, but I doubt they had much interaction. Those were always stiff, formal affairs. Everyone stayed in their lane except for Uncle Mal." She paused again, then snapped her fingers. "Oh, yeah, there was one thing I overheard a long time ago. Before Donny started working at the gun shop, he bought a landscape business. I think Uncle Mal helped finance it, but I was in college then and out of touch. Anyway, I think Uncle Mal asked Nielsen to mentor Donny, you know, since Nielsen was good at business." She shook her head and curled her lip. "I overheard Gloria talking about that on the phone a few years ago. Apparently, Donny flew the business into the ground. That's all I know about it."

"Do you remember the name of the company?"

"Stumptown something or other, maybe Stumptown Landscaping." She eyed me. "You think Donny's been doing Nielsen's dirty work?"

"Maybe. Nielsen told me he didn't remember Donny, which struck me as a bit odd. I'd just like to check that out."

"Donny kills Uncle Mal to benefit himself and Nielsen? That I get. Then he turns around and kills this guy Trenton out of jealousy? *Really?*"

"He was certainly jealous," I countered, "but Trenton was set to speak to the police before he was killed." I went on to describe my last conversation with him and the resulting meeting that was planned with Harmon Scott.

"Oh, so Trenton suspected something about Uncle Mal's murder and Nielsen found out. He dispatches Donny to take care of him, which is an easy sell, because Donny's jealous as hell. Is that the deal?"

"Something like that," I said, amazed once again at the quickness of my young client. "But it's just a theory without proof."

"How do we get the proof?

I absently rubbed the back of my neck and scowled. "We need a couple of breaks. The cops need to find Donny, and Benny Boykin needs to get off the ventilator so he can tell us what the hell he knows."

"And something that ties Donny and Nielsen together?" she added.

"That, too."

Our conversation about the case wound down from there. After she'd packed up her camera and was about to leave, I said, "Look, Willow, I know how worried you are about the photographs in St. Helens, but I don't want you going out there again. There are just too many unknowns right now. You need to be careful until we get our hands around this thing."

She folded her arms across her chest and drew her eyebrows in. “Okay.”

I wasn’t sure I believed her.

CHAPTER FORTY-ONE

AFTER WILLOW LEFT TO GO PHOTO SHOOTING, I CALLED Timoteo. He'd taken some time off to study for his midterms. He got paid just the same, because we had an agreement that studying counted as work for me. It was a small incentive and one he never abused. I gave him an update on Zoe next, then said, "How are things at the vineyard?"

He sucked a breath and went on to tell me the trend was not good, that three of his dad's workers were out sick now. We discussed the latest pandemic news without finding anything to be encouraged by. It seemed a perfect storm was gathering for workers who had little or no access to healthcare.

"Interested in a study break tonight?" I asked, finally getting around to the reason for my call. He said he was, so I brought him up to date on the Trenton murder, Donny's disappearance, and my renewed interest in Bradley Nielsen. "Following Nielsen is another long shot," I summed up, "but he seemed antsy. Maybe he'll lead us somewhere in the cover of night."

"Like to Donny Romano?" Timoteo said.

"We should be so lucky."

Timoteo called at ten thirty that night. "No action here, but I got two poly sci chapters read."

I told him to call it quits, and we agreed that he would continue the surveillance for the next three nights.

Hope springs eternal.

—//—

I was in my Dundee office the next morning when Gertie called. "I've got some great news," she said. "Zoe's blood oxygen saturation level has increased from eighty-eight percent to ninety-one percent. She's still on oxygen, but the increase is significant, according to Julia. They might upgrade her condition to fair or even good."

The news brought me out of my chair and spread a silly grin across my face. "That's incredible, Gertie! What else did she say?"

"The normal range is ninety-five to ninety-eight percent, so Zoe's still not where she needs to be. Julia cautioned me, too, Cal. She said there can be fluctuations with this virus."

"Of course," I said, "but I'm taking this as nothing but positive news. Zoe's a fighter like you, Gertie, and she's not going to give up ground she's gained. That's not going to happen." What I said simply burst out of me, but I'd never been more certain of anything in my life.

"Well," Gertie said, her voice cracking, "I hope to God you're right."

Hearing the emotion in my voice, Archie came over to check on me after the call ended. I sat at my desk for I don't know how long, scratching him behind the ears, until a rap at the streetside door interrupted us. It was Clete Bower.

"You drove all the way out here just to see me? I'm honored," I said with deliberate sarcasm. I'd managed to stop him at the doorway by warning that I had a sore throat and a cough, which I didn't.

"Don't flatter yourself," he said with one foot in the door. "I have a court date in McMinnville. I just dropped by to tell you Donny's still AWOL."

I didn't buy the court story, since he needed a shave, and even six feet away smelled faintly of stale cigars. "There's more," he went on. "Gloria was banging some hot-shot scientist at Spectro Systems. He got murdered at his house yesterday, choked to death. The Portland cops want to talk to Donny in the worst way. They raked me over the coals last night, like I was hiding the little bastard or something. Same with Gloria." He fixed me with his squinty eyes. "Know anything about this?"

I feigned a puzzled look. "Why would I? Do you think Donny could have done something like that?"

He shrugged. "I don't have a good feeling about it. The kid's unpredictable, and he's got a low flash point. If he gets in touch, I'm going to tell him to turn himself in."

"That's wise," I said.

He scratched his bent nose and swung his eyes back to me. "Still don't understand how the cops landed on Donny so quick, you know? And how they knew about Gloria and this guy...?" He let the question dangle there in the space between us.

"Phone records, text messages? I said, filling the void. "The cops have their ways. How is Gloria taking this?"

"She's all broken up, like it was her fault or something. I told her that was stupid." He rolled his eyes. "Jesus Christ, I took this gig figuring it was easy money. Get Donny through his uncle's probate and collect a nice fat fee. Now he might wind up with his ass in jail for murder. How's he gonna pay me?"

"If I hear anything, I'll let you know" I said, my tone dismissive. "Good luck on your court case." Bower turned to go, and I added, "One other thing—you told me you and Donny were at a Blazer game the night Bainbridge died. Did Donny stay for the whole game?"

Bower shrugged and said over his shoulder. "I didn't babysit him, for Christ's sake. It's a ball game, you know? You have a few beers and try to move down to better seats at halftime." With that he headed back to his car, his shoulders hunched in dejection.

Since my foul-smelling guest had told me about the murder, I realized I was free to talk to Gloria Talbot without giving away my knowledge of the case. But first Archie needed a walk, and I needed a coffee. We'd crossed the Pacific Highway and were headed up SW 7th when Darcy Tate pulled alongside in an unmarked Newberg-Dundee police cruiser.

"Thought I'd find you here," she said with a knowing smile. "You and that dog of yours are going to wear a groove in the pavement between your office and the Red Hills Market."

Archie whimpered a couple of times and wagged his butt. He liked Darcy as much as I did. I said, "Caffeine and sugar, the two basic food groups."

She laughed. "Just a heads up. That Portland forensics tech you recommended may have come through for us. He found three human hairs in the Jeep that appear to match—at least under a microscope—the ones he found in the truck that killed Wanda Jenkins. There's a small fragment of root material on one of the hairs, so the hope is we can get a DNA profile. We're trying to get priority at the state lab, but you know how slow that can be."

"Told you the two crimes were related," I said in a playful tone. "Seriously, that's great news, Darcy."

"Well, we still won't know if the hairs belong to the perp or the contract car thief."

"Either way, we'll have a leg up," I said. "Make sure Harmon Scott's pushing the state lab, too. He's got some clout there."

She said she would and was on her way.

—/—

"I feel like shit right now. I don't want to talk to anybody," Gloria Talbot said over the phone after Archie and I got back to the office.

"I can understand that, Gloria," I said quickly to avoid her hanging up on me. "I just have a few questions, since I'm involved on the periphery here. The person who killed Eric Trenton needs to be brought to justice." I was walking on eggshells, not knowing for sure whether justice was something she wanted or not. I held my breath.

After a long pause, she sighed heavily. "I can't talk right now. Why don't you meet me at the same bar as last time after I get off work, say around five forty-five. The Haymaker on Killingsworth."

I agreed to the meeting, although I wasn't that crazy about swapping air with bar patrons. Suck it up, I told myself. Gloria could have vital information. After all, I rationalized, the ceilings are high there so the ventilation should be decent.

The Haymaker was sparsely populated, mainly by the serious drinkers every neighborhood bar attracts, the ones tucked up to the rail and focused on their drinks. Gloria waited at a table in the back, unsmiling, her ice-blue eyes guarded but attentive and the stylish tousle in her blond hair combed out. Her lower lip was still swollen, and a halfmoon below her left eye was the color of an eggplant, only faded. She looked older, much older.

I pulled a chair out to increase the space separating us and sat down. "I'm trying to keep a safe distance," I explained. "I don't want—"

"Oh, please," she cut in with an annoyed expression, "Surely you don't believe all the scare tactics we're being fed. This corona virus thing's just another flu. It'll vanish as soon as it warms up."

I forced a smile. "Well, even the flu knocks the hell out of me, so I'm going to keep my distance."

She responded with a smile tinged with pity at my apparent naivete. "You shouldn't believe everything you read."

I let the comment go, saying, "I'm sorry to hear about Eric Trenton's death. It must have been a shock."

Tears welled up in her eyes. "Yeah, you could say that. He was a really sweet guy. He didn't deserve that. Nobody does, I guess."

A young waiter appeared. Gloria ordered a whiskey sour with a straw, and I asked for my usual. When the waiter was out of earshot, I said, "Bower told me you talked to the police last night. Has anything come to light since then, something you might've just thought of?"

She eyed me. "Here you are again, snooping around. I agreed to meet out of curiosity. What's your interest this time?"

I held her gaze. I'd been open with her before and no apparent harm had come of it, so I decided to gamble again. "I think Eric's murder is connected to Bainbridge's death, Wanda Jenkins' hit-and-run, and the attempt on my life. So, it's both professional and personal for me."

She stiffened. "Connected? Like one person did all that?"

"It's possible. What do you—"

The waiter came back, set our drinks down, and then retreated to the bar.

I began again. "What do you think, Gloria? Let's start with Eric's murder. Did Donny kill him?"

She put her head back and closed her eyes, squeezing out tears. "Oh, Christ, I hope not. If he did, it's all my fault." Tears streaked her cheeks. "Donny's so fucking volatile there's no telling what he'll do. I should've known better than to get involved with him in the first place." She swiped the tears from her cheeks with the fingers of both hands.

"Do you know where he is?"

She looked at me through wet eyes and sniffed. "No. And if I did, I'd tell you, believe me. Then she added half to herself, "The hell with the consequences."

I caught her drift. "Do you know where the photos are, Gloria?"

She rolled her eyes.

I took that as a 'no' and changed the subject. "Willow told me Donny had a landscaping business before he started working at the gun shop. Do you remember anything about that?"

She laughed, a single, sarcastic note. "That didn't last long. Donny told too many customers to go screw themselves."

"Willow remembered something about Bradley Nielsen

mentoring Donny at the request of Malcolm. Does that ring a bell?"

"Yeah, Bradley did get involved. You know, advice, that kind of thing. Lord knows, Mal would've been useless as a business advisor."

"Donny and Nielsen spent time together?"

"They did." She managed a weak smile. "I think they talked way more about MMA than business."

"Really. How did that work?"

"Well, they were both into martial arts, you know. By that time, I'd taught Bradley just about everything I knew, and Donny, well, like I told you before, he and I used to spar around. They started working out together. I watched a few times. They were impressive, both of them."

"I understand they don't see each other now. What happened?"

A flush crept across her cheeks. "The divorce happened. I think Mal told Bradley why."

"Oh, so Bradley blamed Donny?"

"I think it was more out of respect for his business partner's feelings than any moral judgment on Bradley's part." She curled a lip. "His only concern is that fucking business." She studied me for a moment. "You think Bradley's involved in this?"

"I'm still gathering facts. I haven't come to any conclusions yet."

Her face hardened. "Well, I wouldn't put it past that mercenary bastard. Having his business partner kill himself just before the business is sold is pretty convenient timing, I'd say."

She'd finished her whiskey sour by then, and when she

picked up her purse I said, "Again, I'm sorry about your loss. You've been a great help today. Thanks."

She stood and looked straight at me. "Well, I'm still waiting for my insurance payout to be approved. You can thank me by putting a good word in with that damn insurance investigator. The little bitch is still dragging her feet." With that, she turned and left.

I shook my head and let a breath out as I watched her go. I'd been on the brink of feeling sorry for Gloria, but her parting comment disabused me of that notion in a hurry. As for Bradley Nielsen, well, he either had early onset Alzheimer's or he was a liar. I was pretty sure which it was.

CHAPTER FORTY-TWO

I WAS STILL WARY OF JOGGING IN THE RED HILLS, SO after leaving the bar I stopped at Caffeine Central, where I had sweats and a pair of Asics stashed. A run along the river was just what Archie and I needed. Thirty minutes later we were heading down the Tom McCall Parkway with Archie out front. The sky had cleared, and in the fading light the river looked like a dark blade slicing through the center of the city. We crossed at the Hawthorne Bridge and were nearly to the Steel Bridge when my phone went off. Archie knew that a call meant a pause in our jog. He pulled up and looked back at me with an annoyed expression.

"Come on, Arch," I said. "You know the drill."

"Cal?" Stuart Burgess said. "Did you hear about Eric Trenton getting murdered?"

"Yes. I was called by the lead detective. He's a friend of mine."

"We just heard about it today from Bradley Nielsen. Everybody's in shock around here. I mean first Dr. Bainbridge and now Dr. Trenton. Both dead. Maybe this company's cursed or something. Do the cops know who did it?"

"It's an ongoing investigation."

"The real reason I called is that Eric Trenton's TA, a guy named Charlie Givens, cornered me in the parking lot this afternoon and asked me if I knew a lawyer, you know, someone he could go to and trust. Charlie's not real popular around here since he got a big promotion after Trenton became Principal Scientist."

"Why did he come to you?"

"Well, I haven't talked any shit about him, and I guess he knows it. I figured Charlie was at the right place at the right time, could've happened to any one of us TAs. Anyway, I told him he should talk to you, that what he told you would be confidential and that you'd be able to steer him in the right direction."

"Good," I said. "Do you know what's on his mind?"

"He wouldn't say, but it's obviously something about Trenton's death. He was totally freaked out about the murder. He wants to talk to you, like tonight if possible."

I glanced at my Fitbit. "Okay, give him the Caffeine Central address and tell him to meet me there at seven. Tell him to wear a mask."

"I won't have to."

—/ /—

Charlie Givens arrived at six fifty-five. Mid-forties, he was tall with salt and pepper hair, an angular face, and dark, watchful eyes. He entered my office wearing an N-95 mask. Archie watched from the corner as we exchanged introductions, and I offered him a seat. "Thanks for wearing a mask," I said.

A curt nod. "I'd be an idiot not to. I see you're wearing one, too. They're hard to come by these days."

I got right to the point. "So, how can I help you, Charlie?"

He leaned forward, clamping a hand on each thigh. "I, ah, need some legal advice. Stuart Burgess said you were a good man, that you might be able to help." His eyes had grown anxious.

"I'll be glad to help you if I can. Why don't you describe the situation, and we'll go from there?"

He leaned back and tugged absently at one side of his mask. "Well, it was two days after Dr. Bainbridge died. My boss, Eric Trenton, called me into his office and shut the door. He, ah, he asked me if I knew the location of Dr. Bainbridge's laboratory notebook, the most recent one he was using to record his work on InstaVision. I told him I did, and he said, 'I want you to bring the notebook to me, and don't let anyone see you do it. Can you do that?' I said I probably could—"

"Did Trenton give you a reason for the request?"

"Yes, he said that our CEO, Bradley Nielsen, had requested it, that I was chosen for the task because I was, ah, trustworthy. He told me it was for the good of the company and that I was absolutely forbidden to mention it to anyone."

"Where was the notebook?"

"It was in Dr. Bainbridge's lab, on a workbench in the back. I knew that because I saw it the day before when I was looking for Marsha Coates, his TA. I'd gone there to express my condolences. She wasn't there, and I later found her holed up in her office. I mean, everyone was so upset by what happened. Anyway, when I went back the next day she was still grieving in her office, and I took the notebook and gave it to Eric."

"Do you know what he did with it?"

Givens shook his head while wringing his hands. "I assume he used it to support the provisional patent he filed and in the technical briefings he gave our new owners, but I don't really know."

I nodded encouragingly. "I see. I'm curious about one thing—Nielsen made a big show of looking for the notebook after Bainbridge's passing. How did you feel about that? I mean, you're the one who took it, and you must have heard about the search at Bainbridge's house and at Spectro Systems."

He wrung his hands some more. "Oh, yeah, I knew about that. I went to Eric and asked him what was going on. He told me not to worry about it. Then he said I was in line for promotion to Senior Lab Technician and a big raise." He lowered his eyes and studied the surface of my desk for a moment. "It was pretty clear that he was buying me off to keep me quiet."

"And you went along with it," I said.

He raised his eyes. "It was a forty percent raise and a new title."

"Why do you think your bosses were so interested in the notebook?"

"Maybe something to do with the patent or the sale of the company. I just don't know."

"That's okay," I said, my tone reassuring. "Why have you come to me now?"

He lowered his gaze again. "What I did feels wrong. I shouldn't have taken the damn thing, and I shouldn't have kept quiet about it. And I'm wondering if I broke any laws?"

I shook my head. "Your immediate boss and the CEO told you to do something, and you did it. It was a breach of ethics, perhaps, not to have spoken up, but you did nothing criminal that I can see. However, if you come forward now,

I can't say how your soon-to-be new management would view your actions."

He brought his eyes back up. They'd morphed from anxious to fearful. "I don't care what Endeavor thinks. The truth is, I'm scared to death. I've heard the rumors about Dr. Bainbridge's death not being a suicide, and now Eric is murdered. I feel like I might be involved in something dangerous, something I don't understand." He swiped his arms like an umpire calling a runner safe. "I don't want any part of this." He paused before adding in a pleading tone, "What do you think I should I do, Mr. Claxton?"

"First of all, Charlie, I think your instincts are right about the possible risks and the need to get this out in the open, and I commend you for your honesty. I'm not your lawyer and I don't think you need representation, but my advice is to go to the Portland Police with your story. I know the lead investigator on the Trenton case and can facilitate this if you want."

"Yes, I'd appreciate that very much."

"One other question," I said. "Do you have any idea, or can you speculate on what Eric Trenton did with the notebook?"

"No. I don't have a clue. He never said a word about it after I gave it to him."

I told Givens I'd be in touch, and when he got up to leave I added, "I don't want to alarm you, but you should be careful until this gets cleared up. Keep your house locked and be alert to anything unusual around you."

I called Harmon Scott immediately after he left my office and related what I'd just learned. "You think that's what the perp was looking for at Trenton's place—a missing scientific notebook?" he asked when I finished. He chuckled, which was out of character. "Sounds like a Nancy Drew mystery."

I ignored his attempt at humor. "Look, Harmon, I don't know how it fits yet, but that notebook could be key. The company was just sold for four hundred and fifty million dollars based on technical information of the type recorded in it. Maybe there was something in there that Trenton and Nielsen didn't want the new buyers to see." I went on to describe what Gloria Talbot had revealed about the relationship between Donny Romano and Bradley Nielsen.

"Nielsen had Romano throttle Trenton to keep him quiet about something in the notebook? Is that what you're saying?"

"Why else would Nielsen lie to me about not knowing Romano?"

"Maybe Nielsen didn't like the optics of being associated with the guy who killed his star employee, but okay, get Givens in to see me ASAP. Meanwhile, let me see what I can do about going back to look for that damn notebook. Chances are the perp found it, but I guess it wouldn't hurt to have another look."

"Agreed," I said, then added, "How did the interviews go with Talbot, Bower, and Nielsen?"

He puffed a dismissive breath. "Nobody knows a thing about Donny Romano's whereabouts or anything else remotely useful to the investigation. When I got around to asking where they were at the time of the murder, Nielsen and Bower got all huffy, like how dare you? It turned out Gloria Talbot has the best alibi. She was working. Nielsen was home with his wife, and Bower was at his one-man law office."

"At home with his wife, huh? That's what Nielsen told me when I asked him about the Bainbridge suicide. And

I have it on good authority his wife is firmly under his thumb."

"Oh, so Nielsen could have throttled both of them?"

"That's a possibility. He certainly has the martial art chops." I had to chuckle. "Hey, I never said this case was going to be easy."

"Yeah, thanks," Scott said, "but I still like our boy Donny for Trenton's murder."

"No sign of him, I take it?"

"Nada."

"What about the crime scene? Find anything interesting?"

"A few fingerprints we need to check out, but that's about all."

"No human hairs?"

"No hairs."

After we disconnected, I sat back in my chair to reflect for a few moments. Notwithstanding Donny's fugitive status and the alibis of his possible accomplices, I felt like the case finally had some forward momentum. It was a welcome feeling.

Back at the Aerie that night, I got out to open the gate. Archie followed and as was his habit, went racing into the darkness, barking at deer I knew were there but couldn't see. I got back in the car, and as I started down the driveway a great horned owl swooped out of nowhere, as if to guide me in. Its wingspan was easily four feet, and as it became illuminated in my headlights, I could see the horizontal bars on its breast and its stark white throat patch. The apex predator glided in front of me before flying off just before I reached my garage.

I got out of my car with my heart racing. This was the creature who'd serenaded Zoe and me so often, but he'd never shown himself until now.

After herding the deer, Archie joined me as I entered the house. "You missed it," I told him. "I'm taking it as a good omen, Big Boy." He cocked his head with the equivalent of a doggie shrug. I didn't really believe in omens, but I was left with a positive, if apprehensive, feeling in my gut I couldn't shake. Things were moving.

CHAPTER FORTY-THREE

I WAS TIRED BUT FAMISHED, SO AFTER FEEDING ARCHIE I peeled and grated some potatoes, dried them with a paper towel, and pressed them down in a skillet with hot oil. When they were crispy brown, I flipped them over, dropped a couple of eggs on top, and put a lid on the skillet until the eggs were done—a quick and dirty version of Swiss rösti. I got out a jar of local honey, toasted up a couple of pieces of Dave's Killer Bread, and ate the entire meal with gusto.

I cleaned up the kitchen and went into the study to check the news online. Bradley Nielsen was right about the virus—a guy named Tedros Ghebreyesus, Director General of the World Health Organization, had just officially declared Covid-19 a pandemic and said at a briefing in Geneva that the agency was "deeply concerned by the alarming levels of spread and severity." In Oregon, cases were climbing, and in response the governor issued new guidelines restricting visitation at long-term care facilities. No question about it, the outbreak was gaining momentum.

This won't make the investigation any easier, I told myself.

I finished with the news and was reading through my email when Timoteo called. "Nielsen came through his automated gate tonight in his Lexus, and guess what? He drove straight to Gloria Talbot's place, parked right in front, and she let him in."

"Is he still there?" I asked, feeling a jolt of concern for Gloria.

"Nope. He stayed for twenty-eight minutes, then came out and drove back to his estate. I saw her at the door when he left, so no worries about her safety."

"Good," I said with relief. There was a lot I didn't like about Gloria, but at the same time I admired the grit and toughness that lay beneath her vulnerability.

"That's an interesting move on Nielsen's part," Timoteo said. "What do you think?"

"I'm not sure what to think. They know each other, of course, but I wasn't aware of any current connection between them. I've been working on the assumption that Gloria's not a part of the murders, but I could be wrong." We kicked the possibilities around for a while, but finally I told Timoteo to go home and get some sleep.

"Should I keep following Nielsen?"

I turned the question over for a few moments. "Stay on him the rest of this week, and Timoteo, don't let your guard down for a second."

After we disconnected, I leashed up Archie, but not before loading my Glock and placing it in my waistband. He needed a walk and I needed to think. We were halfway to the gate when Gloria Talbot's name lit up my cell phone screen. "I'll be damned," I said before answering.

"I thought you might be interested to hear that I just had a surprise visitor, Bradley Nielsen," she began. "He stopped by to offer his condolences for what happened to Eric, said he'd been contacted by the police same as me."

"He knew about your relationship with Eric?"

"Apparently everybody in Portland does. Anyway, he said he was very fond of Eric, and we talked for a while about him." She paused and said in a softer voice, "It was kind of sweet, even though I didn't buy his sincerity for a millisecond."

"I see," I said, waiting for her to get to the point of the call. I knew she had one.

"He told me the cops suspected Donny, and I said I knew that. He asked if I thought Donny had done it. I wasn't going to tell him what happened between Donny and me, so I just said I didn't know, that I hadn't seen Donny lately." I waited and she went on, "Then he says something like, 'Did Eric ever mention a scientific notebook, one that's important to that invention he was working on, you know, the rapid Covid test?' He said it innocently, but the urgency in his eyes kind of scared me. He wants that notebook, and that's why he came to see me."

"What did you tell him?"

"I told him no, he never mentioned anything like that."

"Is that true, Gloria?"

The line went quiet for what seemed an age. Finally, "Eric did mention something. He said he took Mal's notebook after he died to make sure he got the patent and not Mal. It was pillow talk one night. You know how that goes. Later, he told me he was having second thoughts about it, like he'd done the wrong thing."

"Do you have any idea what he did with the notebook?"

"He never said, but I'm sure he kept it. At the end of the day, I think he respected Mal a lot and couldn't bring himself to destroy the record of his work." She sighed deeply. "I called you because for some damn reason I feel like I can trust you, and I'm worried Bradley thinks I know where the notebook is."

"Why are you worried?"

"People are dying, and people are missing. What do you expect?"

Was she telling the truth? Once again, my gut said yes. "Okay. I advise you to get in touch with Captain Scott and tell him about the visit and Bradley Nielsen's relationship with Donny right away." *And so will I*, I thought but didn't say.

She sighed again. "The cops worry me almost as much as Bradley. I don't want to get blamed for stealing those goddamn photographs. That was Donny and Bower's idea. All I agreed to do was back up Donny's story, which was a stupid mistake on my part."

"I figured that out a long time ago, Gloria. Don't worry about the Ansel Adams collection. Much bigger fish are frying here."

"Well, if Bradley put Donny up to killing Eric, I want them both to burn for it." She paused for a moment. "Oh, mother of God, that means they also killed Mal, his housekeeper, and damn near got you. You're right. That's some big fish."

We ended on that note. I turned around and headed back. The moon was full enough that I was casting a shadow, and when I was almost to the house, my friend the owl gave me a four-note salute from high up in one of my Douglas firs. Maybe I was right about his flyover being an omen of the good kind.

I felt like jumping up and clicking my heals. Bradley Nielsen and Donny Romano were looking good as suspects. Now all I needed now was hard evidence.

CHAPTER FORTY-FOUR

"DAMMIT, CAL, I HAVEN'T GOTTEN AROUND TO IT YET," Harmon Scott told me the next morning. "I can't just drop everything and go search Trenton's place for that notebook." He coughed and excused himself before continuing. "We already gave the house a going over and removed the crime scene tape."

"Come on, Harmon, you said it wouldn't hurt to have another look," I countered. "You were keying on his computer and his personal correspondence the first time, not a specific *object*, something he might've kept well hidden. That notebook might give you probable cause to get a search warrant for Nielsen's home and office."

"Yeah, and I'll probably win the lottery today, too," he said, then coughed again, a rasping sound that alarmed me.

"Are you okay?" I asked.

"Yeah, I'm fine," he said in an irritated tone. "Just a little scratchiness. Okay, I'll get the search done. Stay tuned."

"I will, and Harmon, that's a nasty cough. Maybe you should get a Covid-19 test."

"I'm fine."

I checked on Zoe's condition next. She'd been upgraded to "good." I was ecstatic. "If she's in good condition, when can she come home?" I asked the attendant.

"I don't have that information, sir, but the indications are favorable. She's made a surprising turn-around."

"Can I talk to her?"

"She's still in the PCU, which isn't phone accessible. Try again tomorrow."

I tapped out of the call and looked over at Archie, pumped a fist, and shouted "YES!"

He sprang to his feet and followed suit with a flurry of ear-splitting barks that roughly translated to, 'Whatever it is, count me in."

After calling Gertie with the good news, I got a prodigious amount of work done that morning, including filing a brief in a lawsuit that was soon to be litigated, taking on a DUI case involving the pastor of a Baptist church in McMinnville, and conferencing by Zoom with Phoebe Tyson, my soon-to-be-divorced client.

Phoebe appeared on my screen wearing an unusually bright smile, the bas relief of the two Khmer warriors in its usual place on the wall behind her. Had it only been two weeks since that image triggered the first breakthrough in this case? Hard to believe.

After we exchanged greetings, she said, "I have a surprise." With that, a much younger man with dark wavy hair and a dimpled chin came within camera range, draped his arms around Phoebe possessively and kissed her on the cheek. "This is my husband, Arnold." He looked into the camera and smiled. It might have been me, but I thought the smile had a tinge of smugness.

"We're back together," Phoebe said, "I won't be needing your services any longer."

"That's right," Arnold chimed in, staring back at me, the smugness now impossible to miss.

I wished the happy couple the very best, signed off, and left a note for Timoteo to prepare a bill. *All's well that ends well,* I told myself, although I had a feeling I might be seeing Phoebe Tyson again.

—/—

The call came in late that afternoon from a local number my phone didn't recognize, so I had no inkling. "Cal? It's Zoe. Can you come get me?"

I was stunned into silence for a couple of beats. *"Now?* Come get you *now?"* I finally stammered.

"Yes, now," she answered, and I could picture her amused expression from the tone of her voice. "They wanted to keep me another night, but I convinced Doctor Hidalgo to let me go. I'm the miracle patient around here. Can't wait to see you."

"Me, too," I said. "I'll be right there."

"Bring Archie, okay? They said you should pull up to the main entrance, and they'll bring me out."

"Of course. Shall I call Gertie?"

"Let's wait until I get situated. I'll need to be isolated for ten days or so."

I drove into the hospital parking lot in Newberg fifteen minutes later. As I pulled up, the entrance doors opened and out came Zoe in a wheelchair. My heart did a backflip. She was accompanied by several beaming nurses, who had come to say goodbye to someone they obviously cared about.

Behind the mask, Zoe's face was pale, but her deep blue eyes were radiant. Her hair was covered with a scarf one of the nurses must have given her. I jumped out of the car, and my mask could barely contain my smile. I wanted to gather her up and never let her go. "You look great," I said.

Her eyes smiled back. "So do you," she answered as her eyes locked onto mine. "I want to go home."

"Consider it done."

She introduced me to the nurses as if they were her best friends. I was handed a list of aftercare instructions and watched as they said their heartfelt goodbyes. I thanked them all and helped Zoe get into the back seat with Archie. His butt wags, whimpers, and doggie kisses made it clear how much she was missed.

We agreed that it made sense for Zoe to isolate in my guest bedroom until she felt ready to move back into her place. Refusing my help, she took the stairs up to the bedroom slowly but with determination. She made a list of needed items, and I went to her house and packed a bag for her. I was low on provisions, as usual, but I had a couple of cans of cannellini beans and chicken stock along with some onions, carrots, celery, and chard, so I whipped up a big batch of white bean soup for that first night. When I took a tray into her, she was in bed after showering. She'd blown her ash blond hair dry, and it lay curled on her shoulders smelling faintly of lavender.

My heart swelled in my chest.

"That was the best shower I've ever taken in my life," she quipped as I set the tray down on her night stand and backed away. "Thanks. I'm hungry, but my sense of taste isn't all the way back yet."

"No worries," I said. "The nurse said it could take some time." I stood in the doorway watching her eat. She looked at me and cocked her head slightly. "Don't mind me," I said. "I just want to be here, you know, to see you, to talk."

"Me, too," she said, "but no closer. You don't ever want this virus, believe me." She took a sip of soup and rolled her eyes toward the ceiling. "Oh, God, this is delicious, Cal." She ate in silence for a while before leveling her gaze at me. "How did you scratch your face and ear all up?"

My hand went to my left cheek unbidden. "I'm surprised you noticed. It's almost healed."

She smiled knowingly. "I saw it the day you and Gertie came to see me on the way to the PCU, despite your effort to hide it. It looked pretty bad then."

I resisted an impulse to play down the injury. Zoe deserved to know where things stood, and I was determined to tell her and let the chips fall where they may. "I, uh, had a close call." I recounted the hit-and-run attempt on Archie and me.

When I finished, she closed her eyes for a few moments before speaking. "If whoever tried that thought you knew too much, then you must be in even greater danger now. Are you taking precautions?"

"I am." I paused to gauge where she was coming from. "Look, a lot has gone down while you've been in the hospital, but we don't have to discuss it now. You need to finish your soup and get some rest."

Her eyes flashed at me. "I can eat and talk, you know. I've been in mental limbo for two weeks. I want to know everything you've learned. Maybe I can help in some way."

I was both surprised and relieved at her seeming acceptance and even support of my investigation. I took her through how the blood choke hypothesis came about and what I'd uncovered about the mixed martial arts expertise of Gloria Talbot, Donny Romano, and Bradley Nielsen.

Then I went on to describe Gloria's beating at the hands of Donny and the way Eric Trenton was murdered.

She ate while I talked, and when I finished she set her tray aside. "Okay, big picture—Donny has the know-how to pull off both chokeholds, and his motive is financial in the Bainbridge murder and jealousy in the Trenton murder. There are other suspects, as you point out, but he's the most compelling since his truck was seen at the Trenton scene, and he's hiding out now."

"His whereabouts the night Bainbridge died is in question, too," I added. "Bower more or less told me Donny vanished at half-time from the Blazer game that was his alibi." I paused for a moment. "But there may be an even bigger scheme at play." I recounted the relationship between Donny and Nielsen, the fact that Nielsen lied about it, and the questions surrounding the sale of the company and the missing laboratory notebook.

She smiled the smile I'd missed, and her eyes lit up. "Oh, I see. Makes sense. Bradley Nielsen has the most to gain by far and is smart enough to have manipulated Donny into doing his dirty work."

"Yep. And Nielsen's already got his private island picked out and plans drawn up for a yacht harbor."

"No surprise, of course," she said. "Greed is a powerful motivator. Like all addictions, it creeps up unawares, gains a psychological grip, and takes complete possession of a person before they realize it. Pretty soon they're doing things they never imagined they would do, bad things. It's a fatal flaw. It rots your soul from the inside."

I nodded. "Seems like there's a lot of soul rot going around these days."

We fell silent for a few moments. Finally Zoe looked at

me and said, "What about the notebook? How does that fit in?"

"I don't know yet, but it could have been the real reason Trenton was killed. I think he may have grown a conscience, and that became a threat to Nielsen's scheme to cash in. Gloria Talbot told me she didn't think Trenton would've destroyed it, so I'm hoping it'll turn up. It's a strong theory, but I'm short on hard evidence."

She met my eyes. Hers were moist with unshed tears. "You've made great progress, Cal. I know I've been critical of your efforts, but I've had some time to think about my actions. This is what you do, it's who you are, and it was selfish of me to whine about it. I realize now it was just fear on my part, fear I might lose you." She shook her head and dabbed a tear. "Turns out we're all at risk in this life. There just isn't any way to play it safe. Can you ever forgive me?"

I was speechless for a moment. "Of course I can. And I know how upsetting to you it must have been for me to jump right into this case. Can you forgive *me?* Believe me, I had no idea this thing was going to blow up in my face."

We both laughed at that. Holding my gaze, she said, "I know how much you mean to me, now. I'm in for the long haul, if you'll have me."

My heart did a little flip-flop. "I'm in, too, if you're willing to put up with me."

That's where we left it. No violins, no romantic embraces, just quiet vows of commitment exchanged across a room. But it sealed the deal between Zoe and me.

CHAPTER FORTY-FIVE

THE FIRST DAY OF SPRING WAS STILL A WEEK AWAY, BUT the next morning broke clear and bright. Sensing Zoe was in a vulnerable state, Archie had slipped into her room and slept next to her bed that first night and continued to do so for the duration of her stay at the Aerie. I slept better than I had in weeks, got up early and after feeding Archie, made Zoe a breakfast of poached eggs, toast with Scottish marmalade, and a pot of Earl Grey tea.

When I brought in her breakfast, she was sitting up focused on her computer. She looked up at me, smiled, and said, "How did I get so lucky?" But her eyes were troubled. "The governor has declared a moratorium on gatherings of more than two-hundred and fifty people, and she's closing all elementary and high schools beginning in four days."

I set the tray down. "Whoa, that sounds draconian, but I'm glad she's trying to get out ahead of this thing. Maybe shutting down large gatherings will put the brakes on," I said with an inflection of optimism in my voice.

"I hope so," she said. "I don't think it helps that the guy in the White House is comparing Covid-19 to the flu."

I had to laugh, thinking of Gloria Talbot's comments. "Yeah, I had someone tell me the same thing the other day. From what I've read it's wishful thinking."

Zoe smirked. "What I had was no flu, that's all I know."

"Surely, we'll get our act together," I offered. "After all, a pandemic is not a political issue."

Me, the eternal optimist.

—//—

Archie—who could avail himself of the wall-mounted pet door in the kitchen—stayed with Zoe, and I drove to my office in Dundee. It was a morning of incoming calls, none of them bearing much in the way of good news. First, Sonny Harper, the other detective on the Trenton murder case, called to inform me that an additional search conducted at the Trenton's house came up empty. The tone of the call made it clear he thought the second effort was a complete waste of time. When I asked about Harmon, he told me he'd called in sick without giving me any other information.

Worrisome.

Later that morning, Darcy Tate rapped on my Dundee office back door and stuck her head in. "Just heard the DNA analysis on the hairs from the truck that hit Wanda Jenkins failed," she informed me. "Not enough root material to get a decent profile. We're still hopeful the hairs from the Jeep that forced you and Archie off the road will give us something. I'll let you know as soon as I hear." That said, she ducked out and was on her way.

Was this the new normal? I asked myself. Either phone calls or the briefest of direct contact? It wasn't an uplifting prospect.

Esperanza Oliva called shortly after that. "How's Nando?" I asked.

"He is fine, no sickness. Our Lady of Guadalupe must have heard my prayers. But I'm going crazy trying to get him home. I have had two return flights cancelled, and I just booked another flight today for April tenth." She sighed softly. "He is going as crazy as I am. He loves his mother and sisters dearly, but I think he's had enough of Cuba."

"Let me guess," I said, "he's worried about his businesses."

"He is *always* worried about his businesses, but yes, he thinks the virus will be big trouble here. He thinks Americans may not be willing to make the sacrifices needed to beat it, but that is not why I called." She paused for a moment. "Benny Boykin died this morning. I'm sorry to tell you, Cal."

"Oh," I said, as the news hit me like a gut punch. "I'm sorry to hear that."

After we disconnected, I sat in a funk for a long time, and I didn't even have Archie to commiserate with. Benny Boykin was my ace in the hole, and now he was dead. I was mad, I was disappointed, I felt let down, but most of all I felt embarrassed. I had convinced myself I had the whole plot figured out, and in some leap of faith that now seems stupid and arrogant I assumed the evidence to prove it would simply materialize.

I decided that was enough bad news for one day, so I locked up the office and was nearly to my car when my cell phone went off again. "Mr. Claxton?" a young voice inquired, "I'm Virginia Gaines, a senior administrative assistant at Adventist Hospital. I'm calling to inform you that a patient of ours, Benjamin Boykin, passed away this morning at 9:16. Myself and the entire staff here at Adventist are sorry for your loss."

"Uh, thank you. I really didn't know him that well," I stammered, not having a clue why she would contact me about the death.

"Well, the reason for my call is that Mr. Boykin left something for you. He made it clear when he first checked in that you and only you were to have it if anything happened to him."

"I see. Can you tell me what it is?"

"It's a set of keys, three in all."

"That's it?"

"Yes."

"Can I come to the hospital now and pick them up?"

"Of course. Just ask for me at the main desk. Virginia Gaines."

"I'll be there within the hour, Virginia."

"Keys?" I said out loud after hanging up, "BB left me a set of keys? What's up with that?"

CHAPTER FORTY-SIX

VIRGINIA GAINES WAS MAYBE THIRTY WITH THE KIND OF bearing that made you think she might wind up running the hospital someday. She made me show my driver's license and sign a release before handing me a sealed envelope with my name written on it. I waited until I got back to the car before tearing open the envelope and extracting three keys on a simple key ring. One was a Honda car key and the second, the largest, looked like a house key. The third was the smallest, a key that looked like it might open a cabinet or a desk drawer.

I turned the situation over in my mind. Why did BB want me to have these keys? I couldn't fathom an answer, but it was clear the only way to find out would be to locate the locks they opened. That thought took me directly to an ethical dilemma. If I assumed the large key was to BB's house, did that mean I had permission to enter and search it? After all, why else would he give it to me? It was a gray area, so I called Harmon Scott, hoping he might pick up, but the call was forwarded to the central number of the Portland Police, where I was told he wasn't available. No way I was calling Detective Harper. I didn't trust him. The ball was in my court, I decided.

I put the keys in my pocket and drove home. Zoe and

Archie were both glad to see me. After I took my dog out for a raucous game of slobber ball, I fed him and then cooked dinner for Zoe and me. She was in a particularly good mood, having re-started work on her novel. "I got entire chapter done today," she said, beaming a smile as I brought her tray in.

"Laid down some good dialogue, did you?" I said with a smile.

"Elmore Leonard would be proud," she said with a deadpan look, and we went on to discuss her story at some length. I mainly listened, marveling at her passion for the project. When the discussion wound down, I pulled BB's keys from my pocket, held them up, and recounted how I'd come to possess them.

"He wanted you to *use* the keys, Cal," Zoe said when I finished. "There must be something either in his car or his house he wants you to have."

"I hope it's not his car," I said. "He was taken by ambulance from a motel, and his car's probably been towed by now. God knows where it is."

"The house then. See if the large key fits his house," she said, her eyes alight. "Surely you won't risk your law license by doing that. Isn't that what giving someone a key means, that they want you to *use* it? You owe it to him to go look, don't you? It was his dying wish."

I had to laugh. "You should have been a lawyer, but seriously, it's a stretch from a legal standpoint, particularly if I start looking around in his house."

She rolled her eyes. "I don't get it. You risked your life taking this case, but you won't risk a potential dustup with the Oregon Bar?"

I shrugged. "It's the law, I guess. I have a lot of respect

for it...but you're right, damn it, this is worth the risk. I'm going tonight."

—/ /—

Two hours later I parked a block and a half down from BB's bungalow on SE 82nd. The street was deserted and poorly lit, and the weeds in his yard had grown another foot. The porch steps creaked in the still air, and the mailbox next to the front door was stuffed to overflowing. After donning a pair of gloves, I held my breath as I tried the large key. It grated a little against the worn lock but slid right in, and when I turned the key, the lock released with a loud click.

"Whataya know?" I said under my breath.

The stench hit me as I crossed the threshold—rotted garbage, sour milk, and something worse. I hoped it wasn't a dead cat. I eased the door shut and pulled down the shade on the living room window. I switched on a small flashlight, and with the beam directed downward, moved through the one-story house, lowering the rest of the shades as I went. Intending to leave the smelly kitchen for last, I didn't see anything of interest until I came to a spindly-legged bedside table in BB's bedroom. I tried the drawer. It was locked. I took out the key ring and inserted the smallest key into the vertical slot in the small circular lock. Smooth as silk, the drawer was open.

"On a roll," I said, rather pleased with myself.

The drawer had only two items in it—a box of thirty-two caliber shells, half full, and an opened, padded security envelope addressed to Benjamin Boykin with no return address. I figured the bullets were for the gun

BB smacked me with in our first encounter. He probably stored the gun in the drawer and took it with him when he went into hiding. The envelope held a prepaid cell phone. The phone was dead, but I spotted a charge cord partially hidden on a dresser by a stack of underwear and socks. I slipped it and the phone into my coat pocket, and after making one more sweep through the house, got the hell out of there. With luck I could charge the phone in my car by the time I got back to the Aerie.

Someone had mailed BB a prepaid cell phone, and it was almost certainly what he wanted me to find. Why?

CHAPTER FORTY-SEVEN

I THOUGHT ABOUT CALLING ZOE TO TELL HER ABOUT MY find but was afraid I might wake her. She was indeed sound asleep when I got back. After taking Arch for a quick walk, I went directly to my study and powered up BB's phone. The only thing on it was a series of text messages between it and a 971-prefix number. I tapped open the first message in the thread:

> Hello Benjamin, thanks for following the instructions in the envelope. I hope the $500 will come in handy. How would you like to earn $5,000 more, no questions asked? If you are interested, text "yes" back to this number. This is not a scam. The $500 demonstrates our sincerity and is yours with no obligation.

The date of that first text was fifteen days prior to the death of Malcolm Bainbridge, I noted. BB texted "yes" back eight minutes later, and the next message followed an hour later:

> Excellent! We need you to borrow Malcolm Bainbridge's Ruger-57 pistol. Your job is to remove it from the vault, relock the vault, and leave the

> gun at the location we specify. Your sister knows it's location and his schedule. If you agree to help us, we will send you the vault combination and immediately mail you $1,000 as a good faith down payment on the $5,000. Text your decision back to this number.

I chuckled when I read BB's response, which he texted back a scant three minutes later:

> I can do this. But I want $10,000 with $2,000 up front. Let me know.

It took even less time for BB to make up his mind this time, and the man drove a hard bargain. The answer came back in the affirmative thirty-four minutes later. Apparently, the killer had to think about it before agreeing.

I leaned back in my chair and thought about the exchange. From BB's perspective it was easy money, and he intuitively understood that he had the leverage to up the price because he was Wanda Jenkin's brother, the one person who could easily pull the job off. From the killer's vantage point, it was a clever plan. Once BB learned that Bainbridge had been shot with the gun he'd stolen in a burglary, it would undoubtedly dawn on him that what he helped facilitate was a murder. No way BB was going to the cops with that.

The next text detailed directions for the Ruger drop using a locker at the Portland train station. The text arrived the day before Bainbridge's death. Directions for BB's ten-thousand-dollar payoff arrived two days after the murder. Another text came in after his sister's death, expressing condolences for his loss and the hope that the driver responsible for the "tragic accident" would be brought to justice. A couple of brief texts arrived before BB fell ill, asking if he was interested in more "high paying work." BB didn't answer any of those texts.

After I finished reading, I shut down the phone and went into the kitchen to brew a cappuccino. Archie heard me stirring and came down to join me. I stood at the kitchen window, sipping my coffee as the sky to the east bloomed a deep rose color and the birds started hitting the feeders.

That's when it came to me.

I set my coffee down, rushed back into the study, and looked again at the second text in the string. I'd skimmed it so rapidly the first time that I almost missed it.

I looked at Archie, who was sitting in front of me with his head cocked, his eyes anxious. "The possessive of 'it' does *not* have an apostrophe, Big Boy," I told him. "Most sixth graders know that, but I'm willing to bet Clete Bower doesn't." I sat back, recalling that first meeting with Bower in my office. It came back to me with crystal clarity—the *exact* same grammatical error on the first page of the draft agreement he'd given me.

I looked at Arch. "Two misused apostrophes? Happenstance or something more? Maybe I've been looking at this damn thing all wrong." I recalled my suspicion of Bower after the break-in at Caffeine Central, the fact that he knew I was a jogger after that night, and that the color of his car was consistent with the hit-and-run attempt on Arch and me. I thought of his thick forearms, which were more than sufficient to pull off a blood choke and an air choke, for that matter. But most of all, I thought about his alibi for the Bainbridge murder—he led me to believe Donny had slipped away at the halftime of the Blazer game. It could have been the other way around. Bower could just as easily been the one that left and committed the murder.

That last thought made me think of Donny Romano. If I was right about Bower, then Donny was the fall guy. Was he still alive? I wasn't so sure now.

How did Bower know about the Ruger? Wanda Jenkins certainly knew about it but perhaps not the combination to the vault. That made me think of Gloria Talbot. She certainly knew the combination. Was I wrong about her? Was she in this thing with Bower? My gut still said no, and I felt talking to her again might be worth the risk. After all, the killer already thought I knew too much, so what was there to lose?

By that time, Zoe was awake, so I fed Archie and made her breakfast. I was anxious to tell her what I'd found, but when I brought in her tray, she had fallen back into a peaceful sleep. I tiptoed out of her room, took the tray to the kitchen, and went back to my study. I knew it was too early to call Gloria, but I did it anyway.

"Jesus Christ, Cal, you woke me up. What is it now?"

"Sorry, Gloria. I need your help again." She groaned but didn't hang up. "Did Clete Bower have anything to do with your decision to ask for a large life insurance policy when you divorced Malcolm?"

"That's none of your—"

"Come on, Gloria, I need the truth here. Trust me on this." I held my breath, knowing it was a big ask.

After a long pause, she said, "I'm curious where you're going with this. Yeah, he told me it might be a smart thing to do. You know, I'd been popping off about how unstable Mal was, might've even said he was suicidal. I thought it was brilliant—you know, out-of-the-box thinking—so I went along with it. I had to give up some cash in the settlement, but I decided to take Bower's advice."

"What kind of deal did you cut?"

"He wanted five thousand on top of his fee if he could get me a policy for two-and-half million, which he succeeded in doing. If the policy paid off, he wanted an additional one hundred and fifty thousand. He called it a bonus."

"I see. Did he know about the Ruger in the pistol vault, the one that killed Malcolm?"

Except for her breathing, the line went silent for a few seconds. "Ah, yeah, it came up when we were splitting up the possessions. The gun was on a master list of everything in the house, and Clete asked me about it out of the blue, come to think of it. I figured he was into guns or something."

"Did he know the combination to the vault?"

Another pause. "I don't think so. I didn't tell him, if that's what you're suggesting."

"Could he have gotten it from Donny?"

"Oh, yeah, that's very possible. He had a lot of influence on Donny." I heard her swallow. "I get your drift, and it's weirding me out."

"Bear with me," I said. "Has Donny been in touch?"

"No. The little bastard's still on the run, I guess. Unless...good God, you think something's happened to him, that Clete—"

"I'm just working through the possibilities, Gloria."

"A couple of days ago you were hot on Bradley Nielsen," she shot back. "Now it's Clete Bower. Which is it?" When I didn't answer, she added, "Either way, I'm too damn close to the action."

"Could Bower have blood-choked Malcolm into unconsciousness and then shot him with the Ruger?"

"That's how you think it happened? Oh, fuck. If Donny taught him the move he could have." She paused. "Jesus, now I'm really scared. What should I do?"

"Nothing right now. Just make damn sure Bower doesn't think you suspect anything, and don't tell him you talked to me. He could be a ruthless killer, a psychopath… I'll be in touch."

After we disconnected, I sat there, deep in thought. Sure, there were still questions to be answered about Bradley Nielsen, his relationship with Donny, and the significance of the missing notebook, but those questions seemed less compelling now.

I laughed out loud, thinking of the two errant apostrophes. *Could this whole thing really come down to bad grammar?* It looked possible, especially after Gloria answered the remaining questions I had about Bower. As for Donny Romano? I hoped Bower hadn't used him, then killed him.

BB's prepaid phone was now the issue. It provided solid evidence backing up my theory of Malcolm Bainbridge's murder, but could I use it to somehow identify who the mystery texter was? It was one thing to have removed the phone from BB's house, but it was quite another to start using it try to catch a killer. I needed to talk to Harmon Scott.

I called Scott's number, and my call was again forwarded to the Police Bureau. Out of frustration, I called Sonny Harper. "Harmon's sick in bed," he told me.

"Is it Covid-19?" I asked, my chest tightening.

"We don't know. We're trying to get him tested, but he's being stubborn, says it's just a sinus infection. What can I do for you?"

I hesitated, thinking about how long it would take to brief Harper on the case and the fact that his reaction was likely to be negative and uncooperative. "Thanks, but it's just a personal matter," I told him. "I'll try him later today. If you hear anything about his condition, let me know, okay?"

I was packing up my briefcase and worrying about my cop friend when I heard the unmistakable ping of an incoming text. I instinctively pulled my phone from my pocket, but that's not where the ping originated. I swiveled around and saw that the screen of the prepaid phone was alight with a message:

> Hello Benjamin, haven't heard from you in a while. Are you interested in some more well-paying work?

The hair on the back of my neck stood at attention, and before I had time to talk myself out of it, I texted back:

> What do you have in mind?

Once my text vanished into the ether, I sat there staring at the phone, trying to justify what I feared was a rash decision. Or was it? If I hadn't answered the text and instead opted to go through channels with the Portland Police, it could take days to define a course of action—even with Harmon Scott's support—since the Bainbridge death was still classified a suicide. A delay might result in losing connection to the killer, at least that's what the impatient corner of my brain argued.

On the other hand, the timing bothered me. The text arrived the day after I came into possession of the phone. Could the killer know BB had died and passed his phone onto me? That was always a possibility, although the fact that the killer had sent a couple of similar texts a few weeks earlier seem to suggest this was just more fishing.

In any case, I opted to take action, even if it brought danger. And that's exactly what I got.

CHAPTER FORTY-EIGHT

THAT THURSDAY IN MID-MARCH PASSED MORE OR LESS routinely. BB's phone stayed silent, there was no word on Harmon Scott's condition, and I decided to suspend the surveillance of Bradley Nielsen after Timoteo's work the night before yielded nothing. I didn't tell my legal assistant about the phone or that my interest had shifted from Bradley Nielsen to Clete Bower for the same reason I hadn't told Zoe—I was tired of speculation. I also had a sense, bordering on premonition, that something was about to break that would end the damn guesswork.

Zoe was getting stronger each day, and on that Friday morning when I brought in her breakfast she was dressed and typing away on her keyboard at the small desk facing the window. Her hair bounced on her shoulders with the effort, and when she turned to me her eyes gleamed with the same kind of happiness I felt.

"Okay," I said in a faux stern voice, "knock it off. I made you steel-cut oatmeal with brown sugar, walnuts, craisins, and shredded coconut. It's best eaten hot." I set the tray down, and she blew me a kiss with a suggestive smile. "Enough with the brazen temptations," I quipped. "This isolation thing's already hanging by a thread."

She laughed. "Promises, promises."

I left for Portland shortly after that. Archie stayed with Zoe with instructions to take good care of her. One of my Facetime callers that morning was a young girl who had a bad cough and looked flushed. As the call concluded, I suggested she go to the free clinic at Outside In over on SW 13th and have them check her out. That left me wondering how people on the street would fare if the virus kept spreading. It had the makings of a humanitarian crisis.

I packed a lunch that day on Zoe's urging, so I wouldn't have to go out to eat. I'd just finished a peanut butter and honey sandwich when Willow called. "Hi, Cal," she began, "are you in town today?" I told her I was. "My food order didn't come in again, so I shut Plat du Jour down and went photo shooting. I, um, I've had a little car trouble."

"What's wrong?"

"It won't start. I push the button and nothing happens."

"You've got your foot on the brake, right?

"Of course. Could you give me a hand? I'm out here with Tater, and my cheap insurance doesn't include towing."

"Sure, I can help. Where are you?"

"That's the embarrassing part. I'm at Donny's cousin's cabin."

"*What?* Dammit, Willow. I thought we agreed you should stay away from there."

"I know we did. I was shooting some of the derelict ships on this stretch of the river, and I was so close I just dropped by to check things out. Cal, the lock on the shed looks tampered with."

"Okay, I'll be there in thirty minutes. Sit tight. And stay away from the shed."

I locked up Caffeine Central, threaded my way across town to I-405 and was headed north on the Columbia

River Highway when Harmon Scott called. "He lives," I answered. "How are you feeling?"

"Fine," he replied, his voice grumpy. "I think I disappointed a lot of people around here when I tested negative for Covid. Sinus infection. Get 'em every spring for some reason. What's up?"

"I have solid evidence backing up my contention that Bainbridge was murdered, and I think I know who's behind this whole crime spree, and it's not Bradley Nielsen."

"The lawyer, huh? Could be." he said, after I summed up what I had. "Bower's alibi for the Trenton murder isn't worth a damn either. We talked to some people who work near where his law office is located. No one remembers seeing him or his car that afternoon." He paused. "Why didn't you tell Harper any of this?" When I didn't answer, he said, "Okay, he's a butthead. Bring the phone in ASAP and we'll go from there."

I told him I had an errand to run first. By the time I passed through St. Helens and turned off at Fox Creek Road, a soft rain was falling. I turned in at the listing mailbox and followed the drive around and through the trees. Willow's Prius was parked adjacent to the house. I parked behind it, and not seeing her and Tater, I walked around to the back of the house and over to the garden shed. The lock on the shed didn't look tampered with to me, which I found odd. I called out her name.

"I'm down here," she called from the boathouse on the river. "You won't believe what I've found. Come on down." She went back into the boathouse.

I made my way down to the dock, crossed on the gangplank, and when I pushed open the boathouse door, I smelled it—stale cigar odor. When my eyes adjusted, I saw

Willow standing stock still and behind her, Clete Bower. He held Tater in the crook of one arm and a semiautomatic in his free hand. The gun was pointed at the child's head. Tater's eyes were wide with fear, but she wasn't crying.

"Welcome aboard, Cal," he said, and with a slight nod to Willow added, "Nice job getting him in here. You get a good-mommy-medal for that." To me, he said, "If you try anything, I'll shoot the kid right in front of mommy. Got it?"

I nodded, then glanced at Willow, my throat and chest constricting. Believe me, I took no satisfaction in having my suspicions confirmed. Instead, my head reeled as I tried to adjust to the stark reality of what was happening.

She sobbed, her eyes pleading, her lips trembling. "I'm sorry, Cal. He said he'd kill Tater unless I got you to come here. I didn't—"

I raised a hand slightly to silence her. "It's okay. You did what you had to do." Keep him talking, I said to myself. Look for an opening. "It's too late, Bower. I've already told the cops about you. Your best move is to give up right now, plead your case. Don't make it worse for yourself."

He laughed, more of a contemptuous snarl. "You're bluffing. I figured it was you who wound up with that burner phone. I have my own source at the hospital, a nurse who slips accident victims my card for a price. He told me a guy fitting your description picked up a small package belonging to Boykin after he croaked. There aren't many secrets in a hospital." A reptilian smile spread across his face. "When my text was answered, I knew the phone was back in service. Had to be you."

I fought back a wave of guilt and self-reproach. "The cops know you wrote those texts to Boykin. And they know you killed Bainbridge using a blood chokehold to incapacitate him. I told them."

His face registered surprise. "I knew you were a problem, Claxton, but you're smarter than I thought if you figured out how I killed Bainbridge. But what you're saying is bullshit. There's no way to prove that and there's no way the texts or the phone can be traced to me. And once I take care of you two, they won't—"

Willow broke into racking sobs. "No, you can't—"

"Shut the fuck up," he barked and moved the barrel of the gun closer to Tater's head. I inched a little nearer while he was preoccupied with Willow. He eyed me with that closed lip smile again. "I figured the way to get to you was through her. I followed her today, and what does she do? She comes here, which saves me a lot of trouble, being close to the water and all. His normally squinty eyes were wide with anticipation. "We need to get on with—"

"What did you do with Donny?" I said, cutting him off in a last-ditch attempt to buy time, although I had no plan except a final suicide charge.

"Oh, Donny the loose cannon?" he said, looking amused. "He's feeding the sea lions." The smile again. "Better him than the salmon, right? Just doing my part for the environment."

I fought back another wave—revulsion this time. "I can understand you killing Bainbridge and Boykin's sister, but why Donny? I don't get it." Willow sobbed again and when Bower shot her a look, I moved a half step closer to him.

"Donny knew too much, but I was more worried about Trenton. He told Gloria about some notebook he took at Spectro Systems and what happens next? She tells him about our little scam to get the Ansel Adams photographs, you know, lovers playing true confessions." He rolled his eyes. "I was worried Trenton would blow the whistle on me. When Donny beat up Gloria over him, it gave me the perfect out. I knew Donny didn't have the cojones to kill Trenton, so I did it myself. Problem solved."

"So you killed Trenton just to protect the Ansel Adams scam?"

He looked puzzled for a moment. "Hey, those photos are going to make me a bundle. Every dollar counts, you know."

"Where's the notebook?" I asked, continuing to stall.

"Took me a while to find it, but when I did, I took it. I figure I can sell it back to Nielsen. It's right over in the garden shed with the photographs."

With a play to his vanity, I said, "I concede that what you've planned and executed here is brilliant, but why? Why such excess?"

"Excess?" he snapped back, his look incredulous. *"Really?* I need the money. My law office needs renovating, and I haven't been on a decent vacation in four—"

At that instant, Tater Daniels quietly threw up the entire contents of her stomach, a chunky, yellowish stew that cascaded down the front of Bower's shirt. *"Shit,"* he said and reflexively plopped her on the floor, and in that moment took his eyes off me.

It was my only chance. I took two quick steps and leaped forward, grasping the wrist of his gun hand with both of my hands. My momentum knocked him backwards, and when we hit the floor, the gun went off like an explosion in the confined space.

"GET TATER OUT OF HERE!" I screamed as I struggled to knock the gun from his grasp. Movement in my peripheral vision told me Willow had scooped up her child, who was now screaming at the top of her lungs.

Bower was much stronger than I thought. While I continued to pound his gun hand on the floor, he managed to get his free hand in my face, scratching at my eyes and raking my injured ear. His little finger strayed into my mouth, and I bit down as hard as I could. He screamed and ripped his hand free, and at the same time I slammed his gun hand down again, crunching it between the gun and the floor. He grunted, and the gun skittered from his grasp, hit the side of the aluminum boat with a clang, and dropped into the river.

I let go of his wrist and jumped to my feet, figuring I had a better chance of taking him if I was vertical. Breathing heavily, we faced each other. My previously injured ear and his bitten finger were both dripping blood. His reptilian smile and smug demeanor were gone, replaced with a look that was wild-eyed and feral.

We circled each other like a couple of wrestlers looking for an opening. He was strong in his upper body, but I figured I was quicker. When he finally made his move, an awkward lunge, I stepped aside like a matador and pushed him as hard as I could. He crashed through the door and skidded onto the dock.

I followed him out and jumped on his back, trying to get my forearm around his neck. This was a fight to the death, and we both knew it. With more agility than I expected, he swiveled around and elbowed me in the jaw. A meteor shower went off in my head, and I almost lost consciousness.

I let go of his neck and scrambled to my feet. He pressed his advantage by coming at me, but I threw a desperation punch that caught him flush on his bent nose and snapped his head back. He staggered back and wiped blood from his nose and mouth, snarling like a wounded animal.

As we circled each other again the rain intensified to a pelting downpour. He rushed me, and when I stepped back, I slipped on the wet deck. The next thing I knew, he was behind me with his forearm around my neck in an air chokehold, the same hold he used to kill Eric Trenton. I managed to wedge my fingers between his forearm and my trachea, but the pressure he applied was immense, and I felt my air passage begin to constrict.

As we struggled on the edge of the dock, thoughts of what this monster had done flashed through my mind. My breathing became more labored, and my field of vision swarmed with gnats. He ratcheted up the pressure even more, forcing me to croak like a dying frog. I summoned the rage I felt to steel myself for what I was about to do... My only choice.

I gathered all my strength, twisted my body with everything I had, and we both tumbled into the river.

We sank like a couple of bricks and landed upright on the river bottom in the mild current. Bower's forearm was still clamped on my neck, and I was still trying to wedge my hand in to break his grip. We drifted in the current with each of us struggling to gain an advantage. Only one of us was going to surface alive. Images of Zoe and my daughter and my dog flashed through my mind as my lungs cried out for air. The reflex to breathe—even water—became stronger and stronger.

Suddenly, Bower released his grip and pushed off for the surface, which glowed like a yellowish green beacon, a chance to breathe. But I grabbed his legs and pulled him back down and clamped him in a bear hug. He struggled to free himself from my embrace, but I held him tight, looking straight into his eyes, which were wide with fear and panic.

An eternity passed while my lungs scavenged the last available oxygen molecules. Finally, his pupils rolled back into his head, he shuddered, and I felt him suck in a lungful of water. He shuddered again and went limp. I pushed off the bottom, and we both burst through the surface of the river.

He was unconscious, but I was able to take a huge breath of sweet, fresh air.

I pulled Bower's body to the shore and dragged him out of the water. I sat next to him in the river mud and watched his chest. He wasn't breathing and no blood oozed from his mangled little finger. I didn't care. I would enjoy watching him die, I decided.

I put my hand on his chest, which remained motionless. The rain had stopped and sunlight streaming through a break in the cloud cover began to warm my body. I heard a familiar screech, and my attention was drawn to a bald eagle out over the river. I watched the big raptor cut lazy circles high above the water, and that's when my conscience got the better of me.

I turned Bower's head to the side and began administering chest compressions. After what seemed too long a time, he coughed violently, and river water gushed from his mouth and nose. He continued to cough, and his breathing was labored and ragged, but it seemed self-sustaining. He wasn't going anywhere, so I went back on the dock, fetched a coil of rope from the boat, and tied his hands and feet.

I left him on the bank of the Columbia River and walked back to my car. Willow's Prius was gone, as it should have been. The car trouble was part of the ruse to lure me in, of course. Since my cell phone was ruined, I used BB's prepaid phone, which I'd left in the car, to call Harmon Scott.

"It's not your jurisdiction, but you need to come to St. Helens right now," I told him.

"Why," he asked.

I gave him the address. "Just come, damn it. It's over."

As I walked back to the river, I glanced down at my left wrist and saw my Fitbit had been torn off in the struggle. But my Huichol bracelet was still intact. Maybe Zoe was right about it being a good luck charm, I mused. I heard a siren in the distance, the local cops that Willow had undoubtedly summoned. A stiff breeze came off the water. The air smelled fresh and pure, and Mt. St. Helens gleamed white in the distance.

CHAPTER FORTY-NINE

Two Months Later

"GOG GOG, GOG GOG," TATER DANIELS SAID, LAUGHING and pointing at Archie as I held him up in front of the computer screen for her to see. Timoteo had arranged a Zoom meeting so I could fill everyone in on the status of the case and provide an opportunity, if not to celebrate, at least to be thankful for the way things worked out.

The probate hearing had taken place, and all the Ansel Adams photographs were back on the walls at the Bainbridge house. Willow became the sole heir of her uncle's estate after Donny Romano's body was recovered from the Columbia River. "What are your plans, now?" I asked her on behalf of everyone present.

"I'm going to sell Uncle Mal's place and buy the old Craftsman house I'm renting now. I've talked to the owners, and we've agreed on a price. I'm going to restore it back to the way it looked when it was built in 1918, and add a photographic studio, of course."

"Will there be room in your Craftsman for the Ansel Adams collection?" I asked.

Willow laughed. "Not all of them. I'm going to cherry-pick several of my favorites and give the rest to the Portland Art Museum."

"What about your bridge series show?" I asked next, knowing everything in Portland, including the Alberta Gallery, was shut down.

"The gallery is going to have a virtual showing of the entire collection. It'll be the first time they've tried it, so we'll see how it goes."

"If your photos are anything like the one you gave Cal," Zoe chimed in, "I predict the show will go viral."

Zoe was with me that afternoon, and although she had moved back to her place, she was spending a lot of time at the Aerie. The view inspired her writing, she said, but I think it's because she likes my cooking.

Nando had finally escaped the island of Cuba and was home enjoying the fruits of capitalism once more, such as joining our Zoom call on his eighty-five-inch smart TV. Esperanza, who moved heaven and earth to get her boss home, was busy with family that day. Nando told me that despite the downturn in his numerous businesses, he had given her a hefty raise—by his standards, at least—for the deft way she'd handled his affairs while he was gone.

"Regarding the case," I said at that point, "the first person I want to acknowledge is Tanya Daniels for her epic upchuck. Thank you, Tater. Your timing was impeccable."

Willow held her daughter up, and we cheered and clapped. It was all in good fun, but the horror of the encounter on the Columbia River was still with Willow and me. The young mother—who was working through the trauma with the help of Zoe—smiled and said, "Tater and I want to thank you again for what *you* did, Cal."

More cheering. I laughed. "Well, I'm just lucky that I happened to be a slightly better swimmer than Clete Bower. His cigar habit gave me a definite edge, I think."

That's all I was willing to say to people about my encounter on the river, with the exception of Zoe, to whom I'd told everything. She said that confronting the savagery of our nature can be unsettling. "But it's there when you need it, Cal," she explained, "for self-preservation and maybe even for exacting retribution." She was right on both counts, but I was still haunted by the thought if it hadn't been for an eagle looking for its lunch, I might've let Clete Bower die on that riverbank.

"How's the case against Bower shaping up?" Timoteo asked.

"It looks strong. So far, the Multnomah County DA has charged him with the aggravated murders of Malcolm Bainbridge, Donny Romano, and Eric Trenton. Bower confessed to all three in front of Willow and me, so we're key witnesses. But it's not just our word against his. Willow had the presence of mind to switch on the recording app on her phone, so she got every word he uttered in that boathouse."

"Bravo, Willow," Nando said, "You young people are so good with the technology."

"Charges are also pending in Columbia County for the kidnapping of Willow and Tater," I went on. "That won't be hard to prove, either, since a surveillance camera set up to watch the storage shed literally caught Bower in the act."

Timoteo laughed. "I take it the misplaced apostrophes won't be needed as evidence?"

"No, but they should at least be grounds to yank Bower's law license," I said to a round of laughter. "And he's looking at another charge, too—the attempted murder of me—"

"And Archie," Zoe added.

Willow asked, "What about Wanda Jenkins?"

"The police have nothing on her hit-and-run so far," I

said. "There's a great irony there. Bower made very few mistakes. His undoing was his paranoia—he thought I knew way more than I actually did. I wonder if he'd ever been caught if he hadn't gone after Willow and me."

"Is the man insane?" Timoteo asked. "All this so he could renovate his office and take a vacation?"

Zoe said, "Bower knows fantasy from reality, but he sees the world through a lens of greed and narcissism, so anything goes to get what he wants, *anything*."

"And of all the suspects, he had the least to gain monetarily," I added. "That's one of the reasons why it took me so long to land on him."

The call went silent for a few moments. "Where does all this leave Gloria Talbot?" Willow finally asked.

I had to laugh. "It leaves her very pissed off and very frustrated. The insurance company is still refusing to make good on her policy. The investigator suspects she might have had something to do with Bainbridge's murder, so she's not budging until the case is completely adjudicated, which could take a couple of years."

"Could she have been involved?" Stuart asked. He was on the call with Willow.

"No, I don't think so. Gloria has her issues, but she was instrumental in helping me understand this case." Changing the subject, I said, "Stuart, what's the status at Spectro Systems?"

"Oh, man," he said, "it's pure chaos. Once Bainbridge's notebook was recovered from that shed in St. Helens, it was returned to Nielsen, but our buyer, Endeavor, managed to get a copy. As a result, they've pulled the plug on their offer and are suing Nielsen for fraud. Apparently, Bainbridge's work showed that the InstaVision technology worked in principle, but it wasn't accurate enough—"

"My uncle would've found a way," Willow interjected.

"I'd like to believe that, too," Stuart said, "but his final experiments predicted the test would show fifteen to twenty percent false negatives, which is totally unacceptable. There simply isn't enough resolution in the spectroscopic method to tell one virus from another. The problem is fundamental."

"I have heard it said that you cannot fool Mother Nature," Nando quipped.

"That's right," Stuart said. "Anyway, Trenton told Nielsen he could fix the problem, and Nielsen bought it because he was desperate to unload the company. That's why he had Charlie Givens take the notebook after Bainbridge turned up dead, and that's why they hid it from Endeavor's management."

"So, what's the future at the company?" I asked.

"Bankruptcy, I'm afraid," Stuart said. "And civil lawsuits and maybe jail time for Nielsen."

There goes the island and the yacht, I thought but didn't say. "What about you?"

He looked at Willow. "We're working on a plan to open a restaurant after the pandemic's over. It's going to be a fifty-fifty partnership."

Willow beamed a smile. "That's right. It's going to be French and Northwest fusion just like my food cart, only served from a full-blown restaurant."

We going to call it the Plat du Jour Deux."

Willow told me earlier that their arrangement was strictly business. I wasn't so sure, but I kept my mouth shut. Less is definitely more with Tater's mom.

—//—

After the Zoom call, Zoe and I put on our jogging shoes and headed out for the Pioneer cemetery with Archie leading the way. It was a clear, cool June day, perfect for running. Bud break had finally come to the Red Hills a month earlier, a welcome reminder that life relentlessly renews itself. The vineyards were now fully leafed, the rich green foliage masking the gnarly vines that formed the winter understructure.

When we reached the cemetery, we turned and took in the view. A thread of reflected light marked the Willamette River, and bounded by the Cascades and the Coast Range, the valley stretched to the southern horizon like a multi-colored carpet. Zoe took my hand. "I love it here, right here. I don't want to go back to Washington."

"Good," I said.

ACKNOWLEDGEMENTS

ONE MIGHT THINK THAT THE SLOW DOWN AND ISOLAtion caused by the virus crisis might be conducive to fiction writing, but that wasn't the case for me. However, thanks to the encouragement, support, and editing prowess of Marge Easley, I finished this manuscript and feel satisfied that it says what I set out to say. I couldn't have done it without you, Marge.

Thanks again to my *amazing* critique group, Janice Maxon, Debby Dodds, LeeAnn McLennan, and Lisa Alber for crucial insight and input. My writing IQ always goes up when I'm around these fine authors! I'm also indebted to first readers Lanie Douthette and Barbara McReal, who provided suggestions that helped strengthen the manuscript. Also, special and heartfelt thanks to Barbara Peters, who read and edited an early draft of the manuscript and encouraged me to publish it.

ABOUT THE AUTHOR

Formerly a research scientist and international business executive, Warren C. Easley lives in Oregon, where he writes fiction, hikes, skis, and fly fishes. As the author of the Cal Claxton Mysteries, he received a Kay Snow national award for fiction and was named the Northwest's Up and Coming Author by Willamette Writers. His fifth book in the series, *Blood for Wine*, was short-listed for the coveted Nero Wolfe Award and his eight book, *No Witness*, won the Spotted Owl Award for the best mystery written by an author living in the greater Northwest. For more information visit: warreneasley.com and facebook.com/WarrenCEasley.

Milton Keynes UK
Ingram Content Group UK Ltd.
UKHW021827131023
430526UK00015B/618